[...] n ha[...]
in Texas anthologies toge[...] one book. Now for those of you who would like my stories all together we have *One Texas Night*. I rarely call the folks in my stories characters. To me they come alive and tell me their stories. May they come alive for you as well in these four short adventures.

In the first story, "Amarillo by Morning," I picked my hometown as the setting and wrote one of my favorite characters of all time. You're going to like meeting Hank.

In "Silent Partner," I wrapped my story around an early rodeo. When I was a kid I loved the rodeo and by the time I was eight I rode in the Grand Entry. It was great fun doing the research about the history of rodeo and watching two people who needed each other turn to loving.

In "The Outlaw," I enjoyed creating an outlaw who wasn't all bad and a girl he meets in church who wasn't all good.

"The Ranger's Angel" gave me a chance to show just how hard it was to be a Texas Ranger. When Wynn's hurt, Anna whispers her dream to him and he vows to make it come true. A hard Ranger and a caring angel find newborn love.

Step into the past with me and come along on the journey. I promise you'll meet some great people.

Jodi Thomas

Other Books by Jodi Thomas

BENEATH THE TEXAS SKY

With Linda Broday,
Phyliss Miranda, and DeWanna Pace

GIVE ME A TEXAN

GIVE ME A COWBOY

GIVE ME A TEXAS RANGER

GIVE ME A TEXAS OUTLAW

A TEXAS CHRISTMAS

BE MY TEXAS VALENTINE

Published by Kensington Publishing Corporation

One Texas Night

JODI THOMAS

ZEBRA BOOKS
KENSINGTON PUBLISHING CORP.
http://www.kensingtonbooks.com

ZEBRA BOOKS are published by

Kensington Publishing Corp.
119 West 40th Street
New York, NY 10018

All Kensington titles, imprints and distributed lines are available at special quantity discounts for bulk purchases for sales promotion, premiums, fund-raising, educational or institutional use.

Special book excerpts or customized printings can also be created to fit specific needs. For details, write or phone the office of the Kensington Special Sales Manager. Attn.: Special Sales Department. Kensington Publishing Corp., 119 West 40th Street, New York, NY 10018. Phone: 1-800-221-2647.

ISBN-13: 978-1-4201-3141-3
ISBN-10: 1-4201-3141-9

First Mass-Market Paperback Printing: April 2013

eISBN-13: 978-1-4201-3157-4
eISBN-10: 1-4201-3157-5

First Electronic Edition: April 2013

10 9 8 7 6 5 4 3 2

Printed in the United States of America

Contents

AMARILLO BY MORNING

This story is dedicated to a real Amarillo hero.

Happy birthday, Hank.

Chapter 1

Fort Worth, Fall, 1889

Hank Harris squared his shoulders, forcing himself not to slump as he passed through the doorway of the Tucker dugout. He stepped into the one-room home with dread settling around his heart like sand.

At six feet six he knew he was destined to hit his head any time he ventured indoors. Seemed like houses all got too short about the time he started growing whiskers. Now, at thirty-one, he'd spent half his life watching out for low rafters.

He caught himself wishing that was all he had to watch out for tonight.

"Welcome, Mr. Harris!" a female bellowed as if he wasn't standing within reach of her. "Trust you made the five miles from Fort Worth without any problem. That north wind has sure been howling all day." The woman winked boldly. "I'll bet you think it's calling you home to that mound of dust folks call Amarillo."

Hank removed his hat and nodded, not wanting to encourage conversation. Dolly Tucker's shrill voice could strike kindling in a dry stove. He only prayed that her tone wasn't hereditary.

He couldn't stop the smile that wrinkled his normally hard mouth. Maybe he should be praying for himself. After all, he was the one fool enough to agree to meet Dolly's little sister. Most folks would say he had no right to be criticizing others. He wasn't the kind of man anyone would mistake as good-looking and, with the price of cattle dropping, any wealth he had lay far in the future.

I'm a hard worker though, he reminded himself. And honest. If I ever get a wife, I'll never mistreat her. That should be worth something in this world.

"You're looking all cleaned and pressed," Dolly yelled as she patted his arm. "You must have stopped at the creek." She waddled around him like a round little toy. "Your hair still looks wet."

Hank didn't know how to answer. He had no intention of discussing his bathing habits with the woman. In truth, he could never remember discussing anything but the weather with the fairer sex.

When he'd seen Dolly's husband, Charlie Tucker, at the stockyard in Fort Worth a few hours ago, it had seemed simple. Dolly's sister was visiting from Chicago and Charlie said they'd like him to meet her. He had even insisted that Hank stop by around suppertime.

Hank knew what that meant. They were introducing her to all the single men in West Texas. He'd played the game before a few times in the ten years he'd been ranching. He was respectable enough for a brother-in-law to introduce. He owned his own spread, was single, didn't drink to excess. But Hank also guessed that if Charlie was rounding up prospects, he might as well take his place at the back of the line.

On the bright side, he'd get a home-cooked meal for his trouble and Hank figured that made the ride out worthwhile.

"Would you like some coffee, Mr. Harris?" Dolly didn't give him time to answer before shouting, "Charlie Ray, pour him a cup while I go to the barn and find Agnes. It's almost dark. She should be able to guess it's about time for supper. The world can't always run on *her* schedule."

Hank swallowed hard. Agnes was close to the ugliest name he'd ever heard. That must be why they keep her in the barn. Either that or the girl talked like her sister and poor Charlie would be deaf if he heard the voice coming from two directions at once.

Another thought crossed his mind. What if Agnes wasn't bright enough to know the time of day? Some men in this part of the country weren't too particular, but knowing the time seemed a necessary skill.

Dolly's husband moved to the iron stove and burned his hand grabbing the pot. Hank fought down a laugh. What was it about some men? They seem to live perfectly well by themselves for years. Then they get married and act like they've never been near a stove.

"I appreciate you stopping by," Charlie mumbled as he finally managed to pour a cup.

Hank nodded, knowing he was just doing a favor for a friend. Men like Hank lived alone. No woman would have wanted to start out with nothing like he'd had to and, by the time he could afford more than a three-room house, he'd be too old and hardened for a woman to be interested.

Before Hank's coffee cooled enough to drink, someone tapped at the door.

Hank stood ready to offer his hand as more guests arrived. He wasn't surprised to see the young banker most of the cattlemen used while they were in Fort Worth. William J. Randell always seemed fair and wore clothes that looked like he must have ordered them from somewhere up north without bothering to take his measurements. He had a habit of playing with his watch fob when he was nervous, which would have made him easy pickings at a poker table. His hair curled in thin waves over his head making him look older than Hank guessed him to be.

The man behind Randell looked almost the same age, only Hank had never seen him before. He was stockier and stood with his feet wide apart as if expecting a fight to break out as he entered the dugout.

"Potter," the stranger said as he shook hands without waiting for Charlie to introduce him. "Potter Stockton at your service." His smile never reached his dark eyes.

Hank felt like counting his fingers to make sure they were all still there when the handshake ended. Something about Stockton didn't seem right. He was too friendly, too eager, too forward for a man not running for office. Hank found himself thinking a little less of the banker for keeping company with Potter.

Charlie Tucker didn't seem to notice. He offered the two men a seat and grinned. Before he could pour more coffee, Dolly returned alone from the barn. Her little marble blue eyes sparkled as she counted the bachelors at her kitchen table.

Within minutes, Hank was forgotten, which suited him fine. Dolly made over first the banker, then Potter Stockton, who explained he worked for the railroad. As Dolly served the food and insisted they eat, she kept the questions coming in rapid fire.

William J. Randell told all about the big family he came from in Ohio and Potter Stockton said he had relatives in Tennessee who were related to the royals in Europe. Hank kept quiet. As far as he knew he had no living relative. His mother left them when he'd been three and his father worked their small farm around Tyler, Texas, until he died before Hank turned twenty. The sale of that farm had given Hank his start near Amarillo.

They were halfway through the meal before Charlie got a word in to ask about his sister-in-law Agnes.

"She'll be along," Dolly scolded her husband as if no one would have remembered the reason they'd all been asked to dinner if Charlie hadn't mentioned it. "We'll be eating at midnight if we wait on her."

Hank pushed food back and forth on his plate, feeling like the walls were closing in around him. He'd always hated dugouts. Everyone said they were warm and protected from the weather since they were built half into the ground, but he felt like he was half buried in them. Even through the cooking odors, he could smell damp earth.

When he stood, mumbling something about taking care of his horse, no one in the room noticed him leave. He felt cheated. Though he had no hope of finding a bride, he had thought Dolly could cook. He would have had a better meal at the café by the train station.

Once outside, he stepped into the blackness between the two small windows and took a deep breath, wishing he could ride back to town. Waiting on the platform for the midnight train north would be better than going back inside. But if he just left, it would be an insult to both Charlie and the invisible Agnes. There was an unwritten law that said the girl, no matter how homely or dumb, had the right to turn away any man who came calling.

And he'd been dumb enough to come calling, even if it was wrapped in a dinner invitation.

He knew he'd be leaving alone. Both men inside were better-looking, better dressed, and probably had more money than him. Potter said he could dance and was a crack shot. Hank had never shot at anything he couldn't eat. William Randell bragged about building a two-story house in town and said he was up for a promotion at the bank. Potter swore he'd be in the cream of Fort Worth society in five years. They were dueling braggarts and Hank wanted no part of it.

"It's bad in there, isn't it?" a voice whispered from the blackness on the other side of the window.

Hank jerked away, almost knocking himself out on the low-hanging roof. He had no doubt the voice belonged to the missing sister, but she'd scared a year off his life when she spoke. In the night, he couldn't make out even an outline of her. "Yep," was all he could think to say.

"Dolly and Charlie Ray mean to marry me off," she whispered after a long silence. "Dolly's been planning it all day."

He wasn't sure if she talked to him or herself. "You Agnes?"

Dumb question, he thought. Who else would be out here this time of night?

"Yep," she echoed him, but without the accent it didn't sound natural. "I'm the old maid sister who's being passed around. If I don't get married here, I'm due in Austin at my oldest sister's place next month. Kind of like a traveling sideshow. Dress me up and put an apple in my mouth."

Hank couldn't stop the laugh. "I'm sorry," he quickly added. "I never gave much thought to the other side of this game."

"Sorry for what? For laughing or for me?"

"Both, I guess."

"My poppa sent me west before I rotted on the vine in Chicago. You see, I'm the last of five girls. The only one not claimed. As soon as I'm married, my poppa plans to take another wife. There's not room in the little apartment behind his shop for two women. I'm delaying his plan. I'm as much in the way in my home as I am here."

Hank smiled. He knew how she felt. "The runt of the litter, last to be picked," he mumbled, then thought he might have offended her.

Before he could say he was sorry again, she laughed. "That's right. I'm only half the woman my sister is."

Hank glanced in the window and watched Dolly waddle past. He couldn't say anything without insulting Charlie's wife so he changed the subject. "Don't you want to get married?"

"Not really. Do you?"

"No," he said honestly. "I like living alone. Running on my own clock."

"Me too."

His eyes had adjusted to the night enough that he could make out her shadow. She appeared short, like her sister, but not as round.

"But why not marry? For a woman, it seems like the best life." He couldn't help but add, "Unless you hate the cooking and cleaning part?"

The shadow lifted her head with a snap. "Women do more than cook and clean."

He'd said the wrong thing. She couldn't even see how homely he was and she was still rejecting him. "I know, but it helps if they can cook a little."

Agnes laughed suddenly and he liked the sound.

"You've been eating Dolly's pot roast, haven't you?"

"Trying to." He wished she would step into the light. "What *do* you like to do . . . Agnes?" Her name stumbled off his tongue.

"Back home, I helped my father in his workshop. He was a gunsmith. Sold the best weapons in the state and repaired the others."

"You liked working in his shop?"

"No," she answered. "I liked repairing guns in the back. I wish I'd been born a man. I'd love working on my own little workbench all day and coming home to a hot meal. It's always appeared to me that a wife was more an unpaid servant than a partner. I'd hate that, so I don't see much point to marriage. If I could, I'd open my own repair shop, but I have no seed money and none of my family thinks it would be a respectable kind of place for a woman to have. So, I'm cursed to circle my sisters' houses looking for a husband."

Hank leaned against the building. He could hear Dolly's voice asking if anyone wanted more pie, but he didn't glance toward the window to see if any victims had volunteered.

"Would you marry someone if it was a true partnership? Each taking care of himself, taking turns with shared duties. Each supporting the other in whatever work."

"No one bossing the other, or controlling?" She leaned closer, almost crossing into the light.

Hank had no idea where his thoughts were going, but for once he wasn't talking to a woman about the weather, so he decided to keep talking. "Right. Just two partners sharing the same house. Both bring in what they can as far as money goes. Both respecting the other's privacy."

"No wifely duties? No children coming every year?"

Hank thought he knew what she was talking about. He shook his head, then remembered she couldn't see him and added, "None. They'd each have their own room, their own things, their own lives." He'd seen men who ordered their wife around as if she were a slave. On the other side, he had watched a few women bossing their man in the same tone. In truth, he couldn't remember ever seeing a couple stand as equals.

The one memory he had of his mother circled among his thoughts, not quite substance but more than dream. A tall woman sitting by the window, ignoring all the world around her, including him. Long after she'd gone, Hank remembered asking his father why she'd left. His father had only mumbled that she didn't want children. They'd never spoken of her again.

Hank glanced across the darkness, pushing the image aside, trying to understand the woman only a foot away.

They were both silent for a few minutes, then she whispered, "I'd marry like that. A partnership. In fact, I'd consider it heaven. But even if I found a man willing to follow those rules, what's to make him keep his word? He could lock me in the house and beat me, and no one would stop him."

"You're the gunsmith, Agnes. You should be able to figure that one out. Ask for his guns as a promise. No man but a fool would stand in front of a barrel, even in the grip of a woman."

She laughed, then offered her hand across the light of the window. "It was a pleasure talking to you, but I have to go in and turn those two down before they die of food poisoning."

He took her tiny hand in his. "I wish you luck, Agnes," he said, realizing how much he meant it.

Just before she shoved at the door, she whispered, "My friends call me Aggie."

He placed his hand above her head and added his strength to hers. "Aggie," he said so close to her that he could feel her hair brush his face as the door opened. "I like that name."

Chapter 2

Hank blinked at the light as he stepped inside. Aggie walked ahead of him and stopped just over the threshold as if too afraid to go on.

He looked at the two men at the table. They both glared open-mouthed at her as if she were some kind of creature and not human. His fist clinched, and if she hadn't been in front of him, he might have closed their mouths with one blow. He didn't care what she looked like; she seemed a kind person who had a right to some degree of respect.

"I'm sorry I'm late," she said as if she hadn't noticed the way they stared. "One of the calves Charlie brought home from the stockyard is sick, and I had to make sure he'd eat before I came in."

Charlie smiled a lopsided grin and shrugged as if taking the blame for his sister-in-law's tardiness. "Once in a while they cull out the little fellows too weak to make the trip north. If I don't bring them home, I have to bury them behind the lot."

No one but Hank seemed to be listening.

Potter and William bumped heads trying to stand at the same time. Both were stumbling over words.

Hank stood behind Aggie, proud of her. She timidly offered her hand to each as if these two idiots made sense. The banker started playing with his watch chain and Potter talked even faster than he had at dinner. They were both "honored" and "privileged" to meet her.

The banker pumped her hand up and down so fast Hank feared he might break bone.

Potter kissed her fingers while he mumbled something in French. Hank would bet even money that he learned the phrase in Fort Worth's rough section called Hell's Half Acre.

If Hank didn't know better, he'd swear both men had been drinking.

"And Agnes, I believe you must have met Hank as you came in." Charlie sat down, adding only, "He often does business at the stockyard when he's in town."

Aggie turned to offer her hand to Hank.

"Nice to meet . . ." was all he got out before he saw her face. He'd braced himself for a plain girl, maybe one with pockmarks or scars, thick glasses or a birthmark. But what he saw almost buckled his knees.

She had the face of an angel, with perfect skin and curly auburn hair tied into a mass of curls at the base of her neck. And, he noticed, the devil twinkling in her blue-green eyes.

"Nice to meet you, Mr. Harris," she said shyly. "Would you like a slice of my sister's pie?"

There it was again, he thought. The sparkle in her gaze—daring him—challenging him.

"If the others left a piece," he managed to say. "I'd love one."

He sat down and watched her as she talked with the others. He ate the pie Dolly passed him without tasting it.

Aggie asked the other two men questions, as if she'd been coached, about their life and what their plans were. Hank didn't try to speak up. His life on a ranch would look pretty stale compared to Potter Stockton's travels and parties, or the magnificent house Randell planned to build in the center of town. She'd probably be bored to hear the details of raising cattle in West Texas.

He *was* proud of his house though. She might consider it plain with the high ceilings and wide, uncovered windows. But if Hank could have gotten a word in, he would have told her how from every direction she could see for miles, and how when the clouds hung low, close to the ground, his home seemed suspended between heaven and earth.

The banker and Potter found their footing on her questions and began to compete for her attention. They said pretty things to her, flattering her with words Hank could never hope to put together. Within minutes both men were hinting that she should consider marrying them. William Randell seemed good-natured with the competition, but Stockton's bragging carried an edge. He seemed a man who was used to fighting for anything he wanted, and he claimed Aggie was the prettiest girl he'd ever seen.

Aggie listened politely, without comment. It crossed Hank's mind that she'd probably heard such talk all her life. For a woman who said she liked working alone, the idea of entertaining and the dinner parties that Randell talked of must seem frightening. Potter boasted of traveling with his work and staying in hotels across the country.

Hank seemed the only one who noticed she didn't smile. In fact, if he was reading her right, Aggie was one step away from bolting out of the room.

Hank also noticed that the more she drew everyone's attention, the sharper Dolly became. It must have been hard on four sisters with the baby being so beautiful. That might explain why the father kept her tucked away in the back workshop. Hank wondered if she'd stayed in back because she was naturally shy, or if the sisters had forced her to remain in the shadow. Whichever, one fact was obvious to Hank. Beautiful Aggie was afraid of people.

He watched her carefully. She wasn't believing a word they said. She kept her hands laced tightly together over her frilly dress. He felt her loneliness more than he saw it. She was on display, something to be sold to the highest bidder, and no one stood by to help her. In fact, her sister made it plain that if she could decide for Agnes, little sister would already be packing up her things.

After an hour, Dolly ended the torture, not for her sister's sake, but for her own. Dolly complained that her feet were tired and it was time for bed.

As the banker moved to the door, he held both of Aggie's hands and kissed them. "I'll dream of you this night," he said with practiced flow. "Think of me also."

Potter was bolder. He swore he'd fallen in love at first sight and asked for her hand in marriage. He said she was the first woman he'd seen in Texas who would be perfect on his arm, and now that he found her he saw no need to hesitate. Without waiting for her answer, he began listing his qualities and continued to do so as Charlie showed him the door.

Aggie politely said she'd consider his offer.

Both men stood at the doorway and waited to see what Hank would say, if anything. Obviously, neither considered him a threat, but they had no intention of leaving him inside with the prize.

Hank stood and put on his hat. When he walked past Aggie, she seemed so small. He hoped his height didn't frighten her. She didn't look up, and he wondered if she was embarrassed by all she told him in the darkness. After all, her family had made her options limited and for all her brave talk outside, she might still have little choice but to marry.

"Thanks for the meal." Hank nodded toward Dolly. "And for the invitation," he added to Charlie. "It was a pleasure to meet you, Miss Aggie."

She still didn't look up. He leaned and unbuckled the

gun belt he always wore when he traveled. "There's a train leaving Fort Worth about midnight. If you're on it, you'll be in Amarillo by morning." He lifted her hands and placed his weapons in her grip. "If it's a partnership, equal and forever that you want, I'll pledge my Colts that it will be true."

The silence in the room was complete for the first time that night.

Finally, Charlie whispered what everyone was trying to believe. "You're giving her your guns?"

Hank nodded once.

When William Randell and Potter Stockton finished laughing, they yelled things like, "You don't give a woman a gun, you give her flowers," and "Give a ring." One of the men even suggested that maybe this girl was the first woman Hank had ever been around. Both seemed to be rehearsing the story that they planned to tell many times over.

Dolly swore at Charlie, calling him a fool for inviting someone so crazy to their dinner. "Waste of good food," she yelled as the men mounted.

Aggie stood in the doorway, gripping the Colts and looking up at Hank. He saw the fear in her eyes, the uncertainty, but he also caught a hint of a smile on the side of her lips.

They were all laughing, except her. As he turned his horse, he caught a glimpse of Aggie buckling his gun belt around her skirts, and he knew as sure as he knew the sun would rise that she'd make the midnight train.

Chapter 3

Aggie didn't say a word on the ride into Fort Worth. She sat on the bench of Charlie's old buckboard feeling like she was waiting for her life to start. She barely noticed the cold wind whipping from the north, or the rustle of brittle leaves that still clung to the live oaks along the creek. Her brother-in-law made this trip each morning and evening, so he knew the road well even in the darkness. Five miles was a long way to travel to work, but between her sister and the cattle auctions, she guessed it might be the only silence he knew.

Hank Harris had asked her to marry him, or at least she thought he had. It wasn't like any proposal she'd ever heard. He'd offered a partnership, equal and forever. Then, he'd unbuckled his gun belt and handed it to her. And, for the first time in her life, she found she couldn't say no.

She smiled to herself. Her sister had argued all the while Aggie packed. At one point Dolly even insisted Charlie Ray stop Aggie from going with the crazy cowboy who thought a proper engagement gift was a gun. But Charlie, for once, spoke up and said he'd had enough. He claimed Hank was a good man and if Aggie wanted to go with him the only duty he saw as his was to see that they were married before the train left the station.

Hank and Aggie might be in Amarillo come morning, but they would be wed tonight.

The night air cooled Aggie's tears as she gripped her hands together in her lap. She'd never been brave, she reminded herself, but the fear of everything remaining the same was worse than the fear of the unknown. She had to go. She had to take Hank's offer. She had to end the torture of being passed from house to house.

"I never heard Harris swear," Charlie interrupted as the lights from town blinked on the horizon. "That's one good thing about him, I reckon."

Aggie took a breath. "Yes." She had one brother-in-law in Kansas who thought "damn" should serve as an adjective to every noun he used. Not swearing was definitely a good trait, she decided.

"Though I don't think he has much money, he always pays his bills at the stockyard. Some ranchers, even after they have the cash for the sale, try to slip by without paying." Charlie spit a long stream of tobacco into the night. "Paying your bills is good."

"Yes." Aggie guessed Charlie was trying to calm her. Maybe he thought she might jump out of the wagon and run away wild into the night. But, to be honest, if he didn't hurry she was more likely to bolt and run toward the station. Charlie Ray Tucker was the best of her brother-in-laws and he was barely tolerable. After being passed from sister to sister she'd noticed that all their husbands had bad habits.

Closing her eyes, she tried to guess Hank's.

"If he goes to the whorehouses he ain't one to brag about it." Charlie interrupted her thoughts again.

"That's good." Aggie tried to forget all the lectures her sisters had given her, as though each man she'd turned down had been her flaw. She grinned, realizing that accepting a proposal hadn't halted the lectures. If Dolly had had the time she would have ranted for hours.

All her sisters thought Aggie was weak-minded. Poor, beautiful, slow-witted Aggie. She can't cook, can't sew, can't remember the time of day when she becomes interested in something. The only way she'll find a man, they claimed, was to remain silent until the wedding. They barely noticed what she *could* do, all the things she fixed, how dearly she loved animals. All they saw was the way she hid in corners at socials and refused to talk to strangers.

Charlie didn't seem to notice her silence as they passed the pens of cattle waiting to be shipped. He was on a roll praising Hank. "And he's clean. I swear some of them boys come in smelling worse than the cattle."

Aggie nodded as she watched the station draw closer. She had no trouble making out the tall man standing with his feet wide apart at the end of the platform. He must have been waiting for her for over an hour. She thought she saw a slight nod when they drew close enough for him to recognize Tucker's wagon, but his expression was hidden in the shadow of his wide-brimmed Stetson.

"What's your bad habit, Mr. Harris?" she mumbled to herself. "What will I have to put up with?" With a slight nod, she greeted him, realizing whatever his shortcomings were, they couldn't equal hers. He'd be the one shortchanged tonight.

Charlie pulled up to the platform and tied the reins around the brake handle. "I'll go wake the preacher. He don't live but a block from here," he shouted so that Hank could hear him. "You two might as well get acquainted."

She watched her brother-in-law disappear into the clutter of homes behind the station. For a while she just stared into the darkness wondering what she'd say to this man she was about to marry. Getting acquainted wasn't easy when neither liked to talk.

When she finally turned, Hank Harris looked as nervous as she. He offered his big hand and helped her down from the wagon. As his sleeve slipped a few inches up his arm she noticed a white bandage.

"Are you hurt?" If he'd had a bandage on his arm at dinner, surely she would have noticed.

Hank pulled his shirt over the wound as he shook his head. "It's nothing really. Right after I bought our tickets, some fellow I've never seen before thought I should have a drink with him. When I said I was waiting for someone he pulled a knife." Hank brushed his coat sleeve as if the wound could be dusted away. "The doc in the saloon across the street stitched it up for me. He was well into his whiskey, but he did a fine job. He wasn't much of a doctor and it wasn't much of a cut, so he only charged the price of a bottle. I was more worried about not being here when you drove in than the blood."

She frowned.

Hank continued, "I think the fellow mistook me for someone else. He was drunk enough that, by the time he realized his mistake, he decided to be mad at me instead of himself."

Her smile returned. "I can see how he'd take you for another." She scanned the length of him. "There must be quite a few men your size catching the midnight train."

Hank hated comments about his height, but somehow he didn't mind her teasing. "Be careful or next time I'll tell the guy to stay around until my wife arrives to shoot him."

"Did he try to rob you?"

Hank shook his head. "No, just a drunk wanting company."

Aggie brushed her fingers along his arm, lightly feeling the bandage beneath layers of shirt and coat. When their eyes met, they both turned away, embarrassed at her boldness.

He quickly stepped to the wagon bed. "This all of your

luggage?" he asked as politely as if she were a stranger he'd offered to assist.

She glanced at the carpetbag and two boxes tied with twine. "I've a trunk my father said he'd ship once I settled. That's all." She knew it wasn't much. Most brides came with all the necessities for setting up housekeeping, but without a mother to help her, Aggie had neither the skill nor desire to quilt and stitch a dowry.

He picked up her belongings and loaded them on the train. When he returned, she whispered, "Thank you."

"You're welcome," was all he answered.

They just stood, side by side, as mismatched as any couple she'd ever seen. Her fingers twisted together, she shifted in place, straightened her skirt, retied the bonnet Dolly had insisted she wear.

Hank could have been made of stone. He didn't even seem to breathe. They both stared at the few lights of Fort Worth. On the breeze she thought she heard the tinny sound of a piano and guessed the only thing open this time of night would be the saloons.

"You cold?" He startled her with his question.

"No," she lied, pulling her cotton dress coat around her. She wasn't about to complain or tell him this was the only coat she had. Her father had bought her three new dresses to "go on her courting journey." Only, when she'd left for her first sister's house, it had been late spring. Now, in another month it would be Thanksgiving. Her three fine dresses were worn from washing and pressing, and no brother-in-law had offered to loan her money for winter clothes. Not that she would have taken a single coin from them. All any of them wanted from her was her absence. She was another mouth to feed and something for their wives to complain about. Nothing more.

She watched Charlie hurrying down the platform. A

chubby young man, trying to pull on his long black coat, rushed behind him.

"I finally found a preacher," Charlie grumbled. "We can get this done now."

The preacher introduced himself as Brother Philip Milton. He shook Hank's hand with a strong pumping motion. "First," the young man said, straightening to his full height, "I have to ask if you're still wanting to marry this lady." He looked nervous, as if this might be his first ceremony. "I don't push nobody down matrimony road that don't want to go."

Hank swallowed, then nodded. Aggie wished she could see his face and know for sure that he wasn't having second thoughts. She wanted to warn the lean cowboy that all she'd ever been was trouble. Her mother died giving her birth. Her sisters had to take care of her when they were little more than babies themselves. Her father carted her to work with him until she'd been old enough to go to school. She didn't like, or trust, people, and she smelled of gunpowder and oil most of the time. If this man had any sense, he'd run now while he still had the chance.

Brother Milton patted Hank on the shoulder and turned to her. "You feel the same about him?"

She fought down a scream as she managed to whisper, "Yes."

While the preacher continued, she told herself nothing could be worse than being passed around. At least she'd have a home, no matter how small or plain.

Brushing the Colt at her waist she remembered his offer. A partnership. If he was fool enough to offer, she was crazy enough to take him up on it.

The preacher asked them to join hands as the first whistle to load sounded. Hank's fingers closed around hers and she tried to hear Brother Milton's words over the pounding of her heart. She was doing what her father had ordered. She was marrying.

Steam filled the night air, fogging the lights on the platform as travelers rushed by, unaware that two people were joining their lives together, forever. Aggie gripped Hank's hand and breathed in the damp air. Silently, she said good-bye to all she'd ever known, and hung her hopes on his promise.

The preacher pronounced them man and wife as the second whistle sounded. Hank reached in his pocket and handed Brother Milton two dollars.

Charlie yelled for them to hurry and suddenly they were running—her hand still in Hank's—toward their new life.

Hank paused a few feet ahead of her as the train began to move. Then, without warning, he reached for her and lifted her up to the second step as the train picked up speed. A moment later, he jumped aboard.

Aggie backed up another step, giving him room, and found herself at eye level with the stranger she'd just married. She should have been afraid, but all she saw was a pair of walnut-colored eyes reflecting the questions and uncertainty she felt. She knew without asking that he hadn't come to dinner planning to leave with a wife. He didn't even seem all that happy with the turn of events. He looked more confused and worried.

He might be clean and not swear, but for all she knew he'd murdered and buried several wives out on that ranch of his. No one, not even her brother-in-law, knew Hank Harris well enough to pay him an honest compliment. He might be a raving maniac living way off in a town she'd never heard about. But then, who was she to question his sanity. She'd married a giant she'd talked to for five minutes in the dark.

The wind tugged a strand of her hair free. She turned away from his stare and tried to push it back beneath her bonnet.

When she looked back, he was still staring at her as if she were the first woman he'd ever encountered. He had a strong face, made of all planes and angles. Not handsome, but solid with character.

Aggie let out a breath and told herself that a man's face didn't lie.

One corner of his mouth lifted. "How are we doing so far?"

She couldn't help but smile. "Well, I haven't shot you yet so I guess the marriage is lasting."

"You think we might try sitting down? It'll get mighty cold out here in the next eight hours."

Turning around just as the car shifted, Aggie lost her footing on the narrow step.

Hank's hand touched her waist only long enough to steady her. When he pulled away, she thought she heard him whisper, "Sorry."

They moved inside and found an empty seat. While she slid close to the window, Hank tugged at the top half of the bench in front of them, shifting the back so it made the seat face them. He sat his saddlebags on the empty bench. The tiny square he'd created offered them space and the hint of privacy. With an almost empty train, no one would be close to them for the journey.

He stood, halfway between the seat next to her and the one across from them as if debating where to sit.

"Do you like to ride facing backward?" she asked, thinking he looked so cramped having to lean forward to keep from hitting the top of the car.

"No," he said but didn't move.

She pulled her skirts close against her leg, making room for him.

When he sat, his knee brushed hers and he apologized again.

Relaxing, she almost giggled. Any man who'd said he

was sorry twice in ten minutes of marriage couldn't be as bad as her fears. "It's all right," she said. "We're married. We're bound to touch now and then."

He nodded and tossed his hat and coat on top of his saddlebags. "We probably need to talk about the rules of this partnership. I'd sure hate to do something to make you think you'd just as soon be a widow."

She patted the gun belt at her waist and smiled. "It's a long way to Amarillo. Maybe we should set a few rules so we both know what the other expects."

And they did. He told her of his house and how he'd change one room to be hers. She said she only knew how to fix breakfast, but she'd do that every morning if he'd cook dinner. He explained that his land was less than a mile from town so they could manage to eat at the hotel café some nights.

When he talked of his home, he relaxed, describing it so well she could almost see the ranch with its endless sunsets and room to breathe. From the train window the land turned flat, but he painted the beauty in it with his words so clearly she could almost see it through the night.

Somewhere between Fort Worth and home, Aggie fell asleep on her new husband's shoulder, dreaming of a life where her time was her own and no one ordered her around.

Chapter 4

Hank put up with her wiggling beside him, trying to get comfortable, for as long as he could stand it, then he shifted and circled his arm around her shoulder. Her head settled against his heart. She sighed softly in sleep and stilled as if she'd found the place where she could relax.

He thought back over everything he'd done or said all evening, and for the life of him he couldn't figure out how he'd ended up heading back home with a beautiful woman sleeping on him. Not just a woman . . . his wife. He'd always said he liked his solitude, but he looked forward to seeing what tomorrow would bring for the first time in years.

He felt like a miner who'd been breathing stale air for so long that a fresh breeze made him dizzy. Everything in his life had seemed fine until he met Aggie, then he noticed the emptiness. And, it had happened in the darkness outside, before he'd seen her face. He admired her honesty, her spirit, but her beauty made him nervous.

For a while he worried about what she'd think of his house, then he remembered Charlie's dugout and decided she'd like his place just fine. She wasn't his real wife, he reminded himself. Not in the true sense of it. But to the town, to his friends, she would be. Somewhere in their discussion of the rules for this partnership, they'd agreed to keep the arrangement between them. Which suited him fine. He wasn't sure anyone would believe him even if he tried to explain. She'd told him that he could touch her in any way that would be acceptable in public, but that she'd not be ordered around anywhere. He grinned, guessing she'd had enough bossing with four older sisters.

Her determination to work surprised him. He hadn't missed the way, after telling him of her dream to be a gunsmith, that she'd waited as if she expected him to argue.

He'd told her Amarillo had several places that sold guns, but no gunsmith to repair them. He offered to speak to Jeb Diggs at the mercantile and ask if he'd put out a sign.

Hank smiled again, realizing he'd smiled more tonight than he had in months. Once he mentioned the sign, she'd asked questions, wanting to know all about the possibilities of her working. Aggie told him about her small box of tools and said she could mail order more with the first money she made.

For a few moments her shyness had disappeared. She'd promised him she'd pay her way, buying her own clothes and paying for half the food. The last thing she'd said before falling asleep was that she'd be no trouble to him at all as if by agreeing to marry her he'd somehow taken on an extra burden.

Touching her hand with one finger, he wondered how such a delicate creature could want to work with weapons. Her blue-green eyes had sparkled at the thought though, and if that was what she wanted, he'd do his best to see it happened. He had a feeling, trouble or not, great changes were coming in his life, and all he could think was that it was about time.

He rubbed his chin against her auburn hair. She'd been asleep an hour. They'd be pulling into Wichita Falls soon. He knew all the noise would wake her, but he wasn't ready to have her pull away. They might be strangers, but she felt so right against his side.

The whistle blew as the train slowed. As he knew she would, Aggie straightened and replaced her bonnet. "Are we close to your home?"

"No," he managed to answer while thinking how ugly her hat fitted her face and hid the color of her hair. "We've only made the first leg, but there's a café here that stays open for this train. You hungry?"

She nodded.

"Twenty-minute stop," the porter yelled as he passed. "We don't wait for anyone."

Aggie's hand slid around Hank's arm as they rushed from the train. "Does the wound pain you?"

He covered her cold fingers with his. "I'd forgotten about it." He guided her into the café.

After they ordered, Hank decided to voice his thoughts. "I've been thinking since I just sold a few cattle that you should go ahead and order those tools you need right away. There's a mercantile across from the station." He added in almost a whisper, "We could also pick up any clothes you might need and maybe a hat to protect your face from the sun."

She looked up from her coffee. "I'll keep a record and pay you back."

He nodded, guessing she wouldn't accept the money any other way, and was thankful she didn't take offense at his suggestion of a new hat. "I could build you a bench in the barn to work. I have a bench out there where I'm always intending to build a few pieces of furniture, but I never seem to have the time. You could work with me on warm days, then when it gets cold you could use the kitchen table as a work area."

"You wouldn't mind?"

"I wouldn't. If we're to truly have this partnership, then half the barn, as well as the kitchen, is already yours."

"Thank you," she said as the cook delivered two bowls of chili with corn bread on the side.

When they were alone she added, "Mr. Harris, would you consider telling me why you married me?" She'd talked freely of her work and the rules, but she must think this question personal for her shyness returned.

"Don't you think you should call me Hank?"

She shook her head and looked down at her hands. He finished half his chili before she spoke. "My father told me once that my mother never called him anything but 'dear.' Would you consider it too bold if I did the same?"

No one had ever referred to him as dear. "I wouldn't mind." He wanted to add that she'd just made this bargain worthwhile even if she didn't do another thing, but all he said was, "I married you because you needed me."

She looked surprised. "Not because you wanted me or because folks say I'm pretty or because you needed a wife to help out?"

He shook his head. "You know you're pretty. In fact, I think you may be the prettiest girl I've ever seen, but I wouldn't have offered if that were all there was to you. In the dark, when we met, I saw your dreams, your hopes and, when we went inside, it didn't take much to see that those two fools would never make them happen."

She laughed, but her eyes studied him as if searching for a lie. "And will you?"

"Nope," he answered between bites, "but you will."

They ate the rest of the meal in silence with him wondering if she believed him. When they left the café and ran for the train she huddled close to him. The wind blew hard from the north. Hank could feel a storm coming and he hoped he made it home before it hit.

When they settled back into their seats, the car was empty except for a drunk snoring on the last bench. Aggie tugged off her shoes, doubled her legs beneath her skirts, and shifted so that her back rested on the window. Hank folded his leather coat and made a pillow for her to lean against.

"Thank you, dear," she said as casually as if she'd said the endearment all her life.

"You're welcome," he managed.

Hank had been an only child raised by a father who seldom said more than was necessary to anyone, including him. He was totally unprepared for Aggie. As the train pulled away from Wichita Falls and moved into the night, she began to talk, shyly at first. She told him of her home and her father, then she described all four of her sisters and how they'd married one by one and moved away.

Hank listened.

Tears bubbled in her eyes when she talked about how lonely her father seemed with all the girls gone except her. She loved working beside him and he'd taught her all he knew, but there still seemed to be this big hole in him that didn't fill until he began stepping out with Widow Forbes.

Hank liked the sound of Aggie's voice and the way emotions reflected in her face. He saw pride when she talked about her skill, and sadness when she told of leaving home and knowing if she ever returned she'd be a visitor in another woman's house. Anger also danced in her blue-green depths when she described how her sisters passed her from one to the other, each adding another layer of reasons why she wasn't married.

He could read in her eyes far more than she told. He'd bet the five hundred dollars in his pocket that she'd been her father's favorite and her sisters had resented it. He'd also bet the sisters hadn't wasted much time looking for the best man for Aggie.

Like a top spinning down, she finally said all she had to say. She must have waited a long time to find someone who would listen.

"You tired?" he asked.

She nodded.

"Turn around and lean against me." He shifted.

She pressed her back against his chest and he pulled his coat over her, resting his arm over her to keep the coat in place. "Trust me," he whispered against her hair. "I'll wake you before we get there."

"Yes, dear," she answered, already almost asleep.

Chapter 5

With the dawn came a downpour that seemed to be trying to wash the small town of Amarillo off the map. As the train pulled into the station, Aggie tried to catch her first glimpse. She stared out the foggy window at gray skies blending with the brown landscape.

"This is it." Hank stood as the engine braked. He crammed on his hat as if preparing for a fight. "We're home." Slinging his saddlebags over one shoulder, he moved toward the door. "I'll take your carpetbag now and come back for the boxes when I fetch my horse."

She sat motionless realizing he expected her to follow him.

"You have to be joking," Aggie mumbled. "I can't go out in that." She pointed at the rain pelting the windows. "There are tree branches blowing by bigger than me." She twisted her hands until her fingers turned ghostly white. "I can't go."

Hank laughed. "Train's moving farther north in half an hour and my guess is the storm only gets worse from here. We have to get off now."

When she didn't move, he added, "I'll carry you to the mercantile across the street. It's not far. You'll still get wet, but at least you won't get muddy . . . or blown away. Don't worry. I'll hold on to you."

Neither option seemed possible. Even if she had an umbrella, using it would be like fighting a bear with a twig. Much as she hated it, the only choice might be to run for the nearest shelter.

Hank moved down the aisle as if their discussion was over and she followed, her hands worrying in front of her. Marrying a stranger might have been reckless, but stepping out in that wind bordered on suicidal in her mind. No wonder there were no people in the Panhandle of Texas. They'd all blown into the Oklahoma Territory.

She watched as Hank crossed onto the platform, his legs wide apart and solid against the wind.

Before she could say anything, he swung her up and jumped from the train. Aggie wrapped her arms around his neck and held on for dear life as he ran into a wall of gray rain.

Shivering against him, she was too frightened to make a sound. Once they were off the platform, the street turned more river than road. He slowed, picking his steps. As tiny hailstones joined the rain, she felt his heart pounding even through their clothing.

His face lowered and his hat protected them both. A rough brush of whiskers touched her cheek.

"It's all right," he whispered, his lips near her ear. "We're almost there."

Aggie managed a slight nod and felt her cheek touch his once more. She tightened her grip. He did the same.

When he stepped onto the porch of Diggs Grocery and Hardware, she didn't lessen her hold. Now the rain wasn't hitting them, but the sound of it seemed deafening against the tin roof.

Hank pushed into the store. "We made it," he whispered with a laugh.

Aggie realized she hadn't been nearly as frightened as she thought she would be. She'd felt safe in his arms.

Placing her hand on his jaw, she turned his head slightly so that their eyes met beneath the shadow of his Stetson. "Thank you." She silently mouthed the words as she studied his face. A strong face with honest eyes, she decided. This tall man held far more than her at the moment. He held her future.

Warm air circled around them. Hank took a deep breath and raised his head.

When she looked up, a colorful mercantile greeted her. Everything from clothing, blankets, and food supplies to farm equipment and furniture seemed haphazardly piled around them. One man with a wide smile stood in the center of it all.

"Aggie." Hank cleared his throat. "I'd like you to meet Jeb Diggs."

Jeb Diggs, as round as the potbellied stove he stood beside, hurried toward them. "Well, well, Hank Harris. I didn't expect to see a soul today, much less you. What you got there?" The fat little man wiggled his eyebrows at Aggie.

Hank's hat dripped water as he looked down. "My wife," he answered as if the two words were all that needed to be said. Leaning, he set her feet on the floor.

"Mary Carol! Get out here!" Jeb bellowed. "Hank just found him a wife."

A woman matching Jeb in size waddled from the back. They both stared at Aggie as if they'd never seen such a strange creature.

Aggie straightened slowly. "Nice to meet you," she managed between shivers.

Hank's hand spread across her back, steadying her as though he sensed her fear.

Jeb motioned for them to come closer to the stove.

Hank circled her shoulder as if to draw her forward, but

she didn't budge. All her life she'd hated meeting strangers. Her father had never made her wait on customers in his shop as her sisters did. Now, everything and everyone about her was a stranger, and she longed for her quiet days spent in the back of the shop.

She glanced up at Hank. He smiled slightly, but didn't say a word. He looked like if she planned to remain rooted at the front door, he'd stand right beside her.

Mary Carol misunderstood Aggie's hesitance. "Don't worry about getting this floor wet, we'd outlast Noah, and don't pay no mind to that basket of cats. I found them out on the back porch without no momma to look after them. I couldn't stand them newborns getting soaked in this rain, so I put them as close to the fire as I dared."

Forgetting her own worries, Aggie looked at the basket by the stove. Wet, crying kittens wiggled about. She crossed and knelt, seeing that they were newly born and shivering. Blindly, they searched for their mother.

"If you have a cloth," she asked the lady staring at her, "I could wipe them dry."

Mary Carol smiled down at her. "I'll get one for them, and one for you too."

Aggie removed her ruined bonnet and wet coat, then sat beside the basket to begin rubbing each kitten down.

"She's a pretty one," Jeb Diggs said as he watched Aggie. "An angel you got there, Hank."

"She needs dry clothes and a warm coat. Just put whatever she picks on my bill," Hank said as he shoved back on his hat. "I have to get my horse unloaded."

Aggie looked up, hating that he had to go back out in the storm.

"You be all right here?" he asked, studying her.

She nodded.

Mary Carol waved Hank away. "You hurry right back. Jeb

will put on a fresh pot of coffee and it'll be waiting for you. I'll see to your new missus." She studied Aggie. "I'll bring out the few choices of clothing we have to pick from, and you can change in the storage room when you finish with them cats." As she walked away she mumbled, "You'll be needing boots as well."

The woman disappeared behind the stacks of clothing, but her voice continued, "You're lucky, we got in a huge shipment last week of winter wear. Nothing as fancy as what you have on, but good sturdy clothes."

Aggie looked down at the wrinkled violet dress she wore. Two of her sisters had picked it out, saying she needed something elaborate to attract a man, but the frills and buttons weren't comfortable and hadn't worn well.

Mary Carol tossed clothes over the stacks. A dark, rich, blue wool skirt landed at Aggie's feet, and a blouse cut like a man's, except for the collar and cuffs, followed.

Aggie ran her hand over the outfit. Growing up, her clothes had always been hand-me-downs. Pale yellows and washed-out pinks. She'd never worn anything in dark blue and couldn't wait to try it on.

"I got just the right vest to go with that," Mary Carol shouted as she hurried into sight. She held up a multicolored vest that looked like it had been made from an Indian blanket. "What do you think?"

Aggie grinned. It wasn't like anything she'd ever worn. It was perfect.

Twenty minutes later, when Hank stomped back into the store, Aggie sat by the stove drying her hair. He almost didn't recognize her. From her black boots to her western vest, she put any model he'd ever seen in a catalog to shame. He felt his mouth go dry. How does a man tell a beautiful woman she's just improved on perfection?

Tiny gray kittens, now fluffy and dry, were at her feet wrapped in a towel. Hank tried to concentrate on them as he moved closer, but five feet from her he made the mistake of looking up and froze.

"What's wrong? Is the storm worse?" She stood.

"No, I think it may be letting up a bit," he said, studying the way the mass of curls danced around her shoulders. "I just didn't know you had so much hair."

She frowned. "I'm afraid it curls when it gets wet. I'll . . ." Lifting her hands, she tried to pull it back.

"It's nice. Real nice," he said, wishing he could think of something more descriptive than "nice." He should have told her that the beauty of it took his breath away, but words like that would never make it past the lump in his throat. She must truly have no idea,how beautiful she looked.

Something wiggled in his shirt, demanding Hank's attention. "Oh," he said, pulling a gray cat out before she permanently scarred his chest. "I found this under the porch. Hope it's the momma."

Aggie laughed and took the cat from him. "Of course it's the mother cat. She's probably been frantic looking for her babies."

As she sat the cat in the middle of the towel, the little mother began licking each kitten.

Hank watched. "Guess she didn't think the storm got them clean enough."

Aggie shook her head. "More likely she's cleaning off my scent."

Before either could say more, Jeb entered with a round of coffee. "I was just askin' Mary Carol," he bellowed, unaware he was interrupting a conversation, "how did Hank manage to leave a week ago with cattle and come back with a wife?"

Hank ignored the store owner and moved closer. "I like your choice of clothes," he whispered before Jeb reached them. "They look right on you somehow."

She leaned nearer, almost touching him. "Thanks for bringing the mother cat in."

"You're welcome," he said, liking their whispering game.

Jeb tried again. "When did you two get married?"

"Last night, before we boarded the train," Hank answered without taking his eyes off of Aggie. "And as for how, I asked her, and she said yes."

Jeb laughed. "So that's it. We was figuring she must have held that gun she's wearing to your head and made you marry her—her being so homely and all."

Aggie lifted the Colt from its holster as if she hadn't heard the backhanded compliment. "Hank gave me his gun because, like my father, I'm a gunsmith."

Hank took one of the hot mugs from Jeb and almost laughed at the man's surprise.

When he found his voice, he asked, "A gunsmith?"

Both men stood silently as she opened one of her boxes. She pulled out her tools wrapped in oil cloth, then sat on the stool by the stove and used the checkerboard as her workbench. While they watched in amazement, she disassembled the Colt and cleaned it. She then dried the holster and rubbed the leather down with saddle soap to keep it soft.

Jeb stared at Hank. "Let me get this right. She's not only beautiful, she can fix guns too." He raised both eyebrows as if piecing together a puzzle. "And she married you?"

Hank laughed. "That's about the size of it, except she wants to practice her craft. Do you think you could hang a sign in the window and take in any work folks might need done? We'll come by every few days and deliver back and forth if she gets any business."

"And I'll give you a percent of all I earn, Mr. Diggs," she added.

Jeb shook his head. "Don't want a percentage. It's your work. I'll make any money for my time by selling more from the extra customers the sign will bring in. My guess is when word gets out that you're here, you will have all the business you can handle."

Aggie rolled up her tools. "Thank you. I have a list of tools I need." She pulled a slip of paper from the side of the box.

Jeb took the list. "I could probably get most of them from a supplier in Fort Worth. Wouldn't take more than a few days." He tapped the paper with his finger. "I'll send this order with the afternoon train." He glanced at Hank. "And, of course, I'll put it on your bill."

Hank agreed but didn't miss the surprised look she gave him. He couldn't help but wonder how long she'd carried the slip of paper with her small box of tools.

She accepted a mug of coffee and went back to her seat beside the cats. "Thanks for the coffee and for letting me watch your kittens."

Jeb shrugged. "In a few weeks you can have your pick of the litter."

She grinned at Hank.

He nodded his agreement.

"We'll take the runt," she said and went back to watching the animals while the men talked about the weather.

When his cup was empty, Hank pulled on his slicker over his coat and asked if she was ready to leave. He slipped a new slicker over her shoulders and covered her hair with the hood, unable to resist touching the curls.

Her hand gently brushed his forearm and she whispered, "Should I change this bandage? It must be wet."

Hank shook his head. "It'll just get wet again. Wait until we're home. I've got a good stash of medicine there."

She agreed and Hank heard Mrs. Diggs mumble something about lovebirds.

Before they realized there was nothing between Aggie and him but a partnership, Hank waved good-bye and held the door open for his wife. "I didn't bring the wagon into town. I thought I'd be coming back alone. You mind riding double?"

Surprisingly, she giggled. "I've only been on horseback a few times. My father always drove a wagon."

Hank bumped his head against the door frame, too busy watching her and not where he was going. "I won't let you fall," he mumbled, thinking that if he didn't stop staring at her and start paying attention, he'd have brain damage before the day was over.

Chapter 6

The rain launched an assault to keep them inside, pelting at full force when they cleared the door. Hank motioned for her to wait while he climbed onto his horse and tied her bag and the boxes in place behind the saddle. He rode close to the porch so he could lift Aggie up in front of him.

She might be shy, but her willingness for adventure surprised him. He'd half expected her to refuse to go with him. He'd bluffed her into following when they'd left the train, but he had no idea what he would do this time if she refused. He didn't know her well, but he didn't think Aggie would take too kindly to being tossed over the saddle against her will.

Mary Carol rushed out with two bags. "Here's her wet clothes," she said, pulling her shawl around her head. "I also packed a few supplies—bread, milk, and coffee just in case you don't have any out at your place."

"Thank you." Aggie accepted both bags.

"No problem. I put them on your account."

Hank's arm tightened around his bride as he turned the horse toward home.

"Maybe you should stay and wait out the storm?" Mary Carol yelled as they pulled away.

"Want to wait?" he whispered near Aggie's ear.

She shook her head. "I want to go home."

Hank no longer cared about the weather. He'd been so many years without a family, without anyone, heading home with Aggie seemed almost too good to be true. He had a feeling any moment he'd awake from this dream and find some other man had won her hand. The thought brought to mind Potter Stockton's frown last night. The railroad man had made fun of the proposal almost all the ride back to Fort Worth. Hank hadn't missed the anger in Potter's remarks. He'd hinted twice before they split near the depot that Hank would be smart to go on back to Amarillo alone and leave the courtship of Aggie to a man who knew how to treat a woman like her.

Hank couldn't help but wonder, if he'd missed the train last night, would she have agreed to meet Potter Stockton again, or would she have turned both men down and moved on to the next sister's house? Hank remembered how Stockton talked about her beauty and how he'd laughed and commented that shy ones always "take the bit" without too much fighting. Hank didn't even want to think about what Stockton meant.

If Hank hadn't already asked for her hand, he would have turned around and ridden back to Aggie just to warn her not to see the railroad man again.

If she wasn't cocooned in her slicker, he might have tried to tell her where his land started, but with the rain she could see little. He wished he'd had time to telegraph ahead and have his hand, Blue Thompson, light the fire in the house and put lamps in the windows to welcome her.

When they reached the ranch, even though it was late morning, all was dark. He leaned down to open the gate. She twisted in front of him, holding tightly to his slicker.

He straightened and pulled her close once more. "It's all right, Aggie. I won't let you fall."

Her hood slid back enough that he could see her nod, but

she didn't turn loose of her grip on him. When they reached the long porch that rounded three sides of his house, he lifted her with him as he stepped from the saddle and carried her up the steps. Old Ulysses, his guard dog, barked from beneath the porch.

"Hush, Ulysses, it's just me," Hank mumbled.

The dog growled, but quieted.

When they were well out of the rain, he sat Aggie down beside the only piece of furniture he'd brought north with him when he'd homesteaded—his father's rocker. "Don't worry about Ulysses. He's mean and hates everyone, including me, but he's a good guard dog. He keeps snakes away and warns me if anyone gets near the place."

Hank straightened and gripped the doorknob. "If I'd known you were coming, I would have . . ."

He didn't finish. It was too late for explanations or apologies. "Welcome home," he managed as the door creaked open.

Aggie walked in ahead of him and didn't stop until she was in the center of the polished floor. The storm's gray light shown the open area in layers of shadows. He stood at the threshold and stared at her back. The big main room looked empty with its two chairs and one long table. The fireplace was cold and dusty. The curtainless windows were stark, letting all the rage of the storm inside and holding no warmth.

"There's a kitchen and mudroom behind the fireplace. My room is to the left and yours will be to the right once I get my tack out of it. I'll move my bed in for you until I can build you what you need."

She hadn't moved. Her back was so straight he decided she must be in shock. To him the house had been great, but to her it must look cold and bare.

"The kitchen ceiling is only seven feet. I built an attic above it." He almost said "for kids." "I haven't been up there in awhile, but it would make a good storage room if you need one. All that is up there now is an old trunk someone sent back to my father after my mom died."

"You weren't there when she died?"

He shook his head. "She left my father and me when I was barely walking. Never heard from her. There must have been nowhere to send her trunk. Our address was still written on the top so they shipped it home to my father. We never opened it." His words sounded hollow, even to him, but better that, he decided, than angry, which is how he'd felt most of his childhood.

He watched Aggie closely. "I could move it to the barn if you need the space. I don't even know why I lugged it from East Texas when I moved."

He had no idea what Aggie needed to feel at home here, but he planned to make sure she had it. "We could order more furniture if you want. I never had much use for it until now."

She took a step toward the archway leading to the kitchen.

Hank had to keep talking. "You can't see them for the rain, but there's a bunkhouse and barn about a hundred feet to the north, and we got a windmill and a good well. In the spring the view is a sight to see from every window."

She'd reached the kitchen and still hadn't turned around or said a word.

"I hire hands to help with the spring calving and branding, but during the winter, Blue Thompson and I do all the work. He and his wife, Lizzy, have a place down by the breaks halfway between here and town." Hank felt near out of information. If she didn't say something soon he wasn't sure what to do.

Without warning, she twirled suddenly, her arms wide, her head back, her hair flying behind her.

He watched, hypnotized by the sight of her. If angels

ever touch ground they could look no happier than she did right now.

When she stopped, she faced him, a smile lifting the corners of her mouth. "I love it," she said.

"You do?"

She nodded. "All my life I've lived in tiny little rooms crowded with too many people. Here I can breathe."

Hank relaxed. "Then I can bring your stuff in and you'll stay?"

Tugging off her slicker, she answered as she disappeared into the kitchen. "Yes, dear, I'll stay."

Chapter 7

Aggie explored her new home while Hank brought in her boxes and bag. Like the main room, the kitchen was twice the size of any she'd seen, and her bedroom had enough space for all four of her sisters to join her. The windows everywhere were tall. She laughed, deciding Hank built them that way so he could see out without leaning down. Her father was short, only a few inches taller than she, and always fidgety in movement. Getting used to Hank would take some time. His strides were long and easy, graceful in a powerful way. But when he was still, he was perfectly still.

While Hank moved his bed into her room, she inspected the area above the kitchen and was surprised there was nothing in it but the battered old trunk he'd mentioned. She couldn't imagine a house with so much space that there would be an empty room. It also amazed her that he seemed to think it should be her room to do whatever she liked with. She moved around the attic, touching each wall, each window—silently saying hello to her new world.

"Aggie?" Hank called from below. "Come down and meet Blue."

She hurried to the kitchen and nearly collided with a gray-haired man almost as tall as Hank and twice as wide.

The man shuffled out of her way. "Pardon me," he mumbled, then laughed and added, "I didn't know you'd be flying down from above. Truth is I'd forgotten that room was up there."

Even with his slicker covering most of his body, she could tell his right shoulder was twisted, but there was nothing weak or soft about him. His frown seemed tattooed across his face and mistrust danced in his eyes. The big man looked as afraid of her as she was of him.

She fought to keep from running to Hank.

As if he sensed her fear, her husband moved to her side and looped his arm around her shoulder. "Aggie, I'd like you to meet my friend, Blue Thompson."

She knew Hank wouldn't use the word friend lightly, but Thompson looked like a man who hadn't trusted anyone since birth.

The big man stiffly offered his left hand while Hank continued. "Blue was shot up pretty bad at Williamsburg. When they found him in the cold, he was so near dead he looked blue." Hank offered him coffee.

"I've been called Blue ever since," the big man said. "I kinda like the name too, since I lived."

Aggie's fingers disappeared in his as they shook hands. "Nice to meet you, Mr. Thompson." She didn't miss the way he glanced down at Hank's gun around her waist and nodded once, as if he understood that Hank wouldn't have given his Colt to any woman unless she mattered to him.

"Just Blue," he corrected. This time when he returned her gaze she saw acceptance and maybe a little respect.

"Just Blue." She smiled. "And I'm just Aggie."

The old soldier relaxed. "Hank said your daddy taught you about guns."

"That's right," Aggie said.

"I got a French LeMat I carried in the war. Haven't been

able to fire it since that day I was shot, but I keep it anyway. Do you think you could have a look at it for me?"

"I'd be glad to," she answered, realizing Blue was accepting her a few inches at a time. "I've worked on one of them before. Bring it by when you have time."

Blue frowned. "I'd go get it now. Our place isn't that far away, but there's a fence down." He looked at Hank. "We gotta get to it, boss, or there will be hell to pay by morning."

Hank agreed. "Help me get the tack in the barn, then saddle the paint."

Blue tipped his hat to Aggie and followed orders.

"You'll be all right here?" Hank sounded like he hated leaving her.

For a moment she thought of arguing. This was their first day together. All her life her father never minded postponing work. He'd even stop working to enjoy his pipe, or a conversation. Aggie knew ranching wouldn't be like gunsmithing. Problems couldn't wait. "Go," she said. "I'd hate to pay hell in the morning."

Hank smiled. "I might need to talk to Blue about his mouth." Hesitantly, he leaned and kissed her on the forehead. "I'll be back as soon as I can. If you run into trouble, just fire three shots. If I'm not close enough to hear, Lizzy, Blue's wife, will come running."

Aggie moved to the window and watched the two men disappear into a curtain of rain. It occurred to her that she should feel lonely and abandoned, but even with the storm raging, she felt protected in Hank's house. She needed the time here to settle in.

The walls glowed honey-colored with each lightning flash as she ran from room to room loving the open feel to it. Space was a luxury she'd never known.

* * *

A hundred yards from the house, Hank realized he'd almost run out of the kitchen. He'd known that if he looked at her a moment longer he wouldn't be able to leave. As he lowered his hat and rode into the rain, he wondered at what point his mind had turned to oatmeal. How could a woman he hadn't even known twenty-four hours matter to him? When had she crawled under his skin and become a part of him?

Within an hour, he and Blue were riding the fence line looking for breaks. Compared to most of the ranches, his herd was small. Hank couldn't afford to lose any cattle. The cows he'd saved back from the last sale were all good breeding stock and he'd need them come spring. Last year he'd finally made it to the black after ten years of scraping by. He'd bought more land when the Duncan ranch next to him failed, and still managed to put some in the bank for a rainy day.

His plan had been to build enough to finally sell this spread and buy another, bigger one, farther from town. But, now, with Aggie in his life, he might have to rethink that plan. If she wanted to work, they'd need to live close to town, and the way Amarillo was growing it would overtake his ranch one day. The thought of being so close to town didn't interest him, but he couldn't see himself moving so far away that he made Aggie unhappy.

Smiling, he remembered the way she'd twirled around, her blue skirts flying.

Hank was so deep in thought he almost missed the downed fence. If Blue hadn't yelled at him, they might have ridden past a hole so big his entire herd could have moved through by morning.

As they worked, the storm played itself out. The wind settled to a breeze and the rain to a drizzle. The red Texas mud clung to their hands and boots. By the time they finished, both men were covered in caked dirt. The watery sun blinked its way between clouds, baking the earth to their clothes like shingles on a roof. Hank pushed hard, trying to keep his mind on his job and not on the woman who waited for him at home.

Blue, as always, worked beside him. For a man with little use of his right hand, he managed to earn his wages. Over the years the two men had learned to work as a team, but they rarely talked.

Late in the afternoon when they headed home, Blue turned off along the breaks with a wave and Hank followed the stream. He was bone tired after not sleeping the night before on the train, but he pushed his horse, wanting to reach the house long before sundown.

While he washed and put on his good white shirt in the mudroom, Hank noticed the bandage on his arm was spotted with blood. Sometime during the afternoon one of the stitches must have pulled loose. He wrapped it with a towel so he wouldn't get blood on his clean clothes, then entered the house as quietly as possible.

He found Aggie curled up in the middle of his big bed, which he had moved into her room when he brought her boxes in. The guard dog, Ulysses, slept on the rug beside her. The moment he sensed Hank, he raised his head and growled.

Hank chuckled. "Protecting the lady, Ulysses?"

Aggie awoke with a smile and touched the dog's head. "We had a long talk on the porch. Ulysses promised to be good if I let him come in for a while."

The old dog lowered his head, but continued a grumble as Hank walked to the bed. "How about we see if together we can't find something to eat." He offered his hand to Aggie. "I'm starving and Ulysses is always in a better mood when he's eaten."

Aggie's feet slipped to the floor as she accepted his hand. "First," she said, staring at the towel, "I'll check that wound and put a fresh bandage on it. I may not be able to cook, but I'm a fair nurse. My father was a walking accident looking for a place to pause. I hope Widow Forbes keeps her medicine kit handy."

"We'll send them one as a wedding gift." Hank laughed as he accompanied her to the kitchen.

To his surprise, she raised her hand to his shoulder and pushed. For a second he didn't understand what she was trying to do, then he realized she was attempting to push him into a chair.

He sat.

"I found the medicine box when I went through the cabinets." She pulled the box forward and stood in front of him. "I also found a full stock of beans and peaches." She hesitated, then added, "and nothing more."

Hank watched her clean the wound. "Most nights I come in too tired to fix anything else. Lizzy brings over a good meal every Monday when she comes to do the laundry and clean." He watched Aggie closely. "I pay her twice a year in beef. If it's all right with you I'd like her to still come. They depend on the meat."

Aggie nodded, but Hank wasn't sure she really listened. She worried over the cut.

"You're lucky this isn't showing signs of infection." She poked at the skin around his cut. "I think if we wrap it correctly the wound will stay closed, but I'll want to clean it and put medicine on it twice a day."

"It'll be all right." He shrugged, thinking he'd had far worse cuts.

She let out a huff of impatience and worry. "I'll clean this twice a day if I have to tie you to the chair."

Hank smiled. "Yes, ma'am. I had no idea I was marrying such a bossy wife."

She raised her gaze to his and wrinkled her forehead. "I never thought I would be, but it seems so. You'll just have to put up with it, I'm afraid."

Loving the way she'd lost any fear of him, Hank put his hand at her waist, steadying his arm as she bandaged his wound. His gun belt was missing from around her hips and he wondered if she simply removed it while she slept, or if she felt safe enough with him not to bother with even the pretense of the Colt.

"How are we doing?" He repeated the same question he'd asked on the train steps twenty-four hours ago. "Any complaints, so far?"

She worked silently, her nearness affecting him more than any poking she was doing. Taking a deep breath, he let the scent of her fill his lungs. He'd smelled perfumed women in the saloons, and a few proper ladies who bore the scent of starch and talcum, but Aggie was like neither. She reminded him of spring water just when the land turns green, all fresh and new.

When she didn't answer, Hank waited, figuring out that something bothered her. If he were guessing, he could think of several things—he'd left her their first day, the storm, no furnishings in the house to speak of, no curtains on the windows, none of her family close.

"There is one thing," she finally said as she tied off the bandage.

"What?" He wouldn't have been surprised if she said she changed her mind and wanted to go back to Fort Worth. Maybe the banker or the hotheaded Potter Stockton weren't looking so bad after she'd spent the day here alone. He remained still, his hand at her waist.

"When you left, you kissed me on the forehead."

If she was waiting for him to say he was sorry for *that,* she'd wait a long time. Finally, he managed to mumble, "You'd rather I hadn't been so informal?"

She shrugged. "No, actually, I was thinking that if you are going to kiss me good-bye, I'd rather you didn't do it on the forehead. It makes me feel like a child. I may be over a foot shorter than you, but I'm not a child. I wish never to be treated as such again."

Now he said, "I'm sorry," and meant it. "That was not my intent." He watched her closely, unsure where the conversation was going. "Where would you like me to kiss you when we part?" He thought of mentioning that couples do kiss one another politely when saying good-bye, but in truth he could never really remember seeing any husband do so except at the train station.

She placed her hand on his shoulder and leaned slightly toward him. "The cheek would be all right, I guess, or even the lips would seem appropriate. After all, we are married."

Hank had that feeling of walking on ice. One misstep and he'd disappear. He wondered if he'd ever be able to read this woman. She'd made it plain she wanted a partnership marriage and nothing more, and now she was telling him where to kiss her. It crossed his mind that if all women were as hard to read as Aggie, no wonder the saloons were packed with married men.

He dove into deep water. "Like this," he whispered as he tugged her near and brushed his lips lightly along her cheek.

She leaned away, considering. "That would be acceptable, I think." She smiled. "Your whiskers tickle."

His arm slid around her waist once more but this time when he pulled her, she stumbled, landing on his knee. Before he could change his mind, Hank kissed her soundly on the lips.

When he raised his head, her eyes were open wide.

"Is that acceptable, Aggie?" he said, preparing himself for any answer.

Standing, she whispered, "Yes, dear." She turned, suddenly giving all her attention to putting up the supplies.

Chapter 8

They ate their dinner of beans and peaches at the kitchen table without saying much. Hank would have thought he'd upset her, only her last words still sounded in his mind. She'd said the kiss had been acceptable.

He was thinking of when he should do the acceptable again when she asked, "Where'd you get your dishes?"

Glancing down, Hank noticed the mismatch of china. "I bought them in the discount bin a few months after I came here. When my dad died, I sold the farm and packed up what I could in a wagon. Somewhere between East Texas and here, the box of his china fell off the wagon." He lifted one bowl. "This was the only piece that survived."

Aggie smiled. "This makes me feel right at home. When my first sister married, she took Mother's good china with her. The second packed away the everyday set. Papa bought more, but they left after the third wedding. After that he just bought odd pieces." She lifted the china teacup she'd been drinking coffee out of. "As near as I can remember, my mother's best set looked like this one with the tiny blue flowers around the rim."

Hank had never noticed the flowers, but he was glad he'd chosen the tea set. He bought them because he thought the pieces somehow made his place appear more like a home. Now he thought the cup looked right in her tiny hand.

"After dinner," he said when he realized he'd been staring at her for a while, "we could walk over to the barn. I'll need to measure how high you want your bench. I'm guessing you'll want to do some of the gunsmithing in the barn."

"It's late," she said, glancing out at the night, "and it looks like it might rain again."

"I know, but I want to get started on it at first light tomorrow morning." He grinned and added, "While you're cooking breakfast."

She finally looked at him. "Let's hope I'm better at it than you are at supper."

Hank didn't argue. She'd only eaten half the beans he'd served her. "Blue, before he got married, used to come over for meals from time to time. He said I made a good stew and in the summer I can fry up fish and potatoes regularly." He'd already decided that if the mud wasn't too bad he'd take her in for dinner at the hotel tomorrow night, but he wanted her to know he wasn't going back on his offer to cook. "I plant a garden in the spring. For half the vegetables and a case of jars, Lizzy will can all we can eat next winter."

"What about this winter?"

"I told her all I'd need were potatoes and carrots. They're in a root cellar. I'm not real fond of the green stuff, even floating in stew, but if you like them, I'll barter for black-eyed peas and green beans. Soon as it dries out, we can pick up all the canned goods we need at the Diggs' place."

She pulled a small tablet from her pocket. "I've been making a list of things I need. If you'll loan me the money, I'll pay you back." She looked down at her new clothes. "I'd also like to buy a few more sets of clothes like these. I don't think I want to wear my old dresses. They don't seem to belong here."

He couldn't agree more.

Hank stood and pulled a coffee can from the top shelf. "I have some money in the bank, but this is what I planned for winter expenses. There's a little over five hundred dollars here. You're welcome to however much you need." He started to return the can to the top shelf, then reconsidered and shoved it between the spices so it would be within her reach.

"I'll pay you back. Once we're square, I'd like it if we both put the same amount into the can each year. Then whatever else you make on the ranch or I make working will be for each to decide."

He wanted to argue that it wasn't necessary, but she'd said each year like there would be many. Figuring he'd have time to talk out expenses later, Hank asked, "Did you decide if you want to use the room upstairs?"

"I thought I'd make it my indoor workroom, that way the kitchen won't get cluttered. The light's good up there and on cold days the kitchen fire will keep it warm."

"I could frame you up furniture tomorrow. The good thing about winter on a ranch is there's time to do all the chores I couldn't get to in the spring and summer. The bad thing is I never seem to finish the list before calving." He stood and lifted a lantern from the peg by the back door. "You want to walk with me to the barn and tell me where to put that bench?"

She nodded and followed him out of the house and along a path of smooth stones. Ulysses tagged along as far as the barn door. He growled and barked at the shadows, but before Hank could tell him to be quiet, Aggie touched his head and he moved to her side, standing guard as if something were just beyond the light waiting to hurt her.

They spent ten minutes walking around the barn, determining where would be the best place for a bench, and finally decided on a spot near the door. There she'd get the breeze, the morning sun, and anything left on the bench overnight would remain protected from the weather once the door was closed.

"I'd like to start tonight." Hank knew it was late, but he wouldn't sleep anyway. Too much had happened today, and Aggie would be too close, even three rooms away. "I'll turn in before midnight."

She looked up at him. "All right. I think I'll turn in now. I feel bad taking your bed though."

"Don't worry about it. Somehow it wouldn't be right if you were the one on the floor. I'll talk Blue into helping me string another frame this week, but for now a bedroll will be nothing unusual for me to sleep on."

She hesitated. "Well . . ."

They stood in the circle of light staring at each other. As he guessed she would, she broke the silence first. With her fingers laced together in front of her, she said suddenly, "It's not fair."

Hank fought down a smile. She fired up fast when something bothered her. "What's not fair?"

She fisted her hands on her hips and looked up at him. "If I want to kiss you good night, I have to ask you to bend down first."

A slow smile spread across his face. He grabbed a milking stool from the first stall and set it firmly in the center of the light, then he lifted her atop it.

They were equals. He stared straight into the devil dancing in her blue-green eyes.

He waited as she leaned forward and kissed him lightly on the cheek. When she straightened she said, "Good night, dear." Her hand rested on his shoulder. She made no effort to remove it.

"Good night," he said as his mouth touched hers. This time his lips were soft and slow. He fought the urge to pull her against him. He knew where a kiss could lead, but she was innocent. If he moved too fast, she might be frightened.

Too fast! his mind shouted. When had he crossed some invisible line from accepting her as a partner and nothing more to thinking of what came after the kiss?

Gently pulling away, he smiled when she pouted. "I'll put a stool in every room so all will be fair," he whispered, so near he could feel her quick breaths on his cheek.

He couldn't resist; his lips found hers once more. The kiss remained gentle, but his hands at her waist tugged her slightly so that their bodies touched. He felt her soft breasts press into his chest each time she inhaled, and the feeling was so right.

His fingers relaxed. Aggie could have stepped back if she'd wanted to. But she didn't break the contact. Feather light, she placed her other hand on his shoulder and continued the kiss.

She was learning, exploring, he realized, and he had every intention of being her guide.

Ulysses barked at a shadow somewhere beyond the barn and Aggie lifted her head. For a second their eyes met and Hank didn't miss the fire in her shy gaze a moment before she looked down.

"Aggie," he whispered, ignoring the dog's barking. "Aggie, look at me."

Slowly she raised her head.

"There's no need to ever be embarrassed or shy with me. I'm your husband."

She nodded. "I know, dear. I'm not."

"Then what is it?" Even in the shadowed light he saw the blush in her cheek and felt her fingers moving nervously over his shoulders.

"I . . ." She looked down again, then forced herself to face him. "I just didn't expect it to feel so good."

"The kiss?"

"Yes, that, but also the nearness of you. Even last night on the train I liked you holding me close. And the kissing part, I always thought it was something a man did to a woman. I guess I never considered it as something they did together."

Hank had no idea how to answer. He should have stayed with talking about the weather. He'd never be able to explain what was happening to her. Hell, he couldn't put his own emotions into words most of the time. "Would it help any if I told you I feel the same?"

She smiled. "Not much." He saw it then, that twinkle in her eye. That warning that one day soon she'd understand him better than he did himself.

"Good night, Aggie." Hank decided he'd be wise to stop this conversation while he could still form reasonable thoughts.

As he settled her on the ground, he knew beyond any doubt that he'd be wasting his time building another bed. They'd share the same one soon. It bothered him that he wasn't sure if it would be his idea, or hers. And worse, he didn't care.

Part of him decided it had to be impossible for such a beautiful woman to know so little, but then with four older sisters she must have always been chaperoned. And, for some reason, she trusted him.

He grinned. The perfect wife, a preacher once said, was a woman who made a husband want to be a better man. Hank stared out into the night and silently promised he'd be that and more for her.

He watched the old dog follow her back to the house. She looked like she belonged here. Turning, he set to work on the bench, his thoughts full of Aggie. She was shy, and probably more than a little spoiled. He'd have to tell her that putting her fists on her hips and demanding something wasn't fair might not always work with him.

Suddenly, he laughed, realizing it had.

He heard the back door close and Ulysses run around the house barking at the darkness. Probably a rabbit, Hank thought. That and snakes were the only invaders the place ever had.

Thunder rattled several miles away. He looked up in time to see the next round of lightning. Across the flat land it was easy in the blink to pick out the black outline of the windmill, the bunkhouse, and a lone rider on horseback waiting just outside the yard light.

Hank froze. No one but trouble would be riding up behind the house this time of night. He reached for his Colt and realized it was with Aggie.

Blowing out the lantern, Hank stood perfectly still and listened. Someone was out by the windmill. Someone who wasn't a friend or he would have yelled a hello.

Ulysses had climbed on the porch and was barking wildly now, standing guard, Hank decided, protecting Aggie, just where Hank would have wanted the dog. Whoever moved in the moonless night would not step on the porch without being attacked. Aggie would be all right for now.

The only problem was, the shadow lay between Hank and home.

Chapter 9

Aggie washed and slipped on her nightgown with a blue ribbon at the throat. She'd bought it in Chicago and kept it wrapped in paper in the bottom of her bag. Smoothing the cotton, she told herself this wasn't her real wedding night. But she had to wear it. Dolly had demanded she leave her old one behind. Somehow, even though she'd sleep alone in her bed, it seemed right to start her new life in all new clothes, even a nightgown.

She'd almost finished brushing her hair when she realized Ulysses hadn't stopped barking. At first she'd thought he'd just been running the night like guard dogs do, but now the sound he made was different. Angry, fierce.

Hank was outside with the dog. Surely he'd silence him with a yell soon.

But minutes ticked by and nothing. In fact, if anything the dog's growls sounded near panic.

Her mind began to think of all the possibilities. What if Hank were hurt? What if a wild animal had charged him? She'd heard there were mountain lions and bears in this part of Texas. Her father had often said he'd never go west because it was full of mad animals and crazy people. Her sister told her the Indian Wars had been over for a few years, but what if . . .

She couldn't stand guessing anymore. Grabbing Hank's gun belt, she strapped it around her waist, then pulled on her robe without bothering to tie it. If something was outside, she had no intention of hiding indoors.

Without a lamp, she felt her way through the main room to the front door. The barking sounded like it was coming from the back of the house. If she stayed in the shadow of the porch she might see trouble before it found her.

As she slipped outside, the cold, wet boards felt slippery beneath her, but she couldn't take the time to go back for shoes. Slowly, her fingers sliding along the painted walls, she moved toward the side of the house where she'd be able to see the barn.

Lightning flashed and she froze, knowing that if there was someone, or something out there in the night, they would be able to see her for a few seconds.

But nothing moved.

She continued her progress, one small step at a time. When she turned the corner and saw Ulysses—still barking—facing the barn, she silently pulled the Colt and readied it.

"Easy, Ulysses," she whispered, not wanting to surprise him from behind. "I'm here now."

Ulysses lowered to a growl, but didn't move. Something between the dog and the barn held his full attention. It took her brain a moment to recognize the outline of a man on horseback with something held high in both hands, like a warrior of old wielding a sword.

Aggie waited for the next flash of lightning.

Seconds passed. She and Ulysses stood vigil.

With a sudden flash of lightning, Aggie saw a man again, closer now to the opening of the barn.

As thunder rolled, Hank shouted, "Aggie, get back inside."

He'd seen her, but she hadn't had time to find him in the moment's flash. The blackness that followed swallowed all light. Aggie strained, trying to make out any form, struggling to hear any movement.

The whack of board against bone thundered across the yard. Once! Twice!

Ulysses went wild.

The sound of a horse stomping rumbled near the barn. The animal screamed as a man's voice shouted a curse. A moment later the horse broke into a run. Aggie raised her Colt and fired as a rider blinked past her. Before she could draw aim again, the horse had taken his dark knight out of range.

Suddenly, Ulysses and she were running toward the barn.

"Hank," she cried, not sure if she were screaming his name or praying. "Hank!"

Stepping into the barn reminded her of falling into a cave. Velvet blackness on the moonless night. She clambered for the lantern she'd seen Hank set on a shelf just inside the barn, hoping he had only turned it out and not taken it down.

The lantern was there along with an almost empty box of matches. It took three tries before Aggie brought the match to life and lit the lantern. When she turned, spreading light, she might have missed the heap on the ground beside the stall if Ulysses hadn't been right beside him. At first she thought it might be rags, then she recognized a white shirt.

"Hank!" He lay facedown and far too still. Blood dripped from his head and one of his long legs twisted just below the knee at an unnatural angle. A long two-by-four lay beside him, harmless though spotted with blood.

Aggie sat the lantern a few feet from him and ran for the barn door. As soon as she cleared the roof, she lifted her gun and fired three quick shots. Then she ran back to her husband.

By the time Blue Thompson and a woman who had to be his wife arrived, Aggie had wrapped the belt of her robe around Hank's head and was applying pressure where blood dripped with each of his heartbeats.

"What happened?" Blue asked as he jumped from the buggy.

Aggie couldn't stop the tears. "I don't know. I heard something. Someone. Then he rode off and I found Hank."

"Who would want to hurt Hank?" Lizzy demanded as she knelt beside her husband. Her voice was low, but her hands moved skillfully over Hank's injuries.

"I don't know." Aggie fought panic. "I don't know."

Blue slowly straightened Hank's leg, shaking his head as he worked.

"It looks busted," Aggie cried. "Oh, God, what if it's busted?"

Lizzy grabbed Aggie's chin with bloody fingers. "Don't you worry none, we're going to take care of your man." She forced Aggie to look at her and not Hank. "But we're going to need your help. You understand?"

Aggie pulled in the frayed strings of her emotions and forced herself to take a breath. "All right. We can take care of him. We can."

The no-nonsense directness of the older woman had helped and she allowed Aggie no time to think of what might be beyond this moment, this crisis. "First," Lizzy said in her low, Southern voice, "we get him to the house."

Aggie looked back at Hank. "We can do that." She raised her chin.

Lizzy smiled. "Right you are."

"His leg probably is broke." Blue voiced what they all knew. "We'll have to be real careful moving him. Once he's inside and the blood's cleaned off, we can see the damage. If he's still breathing, I'll ride for the doc."

It took all three of them to lift Hank without moving his leg more than necessary. He moaned once, telling Aggie he was still alive, but his normally tanned face looked almost as white as his shirt.

Aggie held his head while Blue and Lizzy removed his boots and trousers. There was no doubt the leg was broken; a jagged bone had ripped the flesh from inside out. Blue straightened it as best he could, then tied both legs together with a strip of bandage. He explained that he'd seen doctors do that in the war when there was no time to look for splints.

With only a nod toward his wife, Blue left to get the doctor.

Lizzy brought cold water from the well and handed Aggie bandage after bandage for his head. Each time they switched, blood covered the cotton. They talked, trying to convince themselves that his being unconscious was better than if he were awake and in pain, but Aggie could tell Lizzy didn't believe their reasoning any more than she did.

In what seemed like minutes, Blue was back with the doctor, a man who barely looked old enough to shave, much less finish medical school.

To Aggie's surprise, the doctor asked her if she wanted to stay while he examined her husband. Part of her wanted to run as far away from the smell of blood as she could get, but another part knew she belonged here. She was bound to this man she'd known less than two days. Bound by honor as well as the law.

As the doctor worked, stitching up the long gash in Hank's hairline, Aggie gently held his head in her lap. The wonder that she could care for a man so quickly danced in her mind with the grief that would come if she lost him.

In the few hours they'd been together she'd taken him into her heart, and there he would remain whether she loved or mourned him for a lifetime. Closing her eyes, she tried to remember the moment she'd known he could be someone to depend on and trust. Though she liked his laughter and the way he gently teased her, it had been something far more basic that drew her even during their conversation outside the dugout. Hank listened. He really listened to her. Could something so simple form a bond that would weather them through hard times?

She looked down at his lean body. Strong and tan from hard work. It occurred to her that she'd never seen so much of a male body before and she should be embarrassed, but she wasn't—somehow this man belonged to her—was a part of her.

"Keep his head as still as you can, Mrs. Harris," the doctor ordered. "I don't want him thrashing about when I set this leg."

Aggie placed her hands on Hank's cheeks and noticed her tears were falling across his face, but it didn't matter; nothing mattered but Hank. She could not, would not, lose him.

When the doc and Blue set the leg, pulling the bone back in place, Hank groaned in pain. Aggie pressed her face close to his and whispered over and over, "You're going to be all right, dear. You're going to be fine."

Aggie watched, feeling the pain with him as they sewed up the cuts and strapped his leg to a board that ran from his knee to his foot. She washed his face and chest, keeping him cool as the doctor checked his head wound again and again.

Finally, a little after dawn, the doc packed up his things, saying all that was left to do was to wait and see. Hank seemed to be resting comfortably, which was the best medicine.

An hour later, Aggie heard Blue talking to the sheriff. The lawman insisted on speaking to her, but she wouldn't leave Hank's side to go into the main room. Her new nightgown was spotted with blood and she didn't remember when she'd removed her robe or where. Hank's Colts hung on the headboard, within easy reach if she needed them.

Finally, Blue opened the door and asked if it would be all right if the sheriff came in for a minute.

Aggie pulled a thin blanket over her shoulders and nodded. The sheriff walked in, took one look at her, and didn't waste time with small talk.

"Did you see the man who did this?"

"One man." Aggie tried to focus on something besides Hank's breathing. "I only saw his shadow. He wasn't tall but he seemed thick, barrel-chested, or it may have been his coat that made him look so. His horse was dark, black or brown and bigger than most. I don't remember any markings. I heard him swear as he rode from the barn, but he was only in my sites for a moment."

The sheriff looked up from his notes. "You fired at him?"

"I hit him," she said.

"How do you know? He didn't stop. How can you be sure, Mrs. Harris? Maybe you only thought you hit him?"

Suddenly too tired to keep her eyes open, she curled beside Hank. "I hit him," she mumbled, "because I always hit what I aim at."

"And where did you aim?"

"Left shoulder," shc answered as she rested her head on Hank's arm. "Look for a man wounded in the left shoulder and you'll find the man who attacked my husband."

She fell asleep without seeing the look the sheriff and Blue gave each other.

Chapter 10

Hank came to one painful inch at a time. His leg felt like he'd left it in a campfire. His head throbbed.

He turned slowly. Something soft brushed his chin.

Opening one eye he recognized Aggie's hair. She was curled up in a ball, sleeping beside him. The thin blanket barely covered her.

"She's been asleep like that for a few hours." Blue's voice sounded from the doorway. "Stayed up with you all night. Refused to leave your side even when the sheriff wanted to see her this morning."

Hank forced through the pain and moved his head enough so that he could watch his friend cross the room. "She okay?"

Blue chuckled. "Sure. Says she shot the guy who clubbed you." The older man added, "Said it as calm as if she weren't doing nothin' more than shooting rats in the barn. Just from what I've seen today I'd say she might be a tiny thing, but there ain't nothin' frail about her."

Hank closed his eyes, trying to remember what had happened in the blackness of the night. Someone had been outside of the barn. He remembered stepping to the door. Then he'd seen Aggie on the porch, her white gown billowing around her, waving danger her direction. His last thought had been that he had to get to her.

Slowly, he lifted his hand and felt the bandage across half his forehead. He must have been hit, but he couldn't remember the blow. The only thing in his mind had been panic that Aggie was in danger.

"What's the damage?" he asked as if he were talking about a machine and not his body.

Blue shrugged. "Not as bad as it could have been. Four stitches in your head. Left leg broke about three inches below your knee. Doc said it should heal clean."

Hank mumbled as Blue offered him water. "Any idea who or why?"

Blue shook his head. "Didn't know you had an enemy in this world, boss, but one thing is for sure, whoever attacked you meant to hurt you. The second blow broke your leg, not the first. A man planning to rob you wouldn't have done that. No need. You were already out cold."

Hank tried to reason as he cobbled together all that had happened. Maybe the traveler was afraid he'd shoot him for being on his land. Or maybe he was an outlaw running from the law and wanted to make sure no one followed. Why else would the stranger break his leg?

"Get some rest." Blue pulled a heavy quilt over Hank. "It looks like it's going to rain the rest of the day. Lizzy and I are going home to get some sleep. We'll be back long before nightfall to check on you and bring some soup. My guess is that little wife of yours won't leave your side to cook any more than she would for other reasons."

Hank touched the gun belt on his bedpost. "We'll be fine." He forced his voice to sound stronger than he felt. "Let the mutt in before you leave. He'll warn us if anyone tries to get into the house."

Blue nodded. "I'll find you a stick to use for a cane. The

doc says you can climb out of that bed as soon as you feel up to it, but don't put any weight on that leg for at least a week."

Hank nodded, hating the idea that he'd lose days of work. The cane might get him around the house, but he wouldn't be able to go outside until the mud dried out, and even then he couldn't ride. Being laid up was going to cost him dearly.

"I'll keep an eye on things until you're getting around better." Blue's face seemed to have added a few new wrinkles in the past hours. "Lizzy or I will check on you two a few times a day just to see if we can help, and I'll go in for any supplies you need." He glanced at Aggie. "Hell of a first day for the little missus."

"Much obliged." Hank hated needing help, but he knew he'd offer the same to Blue if need be.

Blue disappeared out the door.

Hank stayed awake long enough to hear them leave. They let the dog in and Ulysses hurried to the side of the bed where Aggie slept. The old dog laid his head on the edge of her blanket and waited for her to pat him.

"Lay down, Ulysses," Hank whispered as he drifted off. "She'll pet you when she wakes."

An hour later, Hank moved slightly and pain brought him back from a dream. He rolled his head and faced sleepy blue-green eyes watching him from a few inches away.

He didn't move. Their heads rested on the same pillow.

"Do you need anything?" she whispered.

"Sleep," he answered. "How about you?"

"I'm cold," she admitted as she crawled off the bed.

Her crimson-spotted nightgown was stiff in spots with Hank's dried blood, and so wrinkled it looked more like a rag.

He lifted the side of the heavy quilts covering him. "Climb in," he offered. "We can go back to sleep. With this rain it seems like twilight outside."

She shook her head as she tried to straighten her gown. "I

can't sleep in my clothes and I have no other gown. Maybe if I get dressed and wash this it will dry in a few hours."

Pointing toward the door, he ordered, "Grab one of my flannel work shirts from the mudroom. It'll be warmer and probably as long on you as that gown."

She hesitated, but the night without sleep must have won out. She disappeared.

Hank relaxed as he listened to her bare feet run across the main room floor. He should have told her to grab socks as well.

A few minutes later, she stepped back into the room, buttoning the last button of his favorite shirt.

The flannel clung to her body and stopped at her knees. Though the shirt covered almost all of her, the sight of it on her warmed Hank more than the cotton warmed her.

Without a word, he lifted the corner of the quilt and she slipped in beside him, careful not to touch him.

When she shivered, he raised his arm and pulled her close. Her feet brushed his uninjured leg with the shock of an icicle sliding across his skin, but he forced himself not to flinch.

Her hand pushed against his bare chest. "I'm too close. I'll hurt your leg."

Hank couldn't help but laugh. "Believe me, Aggie, your nearness isn't affecting my injury at all."

When she wiggled, cuddling, Hank fought down a groan. His left leg was about the only part of his body not reacting to her.

"Go to sleep," he said more harshly than he meant to.

"Yes, dear," she answered as she settled beside him.

Hank lay awake and listened to her breathing slow. If he'd known all it took was a few blows from a two-by-four to get the most beautiful woman he'd ever seen in his bed, he might have taken the hits earlier. She felt so good next to him. As her body relaxed in sleep, her softness melted against him, alive and comforting like he'd never known.

Moving his face against her hair, he took a long breath, pulling the scent of her deep into his lungs. Blue had said she'd refused to leave him last night when he'd been out. Hank curled a strand of her hair around his finger, wondering how he could matter so much to her. One look at her and anyone could love her, but how could it be possible that she cared even a little about him? He was nothing special to look at and he sure couldn't offer her much. Even his own mother hadn't stayed around.

But Aggie had. She'd stayed by his side.

He knew he had been little more than her way out of a bad situation. For a shy woman traveling around, being put on the marriage block for first one group and then another to offer for, must have been torture. Why had he been the one she went with? The one she wasn't afraid of?

He watched the storm play itself out, then finally drifted to sleep with his hand resting at her waist.

Around sunset, he awoke to find her gone. He took her absence like a blow even before reality fully registered on his aching brain. Glancing at the side of the bed, he noticed the mutt had also vanished. Wherever Aggie was, Hank would bet his saddle the dog would be with her.

He didn't have long to wait. Five minutes later, she backed her way into the room carrying a tray of food. Seeing her fully dressed made him frown. He'd give up food altogether if she'd crawl back in bed with him.

"I brought you some of Lizzy's soup and bread. They headed home, wanting to be settled in before it got dark." She didn't meet his gaze. Her shyness had returned. "Do you want me to feed you?"

Hank pulled himself up until his back rested against the

headboard. "I can feed myself, Aggie," he grumbled. "My leg is broke, not my arms."

She nodded without looking up as she carefully sat the tray beside him. "The doc said I'm to check the bandage on your head at sunset. If there is no new blood, I can leave the dressing off."

Hank lifted the bowl of soup and drank it down without taking his eyes off her. He couldn't believe, after how they'd slept together all day, she could go back to being so shy again. She busied herself getting everything ready while he ate, but not once did she look at him.

Finally, he could stand it no longer. "What is it, Aggie? What's wrong?"

"Nothing," she said as she removed the tray and began tugging the bandage on his head away. "How do you feel?"

"Fine." He returned a lie for a lie.

"The stitches are holding. I don't think you need a bandage again." She brushed his hair away from his forehead and moved to the wound on his arm. "The cut looks good. You heal fast."

Hank didn't want to talk about his injuries. He wanted to know what had changed between them when she'd cuddled next to him this morning and now. Until this moment he'd thought he missed little by not having a mother around. Now he realized how much he had to learn about reading women. No. Not women, he corrected. Aggie.

When she tucked the blanket around him, his fingers gently closed over her hand. "What's wrong?" he asked again, his tone more demanding.

When she tried to tug her hand away, he held fast. He'd never learn if he didn't start right now.

Finally, she looked up at him, her eyes filling with unshed tears. "We've only been married two days and you've been injured two times. At this rate you'll never last a week." Her chin rose slightly as if she were forcing herself to face facts. "My sisters were right. I'm nothing but trouble. Dolly said once that having me around is no different than having the plague circling. All my sisters were glad to help my poppa get rid of me."

Hank laughed, then realized she didn't see the humor. "Aggie, it wasn't you who had a knife at the train station, or who wielded the board in the darkness of the barn." He tugged until she sat beside him. "But it was you who took care of me. And the reason your sisters wanted to marry you off had nothing to do with you being bad luck, trust me on that."

She nodded once, obviously not believing him. She pulled her hand away.

He fought the urge to reach for it and hold on tightly, but she had to come to him on her own time if there was ever to be anything more between them.

The rain tapped on the windows again, drawing their attention. Aggie turned up the lamp by the bed, then watched gray streaks run down the long windows. "Tell me about the beauty of this land again, dear. I'm having trouble remembering."

Hank laughed, realizing this time of year it would be hard to see any beauty, but she seemed to need calming. Worry wrinkled her forehead, so if she needed to talk of something besides what had happened, he'd give it a try.

He told her of the first day he'd ridden over his land. How spring turns the world green and the colors in the rock walls of the canyons seem to wave and billow like the skirts of Spanish dancers. He described a summer shower that came up all of a sudden like a phantom riding the wind, dumping a bucket of water that sparkled like diamonds over the wet grass. He told how a dust devil seemed to chase him over the open range, following behind no matter which way he turned his horse.

He caught her glancing out the window from time to time as if she didn't quite believe his tale. The tapping grew louder as the rain turned to hail. The tiny balls of ice hit the ground and bounced almost like popcorn jumping in a skillet. Within seconds the ground was white as snow.

Hugging herself, Aggie asked, "Should I light the fire in the main room?"

"No." Hank chose his words carefully, knowing there might be a long way between what he wanted and what was about to happen. "We'll be warm enough under the covers." He kept every word level, without emotion, as if he'd said the same words many times before.

She nodded, and to his surprise picked up the flannel shirt. "I'll wash up in the kitchen and change."

As soon as she left, Hank grabbed the stick that Blue had left to serve as a cane. Slowly, he moved off the bed. Without putting any of his weight on the broken leg, he crossed the few feet to the washstand and chamber pot.

Aggie might be his wife, but there were some things Hank had no intention of asking her to help with. By the time he was washed up and back to the bed, sweat covered his forehead. He sat down with his back resting against all the pillows and pulled the covers up to his chest. He wished he'd had the sense to buy a nightshirt sometime in his life. Having lived all these years alone, he'd seen no need. But Aggie might find his bare chest shocking.

Hank smiled suddenly. She hadn't commented on it earlier. Maybe she didn't notice. One leg of his long-handled underwear had been cut off at the knee just above where the splint started. The other leg was spotted with dried blood, but he'd wait until morning to put on a clean pair. He wasn't sure he had the energy tonight.

Aggie appeared wearing his shirt. "I washed my gown earlier," she began, "but it didn't get dry."

"You look fine," he said, and then wished he'd thought to say something more. In truth, she looked adorable.

She sat on the end of the bed and folded her legs beneath her. "I was hoping, if you're not too tired, that we could talk a while."

Hank didn't move. Bedtime conversations were totally new to him and he had no idea what to talk about. She, on the other hand, looked like this was part of her nightly routine, and with four sisters it may very well have been.

She placed her elbows on her flannel-covered knees and rested her chin in her hands.

He swore she looked twelve years old.

"Blue and I have been talking and we don't think the attack on you was an accident. No one would be just riding by this place. It's too far off the road."

"So, what are you saying?" Hank watched her as he tried to follow the conversation. She had shifted and now the soft roundness of her left breast molded against the shirt. Suddenly, nothing about her seemed childlike. There was no doubt she was all woman.

"I'm saying . . ." She moved again and Hank closed his eyes so his ears would work. "I'm saying," she repeated, "that someone wants you hurt . . . or dead."

Hank shook his head, then regretted the action. "I don't think so. I don't make a habit of crossing folks if I can help it, and it's been years since I even had a heated discussion with anyone."

"Try and think," she coached. "Who lately would benefit from your being hurt or dead? Who has threatened you?"

"Nobody but Potter Stockton on the way back to town the other night. He told me I'd be wise to get on the train and forget about you, because I must know you'd never come." Hank told the account in passing, nothing important, he thought . . . until he saw Aggie's face. "You can't believe

Stockton would send someone to hurt me? Sure, he was probably disappointed when he learned you left with me, maybe even mad. But mad enough to try and kill me?"

Aggie nodded. "On the way to the station, Charlie told me he was glad I didn't pick Potter even though Dolly thought he was the best choice. Charlie said he heard Potter beat a man near to death one night after losing a few dollars in a poker game. He said the railroad man had gunfighter eyes—cold and hard as casket wood."

Hank raised a doubtful eyebrow. "But Charlie still invited him to dinner?"

Aggie shook her head. "He only invited the banker and told him that if he knew a man looking for a wife, to bring a friend along."

That explained Charlie's coldness to Potter Stockton, but Hank still found it hard to believe any man would try to kill another over a woman he'd just met.

Then he looked at Aggie with her beautiful hair and shining eyes and he knew it must be true.

"When did the man insist on having a drink with you?" she asked.

Hank tried to remember exactly the order. "He was standing behind me when I bought our two tickets."

Aggie frowned. "So he knew you were expecting me?"

"He also knew I didn't have time to wander over to the saloon."

She leaned closer. "Do you think, when the offer for drinks didn't work, that he pulled the knife thinking one way or the other he'd make sure you missed the train?"

Hank didn't want to admit it, but she made sense. The fellow hadn't acted all that drunk at first, then as soon as he'd slipped the knife over Hank's arm, he'd run away. "Maybe," Hank admitted. "He knew if I wasn't at the station you wouldn't be going anywhere that night."

Aggie finished the thought. "And if you weren't there, I would have turned around and gone back to Dolly and Charlie's place."

Their eyes met. Hank felt like he could read her thoughts. There was no need to continue piecing the puzzle; they'd both seen the picture it made.

Lacing her fingers together, she leaned an inch closer and whispered as if saying her words too loud might make them come true. "Do you think the hired gun might come back?"

Hank wished he could say no, but he didn't want to lie to her. "He might," was the best he could do.

Aggie swallowed and nodded. "Then, would you mind if I slept in next to you? I'd planned on making a pallet in the kitchen, but I'd feel safer here."

Hank wouldn't have trusted any words. He simply lifted the covers beside him.

She smiled and joined him.

When he stretched and turned out the light, she whispered, "Thank you, dear." As if he'd done her a favor.

Hank wouldn't have been surprised if lightning came through the second floor and struck him any moment. He wasn't worried about anyone trying to kill him; his shy little wife was going to give him a heart attack by doing something as simple as trusting him.

This time she didn't wait for him to pull her next to him. She snuggled against him and laid her hand on his bare chest.

Then, before he could think to breathe, she laughed.

He covered her hand with his. "What's so funny?"

"Your chest hair tickles."

"Aggie?" His fingers stilled her hand.

"Yes, dear?" she answered.

"Kiss me good night," he whispered as she looked up.

This time, when his mouth covered hers, he couldn't hold

back. He had to kiss her the way a man kisses a woman . . . the way a man kisses his wife.

His arm pulled her against him. The thin layer of flannel did little to mask the feel of her. He kissed her long and hard, drinking her in, needing to end the drought in his life, needing to need another.

When he finally let her go, Hank rolled an inch away and tried to think of something, anything to say, but no words would come.

He could feel her tugging at the covers, pulling a blanket over her shoulders, snuggling into her own pillow. "Good night, dear," she said in almost a whisper.

"Good night?" he answered. "Don't you have anything else to say after what just happened?"

She rose to one elbow. "What just happened?"

Hank closed his eyes and swore beneath his breath. She was going to make him say it, then there would be no doubt what he was apologizing for. "About the way I kissed you. I didn't plan it, but I'll not say I'm sorry."

"All right," she said as if she'd given it no thought.

He had the feeling she was staring at him in the darkness. Probably thinking of ways to kill him herself since he was stepping way over the line of being partners.

"You're not mad about the kiss?"

She laughed again. "No, dear," she answered. "I rather liked it. I'm surprised that something I've given little thought to in my life could be so pleasant."

He was back to step one of trying to understand Aggie. "Then you wouldn't mind if we did it again?"

This time she rolled toward him. "I wouldn't mind at all. I rather like the feel of you." Her lips lowered above his before he had time to move. With her mouth brushing his, she whispered, "I find I like kissing you very much."

This time he didn't try to hold her to him. He let her lead.

Her kiss was softer, sweeter than his had been. But the weight of her breast resting on his chest drove him mad. "I love this shirt," he whispered against her mouth. "I love the way . . ." She didn't let him finish. She was busy learning.

When she finally raised her head, she stared down at him. Even in the darkness he could see the devil dancing in her eyes. She shifted, using his chest to lean on and propped her head on one elbow. "What comes next, dear?"

"You really want to know?"

She nodded. "I didn't think I ever would. I thought things between a man and a woman were for the man's pleasure, never the woman's. Since you kissed me I've been reconsidering."

"I'll show you," he said, wondering how she could possibly want him to be her teacher. "But how fast we go down this road, and when we stop, will be up to you."

"Fair enough." She nodded as if they'd made an agreement. She waited.

He hesitated. "Aggie," he finally said. "What do you know about how it is between a man and a woman?"

She shrugged. "Mostly what my sister told me. About how it's something to be endured. I wanted no part of that. But your kisses don't seem that way." She looked down, embarrassed by her own boldness.

Hank placed his hand on her waist. "And my touch? Would you welcome my touch?"

She nodded slowly.

"Aggie," he whispered, "look at me."

She raised her head and he saw her eyes in the moonlight. Nervous. Shy, but not afraid.

His hand moved slowly up her rib cage, a light touch against soft material and softer flesh beneath.

Her eyes widened, but she didn't move.

His first finger touched the bottom of her breast and gently pressed against its weight. Then, as slowly as cold molasses, his fingers moved over the fabric covering her breast. The full mound ripened beneath his caress, and he explored.

Hank's breaths came faster as if there were not enough air in the room to fill his lungs. He cupped her in his big hand and thought he might die from the pleasure the feel of her brought. His fingers moved gently across her and she closed her eyes for a moment and smiled.

He'd never wanted a woman the way he wanted Aggie. For the first time he understood why men of old fought dragons for their women. The need for her was a physical ache so deep within him he thought his blood must surely be heating to boiling level. He stared at the cotton covering her breast as his hand twisted the material into his fist.

She pulled a few inches away. "You'll rip the cloth."

"Then take it off." He spoke his thoughts in a voice so low he didn't recognize it as his.

She rose, stood there, and stared at him. If she decided to walk away, he couldn't even follow. With his leg, he would never be able to catch her if she ran. And he had a feeling that if he frightened her and she ran, she'd run all the way to Dallas or Austin or Chicago before she stopped.

Hank closed his eyes and groaned. What did he think he was doing? A man with a broken leg doesn't seduce his wife. He'd almost passed out moving to the washstand and back. If he even tried to make love he'd probably succeed only in making a fool of himself.

When he finally opened his eyes, Aggie was still sitting next to him. She'd unbuttoned two of the buttons of the shirt.

"If I get to pick when we stop," she whispered, "I pick one touch tonight. I know there is more, but I have to think about it first."

Hank took a deep breath, almost saying thank you. He

wanted their first time, if there was to be a first time in this partnership, to be perfect.

"One touch," he agreed. "Only, if you've no objection, I'd like to do so while we kiss good night once more."

She nodded and moved off the bed so he could lift the covers. When she scooted beneath the quilts, another button had come loose.

Chapter 11

Aggie lay on her back and waited while Hank shifted onto his side without moving his broken leg any more than necessary.

Her heart pounded faster than a sparrow's as she unbuttoned the entire shirt and spread the soft material away from her chest. She didn't move when Hank lifted the covers away to her waist.

"Are you cold?" he asked, staring at her body in the shadows.

She shook her head, too afraid to speak. In truth, her skin felt hot and she was sure he would notice when he touched her. She told herself she'd agreed to one touch, even wanted it, but she hadn't thought ahead to realize that he'd also look at her. Not just look—study.

Before she lost all courage, she turned her face toward him and his lips gently met hers. She'd thought he'd touch her breasts first, but he took his time tasting her lips. She liked the way the hard line of his mouth turned soft when it touched her. His rough cheek brushed against hers as he moved slightly. His tongue slipped across her tender lips and pushed inside. Her cry of surprise blended with his sigh of pleasure.

When she didn't pull away, his kiss softened once more, offering her paradise, but still, his hand remained at her waist.

With his coaching, she opened her mouth wider, enjoying the newness of her husband's kiss. She thought that marriage was so much more than she'd imagined it would be. Nice, she decided; marriage was nice—then his hand spread across her abdomen. And nice moved to pure bliss. The warmth of his mouth, the slight weight of his fingers on her skin, made her whole body warm with an awareness she'd never experienced.

Her fingers reached up and brushed the hair just above his ear, liking the way the thick coarseness of his straight hair felt to her touch. He was her man, she thought, hers. She liked his strong body and his gentle ways. She liked his voice and the way he worried about her. She liked everything about him.

Just when Aggie was reaching a flat plateau of shear enjoyment, he broke the kiss.

Gripping his hair in her fist, she tried to tug his mouth back to her, but he'd already found somewhere else he wanted to taste. As his open mouth moved down her throat, she let out a sigh of delight. Roughly, he pushed her chin aside so that the length of her throat lay open to his exploring.

His hand pressed gently into her middle, anchoring her to earth while she floated toward the heaven of his kisses against her skin. When he brushed his lips across her ear, he whispered her name then added softly, "Aggie, my love."

She thought he'd return to finish the kiss, but slowly she realized his mouth planned to play along her skin until he had his fill of the taste of it. He opened wide and touched his tongue to the spot where her pulse pounded, then dipped low until the whiskers of his chin brushed across the top of her breasts.

She lay beyond words, beyond thought as his mouth took hers once more, giving and demanding fire all at once. As if her body had a will of its own, she arched, pushing against his hand, fighting to get closer to him.

He held her fast to the bed, but his mouth told her of his

pleasure at her attempt. He was tasting deep of her now, taking all he wanted from the kiss, and giving more than she'd ever known to ask. His fingers gently stroked her stomach, and she felt the light embrace all the way through her body.

She grew dizzy with wanting, all shyness, all hesitance shoved from her mind by the taste of him.

When she thought she could stand no more of paradise, he gentled the kiss, bringing it back to soft and loving, almost pure, almost chaste. Only slim memory of its former fire, but the memory forever seared across her mind. Now, even his light touch stirred her blood.

With his lips whispering against hers, he began to move his hand across her flesh and this time there were no boundaries just below her throat or at her waist.

At first he circled her breasts, pushing lightly at the underside of each with his thumb—letting her know and long for what was to come.

The circles made her skin tingle with tiny points of joy, and her breasts ache with need. When he stretched his fingers over her fullness she was ready, arching toward him. This time, he let her move, filling his hand, pressing hard into his palm.

She felt his laughter against her lips as his hand took its time molding her softest flesh to his will. He knew he was pleasing her just as she knew her soft moans pleased him.

Without warning, he deepened the kiss once more. When she responded in kind, he tightened his grip over her, branding her forever with his "one touch."

Chapter 12

They didn't say a word when he finally pulled away with one last tender kiss on her cheek. She buttoned her shirt. He straightened flat on his back once more. Both knew the other was awake. Both were too lost in their own thoughts to talk.

She stared out the window. A sliver of a moon was slightly visible between two clouds. She could still taste his mouth on hers. She could still feel his hand over her breast. He'd kept his word. He'd kissed her good night and he'd touched her once. A kiss that had taken her to heaven. A touch that she felt all the way to her very soul.

How could the gentle, quiet man do such a thing? Why had he?

A smile slowly spread across her bruised lips. Because, she answered herself, I asked him to. She felt a power build inside her, a power she'd never known. She'd always been the little sister, the daughter who obeyed, who would have been the old maid taking care of her poppa in his aging years if he hadn't found the widow to marry. No one had ever let her set the rules for anything in her life, and now this strong, powerful man did just that.

She couldn't stop grinning. She might have set the rules, but he'd made full use of his one touch.

"Aggie," he said low near her ear. "Are you asleep?"

"No, dear," she answered, seeing no reason to pretend.

"Why me?"

"What?" She knew what he was asking, but she wanted to make sure.

"Why'd you marry me? There must have been men at every house you visited. Men with more money. Men better-looking."

"There were." She wished she could tell him how many had made fools of themselves, promising her the moon and stars as if they could deliver. Promising her that life would be one endless party when all she wanted was a quiet place to be happy.

"Then what made you meet me at the train?"

"Because," she whispered as she relaxed into sleep. "You saw me. The inside, not just the out. And you liked me—just me—even before we"—she yawned and mumbled the last few words—"stepped into the light."

Hank heard her breathing slow and knew she was asleep. "You're wrong," he whispered. "I loved you—even before we stepped into the light."

Chapter 13

Dawn slowly spread across the sky. Aggie shoved her hair out of her eyes and lifted her head.

Hank lay beside her, looking like he hadn't moved all night. His jaw had darkened with whiskers and his hair covered his forehead.

She smiled, thinking that he was handsome in his own way. Her poppa used to say that most folks "ugly up" after you get to know them. But Hank hadn't. In fact, the opposite had happened. The rest of the world might think him strong, and big and rough, but he'd been gentle with her from the first, and funny. Even when he tried to be stern, she could see through the act.

Laughing, she realized he was more afraid of her than she'd ever be of him. She'd known it even in the darkness when he'd jumped at the sound of her voice.

Without warming, he opened one eye. "Where's breakfast?" he mumbled.

She shrugged and pulled the covers over her. "I think I'll be one of those wives with the nature to sleep 'til noon."

He pulled the blanket off her head. "I don't think so. I'm starving. You agreed to cook breakfast." He frowned, but she could see the cracks in his armor.

She climbed out and stretched, then laughed at the way he stared at her. She was learning to read this man, and if she was right, he'd just forgotten all about breakfast.

"On second thought . . ." He opened her side of the covers. "We could sleep a while longer."

"Oh, no." She laughed. "I'll put on coffee and bring you hot water. Then I'll cook breakfast while you shave."

He groaned.

She grabbed her clothes and disappeared before he had time to argue. Ten minutes later, when she brought him a cup of coffee, he'd managed to sit up but he looked like he'd been thrown by a horse a few times.

"Do you need any help?" she asked.

"I'm fine." He frowned. "Could I get you to bring the washstand over here?"

"Sure." She leaned close and kissed his cheek. "Good morning, dear. Always wake up on the wrong side of the bed?"

"Yep," he answered. "It's my nature."

She moved the nightstand so that he could reach the pitcher and bowl without standing. "Where is your shaving cup and razor?"

"In the mudroom," he answered.

When she returned, loaded down with everything that had been by the back sink, Aggie studied him. Hank was pale and the pain still reflected in his eyes, but he looked better than he had yesterday.

"How do you like your eggs?"

"Any way you make them," he answered as he brushed hot water into the soap cup and began to circle. "Just make it an even dozen."

She nodded and turned toward the door.

"Aggie?" He stopped her with one word.

"Yes."

"Last night was really something."

She grinned, not allowing his fancy words to sway her. "I agree," she whispered, and vanished before he saw her blush.

Thoughts of how he'd touched her filled her mind as she made breakfast. Thanks to Lizzy and Blue, the milk and eggs were in the cold box along with butter. Bread and apples sat on the table. Aggie mixed up a fine breakfast.

Hank had dressed by the time she checked on him.

"Can you make it to the table or shall I bring it in here?"

"I can make it." He stood, then swayed like a tall pine about to tumble.

She moved to his side and helped all she could as they slowly crossed to the kitchen. The stove she'd lit already warmed the room. He sat at the table while she poured him another cup of coffee and served her first cooked meal to him.

He ate as if he'd been starved for days, downing the bread almost as fast as she could spread butter and jelly on it.

They were just finishing when Blue stepped through the back door with a box on his shoulder.

Aggie stood. "Wonderful." She nodded at Blue. "You brought supplies. Hank's already eaten through a week's worth this morning."

"Nope," Blue said, setting the box down on the far end of the table. "The supplies are still in the wagon. Jeb sent this box over for you."

Aggie wiped her hands on the towel she'd been using for an apron and looked inside. Guns, more than twenty of them, all different brands and sizes, each with a tag tied to the handle.

She lifted the first one. "Firing pin broke." The second said, "Trigger jammed." The third read, "Needs a good cleaning."

"Jeb said he has never seen anything like it," Blue mumbled as he poured himself a cup of coffee. "Folks started coming in as soon as the rain slowed yesterday. He told me to tell you that he knew you probably had your hands full with taking care of Hank, but he thought he better have me bring out the first box."

Hank said, "I don't need to be taken care of," at the same time Aggie mumbled, "First box?"

Suddenly, she was too excited to finish her breakfast. She wanted to get to work. While Blue brought in supplies, she carried the box of weapons up to her little attic room. Sitting in the center of the floor, she examined each project. Always before, in her father's shop, she'd been the helper. Now, she was the master.

She had almost finished looking over her work when Blue bumped his way upstairs. "Hank told me to rig you up a table." He carried two six-foot boards. "It won't be perfect but it will work until he can climb the stairs and make you a proper desk. He won't brag on himself, but that man of yours is quite a carpenter."

That man of mine has many hidden talents, she almost said aloud, but all she could manage to say to Blue was, "I know."

The older man made three more trips before he put the boards over empty barrels. Between his loads she managed to slip down and carry up her two boxes of tools. On the second trip, she noticed Hank sitting in the big old rocker on the porch.

She walked to the door. "Will you be all right if I work a while?"

He looked lost but said, "I'll be fine. I'm just not used to staying in the house. I'm usually out by sunup." The mild day didn't reflect in his mood. "When Blue finishes with your makeshift benches, he said he'd carry the leather work up from the barn. I can do it as easy here as there. Maybe tomorrow the ground will be dry enough for me to hobble out there."

Standing just behind his chair, she moved her fingers

through his hair. “Hank,” she whispered and waited until he looked up. “You make me very happy.”

He looked puzzled. “Do I?”

Heat spread into her cheeks. She’d been thinking about her attic room, but realized he thought she meant their good night kiss. “Yes,” she answered, meaning both. The room was a grand place to work, but last night’s “one touch” had been a slice of magic, pure and unreal.

His eyes darkened as if knowing she was thinking the same thing he was, but he didn’t move to touch her. Both knew it wouldn’t be proper in the daylight. Both knew they’d wait.

When she returned to her work space, she decided the stool Blue had brought wasn’t high enough for the makeshift bench, so she tugged the old trunk over. Surprised at how heavy it was, Aggie looked inside the one thing Hank said was sent back home after his mother died.

Layered between tissue paper and smelling of cedar were several finely made quilts.

Odd, Aggie thought. The paper looked as neatly pressed as it must have been the day Hank’s mother packed away the quilts, and Aggie couldn’t help but wonder why Hank, or his father, had never bothered to look inside. Maybe the chest was simply something Hank didn’t want, but couldn’t leave behind for strangers to discover.

She spread the quilts out, realizing each was a work of art, made with great care. They transformed the tiny attic room into a field of flowers and plants, each reflecting a different season.

Finally, she folded them away—all but one. The last, a beautiful spread of bluebonnets, she couldn’t make herself fold. If she put it away the room would go back to being colorless. On impulse, she reached for two small tacks among her tools and hung the quilt on the wall. When she stepped back, she couldn't help but smile. One wall with windows framing a view of winter across Hank's land. The other wall now showed a spring field with all the warmth of a quilt made with love. She'd found the perfect place to work.

Time flew as she practiced the skills her father had taught her. In a strange way she felt at home with her hands moving over the weapons that belonged to strangers.

She checked on Hank several times during the day, but his mood never lightened. He was a man used to action who didn't take to doing chores from a rocking chair. When she came down for the last time, she found him already in bed, asleep.

She felt guilty that she hadn't thought about the time, or his supper. As wives go she must rank near the bottom. Setting the box of repaired guns by the door, Aggie ate an apple, then slipped into her nightgown and crawled in beside Hank.

He'd had a hard day, she guessed, and she hadn't been there to comfort him. She moved her hand to his arm and touched him lightly. "It will be better tomorrow," she whispered just before she fell asleep.

When she awoke, Hank was gone. As she slipped into her clothes, she heard voices coming from the kitchen.

"Now Hank, we've done all we can do." The sheriff's deep baritone voice rattled through the house.

Aggie slipped on her boots. She heard Hank, but couldn't make out his words.

As she hurried from the bedroom, the sheriff's voice sounded again. "You can't go after them. You can barely walk, man."

Aggie slowed her steps as she walked into the kitchen. Three men were sitting at the table drinking coffee. Blue, the sheriff, and her husband.

"What has happened?" she asked as calmly as she could muster.

Hank looked at his cup but the sheriff faced her. "You were right about shooting that fellow. He got as far as Clarendon before he knew he had to see a doctor. He was hit in the left shoulder, just like you said. The doc wired me as soon as he patched him up, and turned him over to a marshal who was in town investigating a cattle rustling gang near there."

Aggie frowned. Hank still wasn't looking at her. "Did he say why he tried to kill my husband?"

The sheriff nodded. "He said a man in Fort Worth paid him. Said this fellow made an offer in a bar to anyone interested that if they'd see you had a horrible honeymoon he'd give a hundred dollars."

Aggie couldn't believe it. "You mean someone tried to kill Hank for a hundred dollars?"

The sheriff shook his head. "Not kill, just bother. The fellow you put a bullet in swears he planned to knock Hank out and set the barn afire. But he panicked." The sheriff pulled out a chair for her as Aggie melted into it. "The good news is he's in jail. It seems he was wanted for a few other crimes as well, and we'd been looking for him for months. We know the man who made the offer in the bar, but it'll just be his word against this lowlife, and no jury would take the story of a criminal over a railroad executive."

Aggie felt horrible. Hank being hurt was all her fault. She didn't have to ask a name, she knew only one railroad man, Potter Stockton. "What's the bad news?" she managed.

The sheriff looked at Hank as if waiting for permission to continue.

Hank covered her hand with his and nodded.

"The bad news," the sheriff mumbled, "is that the guy says there were two men that night in the bar who took the railroad man up on his offer."

Aggie felt as if someone was choking her. "Someone else is out there?"

The sheriff nodded. "He may have given up and gone back, but I came out to warn you to keep a lookout for trouble."

The sheriff left, with Blue by his side. Blue had picked up the box of repaired guns and said he'd be back from town in an hour.

When they were gone, Aggie stood beside Hank's chair and waited for him to say the first word. If he hadn't married her he would have been working today, not losing money while laid up with a broken leg. She wasn't even good company since she'd spent the day upstairs. He couldn't have even climbed up to see her.

Finally, he reached for her hand. "I should have guessed Potter was a hothead. He must have sent that drunk at the train station to stop me, and when that didn't work he planned to at least see that we couldn't be happy."

She moved closer and leaned her shoulder against him. "I am happy, dear. I hate that he broke your leg and somehow I'm probably to blame, but you must know that I'm happy—here on the ranch—with you."

He looked up at her then as if he wanted to believe her, but something deep inside stopped him. She thought he was about to argue, but he only said, "I want you to promise to wear my Colts today. Don't take them off."

She nodded.

"I can't just sit here and wait for trouble to come, but I can work in the barn. I'll have Blue move my workbench so that I can keep an eye on the house and my rifle will always be within reach."

"I'll bring my tools out. It's warm enough for me to work in the barn."

He pulled her into his lap and held her gently. She thought of a hundred things that needed doing, but it felt so good to have him holding her. She'd almost woken him last night to ask if he would. She knew he liked her here but didn't completely believe her when she'd told him she was happy. Maybe it was the way they married with no promises of love. Or maybe it was more deeply rooted in his past, when his mother left him and never returned.

Aggie kissed his throat and Hank stilled as if returning to reality.

"We'd better get to work," he said.

She nodded and stood, wishing he'd kissed her back just once.

An hour later Blue returned with another load of broken revolvers and a few rifles from Jeb, and a box of new tools shipped in from Wichita Falls. Aggie was so excited she went right to work, hardly noticing Blue moving Hank's bench to the other side of the barn doors.

They worked all morning, their backs to one another. Hank sat on a stool with his leg propped on the crossbar of his workbench. She preferred to stand when she worked with rifles. He asked her to pick up a hammer he dropped, and once she asked if he'd help her pry a jammed cartridge shell out. Neither talked of anything else.

At noon Aggie went to the house and brought back leftover meat and cheese for lunch. She insisted he rest his leg while he ate. She talked about a few of the problems with the rifles, but he said little. His eyes were always looking beyond the barn.

When Blue returned that evening, Hank asked if the hired hand would lend him a shoulder to brace against so he could make it to the house.

Aggie almost cried. He'd worked too hard. He should have turned in hours ago and gotten all the weight off his leg. She grabbed her tools and ran for the house. "I'll work upstairs for a while," she said as she passed the two men. "You rest, dear."

"I'll want no supper," Hank answered. "I think I'll call it a night."

She wanted to argue that he needed to eat, but she didn't want to nag in front of Blue. Instead, she went to her little space above the kitchen and worked, telling herself tomorrow would be better.

She worked until the box of guns was repaired. When she finally crawled into bed, she wished there was something that could make Hank happy, or at least make him believe that she was happy. At some point, when he'd been little, he'd stopped believing he could be loved. That's why he could offer the partnership—it had been safe, there wouldn't be a disappointment, for love wasn't part of the deal.

Shoving a tear away, she silently scolded herself for crying, then she realized why she couldn't stop. Hank didn't believe in love and she loved him. She might never be able to say the words or make him believe, but she loved him.

An idea struck her. Slipping from the bed, she ran back upstairs. Within minutes another quilt was hung, this one on the blank wall of their bedroom. Tomorrow, no matter what the weather, Hank would wake to a sunny day filled with sunflowers and morning glories.

Laughing to herself, Aggie slipped out of her nightgown and into his flannel shirt. Then she crawled in beside her husband. As she moved close to his warmth, he circled her and pulled her against him. His slow, steady breathing told her that his action was more instinct than thought. She molded against him and whispered, "Good night, dear," a moment before she fell asleep.

Chapter 14

In the darkness Hank came awake one pleasure at a time. Aggie's hair tickled his nose, her cheek lay against his heart, and her breast pressed into his side. For several minutes all he could manage was breathing. He'd been in a bad mood all day yesterday, battling pain and the fear that someone might try to hurt Aggie. After an hour of berating himself, he'd decided she probably didn't want to come to bed with him.

But she had. She'd not only shared the bed, she'd curled up against him. He'd managed to live another day without her running out on him.

Finally, he slipped his hand along her back and cupped her round little bottom. She wiggled with his movement, then settled against him. Hank smiled, thinking he'd try harder. "Aggie," he whispered.

She raised her head, her hair wild around her. "Is it morning already?"

"No." He shoved her curls away from her face. "But close. The horizon is already beginning to glow."

"Are you all right?" She rose to her elbow.

"I'm fine. I'm sorry I woke you. I hadn't meant to say your name out loud."

Aggie fell back against the pillow and pretended to snore.

Hank laughed. "Don't you want to stay awake and watch the sun come up?"

"I'll catch it tonight, then turn it over in my mind."

He scooted up and propped the pillow behind his back. "Come on. Wake up and watch. Sunrise is the best part of the day."

Like a grumpy groundhog, she crawled out of her warm hole and sat beside him.

After a few minutes, he asked, "Are your eyes open?"

"Is it here yet?"

"Almost."

"Just let me know and I'll open them then."

Hank couldn't resist—he tugged her to him. He wanted to pull her shirt off and repeat all they'd done before, but for now, he had to let her set the pace. Just because he couldn't advance physically with making her his, didn't mean he couldn't move forward.

"Listen, sunshine, I've been thinking."

She was busy settling atop his chest.

"Are you listening?"

She made a slight sound, half yes, half yawn.

"I don't think I'm going to build another bed. If you've no objection, I think we should just share."

He felt her nod.

"I mean from now on, not just while I'm laid up with this leg."

She nodded again. "I understand. Except for the few months I had after all my sisters left, I've always shared a bed. It has advantages. Someone to cuddle with on cold nights. Someone to talk to when you can't sleep."

"Aggie, sharing a bed with a man is different."

She stilled. "I know."

He waited for her to say more. The easiness between them was gone. She lay stiff at his side. "You know," he whispered, "I would never hurt you."

"I know," she said again. "This isn't what I thought it would be like between us."

He understood. When he'd handed her his gun, he'd thought he was making a partnership that at best would keep her safe and offer him company. But now, it was already more, far more.

Without a word, he leaned down and brushed his lips over hers, loving the sweet dawn taste of them. She wrapped her arms around his neck and held him to her as she turned the kiss to liquid passion.

Hank fought to keep it light, but his hands slipped back over her bottom, tenderly gripping each hip and holding her close.

She broke the kiss and shoved away, and reason fought its way into his brain. He tried to find the words to say he was sorry for something he wasn't, but before he could speak, she unbuttoned her shirt.

"Touch me again, dear." She opened the flannel and in dawn's first light he saw her beauty.

All reason vanished as he lowered his mouth to her breast.

She cried out in surprise, then arched her back and allowed him his fill of her flesh.

By the time sanity returned, the sun had cleared the horizon. He kissed her long and hard, letting his hands continue caressing her breasts, now moist and full from his careful inspection. She'd complained only when he pulled away.

In the lazy stillness while they each remembered to breathe, Hank spread his hand across her stomach and made lazy circles over her flesh. "There's more," he whispered, loving the rise and fall of her abdomen as she breathed.

"I figured there might be." She moved her cheek against the side of his head.

"You'll let me know when you're ready." He didn't bother to say "if you're ready." After the way she reacted to his second touch, there was no doubt where they were headed.

She sighed.

"It might mean children." He'd heard of a few ways to prevent pregnancy, but doubted any one would work all the time. "You wouldn't mind children?"

She frowned. "I wouldn't mind your children. I think I'd love them dearly."

He tried to keep the sadness from his voice. "That's more than my mother did."

"That's not true." She shoved away, unaware how the sudden sight of her beauty stopped his heart.

He shrugged. "I'm afraid it is. My mother left me before I could talk and never looked back."

"No," Aggie shouted as she scrambled off the bed. "No!"

As she backed against the wall, he saw the quilt for the first time. "Where did that come from?" He knew nothing of crafts, but he could see that he must be looking at a work of art. No clumsy blocks, no crazy designs, but an intricate picture painted with tiny bits of fabric and fine stitching.

"Your mother. She loved you and must have spent years making these."

"These?"

"Didn't you know they were in the trunk? Beautiful masterpieces of the seasons. The finest work I've ever seen."

Hank shook his head. "I never looked. I figured it would be her clothes and I didn't want to see them. I didn't want to be reminded of a mother who never touched me." All his old feelings of being abandoned washed across his thoughts. "Besides, quilts in a trunk mean nothing."

Aggie had reached the edge of the quilt. Without a word she turned the fabric over and he saw a small square in the corner. Even from five feet away he could see the stitching. Three words: "For my son."

He sat staring at the quilt as Aggie buttoned her shirt and ran upstairs to get the others. When they were all spread out on the bed, Hank could no longer deny they were for him. Each one had the same three words carefully embroidered on the back. She might have left him, but she hadn't forgotten him.

A knock sounded a moment before they heard the front door creak. Aggie jumped like a rabbit at the sound of gunfire, and in seconds she was dressed.

"Hank?" the sheriff's voice boomed. He opened the bedroom door while Aggie stood behind it finishing buttoning her shirt. "Oh, there you are. I didn't think you'd be in bed. You all right?"

Hank tried to think of some reason he'd still be in bed after sunrise. He knew a very good one, but he wasn't about to tell the sheriff. "I was just getting dressed."

Aggie slipped out behind the sheriff, then managed to act like she was just walking in. "Oh," she said, "good morning, sheriff."

"Morning, ma'am. I got some good news. They found that other fellow in Fort Worth who Stockton hired to bother you. He was still drunk in the same saloon, claiming he thought the offer was a joke. So you can stop worrying."

"Good." Hank drew a long breath. "How about some coffee?"

The sheriff nodded. "I wouldn't mind if I do. I saw Blue in the barn. I'll run over and tell him the news and be right back."

He disappeared. Aggie ran to put coffee on and Hank dressed. When the sheriff returned they were both at the kitchen table.

After a cup of coffee and small talk, the sheriff stood. "I best be getting back." He lifted his hat. You folks have a good day." He took a step toward the door, then added, "That sure is a fine little rocking chair you're building out there, Hank."

Hank smiled, remembering how he'd worked all day on it and Aggie had been so busy she'd never asked what he was making. "It's for my wife. The one on the porch is too big for her."

The sheriff looked at Aggie. "You'll like that, Mrs. Harris."

"I'll need it," she said calmly. "I'm going to have a baby."

For a moment Hank thought he'd be embarrassed, but suddenly he couldn't stop smiling. He shook the sheriff's hand and limped to the door to say good-bye.

Aggie moved beneath his arm to steady him while they waved the lawman away.

When they were alone once more, Hank whispered, "I think I'm falling in love with my partner."

"I'm afraid I am too." She smiled up at him.

"But, Aggie, you're not pregnant."

She frowned. "We'd better work on that, dear, before the sheriff finds out I lied."

Hank looked up at the bright morning sun. "Lucky for us it's almost sundown."

They turned toward the house and stepped inside. For the first time since he'd built the place, Hank locked the door and they made love beneath each season of quilts.

SILENT PARTNER

Chapter 1

Dust circled around Rowdy Darnell's worn boots as he stepped from the noon train. The reddish brown dirt whirled, trying to wipe his footprints away before they were even planted in this nothing of a town called Kasota Springs, which suited him fine. If he could, he'd erase every trace of him ever having lived here.

Beneath the shadow of his hat, Rowdy looked around, fearing he'd see someone he knew. Someone who remembered him.

But only strangers hurried past and most didn't bother to look in his direction. Not that they'd recognize him now. Prison had hardened the boy they'd sent away into a man, tall, lean and unforgiving.

Rowdy pulled his saddle from among the luggage, balanced it over one shoulder and walked off the platform toward Main Street. In the five years since he'd been gone, the place had changed, more than doubling in size, thanks mostly, he guessed, to the railhead. New storefronts and businesses framed a town square in huddled progress. To the north a line of two-story roofs stood behind the bank and hardware store. One end of Main was braced by the railroad, but on the other end houses and barns scattered out for half a mile, uneven veins leading into the heart of town.

Rowdy was glad for Kasota Springs' growth. Maybe he'd be able to sell the nothing of a ranch his father had left him and be on his way. He had a hundred places he wanted to see and five years of catching up to do. The sooner he got out of this part of Texas and away from memories, the better.

He walked straight to the livery and picked out a horse to rent. All the corral stock looked better than any horse he'd worked with in years. Prison horses were either broken down or wild and crazy-eyed. A guard once told him horses too tough to eat were sold to the prisons. Rowdy almost laughed. The stock reminded him of the prisoners, he decided, wondering which category he fit into.

"You here for the rodeo?" the blacksmith asked a few minutes later when he pulled the bay Rowdy had pointed out from the herd.

"No," Rowdy answered without looking at the man.

"I'm surprised. You look like you could rodeo. Got the build for it."

Rowdy didn't answer. He'd spent too many years avoiding conversation to jump in.

The man didn't seem to notice. "If I were younger, I'd give it a try. All the ranchers have gone together and donated cattle. They say the all-around winner will walk away with a couple hundred head. Imagine that. Biggest prize I ever heard of. We're expecting cowboys from three states to be riding and the cattle are in the far pen, ready."

Rowdy moved to the horse's head, introducing himself with a touch before he looked back at the blacksmith. "You mind if I brush him down and check his hooves before I saddle up?"

The barrel-chested man shook his head, accepted the

dollar for the rental, and turned his attention to the next customers riding in.

Rowdy picked up a brush and began working some of the mud out of the horse's hide. The familiar action relaxed him. One thing he'd learned in prison was that animals were a great deal more predictable than humans. Treat them right and they tend to return the favor.

As he worked, he watched a fancy red surrey pull up to the livery with three girls inside and one cowboy, dressed in his best, handling the rig. Another cowhand rode beside the buggy as if on guard.

"Sam!" the driver yelled. "Can you check this rigging? I'd hate to tell the captain I risked an accident with this precious cargo of sisters." He turned back and winked at the two girls sitting on the second seat.

They giggled in harmony.

Rowdy noticed that the third girl sat alone on the backseat looking out of place. She didn't laugh, or even look like she was paying attention. Her dress was far plainer than her sisters', and her bonnet held no ribbon but the one that tied just below her chin. A stubborn chin, he thought. Sticking out as if daring anyone to take a swing at it.

"Give me an hour," Sam yelled as he crossed into the barn. "I'll oil the wheels and have it checked."

The driver tied off the reins and jumped down. The silver on his spurs chimed as he moved. "Ladies, how about lunch at the hotel?" He offered his hand to the first giggly girl, a petite blonde with apple cheeks, while the other cowhand climbed from his saddle and did the same to the second one, a slightly plumper version of her sister.

When the first girl started to step down, the driver moved closer. "We can't have you getting that pretty dress dirty. How about I carry you to the walk?"

Rowdy watched as the cowboys each lifted a laughing

bundle of lace and ribbons. It took him a minute to realize the silent one in the back had been forgotten. She sat, stiff and straight as if saying to the world she didn't care. When she raised her chin slightly with pride, Rowdy saw her face beneath the simple bonnet.

Plain, he thought. As plain as the flat land and endless sky of this country. She didn't look all that old, but she had "old maid" written all over her. She'd be the one to stay with the parents long after the other two had married. She'd age alone, or worse, be forced to live from midlife to old age with one of the sisters and her family.

He glanced at the others, their voices drifting lower as they strolled toward the hotel. Rowdy wondered how often this third sister had been left behind, forgotten.

He moved around his horse and tossed the brush he'd been using in a bucket. For once in his life he wished he had clean Sunday-go-to-meeting clothes. He'd been an outsider enough to recognize another. The least he could do was offer her a way out of her awkward situation.

"Miss," he said, shoving his hat back so she could see his face. "May I help you down?"

She looked at him with a flash of surprise, as if she thought herself alone in the world.

For a moment he figured she'd tell him to mind his own business, but then he saw it . . . a smile that lifted the corner of her mouth. A pretty mouth, he thought, in a plain face.

"Thank you," she whispered and took his hand as he helped her down.

The surrey shifted slightly and he placed his free hand on her waist to steady her. Though she stood taller than his shoulder, she felt soft, almost fragile. He didn't offer to carry her. He had a feeling that would have embarrassed them both, but when she reached the ground, he tucked her gloved hand into his elbow and walked across the road to a boardwalk made from mostly green planks.

Once she stepped on the boards, he touched his hat and turned to leave.

"Thank you, Rowdy Darnell," she whispered.

He froze. Without facing her, he asked, "You know who I am?"

"Of course. We were in sixth grade together the year you and your father moved here." Her soft voice changed slightly. "The year before I was sent away to school."

Shifting, he wished she'd look up so he could see her face again. After his mother died, his father only sent him to school when he wanted an undisturbed day of drinking. Rowdy was there barely long enough to learn the other kids' names. Not that it mattered much. They weren't interested in being friends with the town drunk's boy.

"Laurel," Rowdy said slowly as the memory of a thin, shy girl drifted across his mind. "Laurel Hayes." He remembered liking the way her name sounded.

She looked up. The tiny smile was back. "I'm glad you're home," she said in a voice as gentle as wind chimes whispering on a midnight breeze. "I ride by your father's place once in awhile. Part of the roof on the cabin fell in last winter, but the barn still stands."

He nodded, suddenly not wanting to leave her. "I figured that. The sheriff wrote me when my dad died. Sheriff Barnett said he sold off the last of the stock to pay debts." Rowdy liked the way she looked him in the eye, silently telling him that she had no fear of him. He'd expected to see fear or even hatred in folks when he returned. "But, miss, I'm not coming back. Just passing through. Thought I'd sell the place and move on."

Understanding showed in her eyes along with a sadness

that surprised him. "The water's good on your place. You could make a living running cattle."

He didn't want to tell her that he had less than twelve dollars in his pocket. Not enough to buy even a calf. If he remembered right, she was the oldest daughter of one of the richest ranchers around. She probably shouldn't even be talking to the likes of him.

"Well . . ." He wished he knew more about what to say, but for five years most of the language he'd heard hadn't been something a lady like her should ever hear. "I'd best be going."

To his surprise, the sadness brushed across her pale blue eyes once more. She offered her gloved hand. "Good day, Mr. Darnell. I wish you luck."

He hesitated, then gently took her hand in his. Touching someone was another thing he'd almost forgotten how to do.

When he didn't say anything, or let go of her hand, she added, "I have to go. The registration for the rodeo events ends in an hour and my father wants me to make sure all our cowhands are signed up for at least one event. For a ten-dollar entry fee, each event pays fifty. The best all-around wins cattle. My father says even if his men don't win, it will work some of the orneriness out of them."

"I heard about the cattle prize." Rowdy let go of her hand, thinking that if he entered one event he could walk away with fifty dollars, enough to keep him in food until the ranch sold.

She hesitated another moment, but neither could think of anything else to say. Rowdy watched her walk toward the post office where a banner flew announcing the rodeo.

He fingered the ten-dollar bill in his pocket. If he signed up and lost, he'd starve until he could sell his land and no one in town would likely offer him a job to tide him over. In fact, Laurel Hayes was probably the only person who would talk to him, and she wouldn't be allowed after her bear of a father found out who he was. After all, at fifteen, they said he killed a man. The facts hadn't mattered to the town when he'd been fifteen and they wouldn't matter now.

Rowdy thought of the past five years and how he'd been in the saddle from dawn to dark most days. He'd loved working the prison herd and hated each night when they took him back to his cell. He knew he was good at roping and riding. If he entered the rodeo, he wouldn't be just riding for the fun of it. He'd be riding to survive. He'd pick the category with the fewest entries, give it his all and collect his winnings.

Walking across to the post office he made up his mind that three days from now he'd be fifty dollars richer no matter what he had to do.

When he reached the registration table on the porch, several cowhands were standing around, but none seemed in line. He walked up and forced himself to stand tall.

"How can I help you, mister?" a man, who looked like a banker, said around a cigar.

"I'd like to enter one event." Rowdy scanned the choices. Calf roping, bull dogging, tying down for branding, horse racing, saddle bronc riding, steer wrestling.

"Ten dollars for one event, but you can enter all you want for twenty. Then you'd have a chance at the grand prize. A whole herd of cattle." The banker pulled out his cigar and pointed it at Rowdy. "Now that would make a cowboy a cattleman." He laughed and waited.

Rowdy stepped away to think. Ten dollars more didn't seem like much. Maybe he could find something to sell on the old ranch. His father used to have a box of tools in the barn. All together they might be worth ten dollars. But he'd never make it to the ranch and back in time, much less make the sale. The only thing he had of value was his saddle and if he sold that he'd have no way of winning any event.

Turning the corner of the building, he bumped into Laurel

in the shadows. His hand shot out to steady her. "Sorry, miss." With his fingers curved at her waist, he realized he would have known the feel of her even if the shadows had been black as night.

She looked embarrassed that they'd been so close, but she managed to nod her acceptance of his apology.

He relaxed. "Hiding out?"

She nodded again.

Her plan was painfully obvious. She hadn't been invited to lunch. It was too early to go back to the surrey, and she couldn't just wander the streets. The small alley between the bank and the post office offered refuge.

He tried to think of something to say. "I'm thinking of entering the rodeo."

She managed to look up, her cheeks still spotted with embarrassment. "Best all-around?"

"No, it's too expensive." Now it was his turn to look down. He shouldn't have told her that. The town idiot could figure out that he had more than ten and less than twenty dollars to his name.

They stood, silent for a while. He was too tall to see her face unless she looked up, but he felt good just standing near her. He'd been more boy than man when he'd been sent to prison. The smell of a woman had almost been forgotten.

Finally, he found words. "I thought I'd go take a look at the stock being brought in. They were starting to unload them when I got off the train. Would you like to walk over with me?"

"Yes . . . I'd like that, Mr. Darnell." She didn't look up.

He thought of telling her that he liked her voice, but offered his arm in silence for fear she'd change her mind if he talked too much.

She hesitated, then laid her gloved hand lightly atop his elbow.

"Call me Rowdy, Laurel," he finally stammered. "After all,

we've known each other since the sixth grade." In his memory he could almost see her sitting in the back of the classroom, curled around a book, looking at no one.

She nodded and said in a very practical voice, "You're right. We've known each other for years."

They sliced between the buildings and circled to the corrals beside the railroad. Chuck wagons from the big ranches were already setting up camp at the far end. Rows and rows of pens and shoots framed a small arena. He found himself far more interested in her than the stock as they discussed the horses and cattle. To his surprise, she knew livestock, pointing out things he wouldn't have noticed about the animals.

They walked, stopping now and then. She'd lean into the fence, getting closer to study the wild horses as carefully as a buyer might. But when she finished, she'd turn and place her hand on his arm as if it were the most natural thing.

When they were at the back fence, she finally faced him. She looked up, letting the sun shine on her face. He saw tiny freckles across her nose and tears sparkling in her eyes. Watery blue eyes, he thought, like a rainy morning sunrise.

"You may think me insane, Mr. Dar—I mean Rowdy, but I've something to ask you." She looked like she was mustering every drop of courage inside her.

"Ask." He studied her, half wishing she'd pull off her bonnet so he could see the color of her hair. Brown, he thought he remembered, light brown. "I've already decided you must be crazy to be walking with the likes of me. So I doubt I'll be surprised by anything you say."

She grinned, her smile almost crossing her mouth. "All right." She raised her hand and opened it palm up. Lying atop her glove was a ten dollar gold piece. "If I pay half your fee, will you ride for best all-around? Will you ride for the cattle?"

Rowdy frowned. "Why would you loan me money? If I

win, I might be beating one of the captain's cowhands. Your father, like most ranchers, want men riding for their brand to win these things. I don't ride for any brand."

"Exactly," she said. "And I'm not loaning you the money. I'm buying into a partnership. If you win, you keep any prize money for any individual entries, but I get half the cattle."

"But—"

"No questions. All I ask is that I'm your silent partner. No one can know of our bargain."

"You've never even seen me ride."

She didn't answer, but pressed her lips together as if debating crying. He realized this meant a great deal to her. "I've never seen those wild horses buck, but I can tell you which will give you the winning ride."

He raised one eyebrow studying her. He knew nothing about women, but he had a feeling this one was one of a kind.

"Are we partners or not?" She bit into her bottom lip and waited. "You've very little time left to register."

He took the money. Her reasons were none of his business. "Silent partners, if that's the way you want it, lady."

"That's the way I want it."

Then the shy Miss Laurel did something he never expected.

She stood on her toes and kissed him lightly on the cheek. Before he could react, she turned and ran. Her bonnet tumbled to her back as she ran.

"Brown," he said, as if she were near enough to hear. "I knew your hair would still be light brown."

He walked back slowly, turning the gold coin over and over in his hand. He'd ride and do his best. Not just for his start, but he had a feeling for hers as well.

Chapter 2

Laurel ran all the way back to her corner between the buildings and tried to slow her heart while she waited. From the shadows, she watched.

A few minutes passed before Rowdy Darnell stepped in front of the table and tossed down ten dollars in bills and her ten dollar gold piece. The boy she remembered was gone, replaced by a man, hard and lean.

She smiled remembering how kind he'd been to her, helping her down from the surrey and asking her to take a walk. Something no other man in town had ever done. He might look like a man most would fear to cross, but somewhere in the man still lived the boy this town had sacrificed so that none of their sons would go to jail.

Laurel waited for one of the men to recognize him, but none seemed to. Too many families had moved in and out in these parts.

Jeffery Filmore, one of the town's junior bankers, fingered the money. "Mighty lot of money to toss away if you're no good."

"I'm good," Rowdy answered without a hint of brag in his tone.

The banker snuffed. "Might be, might not be. That's what

we're here to find out." He shoved a chart toward Rowdy. "List your name and check every event you're planning on entering. You got to enter at least three of the four to have a shot at the big prize."

Rowdy wrote his name and drew a line across all the squares.

The banker raised an eyebrow. "You planning on trying them all."

"I am."

Filmore shook his head. "Most cowhands sit out one or two that they don't think they can place in. It'll give you time to rest and lessen the chances you get busted up on something you don't have a chance of winning."

Rowdy took the number off the top of the pile. "I've spent enough time resting and I figure I got a chance at them all. You got an objection?"

Filmore stared at him a moment, then backed down. "No, none at all."

Rowdy turned and walked back toward the livery. He never glanced at the alley shadows, but Laurel had a feeling he knew she was watching him.

She let out a long-held breath. He was registered. She'd been waiting for two years for this chance. If he won, she'd have enough money to run.

When she'd finished school she'd had offers to go to work in Houston and Austin, but her father had insisted she come home to straighten out his books. Three months later, when she had them in good order, she found her small inheritance from her mother had vanished. Her father made sure she had no money to leave. He wanted her to work for him and remain home under his control. Now, after two years, she saw a way out.

Feeling brave, she stepped out of the shadows and walked into the hotel lobby before Jeffery Filmore had time to notice her. The banker had a habit of looking at her the way he looked at his meal when he came to dinner with her father. She was something he planned to have, maybe even enjoy. He hadn't even asked her yet, but Jeffery Filmore was already talking to her father about setting a date for their wedding. He wanted his ring on her finger and her working in his bank before fall.

Her father's only hesitation seemed to be that he needed her to do his bookkeeping until after roundup. Neither of the men had ever considered what she wanted. With no funds of her own, her father knew she wasn't going anywhere and Jeffery knew no other man in town bothered to speak to her. So, to their way of thinking, she was just something to pass from one to the other when the time was right.

Laurel almost laughed as she crossed the empty hotel lobby and entered the small parlor where ladies could have lunch or tea without being exposed to the noisy bar area near the back.

She wasn't surprised the room was empty. Her sisters would love the thrill and the audience in the back room. It was more a café than a saloon, but Laurel knew her father wouldn't approve of his darlings sitting among the cowhands. She also knew she'd never tell him because if she did, he'd either laugh or tease her little sisters about how bold they were, or blame Laurel for allowing them to go into such a place.

Sitting by the window, Laurel folded her hands in her lap and waited. The room smelled of pipe smoke. Dust reflected off the furniture as thick as fur in places. The innkeeper obviously saw the room as a bother, but probably kept it to promote the appearance of respectability. He made far more money off the drinks and food in the back.

"Sorry, miss"—a young maid, with hair the color of rust,

leaned in the door—"I didn't know you was there. Would you like something?"

Laurel swallowed hard. "No, thank you. I'd like to just wait here if I may."

The girl disappeared without a word.

Laurel closed her eyes. She was the daughter of Captain Hayes and his first wife. Her father was very likely the richest man in the county. She could walk into any store in town and buy whatever she liked on account.

But, Laurel almost said aloud, she didn't have enough cash to buy a cup of tea.

The ten dollar gold piece had been a gift from the headmaster when she'd graduated. Laurel had kept it with her for two years, hoping one day she'd be brave enough to buy a train ticket for as far as ten dollars would take her. Once she'd asked if she could have the salary her father paid the last bookkeeper. Her father had laughed and told her she was lucky to have a roof over her head and food to eat.

"Miss?" The young maid stood at the doorway with a wicker tray the size of a plate. "A lady upstairs ordered this tea, then said she didn't want it. You'd be doing me a favor if you'd take it."

"But I haven't—"

"There ain't no charge for it." She set the tray on the table next to Laurel.

"Thank you." Laurel smiled. "You're very kind."

Rusty curls tossed about her shoulders. "We all do what we can, miss, to help each other."

Laurel felt humbled by the maid. She offered her hand. "I'm Laurel Hayes."

"I'm Bonnie Lynn." The maid laughed nervously. "Pleased to meet you, I am." Now it was the maid's turn to be uncomfortable. "I got to go."

"I hope to see you again," Laurel said. "Thanks for the tea."

Bonnie Lynn nodded and hurried out of the room.

Laurel leaned back and sipped her tea. She'd let go of her ten dollars on a hope. A hope that if it paid off would allow her to go all the way to Kansas City, or Houston, or maybe even Santa Fe. She'd have enough money for the train and then a few months at a boardinghouse. She'd look for a job at a bank or as a bookkeeper. She was good at what she did. Her father's books had never been off a penny since she'd started managing them.

Lost in her daydreams and plans, Laurel didn't hear Jeffery Filmore come into the hotel until he was at the door to the parlor. He always reminded her of a bear someone had dressed up and trained to act proper. When he removed his hat, his hair wiggled across his balding head like thin, wrinkled wool and his complexion always appeared sunburned.

"There you are," he bellowed. "I saw your sisters come in and guessed you'd be about."

Laurel didn't answer. She never answered his ramblings for Jeffery talked only to hear himself.

She expected him to storm off, but he barged into the room and stuck out a piece of paper. "Your father wanted a list of the names of those who entered for best all-around in the rodeo. You can take it out and save me a trip. I know it's not as many as he'd hoped would enter, but after seeing some of the rough stock a few of the men backed out. They say one of the steers turned on a roper and killed him in El Paso last month. Some of the bucking horses look like they're too mean to be worth the bullet it'd take to kill them."

"Isn't that the kind of stock a rodeo needs?" she asked.

"Yeah, it makes for wild rides and a man who puts much value on his life would be wise to stay in the stands and watch."

She lowered her head, hoping he'd leave.

Like a nervous elephant, he shifted from foot to foot.

Finally, she looked up.

He didn't wait for her to ask any questions. "I've come to terms with your father, Laurel. We'll marry the end of August. No frills, just a small ceremony after Sunday services so I can teach you what you don't know that afternoon. My bank records require a higher standard than your father's ranch accounts."

"But . . ."

He rushed on as if he already knew what she might ask. "You're to have a new dress, of course, for the wedding, but nothing too fancy. I see no need for parties, or a honeymoon. I've already had that with my first wife, and your father agrees with me that such things are just a waste of money."

Laurel stared openmouthed at his ramblings. She wanted to shout that she'd never been asked to marry him and, if she had been, she would have said no.

Jeffery didn't stop. "You'll work with me at the bank Monday through Thursday, then I'll drive you out and you can do your father's books Friday and Saturday. Your father said you could ride out alone. You've been making the trip between there and town for years, but I see no need to have to board a horse in town. I'll take you and pick you up."

He paused as if allowing questions in his lecture.

A hundred screams log-piled in her mind, but all she managed to say was, "I'll have Sundays off?"

He huffed again. "Of course. A banker and his family are expected to be in church every week. It adds stability to his name. After church, we'll want to invite your father and sisters to dinner. It's only proper if they make the drive into town. He assures me you're a passable cook. Once they're gone, you'll need time to do the laundry."

Her head felt like mice were eating away inside it. All

rational thought left her. "Family. What family?" she started before he interrupted her.

"Don't be an idiot. You're far too old for it to be cute to play dumb." He frowned at her as if he found her only mildly tolerable. "I'm not a young man, Laurel. We'll have a baby before we're married a year. I prefer a son, but if it doesn't happen, we'll try again until I have an heir who can eventually take over the bank."

He stared at her. "You are a virgin? I told your father I'd have nothing less."

As she reddened, he laughed. "Of course you are. You know little of these things, but I know my seed is strong. My first wife was pregnant within a month of our marriage, but she wasn't healthy enough to stay alive to deliver full term." He stared at her. "Don't worry, your father says you ride every day. Such exercise makes you strong and hardy." He grinned to himself. "My seed will grow in you. You're like rich dirt, from strong stock and ready to be made use of. Lots of children will round that thin frame out nicely in time."

Laurel was too horrified to answer. She lowered her head and focused on the piece of paper Jeffery had given her. Rowdy Darnell's name stood out.

He had to win, her mind whispered. He had to.

The banker heard her sisters and hurried to pay his respects without another word to her. He was all smiles and pats with them. Like her father, Jeffery seemed to think every senseless thing they said was funny. She could imagine what his Sunday dinners would be like.

She almost laughed aloud. They'd be pretty much like they were now. Sunday was the housekeeper's day off. So Laurel cooked and cleaned up while everyone else complained that none of the food was good enough, hot enough or served fast enough.

Laurel closed her eyes and blocked out all the noise coming from the others. She focused on the way Rowdy had touched her waist so gently when he'd helped her down from the surrey and again in the shadows when he'd bumped into her.

She smiled. He'd touched her as if she mattered.

Chapter 3

The sun bore down on Rowdy as he rode toward his father's farm. He'd always hated the place and July was the worst month, hot and dry. But he looked forward to being alone. When he'd first gone to prison at fifteen, he thought he'd go mad with the loneliness, but finally he grew to prefer it. There were so many people in town for the rodeo that he felt like the air had thinned just so it would last. He rode hard until town was well out of sight and land, more prairie than farm, stretched before him.

His father had sold their farm in East Texas and moved here after Rowdy's mom died. He could get almost ten times the acreage for the same money. The old man had planned to get away from the memories of her death, but West Texas hadn't been far enough. He'd continued the journey into a bottle.

Rowdy remembered his father being drunk when they'd pulled up to the place and as far as he knew the old man had never sobered up enough to care where he was. They'd brought fifty head of cattle with them. His dad sold them off one by one. After three years he didn't have enough cows left to sell to pay for a lawyer for his son. The horses he'd bred with pride a few years ago had withered into nags.

Reaching the gate, Rowdy was surprised it had been closed. Sheriff Barnett had written twice over the last five years. Once to tell Rowdy that his father had died, and once to tell him the place was still his. Rowdy guessed the sheriff wanted him to know that he had a home; he couldn't have known how little the place meant to Rowdy. It was just something to sell so he could make a fresh start where no one knew him.

As he saw the shack of a house and the barn, he thought of burning the place down, but he knew memories would sift through even the ashes. His father hadn't been a bad man, only a weak one. He'd loved one woman and when she'd died he couldn't seem to find his footing, not even to finish raising his only son.

When the sheriff and some men came to get Rowdy before dawn five years ago, his father's only words had been, "I'm sorry." Not, "I'll help." Or "I don't believe you could shoot anyone." Just, "I'm sorry."

The night before there had been a gang of boys drinking and firing off guns down by the creek bordering Darnell land. One was shot. With no one to stand beside Rowdy, the drunk's son was an easy target. Everyone wanted to lay the blame somewhere.

Rowdy shoved the memory aside as he rode up to the house. He wasn't surprised to find the sheriff waiting on the porch. Barnett had put on a few pounds in five years and his hair looked whiter, but he still had the same sad eyes that seemed to say he'd seen too much in this world.

"Darnell." He nodded in greeting.

Rowdy swung down. He owed the lawman. If it hadn't been for Barnett, the judge wouldn't have considered his age at the sentencing and Rowdy would have drawn far more than five years. The sheriff had also rounded up a few strays his father hadn't taken the trouble to chase and sold them, along with the corral stock, to pay the taxes on this place for five years.

"I figured you'd be looking me up," Rowdy said as he offered his hand.

Barnett gripped his hand. "Just stopped by to say hello, son."

Rowdy waited. Barnett had been the only man in town who hadn't wanted to string him up five years ago. "I want to thank you for—"

"You don't owe me nothing, but I would like to give you one last piece of advice. If I were you, I'd keep low and just stay long enough to sell the place and move on. No sense looking for trouble."

Rowdy nodded. "I agree. This place has never been home. If I could make a few bucks, I plan to head south. There's a man down near the border who said he'd give me a job breaking horses when I got out. I figured I'd look him up. Maybe buy a little spread down there in time."

The sheriff moved toward his horse. "I'll get the word out that you're looking for a buyer. With the rodeo in town, it should get around fast. I wouldn't be surprised if you don't have an offer within a week. Captain Hayes to the north will probably make you a fair one. He's gobbling up land as fast as he can lately. You'd think he had sons and not daughters."

"That would be fine with me. I don't much care who takes it off my hands."

Barnett shoved his hat back and seemed to pick his words carefully. "You know, son, you were mighty angry when you left."

Rowdy almost said he'd had a right to be, but he knew nothing would change the past. "I still fire up now and then before I think," he admitted, remembering the fights he'd had in prison. "But all I want to do is sell this place and move on now. I'm not looking for any trouble."

The sheriff smiled. "I'm glad to hear that. I'm getting too old for any new worries."

Rowdy watched the sheriff climb on his horse and ride away with only a wave. He wasn't sure he had a friend in Barnett, but at least the man seemed fair and at this point in Rowdy's life that was about the best he could hope for.

He checked the barn, then decided to unsaddle his horse and let her graze on wild grass growing in the corral. Walking through the house, he found it just as he'd left it, filthy. It had to be his imagination, but the smell of whiskey seemed to linger in the air. More to use up energy than out of any need to clean the place, Rowdy opened all the doors and windows and swept a layer of topsoil out of the house.

At sunset he pulled his bedroll from behind his saddle, deciding to sleep on the porch. It was too hot to build a fire. Besides, he didn't even have coffee to boil anyway. The jerky and hard tack in his saddlebags wasn't worth eating.

He fell asleep listening to the sounds of freedom around him. Tomorrow he'd ride into town and win the first event. He hadn't even checked to see what came first. He didn't care.

Just after dawn he woke to the smell of blueberry muffins. He hadn't tasted one since his mother died, but he'd never forget the aroma. He opened his eyes. Laurel Hayes sat three feet away on the steps.

Rising, he raked his hair back and mumbled, "What are you doing here?"

She smiled. "Watching you sleep."

"I don't think that's proper," he said.

"Probably not," she agreed. "I don't think I've ever done anything that wasn't proper. I might as well start with you."

He growled at her and to his surprise, she laughed. It seemed to him that if she had any sense, she'd be afraid of him.

He studied her, all prim and proper in her white blouse and navy riding skirt. She didn't look quite so "old maid" today.

He had a feeling her rich daddy would shoot him on sight if the old man thought he was even talking to Laurel.

When he frowned, she added, "I brought you a good horse."

He stood, dusting off his clothes. "I don't think the captain would like me riding one of his horses."

"It's not his, but if you don't want the mare, I'll just take my muffins and go."

"Wait." Rowdy shook sleep from his head. "How about I think about the offer while I test the muffins?"

"All right." She pushed back her wide-brimmed hat and studied him with the same look she'd given most of the stock in the corral yesterday. "You want to wash up and make coffee first before you eat?"

"No," he said, then backtracked when he saw her frown. "I can't make coffee. No supplies around here. All my father left was the pot, but I could wash up."

She watched as he went to the well and drew up water. "I'm surprised the rope and bucket are still here," he mumbled as he washed.

"I put them there last year," she said. "I ride this way often and I like to stop to water my horse. Hope you don't mind."

It hadn't occurred to him to mind. "You happen to bring a towel too?"

She laughed and tossed him the towel she'd spread over the basket of muffins.

He dried and placed the towel on the nail by the well. "Great, I got the towel wet so now I guess I'll have to eat all the muffins." He took the first one from her hand and asked, "Now tell me how come you own this horse?" If she had horses and maybe even cattle, she'd have no use for half the herd they might win.

They walked toward her mount. A lead rope had been tied to the saddle horn. A chestnut mare was at the other end of the rope. At first glance it appeared ordinary, but Rowdy didn't miss the look in the animal's eyes. Intelligent, he thought. He downed another muffin while he circled the horse.

"I don't own him," she said when he returned to her side. "You do."

When he showed no sign of believing her, she added, "When the sheriff came to get the stock after your father died, she was only a colt limping around the corral. The sheriff didn't figure she'd last to town so he turned her loose." Laurel brushed the roan's neck. "I found her the next day and knew she'd be coyote dinner if I didn't put her in the barn for a few weeks."

The horse pushed her with its nose as if playing.

"I checked on her every day until she was big enough to run the land. Whenever I was home from school, I rode by to check on her. The wound on her leg healed with a little help from the whiskey I found in the cabin and she began to grow. I was afraid someone might ride by and see her, so I moved her down to the little canyon by the stream. There's water and grass there year-round along with plenty of shallow caves to get out of the worst weather."

Rowdy ran his hand along the horse's withers and back, feeling strong muscles. "Looks like she'd have had the sense to run."

"I thought that too, but every time I came back, she was somewhere on your place." Laurel pulled an apple from her pocket. "I taught her to come when I whistle." She offered the apple to Rowdy. "Here, you feed her. She's yours."

"No." Just because the horse survived here didn't make the mare his.

"You need a better horse than one of the livery mounts. Cinnamon can be that horse."

"Cinnamon? Don't tell me you named her?" He'd called a

few horses names over the years, but nothing he'd want to repeat in her company.

She laughed at the face he made, then handed him the basket and moved away. "You two share breakfast and get acquainted. I have to get back."

He set the basket down and followed her to her horse. He offered her a step up, but she didn't take it. She hadn't needed it. Her long legs flew over the saddle with ease.

"Good luck tonight."

"Thanks," he said, realizing he didn't want her to leave. "When will I see you again?"

"I'll be around. My father insists we all go every night. He goes for the rodeo and my sisters go for the dance afterward."

"And why do you go?" he asked as he took the lead rope from her hand.

She looked down at him. "I'll go to watch my partner win." Kicking her horse, she was gone before he had time to answer.

He watched her ride away. With her height and lean form, she rode like a man, one with the horse, not bumping along like most women he'd seen ride. He decided she probably wouldn't think that a compliment, even though he meant it as such.

He tossed the apple in the air and caught it, proud of the way he'd handled himself. He'd managed to talk to her, even made her laugh. It was only a guess, but he thought that Laurel laughed very little in her life. She'd been different this morning, but he couldn't put his finger on why. Maybe it had something to do with the fact that they were alone, out of sight of any prying eyes or ears.

Winning this rodeo might prove great fun with her as his partner.

Walking back to the mare, Rowdy swore when he realized

the horse had eaten the basket of muffins and left him with the apple.

Laughing, he patted the horse's neck. "Well, Cinnamon, since you've had my breakfast it looks like we'd better go to work. I got about ten hours to turn you into a cow horse."

Chapter 4

The rodeo started with little more than an hour until sunset. Men drew for events and nights. Since the celebration lasted four nights, one-fourth of the men did each event each night. That way anyone coming only to one night got to see all the rodeo had to offer even if he got to watch only one out of four of the men compete for any one event.

Laurel checked the charts. Rowdy had drawn saddleback riding the first night. Good. That would give him at least one more day to work with the horse on steer roping. She was so excited she couldn't wait for the buggy, so she'd insisted on riding in with her father. He didn't talk to her, but it didn't matter. In four days, she would have the money to leave.

Deep down she hoped that if she had the means to leave, he might tell her he wanted her to stay. She knew she was only fooling herself. Since the day he'd married Rosy when Laurel had been four, the captain had always tried to make his oldest daughter disappear. Leftover children never mattered much when the new batch came along. Laurel had a feeling that when she left the ranch Sunday night after Rowdy won, her father would be more angry about losing a free bookkeeper than a daughter.

When they arrived at the rodeo, she stood just behind him

listening to the men talk and hoping to learn something that might help Rowdy. As usual, no one noticed her.

After an hour, Laurel moved behind the row of wagons and buggies pulled in a circle. She'd sat quietly waiting for her chance. Finally, her father had stepped into a crowd of men who were placing bets on a horse race to be run in the morning and passing around a bottle. Her sisters were flirting with half a dozen cowhands who'd stopped by for a cool drink from the pitcher of lemonade in the back of their rig. No one would miss her.

She found Rowdy off by himself in the shadows of a barn. Since he'd drawn bronc riding as his first challenge, he'd be part of the last group to compete.

Without a word, she moved beside him, leaned her back on the barn only a few inches from his arm and handed him a canteen. She could feel the tension in his body.

"A fellow named Dan O'Brien offered to ride drag for me during the calf roping."

"He's all right, I guess," she said without looking at Rowdy. "He owns a little farm to the south of here." She hesitated, then added, "I'm not sure he's much of a cowhand. I think he raises mostly hogs at his place."

"I've already told him I'd trade the favor off for him. He only entered calf roping, so he must feel like he can handle his own."

Laurel nodded once. "All right." She could have suggested a few others who might have been better, but he hadn't asked.

While he drank, she decided to tell him what she knew before he made another mistake, "I've been watching the black you drew for tonight. He goes to his left more than his right and fires up easy even in the pen. I think you should—"

"I know how to ride," he snapped as if resenting her advice. "I'm no greenhorn."

Silence hung still and heavy between them.

"Fine. Good luck." She planted a quick, hard kiss on his cheek and walked away.

She thought he might catch up to her and say he was sorry, but he didn't. A tiny part of her knew she'd done it wrong. She could have said something to him first, maybe let him tell her what he thought. But Laurel would never be like her sisters. She couldn't have conversations that made no sense. She couldn't giggle at nothing and bat her lashes. It wasn't her. It never would be.

"Where you been, girl?" Her father's voice made her jump.

"Looking at the stock," she said in a whisper. She didn't mention that she'd met a cattle buyer from Fort Worth who told her to pass the word along that he'd be willing to buy off the winner's cattle if the all-around cowboy wanted cash.

"That's better than hiding in some corner, I guess." Her father took her elbow in a tight grip. "You remind me more of your mother every day."

Laurel knew better than to think that was a compliment. Her father had often told her that his first wife was a mouse of a woman, plain and boring. Laurel knew he'd married her for money; he'd even joked once that he'd talked her father into paying more just to get her out of the house.

Her father let go of her arm and climbed on the wagon bench. "I'm going home after the saddle bronc riders. You stay and see that your sisters get home in the wagon after the dance."

"But I rode in," she protested. "One of the men will be happy to."

He looked at her with his usual bothered expression. "All right, see that James or Phil drives the girls home. You can ride back alone, but try to stay for at least one dance. You never know, someone might actually ask you to dance."

Laurel knew he didn't care what she did. He probably didn't care if she danced; he just wanted her to stay behind long enough so that she didn't ride back with him. If he hadn't needed her to do the books, he probably would have left her at school until she was thirty. She was a reminder of a time in his life when he'd settled for something far less than what he'd wanted.

She stood silently and watched the competition. The first rider fell off his horse coming out of the shoot. The second rode, but his horse didn't buck enough to earn many points. The third and fourth started well but didn't make the clock. Rowdy's horse came out fighting with all his might to get the saddle and the man off his back.

The crowd rose to their feet. Several people cheered as the animal kicked dust every time Rowdy's spurs brushed his hide.

Laurel watched, mentally taking each jolt with Rowdy. His back bowed back and forth, but his left hand stayed in the air.

When the ride ended, he jumped from the black horse and landed on his feet. The crowd went crazy, yelling and clapping. Laurel only smiled, knowing she'd invested her ten dollar gold piece wisely.

Her father cussed and demanded to know who number forty was. Five minutes later, when his men gathered round him, he said that Rowdy Darnell was the man to beat in this rodeo and there would be an extra month's pay to the man who topped his final score.

Laurel felt proud. She stood and watched the young people move to the dance floor as the last light of the day disappeared. Her father and a few of his men rode off toward the saloon talking of plans for tomorrow. Every night the rodeo would end with saddle bronc riding and they planned to have the captain's men shatter Darnell's score.

When she knew no one was watching, she climbed on her horse and rode into the darkness. She didn't need much light, for she knew the trail by heart. In fact, she knew the land for miles around. For as long as she could remember, she'd saddled up before dawn and rode out to watch the sunrise, crisscrossing the land before anyone else was up and about.

When she was in sight of her home, she remembered what her father had said about staying long enough to dance. If he got home and found her already there, he'd probably yell at her.

Laurel turned toward the cottonwoods along the creek that separated the captain's land from the Darnell place. She rode through the shallow water until she reached a spot where cliff walls on either side of the creek were high enough to act as fence. There, twenty feet into the walled area, she found the slice in the rocks just big enough for a horse to climb up out of the water and through. No one watching from either ranch could have seen her, but one minute she was on Hayes' land and the next on Rowdy's property.

She knew he'd still be at the rodeo grounds. Everyone would want to shake his hand. She'd even heard several say that his ride was the best they'd ever seen.

As the land spread out before her, Laurel gave her mount his head and they began to run over the open pasture. Rowdy's place had always been so beautiful to her. The way the ground sloped gently between outcroppings of rock colored like different shades of brick lined up. The landscape made her feel like every detail had been planned by God. Almost as if He'd designed the perfect ranch. Rich earth and good water. Then, He had set it down so gently in the middle of the prairie that no one had even noticed it.

She rode close enough to the ranch house to see that no light shone, then decided to turn toward home.

At the creek's edge, she thought she heard another horse. Laurel slipped down and walked between the trees until she saw a man standing shoulder deep in the middle of the stream.

Her first thought was that she might have been followed.

But most of the men who worked for her father were at the dance and someone following wouldn't be a quarter mile away from the pass-through wading in the deepest part of the stream.

She stood perfectly still in the shadows and listened. The sound of a horse came again not far from her. As her eyes adjusted, she spotted Cinnamon standing under a cottonwood with branches so long they almost touched the water.

Rowdy had to be the man in the water.

Laurel wanted to vanish completely. She couldn't get to her land, he stood in between her and the passage. If she moved he might spot her, or worse, shoot her as a trespasser for she *was* on his property.

Closing her eyes, she played a game she'd played when she was a child. If I can't see him, he can't see me, she thought.

"Laurel?" His low voice was little more than a whisper. "Is that you?"

She opened one eye. He'd walked close enough to her that the water now only came to his waist. His powerful body sparkled with water. "It's me," she admitted, trying not to look directly at him because there was no doubt that he was nude. "I was . . . I was . . ."

"Turn around," he ordered.

"But . . ."

He took a step closer. "I don't plan to come out until you turn around."

She nodded and whirled. "I didn't mean to interrupt you. I swear. I was just riding and I thought you'd be at the dance, so you wouldn't be home and I could ride on your land without anyone bothering me." She was rambling, but she couldn't seem to stop. She didn't want him to think that she was looking for him, or worse, spying on him. "I know I'm trespassing, but you've been gone so long I didn't think about anyone being on the place."

"Laurel." He barely whispered her name, but he was so near she jumped. "You can turn around now."

Squaring her shoulders, she faced him. He'd pulled on his jeans and had a towel wrapped around the back of his neck. The same towel she'd given him that morning. She couldn't say another word. She could only stare. Until this moment she'd thought she saw the boy she remembered from school when she looked at Rowdy, but no boy stood before her.

"I'm glad you came." He shoved his wet hair back. "I looked for you after the rodeo. I wanted to say I was sorry I snapped at you. I was nervous about the ride and didn't feel much like talking."

"You were right. You did know what you were doing. That ride was magnificent."

He didn't seem to hear her as he continued. "I'm not used to much conversation, but you had a right. We're partners after all." He smiled at her and she swore he could see her blush. "If you ride by here often, I might want to change my bathing habits."

"I'm sorry . . ."

He reached behind her and grabbed his shirt off the cottonwood. "How about we stop apologizing to each other and relax? Deal, partner?"

"Deal," she managed. "Why aren't you at the dance?"

"Why aren't you?" he countered as he buttoned his shirt.

"I . . . I . . ." She could think of no answer but the truth and she didn't want to tell him that. He could figure it out for himself. She wasn't the kind of girl anyone asked to dance. First, she was taller than half the men. Second, she was so shy she couldn't talk to them and, third, everyone knew she was the captain's plain daughter. The old maid.

"I can't dance either," he said.

She smiled. He'd given her a way out.

Without a word, he took her hand and led her to a spot of

moonlight shining near the water's edge. She sat on a log and he stretched out in the grass as if they were old friends settling down for a long visit.

Somehow the shadows made it easier to talk. She told him everything she'd heard about the stock and the other riders. He said he'd drawn calf roping for tomorrow. She mentioned all the extra things going on around the rodeo. Besides the dance, there was a box supper one night and a horse race, as well as a sharpshooting contest.

When they talked of the competition, she told him of her dreams of working in a bank and maybe buying her own little house one day on a quiet street. With the money they'd get if he won, she might have enough for a down payment. Though she planned to put most of the money away for a rainy day. A woman alone has to prepare for that.

He told her of living on a ranch, a busy, productive one, not a dead one like his father's place. She had the feeling as he talked of what he wanted to do that he was voicing a boy's dreams he'd tucked away at fifteen and hadn't brought out again until tonight.

They settled into an easy silence, listening to the sounds around them. Finally, he said, "I talked with Dan O'Brien after I rode. He said he'd heard I'd been in prison and wanted to know if it was true."

"What did you say?" She knew it wouldn't be a secret for long, but she thought they might make it through the rodeo without everyone knowing.

"I said I had." Rowdy stared up at her. "No matter what folks say I've done, I'm not in the habit of lying, Laurel. Not now, not ever."

Even when she looked at the water she could still feel his dark eyes watching her. "What did Dan say?"

"He said it didn't matter to him; he was in the habit of

judging a man for himself, not by what he heard, but he wanted to know from me if the rumors were true."

She'd never given the farmer a glance, but the next time she passed Dan O'Brien on the street she planned to nod politely, maybe even say good morning to the man.

"From the morning I heard about the shooting, I didn't believe you did it," she said, almost to herself.

"You were the only one," he answered.

She agreed. "I went away to school before the trial, but I kept up with it in the papers. No one wanted to believe it might have been a stray bullet, but after you went to prison all the boys who'd been on the creek that night found reasons to leave town. I think they felt sorry for what they'd done."

"Not sorry enough to drop me a note." Rowdy stood and walked to the water's edge. "You have any idea what prison's like when you're fifteen? I spent the first year mad at the world and the second wishing I was dead. No one would have cared, one way or the other."

"I would have," she answered, then hurried on when he glared back at her as if he was about to call her a liar. "I know it couldn't have been as bad as prison, but the school my father sent me to was dark and hard. Most of the girls were two or three years older than me and offered no friendship. I had no one to talk to and my family never wrote. On Sundays, we had to go to chapel and pray." She straightened. "I prayed you were safe."

All the anger melted away from Rowdy. He walked back to her and knelt down beside her. "Why?"

She shook her head. "Maybe because you were the only person I knew who had also been sent away to hell."

She stood, embarrassed by her own honesty, and straightened her skirts as if they'd been having tea in her parlor. "I'd better get back."

He held the reins of her horse. "Let me help you up," he said from behind her as she reached for the saddle horn.

She almost said that she'd been climbing on a horse by herself since she was six. Instead, she nodded. She felt the warmth of his body only an inch away from hers.

Hesitantly, his hands went around her waist. He lifted her up. Laurel closed her eyes and imagined that he was really touching her out of caring and not politeness.

His hands remained at her waist for a moment. "I haven't been around a woman in a long time," he said. "I've forgotten how they feel. I know you're strong, but I'm afraid I'll break you if I hold too tight."

She almost said that she'd never been touched with such care. He'd lifted her as if she were a treasure.

He moved his hand over hers. "I like the way you feel, Laurel. I'll be careful helping you up if you allow me to when we're alone."

When he started to move his hand away, she caught his fingers in hers and held on tightly. She might not be able to tell him how she felt, but she had to show him.

He finally pulled his hand away and whispered, "It's all right, Laurel. I think I understand."

When she took the reins, he stepped back and watched her leave. Neither said a word.

She rode back through the passage and straight home, her thoughts full of the way he'd touched her.

When she walked down the hall, she wasn't surprised to see her father's study light still on. The man never went to bed if he could walk straight.

"There you are, girl," he yelled in a slurred voice watered down by a dozen drinks. "I'm glad to see you stayed awhile at the dance. Filmore mentioned that he worried about you being so shy. A banker needs a wife who can be part of society, not a mouse running to the corner every time someone talks to her."

"Jeffery Filmore never talks to me, only at me." Laurel voiced her thoughts for once.

Her father laughed. "That doesn't matter, girl. I never did have a conversation longer than a minute with my Rosy and we got along just fine."

Rosy had been his second wife. She'd died ten years ago, but he still mourned her, especially around bedtime.

Laurel tried again. "What if I don't want to marry Jeffery?"

The captain gave most of his attention to refilling his drink. "You won't get a better offer. Best take this one. His being twenty years older is a great advantage. He'll die and leave you comfortable." He looked up at her through bloodshot eyes. "In the meantime, he'll make a woman out of you. You're stiffening up, drying on the vine, girl. You need a man to fill your belly with his seed so you'll ripen." He looked down at her blouse. "You look more like a boy than a woman. Most men aren't interested in a woman like that."

She stood silent and took his abuse. All her life she'd never been right, she'd never passed muster. She'd been too thin, too tall, too flat, too shy, too ordinary. But tonight, his cutting ways didn't hurt so badly because Rowdy had touched her if only for a moment and he didn't seem to find her lacking.

She went up to her room, changed into her cotton gown and stood in front of the mirror for a long while. For the first time she saw herself through another man's eyes besides her father's and she liked what she saw.

Chapter 5

Rowdy was up and shaving when he heard Laurel drive a wagon into the front yard. He wiped the last of the soap off and went to meet her. She'd been on his mind so thick all night he didn't feel like they'd been apart.

"I have news," she said as if she thought she needed a reason to visit him. "And breakfast."

"For me or Cinnamon?" He smiled when he noticed she'd left her bonnet at home.

"Both."

She handed him a basket and a campfire coffeepot, still steaming. "I hope it's still hot."

"Looks grand," he said, but he was staring at her, not the breakfast. Something was different about her. She seemed more confident, happier.

They ate on the porch steps laughing about how she'd managed to fix breakfast, even coffee, without waking anyone up. "In my father's younger days he would be in the saddle by dawn, but after twenty years of drinking late, he's decided the sun could come up without him. Since my sisters never rise before nine, the cook doesn't bother to ride over until full daylight."

"And you?"

She looked surprised that he asked. "Me? I like to get up early and ride. Before I hear anyone else out of bed I've usually finished half a pot of coffee and worked on the books for an hour or more."

"With the size of your father's spread, it must be a job to keep up with the paperwork. You like managing the books?" Rowdy shifted to face her. His knee was almost touching her shoulder. He wondered if she was half as aware of him as he was of her.

She shook her head. "It's what I was trained in school to do." She stared down at her hands and added, "My father thought I'd never marry so, 'a girl like me needs a skill,' he said."

Rowdy watched her closely. He'd heard the rumors about her and the banker yesterday and wanted to know if they were true. "Do you plan to marry, Laurel?"

She shrugged. "My father told the banker I'd marry him by fall."

"But you don't want to?" he guessed.

Her eyes were filled with a thousand unshed tears when she looked up. "But I don't want to," she repeated.

Rowdy saw it all then. He knew without asking why she needed the money. Her father thought he could control her. "You plan to leave as soon as I win."

She nodded. "My father thinks room and board are enough pay, so I've never been able to think of a way out. When you win, I know where we can get a good price for the herd. You'll have enough to go somewhere and start a new life and so will I."

She was as much of a prisoner as he'd been. "Then we'd better win." He grinned, wishing he felt half as confident as he sounded. "How soon can we change the cattle into money?"

"An hour after the rodeo. They are already in the pens by the station," she answered. "I plan to make the Monday morning train. Once my father learns we're partners, there will be no going home. I can spend the night in the hotel and be ready to leave at dawn."

"That sounds like a great plan, partner. I might catch it and ride along until a place looks right."

"What are you looking for?"

He shrugged. "Any place but here where the land is cheap and the people scarce. How about you?"

"A city. I've always wanted to work in a big bank."

"Too many people." He shook his head.

"If my father hears about our deal, he'll try to stop me by stopping you."

"He won't hear about it." Rowdy stood and offered her a hand. "But maybe it would be a good idea if you didn't come around me at the rodeo tonight. Someone might notice."

She nodded and placed her hand in his. "All right. I brought you a few things you can use around here. When you leave, you can give them back or leave them for the next owner."

He wouldn't have taken anything from her but a loan didn't seem wrong. She handed him blankets, towels, coffee and a lantern. "They won't be missed. I took them from the chuck wagon that's stored in the barn until roundup."

He set the supplies down on the porch and unloaded a bale of hay and some oats for Cinnamon. "Thanks," he said when the wagon was empty.

"It's only fair. You seem to be doing all the work in this partnership." She picked a piece of straw off his shoulder and then looked embarrassed at her boldness.

She turned to climb in the wagon, but his hand stopped her with a touch.

"No kiss for luck?" he asked as his fingers rested at her waist.

When she leaned to kiss his cheek, he shifted and their lips touched. He felt her jerk like a colt about to run, but she didn't back away.

For a moment they stood in the morning sun, their bodies an inch apart, their lips barely touching. He wanted to pull her against him, but he figured he'd frighten her to death if he did.

He pulled away and stared down into her pretty blue eyes. She looked a little surprised, maybe bewildered, but not afraid, he thought. Then he smiled, thinking that if she could read his mind she'd probably run like hell.

"Good luck," she whispered.

"Kiss me again," he answered back without moving. "I can't believe it felt so good."

She hesitated, then closed the distance between them. Her lips touched his lightly once more.

He moved his mouth in a gentle caress over hers this time and her body leaned into him in response. Her lips were the softest thing he'd ever touched and he couldn't resist tugging one into his mouth for a taste.

He felt her shock, then smiled when she didn't jump away or slap him for being so forward.

"You like that?" he whispered against her cheek as his hand moved around her waist.

She made a little sound of pleasure.

"Then open your mouth just a little, Laurel, and I'll show you something you might like even more."

He could feel her heart pounding against his chest as he moved his lips over her mouth, now soft and full. This time when he tugged on her bottom lip, she melted against him. Before he changed his mind, he kissed her fully, taking her breath along with her small cry of joy before he straightened.

Her forehead rested against his cheek for a moment while she breathed. He drew the smell of her deep into his lungs, and with each rise and fall of his chest, he felt her body against his . . . and she felt so good. Nothing in his life had ever felt so right.

When she finally pulled away, neither said a word, but his touch lingered at her waist as she climbed into the wagon.

Without looking at him, she said, "I'll be watching you tonight."

"I like your hair down." He brushed his hand gently over a curl.

He couldn't think of any more to say as he watched her drive away. Every nerve in his body was fighting to keep from riding after her, grabbing her and teaching her what a kiss was all about. He'd kissed a few girls before he went to prison and a few others when he'd gone with the warden to pick up horses in Mexico. Those saloon girls wanted money he didn't have and were willing to kiss him to show what they had to offer.

But not one of them felt like Laurel in his arms.

Rowdy turned to the barn. Most men at twenty knew all about women. Most had probably had a half dozen or more. Most wouldn't get all worked up over one kiss that hadn't gone deep enough to taste passion.

He worked his frustration off cleaning the barn. If Laurel Hayes had a drop of sense, she wouldn't be having anything to do with the likes of him. He had nothing to offer her. Even his friendship would hurt her reputation if anyone knew. She'd be wise to marry the banker and live in a fine house. But, he reasoned, the banker would never kiss her as he had and she'd never let him. That was what surprised him the most, she'd let him.

By the time the barn was clean, he'd reached one conclusion. He'd win this rodeo and split the money with her. Then, when she was free of her father and on her own, he'd see if she still wanted to be friends. If not, he'd understand. But if she did, she'd need to know that he wanted more than just a partnership. He wanted her.

He worked with Cinnamon the rest of the morning, then rode in and ate supper at one of the chuck wagons that invited any man riding to eat.

Cinnamon was bright and quick, but in the calf roping event, Rowdy only took second for the night. It was little comfort that none of the bronc riders came close to his score from the night before. With another two nights left, he'd be lucky if he placed in calf roping. He figured he could afford to miss one event. Most riding for all-around weren't scheduled in all events. They usually sat out bronc riding or bareback riding because those were the two that had the greatest chance of causing injury. He'd heard two men had dropped out after seeing his ride, figuring they couldn't beat it.

He saw Laurel sitting near her father when he stood directly across the arena and watched the last few events. She didn't look happy, but he had to smile when he noticed she'd worn her hair down with only a small ribbon holding it in place at the back.

One kiss and he'd ached for her all day long.

After the rodeo ended, Dan talked him into walking over to the dance. It was little more than a floor of boards surrounded by poles of lanterns and hay bales to act as benches. The band sat in the grass a few feet away from the dancers. Half the time he couldn't tell if they were playing the same song.

Dan rocked back and forth on his boots. "I'm thinking I should ask a pretty girl to dance."

"I'll watch," Rowdy answered, but he was looking at Laurel standing across the floor from him. She had the banker on one side and her father on the other. Neither man was talking to her, but he had a feeling they'd be none too happy if he walked over and asked her to dance.

If he could dance, he thought, and then he studied the cowhands bumping into each other to the music. None of them looked like they could dance and most of the women seemed more interested in keeping their feet out of harm's way than holding on to the fellow they were with.

"There sure are a lot of pretty girls," Dan sounded in awe.

"How about one of the captain's daughters?" Rowdy suggested.

They both looked over at the two blondes surrounded by cowhands.

Dan shook his head. "I set my standards a little higher than them two. They ain't got a full brain between them."

"I'm impressed with your wisdom, Dan." Rowdy slapped his new friend on the back. "How about the other daughter? The one there by her father."

Dan stared at Laurel. "Not that one. She's the opposite of her sisters. They say she went away to school for years. Say she can figure in her head faster than most folks can on paper. She'd think I was as dumb as a box of rocks."

"You could give it a try."

Dan let out a long breath as if he'd accepted a challenge. "I guess so."

He walked across the floor and stepped right up to Laurel. Rowdy couldn't hear what he said, but he did see both the captain and the banker frown and shake their heads. Laurel, to everyone's surprise, raised her hand and stepped onto the floor with Dan O'Brien.

Rowdy frowned. He wasn't sure he liked the idea of Dan dancing with her. Not one bit. In fact, the idiot who suggested it should be whipped. He stared at Dan's hand resting lightly on her back and knew just how it felt.

His only satisfaction was that neither of them seemed to have any idea how to dance. They stepped first one way and then the other. Dan looked like an ox tromping in mud and she seemed like a feather being blown in the wind. When the music ended, they both looked relieved.

They stepped off the floor a few feet from Rowdy.

“Miss Hayes,” Dan said politely. “Thank you for the dance.”

“You’re welcome,” she managed shyly.

Dan smiled at Rowdy. “I’d like to introduce my friend Rowdy Darnell to you if you’ll let me.”

Laurel offered her hand and Rowdy held it. Neither said a word.

She looked around as if afraid to meet Rowdy’s stare. Afraid she might give away too much, or he would if they looked at each other.

Pulling away, she stepped into the crowd. Both men stood watching her go and wondering if they’d offended her.

Before either could comment, she reappeared with a petite, redheaded girl at her side. “Gentlemen,” Laurel said, “I’d like you to meet a friend of mine. Bonnie Lynn, this is Dan O’Brien and Rowdy Darnell.”

“Pleased to meet you,” Dan said as if practicing what he’d been taught.

Bonnie Lynn smiled and offered him a curtsy. “I’m glad to meet you too. I’ve seen you in town, Dan O’Brien, and I’m thinking you are the biggest Irishman I’ve ever seen.”

They all laughed.

“Would you like to dance?” Dan offered.

She looked down at his big boots and said, “I’m afraid you’d step on me, Dan O’Brien, but I’d still like to dance with you.”

When he took her in his arms, she pulled away far enough to see her feet and stepped onto the toes of his boots.

He laughed and began to move across the floor.

Rowdy smiled at Laurel. “It appears you lost your partner.”

“I’m not sure I would have survived another round.”

He saw the banker coming toward them and knew he had

little time. Turning his back to the banker, he said low and urgent, "Meet me by the cottonwoods tonight."

"I don't know how long I'll be."

"It doesn't matter. I'll wait."

She didn't have time to answer. Rowdy could feel the banker standing behind him and he didn't like the fear he saw in Laurel's eyes.

Chapter 6

Laurel listened to her father rant all the way home. Her sisters had danced with half the cowboys at the rodeo and he hadn't said a word. She'd danced with one and now he swore she would be marked as a tramp. "Why'd you have to pick the pig farmer? One of my men would have asked you eventually."

Laurel didn't answer and her father never gave her long enough to even if she had wanted to.

By the time they reached the ranch, he'd decided that she would attend no more dances until she was married and no longer his problem. When Laurel asked if it were the dance or the man she danced with that made him so angry, the captain said the man, of course.

"I have nothing against Dan O'Brien, but you are engaged. You should only be seen with Jeffery Filmore. He's a fine man and one of the most powerful figures in town. In ten years I wouldn't be surprised if he owns half the land around here and I plan to have the other half. Marrying him would be smart, girl."

"But he's never asked me to marry him," she tried to reason. How could she be engaged if she'd never been asked?

"He asked me," her father announced. "And that is enough. A man like him doesn't have time to waste."

That wasn't enough by a long shot, she thought, but didn't bother to argue. Once her father made up his mind about something, hell or high water couldn't change him. He was still set on building his spread when most men his age were looking for a rocking chair.

"I always thought if I married it would be for love."

"Don't be a fool. You're not the type men marry for love."

When they reached the house, the captain stormed to his study and slammed the door.

Laurel walked through the house and closed the back door softly as she left for the barn. She saddled her own horse and rode out toward the creek, knowing that once her father started drinking he'd forget all about her.

As she rode, she remembered how Jeffery Filmore had gripped her arm just like her father did when he wanted her to follow orders. The banker had walked her all the way to the buggy and hadn't said a word to her. She couldn't tell if he were angry or simply wanted to get her out of the way so he could enjoy the dance with the other older men who sat about drinking and talking without really watching the dancing.

When they'd reached the buggy, he'd pressed her against it before she'd had time to climb in. "Good night," he said and kissed her hard on the mouth. So hard she'd felt his teeth beneath his thin lip.

She'd shoved away, but it took her a few seconds to push his mass off her.

He'd tried to use his weight to hold her between him and the buggy. He fought her for a moment before letting her slip away. She hated the kiss and the feeling. It was as if he was proving something to her.

Filmore had said good night to her father and walked away

without ever saying one word to her. She was a thing to him, nothing more.

When she reached the creek, she splashed across suddenly in a hurry to get away from her life and from the memory of Filmore's kiss. She wished she could erase the feel of him from her mind. His body had been heavy and shifting like a huge flour sack pressing against her.

When the cottonwoods blocked the moon, she saw Rowdy waiting for her. His arms went up to gently help her down.

"I didn't know if you'd come," he said as he lowered her beside him.

For once in her life, Laurel didn't think. She knew what she needed and wanted.

"I'm glad—" he got out before she rose to her toes and kissed him.

It took a few seconds for Rowdy to react. Then, as if he'd also been hungry for another kiss, he pulled her against him and gave her what she wanted. A long, sweet kiss that made her forget to breathe.

When he finally straightened and pulled away, she could see his gaze still staring at her mouth. She'd shocked him.

Laughing, she pretended to pout. "Sorry I forced myself on you."

A slow smile spread across his lips. "You're not sorry at all and neither am I."

"Good." She closed the distance between them. Her words brushed against his mouth. "Then would you mind kissing me again?"

"How do you want to be kissed, gentle Laurel?" he answered.

"Completely," she whispered, leaving her mouth slightly open in invitation.

He met her challenge. With his body pressing like a wall against hers, he kissed her, widening her mouth until he'd tasted all he wanted, then teasing her until she answered in kind. He tugged the ribbon from her hair and wrapped his fingers in the softness.

When she pulled away to breathe, he whispered, "I love your hair. The warmth of it, the softness of it. The way I feel with my hands wrapped in it."

"I could cut it off and give you a few strands." She laughed.

He kissed her quick and hard. "No thanks. I prefer it attached to you. There are a few other parts of you I'm growing fond of having near. This partnership has some very interesting side benefits."

"Like what?" She knew she was fishing, but she needed to hear something other than she was smart and practical.

He hesitated, brushing her cheek with his knuckles. "I like how your mouth fits against mine. I like watching your thoughts sparkle in the pale sunrise blue of your eyes."

"And?"

"Are you sure you want the list?"

She nodded.

He tugged her a little tighter to him. "I like the feel of your body against me."

She buried her face in his shoulder.

His fingers moved gently along her back. "You asked," he whispered against her ear. "And you didn't pull away so I'm guessing you like it too."

He held her for a while, playing with her hair, caressing her gently; then he held her at arm's length. "Want to tell me what's wrong?"

"Nothing," she lied.

"You rode in here like the devil was chasing you, Laurel. Something happened."

He was right. She couldn't believe she was so easy to read. She'd wanted to wash the feel of Jeffery from her and she'd used Rowdy to do just that. Maybe she'd needed affection that had never come from her father. Maybe she wanted to feel like a woman for once and not a thing. Maybe she wanted to prove her father wrong, that she was desirable.

If she told Rowdy any of those reasons he'd think he was being used and she didn't want to make him feel that way.

She couldn't lie to him and she wouldn't tell him the truth. "If I don't tell you, will you still kiss me again?"

He grinned. "Sure. I kind of like communicating without words. Talking is overrated anyway." He kissed her nose. "When I was waiting for you, I was wondering if you'd let me kiss you again. I wasn't prepared for you to attack me."

She started to argue, then reconsidered. She liked the way this conversation was going. "That's me. I look all shy but underneath I'm a wild woman."

He raised an eyebrow. "How many people know about this secret of yours?"

She rubbed her cheek against his and whispered in his ear. "You're the first so far."

He caught her jaw and kissed her playfully, then whispered, "If I give you what you want, maybe this secret can stay between us."

"I want lots of kisses," she announced. "I can be very demanding."

"I think I can handle that, darling."

She felt like she was melting. Locking her arms around his neck, she let him lift her off the ground and whirl her around. When they were both laughing, he said, "Laurel Hayes, you are a wonder in this world."

They stood in the moonlight staring at each other. She brushed his hair off his forehead. He tucked a wild strand of hers behind her ear. When their lips touched, it was as if they had a lifetime to finish one kiss.

When he finally broke the kiss, she sighed and moved away. "Thank you," she said.

He still held her hand. "For what?"

"For making me feel good all the way to my toes."

He raised a wicked eyebrow. "I wouldn't mind testing to see if that's true. From what I've touched so far, I'd guess you do feel good all the way to your toes. You're tall and slim, but you seem to fit against me in all the right places."

She blushed and turned to her horse. "I have to go. It's late."

He stepped behind her as she reached for the saddle horn. His hand glided from her shoulder to her waist. She leaned against the saddle, loving the feel of his fingers moving down her back. His hands spread wide and made a slow journey along her sides. She caught her breath when the tips of his fingers moved around her enough to brush the sides of her breasts.

"Rowdy," she whispered.

He was so close she could feel his breath brushing her hair at the back of her neck. "Do you want me to apologize?"

She tried to control her breathing, her knuckles white as they gripped the saddle. "No," she finally answered.

His hands moved once more along her sides, only this time, when he reached her breasts, he slowed, tenderly feeling the sides, pressing gently as he tested the softness beneath her blouse.

She was glad he couldn't see her face for she felt like it was on fire. No one had ever touched her as he was now.

He leaned down and kissed the side of her throat. "You feel like heaven come to earth, woman. I could spend all night doing this."

"Then do it once more before I go." She couldn't believe her own words. "So I'll remember exactly how it feels."

With the same gentleness, he moved his hand up from her

waist, only this time his fingers covered her breasts, cupping each. As she gulped for air, she pressed into his palms and his grip tightened.

Neither said a word as he held her in his tender grip. As her breathing calmed, she felt his fingers gently brushing against her breasts.

Finally, he pulled his hands away. When he turned her to face him, she rested her head on his shoulder and they simply held each other. What they'd done hadn't been a casual or an accidental touch. She had a feeling they'd both remember it all their lives.

"I'm not sure . . ." He took a deep breath. "I haven't been around many women. I . . ."

She moved so that he could feel her smile against his skin. "I think you did it just right," she whispered and felt him relax against her.

His lips brushed her cheek. "If you get another urge to let that wild woman inside of you come out, you know where to find me. I'll always be there if you need me."

She couldn't believe she'd been so honest with him. In the clear sober light of day she wasn't sure she could face him. But now, right now, she didn't regret anything.

Putting her foot in the stirrup, she felt his hands tighten around her as he lifted her up. "Thank you," she whispered. "For making me feel like a woman."

"You're welcome," he said as if he didn't understand exactly what she was thanking him for. "And believe me, Laurel, you feel very much like a woman."

Leaning down, she brushed his mouth one last time. "Good luck tomorrow."

"Will I see you at the dance?"

"No." She didn't want a repeat of the lecture her father had given her. "I'll meet you here if I can."

He stood on the edge of the creek and watched her ride away. When she looked back, he was still there.

Part of her wondered how she could be so free and wild with him. Then, slowly, she understood what all women come to know. A woman is a different woman in each man's arms. She'd never be like she was tonight with Jeffery Filmore, not if they married and lived together for forty years.

This Laurel born tonight would only live in the circle of Rowdy Darnell's embrace.

Chapter 7

Clouds blocked any sunrise, but Rowdy was up and dressed by the time the first watery light managed to show along the horizon. He'd cleaned the cabin up enough to make it livable but the place was still depressing. Despite the chill of rain, he opened the doors and welcomed the damp air.

Today he would compete in steer roping. Dan O'Brien would try for his only event, calf roping. Both had agreed to help the other. His lead in saddle bronc riding from the first night had held two days and his second place from last night's event had a good chance of making it. The best all-around cowboy didn't have to win every event. When all the events were over, each man competing for best all-around got three points for first, two for second, and one for third. It was possible for a rider not to place in one round and still win best overall. No man's ranking was safe until the last entry rode.

Rowdy worked with Cinnamon all morning. He swore the horse was so smart Cinnamon would be teaching him soon.

Around noon he noticed a basket sitting on his front porch. Laurel was nowhere in sight, but he knew she'd brought it. By the time he brushed the horse down and made it to the porch he saw Dan riding up.

"Join me for lunch," Rowdy offered, knowing Laurel would have packed more than he could eat.

Dan smiled and moved into the shade.

Rowdy set out fried chicken, mashed potatoes and corn on the cob. Dan's eyes were bulging. The quart of buttermilk made his mouth drop open.

Rowdy offered him the best plate he had and one of the two forks he owned.

Dan frowned. "Either you were raised in the kitchen and travel with a coop of chickens and a cow, or you didn't make all this." He looked around. "I don't see any fire going."

"I didn't make this." Rowdy laughed. "I can't roast a rabbit fit to eat." He took a bite and smiled. "And," he added when he could speak, "I'm not telling you where it came from. So eat, not knowing, or watch me. It's up to you."

"I'll eat." Dan dove into the food.

Rowdy had a feeling the man hadn't eaten all morning. They devoured the food. When they found an apple pie at the bottom of the basket, they split it in half.

Finally, Dan leaned back on the porch and stretched his long legs. "I ain't asking no questions," he yawned, "but if food like this falls from heaven again, would you invite me over?"

Rowdy laughed. "Sure." He liked the big man. Dan didn't ask too many questions.

They spent the afternoon practicing and then rode into town. Dan's calf roping came first. His one event. His chance to win fifty dollars. Tonight was the last ride for this event because the organizers needed time to hand out awards tomorrow.

Dan was the next to the last to ride. Rain had been splattering the dirt for several minutes when they shot out after the calf. Rowdy did his part and Dan had the calf tossed and tied with smooth skill. A few minutes later, the last contestant failed to loop the calf.

Rowdy smiled, knowing he'd just moved to third place and Dan had won first. He looked for Laurel but the rain curtained the other end of the arena from sight.

Fifteen minutes later, he roped a steer almost by the time he cleared the gate and rolled in the mud to twist the horns until the animal tumbled, splattering water and dirt all over him.

Rowdy stood, waved his hat and walked to the gate knowing he'd just taken the lead in steer roping. He stepped behind the pens looking for Dan but the rain was driving so hard he couldn't see more than the dark outline of the barn. He guessed most of the hands sleeping around chuck wagons would be in the dry hay tonight.

Slashing through the mud, he headed toward the barn hoping to find Dan and congratulate him. When he stepped out of the rain at the side of the corral, he heard someone coming up fast behind him.

He swung around expecting Dan, but a fist caught him so hard in the stomach he folded over. All he saw were three men in oil slickers, boots and dark rain-drenched hats. The next blow knocked him against the side of the barn and he thought he heard the chime of silver spurs.

Rowdy shook his ringing head and came up fighting. He knew he hit one man hard enough on the jaw to knock him down and felt another's nose crack beneath his knuckles, but their fists rained down worse than the storm. Finally, when he twisted to avoid one blow, a man behind him hit him hard in the back of the head with what felt like an anvil.

Rowdy crumbled and the dark night turned black. Vaguely, from far away, he thought he felt a few kicks to his ribs and then nothing.

Chapter 8

"Miss Hayes. Laurel?"

Laurel shifted in her chair by the window and looked around the café. Everyone from the rodeo seemed to have moved into the hotel out of the rain. Most of the cowboys were in the bar in the back, but her father had insisted she stay in the parlor surrounded by nursing mothers and whining children ready to go home.

She'd heard rumors that even though the dance tonight had be cancelled, there were still games the men called "outlawed events" going on. There the betting was heavy. Those not out in the rain participating were inside awaiting the outcome.

She had no idea where her sisters were, but her father had gone upstairs with several men to drink and play poker until the rain let up enough to head for home.

Staring out the window she decided that might never be.

"Laurel?" The whisper came again as if it were drifting in the wind.

She studied the people around her. No one was even looking in her direction.

"Laurel," the voice whispered again.

This time she had a direction to follow. Three feet away she saw Bonnie Lynn serving tea to one of the older women.

"Yes," Laurel took a chance and answered.

Bonnie Lynn only spared her a quick glance as she straightened. "Follow me."

Laurel didn't ask questions. She stood slowly, looked around and followed several feet behind Bonnie Lynn as they left the room and moved into a hallway to the kitchen that served both the parlor and the café.

"What is it?" she asked as soon as Bonnie Lynn turned around in the quiet passage.

"Dan's at the kitchen door. He says he has to talk to you."

If it had been anyone but Dan O'Brien, Laurel would have thought it was some kind of joke her sisters were playing on her.

"From the look on his face, I think you'd better hurry," Bonnie Lynn said as she slipped into the kitchen.

Laurel tried not to look at the rotting food and dirty dishes scattered around. The place was so busy it looked as if it hadn't been cleaned in weeks.

Just outside the back door, Dan stood in the rain. Bonnie Lynn was at her side as they stepped onto the tiny back porch. "What is it?" Laurel yelled over the rain and the kitchen noises behind her.

"It's Darnell, miss. He's hurt. I don't know what to do for him."

Bonnie Lynn's hand caught Laurel's arm before she could step into the downpour. "Wait, miss. Take my cape."

It took all her control to stand still as the maid wrapped a cape over her shoulders. She pulled the hood up and Dan offered his arm.

"Where is he?" Laurel asked as she matched the big man's stride.

"In the old barn down by the corrals."

"What happened?"

"One of the men who work the stock said he saw three

cowhands kicking something in the mud. He didn't know it was a man until he almost fell over him when the cowhands walked away. We got him in the barn, but he's bleeding, miss, and I wasn't sure what to do."

"What about the doctor?"

"Rowdy wouldn't hear of us getting him. He says they'd disqualify him if they knew he was hurt."

Laurel could barely speak. Fear blocked her words. "Did he tell you to come find me?"

"No, miss. He's going to be madder than hell when he figures out I came to get you, but I'm hoping you can talk some sense into him."

"But why me?"

Dan smiled. "I seen the way you looked at him that night at the dance and the way he looked at me when I was holding you. I didn't think it was nothing much until I saw that basket of food this morning on his porch. A man don't pack a basket with lace napkins, and the food was too hot to have come all the way from town." He helped her over a mud hole and added, "It made sense it came from the captain's place, and I knew if it was one of your sisters he liked that'd make my friend dumber than a warm cow patty."

She looked away so he wouldn't see her smile.

"Meaning no disrespect against your sisters."

They stepped into the sudden silence of the barn.

"If you won't take offense," Dan said as he pointed to the loft, "I'll swing you up."

She nodded and she was lifted up like a child.

For a moment she saw nothing but hay, then, in the corner, a tiny light flickered.

"Bring another lantern," she called down to Dan and ran toward Rowdy.

He moaned as she tugged his shoulder and turned him onto his back. Blood and mud were everywhere.

"Laurel," he whispered, then tried to push her away.

"Stop it." She shoved back. "Be still. I need to see where you're hurt."

"Pretty much all over," he mumbled.

"Then let me look."

She wasn't sure if he passed out or just decided to follow orders for once. He crumbled like a rag doll.

The light wasn't good enough to see, but she could feel. Laurel tugged off her cape and pressed her hand against his heart. It beat solid and strong. She took a deep breath and began to move over him, feeling the strong muscles of his body beneath his soaked clothes.

When she touched his left side, he jerked in pain but didn't cry out. None of his limbs seemed broken but warm blood dripped from his bottom lip and nose. A cut sliced across his forehead close to his hairline and a knot as big as an egg stood out on the back of his skull. By the time Dan arrived with the lantern, she felt safe in believing Rowdy wasn't going to die.

When Rowdy opened his eyes, she said, "You need to see a doctor."

"No," he answered.

"But . . ."

"No," he repeated.

Dan knelt on one knee. "I figure whoever did this was trying to take Rowdy out of the competition. I don't think it was anything personal. If we take him to a doc, he'll be out no matter how it happened."

"But he can't ride tomorrow like this."

"He has to. I heard one of the judges say if he places even third tomorrow, he'll win best all-around."

"No. His ribs could be broken." She pulled his shirt away and saw the dark bruises already forming.

"Stop talking about me like I'm not in my right mind."

Rowdy swore as he forced himself to sit up. "I'm riding tomorrow. End of discussion."

"I say no. It's not worth risking your life."

He stared at her. "If I don't ride, I'll be risking both our lives. I'm not willing to do that." He closed his bruised hand over hers. "I've been hurt far worse than this. I can ride tomorrow."

Laurel shoved the tear off her cheek. "Dan, can you get him home?"

"I'll borrow a wagon and have him there in an hour."

"Good. Stay with him until I get there. I'll bring bandages and all the medicine I can find."

If the big man thought it strange that Laurel Hayes was crying over Rowdy, he didn't say a word. He helped her get him downstairs to a wagon. She pulled all the blankets from her buggy and packed them around him.

When Dan brought his horse and Cinnamon to the back of the wagon, she whispered her thanks.

"Ain't nothing he wouldn't do for me," Dan answered, then hesitated before adding, "He's a good man, Miss Laurel."

"I know," she answered. "I'll be there as soon as I can."

She watched the wagon move into the rain and then walked back to the hotel.

Bonnie Lynn met her at the kitchen door. "Your father is looking for you."

She handed Bonnie Lynn back her cape and stepped into the hallway. She could hear her father yelling.

He'd lost at poker and was too drunk to notice the mud on her clothes. All he wanted to do was go home. When they reached the barn, he borrowed one of his men's horses and had two of the cowhands ride with the women.

Her sisters complained about the lack of blankets until the men offered an arm around them. Laurel sat in the back too worried to be cold. She ordered the man driving to go faster, but he was in no hurry to get home. The road seemed endless.

When they finally made it, she ran in the house and up the stairs. Minutes later she was dressed in her wool riding clothes and leather jacket. Tossing all the supplies she could find in a bag, she started out of the house.

At the front door she almost collided with her father and one of his men.

"Where do you think you are going?"

Laurel knew better than to tell him the truth. She might be twenty, but he'd think he was well within his rights to lock her in her room if he thought she was leaving. "I'm going to check on my mare."

"At this hour?" He wasn't sober enough to figure out why her story made little sense.

"I couldn't sleep. I think the mare might have hurt her leg." She lifted the bag as if to prove what she was doing.

The cowhand laughed. "The horse isn't the only one hurting tonight."

To her shock, her father laughed and seemed to forget about Laurel. "We need a drink." He put his arm around the cowhand. "You've put in a long day."

Laurel disappeared the minute they turned the corner. She didn't like the feeling gnawing away inside her. Despite all her father was, until now she never would have believed he would have done something so unfair. He wanted his men to win tomorrow and he seemed to be covering his bet with a beating.

She shot out of the barn and rode full out into the rain. Once she reached the water, she had to slow because the banks were slippery. She would do Rowdy no good if she broke her neck getting to him.

Ten minutes later, she stepped into the cabin.

Dan had built a fire and laid down straw to soften the

bedroll. The rain had washed most of the mud off them both, but Rowdy was still bleeding.

Without a word, she set to work. Dan watched, fetched water when she needed more and kept the fire going, but he was helpless in doctoring.

"He started talking out of his head about halfway home." Dan paced as he mumbled. "Kept wanting to know where you were and if you were all right. He thought you might get yourself in big trouble for coming to the barn." Dan stopped and watched her for a while. "You care about him, don't you, miss? That's why you came even knowing it might not set well with your old man."

"I do care," she answered.

"Does your father know?"

"I have a feeling he might know something about Rowdy being hurt, but not about us." She could only guess how angry her father would be. "If he did, they might have killed Rowdy tonight."

Dan nodded, understanding. "I'm going to take care of the horses and then, if you don't mind, I think I'll sleep with my rifle on that porch. You just call me if you need me."

"Thanks," she said as he lifted Rowdy enough so she could circle a bandage around his ribs. "I'll give him enough medicine to ease the pain. Maybe if he can sleep, he'll feel better tomorrow morning."

Dan left, closing the door. Laurel worked for another hour cleaning every cut until the bleeding stopped and keeping a cool rag on the back of Rowdy's head. She knew no one would miss her until breakfast so she could stay until sunup and have plenty of time to get back.

Finally, exhausted, she curled next to him, placed her hand over his heart and fell asleep.

Chapter 9

Rowdy woke feeling warm in the calm darkness. He moved and felt pain rattle through his body.

He smiled, remembering how worried Laurel had looked. She couldn't have known that he'd taken far worse in prison.

Silently, he took inventory. He was hurt but nothing was broken. In prison he'd been in fights where he wasn't sure he'd ever stand much less walk again. This seemed mild in comparison.

He moved his hand over his ribs and encountered Laurel's long slender fingers resting over his chest.

His head ached as he shifted just enough to see her sleeping beside him. She was so beautiful in the firelight, an angel dropped down to watch over him. He remembered how she'd said she prayed for him. He'd thought no one cared and she'd been kneeling in a chapel somewhere saying his name. The image warmed a heart he'd thought long dead.

As if she felt him watching her, she opened sleepy eyes.

"How are you?" she asked, worry wrinkling her brow.

"A little sore, but healing," he answered. "Did you sleep here next to me all night?"

"Yes." She smiled and sat up so she could check each of his wounds. Only the break in skin at his forehead looked like it had bled a little during the night. "I didn't want to leave you alone."

"You were right here next to me and I slept through it. What a shame."

Giggling, she said, "You were in no shape to do anything about it."

"I'd have died trying." He winked and then winced at his cracked lip.

"Shut up and take a deep breath. I want to listen to your lungs."

When she leaned her head against his chest, he took a deep breath and tangled his fingers in her hair. "I'm all right, Laurel. I swear."

She looked up, firelight sparkling in her tears. "I was so worried about you. I don't care if we win. I'll find another way to get free of my father. It doesn't matter. I just didn't want to lose you."

He tugged her against him and held her for a while. "We'll find a way," he finally whispered. "I plan on winning, but if I don't, we'll find a way. I'll stand with you win or lose."

"But you can't ride. You might fall."

"I don't think about how I'm going to fall when I ride. I just think about staying on." He laughed, then groaned. "I don't have to make the best showing tonight, all I have to do is stay on and draw third place. None of the bareback rides have been that good."

He knew she wanted to argue with him. He swore he could almost hear her mind working. But she didn't say a word. They just lay close, listening to the fire and waiting for sunrise. This was the last day. Tonight it would all be over. She'd stay at the hotel and by dawn tomorrow she'd be on the first train. She'd be off to start her new life in some big town and he'd have money in his pocket until the place sold.

By first light, Rowdy had fallen back asleep. She slipped

from his side and put on a pot of coffee to boil, then dug in the bag for bread she'd brought the day before.

When she took Dan a cup of hot coffee, he was hooking up the wagon. "I'm sorry I have no breakfast to offer you but bread. I was in too much of a hurry to think about what we'd eat with it."

"No problem. How's Rowdy?"

"Much better. He's asleep now, but earlier he said he plans to ride."

Dan nodded. "Tell him to sleep as much as he can today. I'll be around when he comes into town and make sure nothing happens to him before the rodeo."

"Thanks." She glanced up at the sun. "I'll try to stay until he wakes, then I have to get back before my family wakes and realizes I've been out all night. You headed home?"

Dan shook his head. "I'm thinking of riding into town and having breakfast at the hotel."

Laurel smiled. "I hear it's good, especially when served by Bonnie Lynn."

He grinned. "I have no understanding of women, but I think she likes me. She told me last night that I make her laugh and I figure that's a start."

"I think she likes you, Dan, even if you don't understand why."

He climbed into the wagon. "And as smart as everyone knows you are, miss, you still like that busted-up cowboy in there, don't you?"

"I do, but we're just friends. Have been since we were kids."

"Sure you are," he said without looking at her.

He waved as he drove away. Laurel sat on the porch and drank the coffee she'd meant for Dan. When she went back inside, Rowdy was awake and sitting up.

She knelt beside him. "How are you feeling?"

"Better." He rubbed his slightly swollen lip with his first knuckle. "I think I could take a little of that coffee."

She poured a fresh cup and shared with him.

When it was empty, he set the cup aside. "Lie back down beside me," he said. "I don't want you to go just yet."

She didn't hesitate as she spread out beside him. They lay in silence for a while, then he said, "I heard what you told Dan."

"That I like you?"

"Yes. And that we're just friends."

He rolled to his side and placed his hand on her middle. "I don't think it's true," he whispered. "I think you feel about me the way I feel about you. Neither of us is looking for love, but we've learned to trust each other. And there is something between us, pulling us closer."

"Maybe," she protested. "I do like being near you."

"No," he answered. "I think it's more than that even if neither of us wants to admit it. We went beyond just partners the first time you kissed me. What I feel for you is deeper than like."

"I don't think so," she whispered. She couldn't admit more, not after only three days. Not when she'd be leaving tomorrow and she might never see him again. "When you win tonight, we'll split the money and go our separate ways. All we can be is partners, Rowdy."

"No, we're already more," he answered as his fingers brushed lightly over the cotton of her blouse. "If your feelings aren't running deep right now with me touching you, then move away. We may not feel love, but I'm definitely attracted to you."

He wasn't holding her, only touching her. His hand slid up between her breasts and began unbuttoning her blouse. "Because if you don't run, Laurel, I'm going to touch you as no one else has ever touched you. If I don't, I'll regret it the rest of my life." He leaned down and brushed his lips over hers.

"There is no time," she mumbled as she answered his kiss with one of her own.

The kiss was so tender she wanted to cry. She felt the first button give way to his fingers.

"Make love with me, Laurel," he whispered against her ear.

She was too shy to say the words, but her kiss answered his question. As they kissed she felt him pulling buttons free, then tugging her blouse from the band of her riding skirt.

When he felt the layer of her camisole, he raised his head. "How many layers do you have on?"

She laughed. "Only one more."

"Good." He frowned. "I'd really like to see what I touched last night."

She turned her head away from him, too embarrassed to look at him. "I'm not—" She couldn't even say the words. Her body curled away from him.

Forgetting about the camisole, he gripped her shoulder and pulled her back. "Not what?" he asked.

"I'm not the kind of woman men want. I'm smart. I can keep books, but that's about all."

He swore and she felt his anger, not at her, but at what she believed. Finally, he calmed down and tugged her chin so that she had to look at him. "Look, Laurel, I don't care if you can count and, as for being smart, I've begun to question that since you started hanging around with the likes of me. And about being the kind of woman men want, I can't speak for all men, but you are exactly what I want."

"You do? How?"

He sat up and shoved his hair back, then winced at the pain. He took a long breath and said, "I thought you would have figured it out by now, but I'll explain so that there will be no misunderstanding between us." He met her gaze and held it. "I want you in my arms. I want you in my bed. I want to be so close that we share air and so deep inside you I forget there is a world other than with you."

"Oh," she said, sitting up to face him.

He laughed. "You know for a smart girl, you surprise me. Or maybe I've had too little practice to get my feelings across. I don't suppose you want the same thing?"

She raised her chin. "I might. What did you have in mind?"

He glanced at the sun coming in the open door. "I would say we do everything right here, right now, but your father will be sending a hunting party for you any minute. How about we start now and finish tonight at the hotel? I don't want to be interrupted."

"All right." She could feel her nerves jumping. "What do we do first?"

"Unbutton that undergarment," he said, smiling a dare. "I think we could call that a start."

She sat perfectly straight and unbuttoned her camisole. Her gaze never left his eyes.

"Now pull it apart, darling, if you don't mind." His voice was lower.

She tugged the thin layer of cotton open an inch at a time and saw only pleasure in his dark gaze.

"You're beautiful," he whispered. "Beautiful."

She closed her eyes as he raised his hand and covered one breast. His other hand slid to the back of her neck as he gently laid her down on the straw bed. When his fingers closed around her and tightened, she let out a cry of joy. He lowered his mouth over hers and caught her next moan of pleasure.

"This is how we'll start tonight," he whispered. "Only the door will be locked and we'll have all night. I don't want to hurry loving you. We need to take our time getting to know each other." He kissed his way down her throat without turning loose of her breast.

When all thought but what he was doing to her had left her mind, she felt him move away and she protested.

"It's begun, darling. There's only one way this is going to end and I plan to make sure you enjoy each step." He stared at her as if she were a work of art. "We'd better stop now while I can. When I ride tonight I won't be thinking of the pain. All that I'll be dreaming of is having you all alone."

He leaned and kissed the tip of her breast, then pulled the cotton back in place. "You surprise me, Laurel."

"How?"

"I didn't think you'd love a man's touch."

"I don't. I love your touch and it is quite possible I may never find another's of any interest."

He grinned, satisfied with her answer.

She sat up and buttoned her clothes.

Watching her hands, he thought about how fine and beautiful they were. He liked her hands. Hell, he almost said aloud, he liked everything about her.

Lost in his thoughts he realized she'd been talking. He only hoped he hadn't missed something important.

"I'll pack and leave my trunk at the hotel. Bonnie Lynn will watch it for me and tell no one. As soon as you ride, I'll find the buyer and have him meet us at the hotel. He said he could bring ten percent in cash and have the rest deposited wherever we like."

He smiled. "You're sure I'll win. You've planned everything."

"I'm betting on it."

"And if I don't?" He had to know what would remain between them if tonight didn't go as planned.

"Then I'll go home as if nothing has changed and pick up

the bag when I'm in town alone." Her blue eyes met his. "It may take me a few hours, but I'll meet you under the cottonwoods before midnight."

He knew what she meant. What was going to happen between them would happen. At the hotel, or beneath the stars. It would happen.

He stood. "Until tonight," he said as he kissed her. The need to whisper that he thought he loved her built inside him, but he couldn't—wouldn't love her. Love had killed his father and he'd never allow himself to crumble. Better never to love than to let it eat you away inside if love is lost.

At the door, he stopped her one step before the sun reached their faces. "Tell me you need me," he whispered against her ear.

"I need you," she answered.

He brushed a kiss into her hair. "Tonight, wait for me. I'll be there in time for a late supper."

He waited for her to answer, then smiled, guessing she wouldn't say the word until he did and as long as he didn't use the word love he could walk away if that was still the way she wanted it after their night together.

Chapter 10

Laurel sat in her tiny office and sharpened each of her pencils to a fine point, then lined them up neatly. If Rowdy won tonight, she wouldn't be coming back. For as long as she could remember this house had been her home. They'd moved here the summer before her father went to New Orleans and brought back a new wife. It had always been a cold house. Her stepmother's mood swings and her father's temper made it impossible for any housekeeper to stay more than a few seasons.

All she'd ever felt in this place was alone. She knew she wouldn't spend one day of her life to come missing it.

"You about ready to go?" her father said from the doorway.

"More than ready." She stood. "All is in order and up to date."

"Good." He smiled. "That schooling of yours was worth the money."

She didn't answer his almost-compliment as they walked to the parlor to wait for her sisters.

"You know that place over the creek, the Darnell Ranch?" he asked as if making conversation.

The attempt was so rare, it surprised Laurel. "Yes, I ride over there now and then."

He nodded, only half listening. "The sheriff tells me it's up for sale. I'm thinking of making Darnell's son a rock-bottom price. He's been gone so long he'll have no idea what it's worth and once I offer I'd be surprised if anyone tried to top me."

"How much is it worth?" Laurel tried to keep her tone bland as if simply making conversation.

"A small fortune, I'm guessing. They say the water's good. In the right hands, it could be a great addition to my holdings." He shrugged. "Since the young Darnell didn't win best all-around, I'm thinking he'll be needing money to move on and will take my first offer no matter how low I make it."

Laurel fought to swallow. "How do you know he won't win?"

"I heard he was hurt last night."

She couldn't say a word without giving away far more than she wanted her father to know.

He patted her pale cheek, seeing only her frailty. "Don't worry, Laurel. When I buy the place you can still ride over there if you like. I might even have a gate cut in the fence so you could cross through." Then as if he'd rationed out all his kindness for the day, he walked away yelling for his other daughters to get downstairs immediately.

A few minutes later, she silently climbed into the wagon. Her father rode his horse, making one of the men handle the surrey's team. Laurel sat alone on the backseat trying to figure out how her father had known Rowdy was hurt. Of course it was possible his men saw Dan carry him into the barn. Maybe the man who almost tumbled over Rowdy in the mud told someone, who told someone. Only they weren't in town that long after she'd visited the barn and, as far as she knew, both her father and his men had been working on the ranch all day.

She walked around and around the obvious answer, hoping

to find another reason for her father knowing than that he somehow had ordered the attack.

When they reached the town square and her family hurried off to watch the children ride lambs and rope pigs, Laurel lay her coat over the small traveling bag she'd used when she went back and forth to school. With her head high, she walked directly to the hotel.

When she found Bonnie Lynn, she asked, "Do you have somewhere you can store this for me?"

Bonnie didn't ask questions, she just nodded and took the case.

"I may be needing a room later."

"We're full," Bonnie Lynn said, "but I wouldn't be surprised if some folks don't head home tonight after the rodeo's over. Don't you worry about your things. I'll put them in my room. They'll be safe there and I'll make sure you get the first room that comes open."

Laurel smiled, silently thanking the girl for asking no questions. "One more favor. Do you know where Rowdy is?"

Bonnie winked. "That is no favor. He's sitting in the bar with my Dan having a piece of my pie."

Laurel took a breath. "I need to talk to him alone."

"I'll have him meet you in the parlor. It's always empty this time of day."

While the maid went to put up her case and tell Rowdy, Laurel stood in the front room and stared out dirty windows at the circus atmosphere outside. Everyone for a hundred miles around seemed to be in town. She watched as people walked only a few feet beyond the window and didn't notice her. That seemed to be how life in this town had always been for her, no one noticed her. She was invisible, or she had been to everyone but Rowdy.

Just as she saw Jeffery Filmore turn up the steps of the hotel, she heard Rowdy's voice.

"Good afternoon, Miss Laurel," he said. He stood politely with his hat in his hand, but she didn't miss the devil of a grin on his face.

When she nodded slightly, he added, "You're looking quite lovely this day."

She heard the front door open and knew within a few seconds Jeffery Filmore would be near enough to see them.

Shoving past Rowdy, she whispered, "Don't sell your ranch."

He'd raised his arms to hold her, but she was already in the doorway.

"Promise me!"

Jeffery's voice boomed. "I thought I'd find you here, Laurel."

Rowdy nodded and backed away so that the banker couldn't see him standing behind her.

"I'm not much for the nonsense on the streets," Jeffery complained. "In fact, I'll be glad when this whole thing is over and we can go back to normal." He was getting closer. "I thought I'd come in and have a cup of tea with you. Your father and I have been talking and there are a few plans you need to be working on."

"No." Laurel held up her hand, trying to think. "No tea. Not now. Since you're here I'm sure it would be all right for me to have tea in the café."

"It's more of a bar. No proper place for you."

Rowdy moved behind the door so that he wouldn't be seen until the banker was well into the room. And he couldn't step inside with Laurel blocking the door.

"I've heard," she said. "But I understand they serve pie in there and I'd love a piece, dear." The endearment tasted sour on her tongue, but she had to get him out of the way before he noticed Rowdy.

Filmore frowned at her as if he thought she had taken ill.

"All right," he finally said, more in answer to the pie than her. "I might have a slice myself."

Laurel tugged the door closed as she followed the big man.

A moment before she let go, she felt Rowdy's fingers reach for hers, but she couldn't take the chance of ruining their dream now. He didn't know what was going on or how her father planned to cheat him, but she prayed he trusted her enough to follow her advice.

Chapter 11

Rowdy moved around the door frame in time to see Laurel disappear with the banker. Filmore laid his hand at the small of her back as if he had the right to touch her and wanted everyone to know it.

Anger washed over him as the scars of five years log-piled in his thoughts.

Who did he think he was kidding? Laurel Hayes was a rich man's daughter and he had one dollar to his name. She'd been sent away to school and he'd been sent to prison. The chance of her caring for him was about as likely as snow on a summer night.

He couldn't deny she was attracted to him. He'd felt the sparks fly whenever they were within touching distance. They both liked the game they'd played the past few days, but it was just a game to her. A pastime to make the rodeo more interesting maybe. She'd have no supper waiting for him in a hotel room tonight. There'd be no lovemaking.

She'd called the pig "dear." That one word kept sparking against his mind, sharpening anger with each memory. He would have thought five years of living with thieves and liars would have taught him not to believe anything anyone said.

He had no idea why she'd told him not to sell his land.

Maybe that was part of the game she played also. She and Filmore were probably laughing about it right now over pie.

All he knew for sure was she left him and went with the banker. She could have told Filmore to wait a few minutes because she was busy talking to him. Or she could have introduced them as if they were equals. But she hadn't. She'd shoved him aside. She'd refused his touch. She kept him out of sight because he was her dirty little secret.

Rowdy hit the hotel door at a run. He stopped by the grounds and took his pick of among the last few wild horses left to ride, then found Dan near the barn.

"What's wrong?" the big Irishman asked the moment he saw Rowdy.

"Nothing."

Dan frowned. "I would have guessed that right off." He slapped Rowdy on the back. "You want to go down to pick out a mount? I'm thinking one of them might look sleepy or tired. That would be the one to ride. All you got to do is stay in the saddle, cowboy, and you'll win this thing."

Rowdy didn't answer or move toward the corral.

Dan watched him closely. "You don't look like a man who cares if he wins."

"I care," Rowdy answered as he checked Cinnamon's cinch, "but I'm not going for third. I plan to win this event."

Dan laughed. "Good way to think," he said. "Then with two first places you'll have a hundred dollars plus the cattle. That'd make you a fine start on that ranch of yours. You could use the money to rebuild the cabin and fatten up a few of the cattle to sell off this fall to get you through the winter. With two hundred head, you could have three hundred by this time next year."

"I'm selling all the cattle tonight, and as soon as I find a buyer for the ranch, I'm never coming back to this place."

Dan played along. "I can understand that. You got a good

ranch with water most of us would fight you for and a woman who looks at you like you're about the grandest thing she's ever seen. If I was in your shoes, I'd run as hard and fast as I could as well."

Rowdy's swear died on his lips as he turned and saw Laurel's father and two of his men walking up the passage between the pens. The old man was headed straight for him.

He and Dan stood staring as if watching a storm moving in over open land. When the captain and his cowhands were within ten feet, Rowdy thought he heard the jangle of silver spurs. The bright day turned into a stormy night of memories, but he didn't move a muscle.

"Rowdy Darnell," Hayes began as if he wasn't sure which man was which.

"Yes." Rowdy didn't offer his hand.

The captain straightened, allowing his years of army service to show. "I'm here, young man, with an offer I think you'll want to hear." He gave Dan a look that made it plain the conversation was only between them and the pig farmer should leave.

"We're listening," Rowdy said, silently letting everyone know that he wanted Dan to stay.

Dan looked like a bull shifting from one foot to the other. He, like everyone in town, knew the captain carried a great deal of weight, but Rowdy was one of Dan's few friends.

Rowdy ended his indecision by adding, "Dan, I'd like you to stay. I've developed a worry over being alone out here after last night."

Dan took the hint. He crossed his powerful arms and stood shoulder to shoulder with his friend.

Hayes, surprisingly, looked concerned. "Oh, why is that, Mr. Darnell? Did something happen last night?"

Rowdy looked at the cowhand whose spurs sparkled in the sunshine. "Nothing that mattered." He lowered his voice.

With the hint of a wild animal growling, he added, "Nothing that will ever happen again."

Hayes seemed bored and drew Rowdy back to him by saying, "I've come with an offer for your ranch. Now I know it's not worth much, never truly been built into anything, but out of respect for your father and my neighbor, I'm here to offer you a thousand dollars more than your father paid for it."

Rowdy knew Dan would react and he did. "That's not a fourth what it's worth, Mr. Hayes, and you know it."

"It's Captain Hayes," Laurel's father corrected.

Dan shook his head. "Changing your handle don't make any difference in what the ranch is worth."

The captain looked bothered. "All right." He smiled at Rowdy. "Your friend may be right. I haven't priced anything for a while. I'll up the offer by another two thousand but that is the best I can do. I don't think you'll find anyone around who'll make you a better price."

Dan huffed. "I would if I had the money."

"It doesn't matter," Rowdy finally spoke, "because the ranch is not for sale at any price."

"There's always a price," Hayes corrected.

"Not this time." As angry as he was at Laurel, her last words echoed in his thoughts, warning him. He couldn't make the pieces fit.

The captain didn't look defeated. "You think about it, Darnell. For most here, you're a stranger and it won't be easy making a go of it. For the rest, you're nothing but a jailbird. They'll remember and never trust you. You'd be better off to take the money and move on."

He started to leave, then turned back. "I just heard that you picked the wildest mount to ride today. Rumor is that horse has put more than one cowboy in a wheelchair."

"A great ride could mean a win," Rowdy said.

Hayes shook his head. "A good one would have made you the winner with a second or third place. But you picked the hardest to ride. I hear he can buck higher than the fence. If you can stay on, you're right, you'll win, but if you don't make the clock, you'll lose not only the event but the best all-around."

Rowdy stared as they turned and walked away. He'd already figured it out and knew the captain was right. If he drew no points in this event and the cowhand with the next best total placed first or second, Rowdy would lose.

Dan leaned close. "You up for it?"

"I can hardly wait," Rowdy answered.

Chapter 12

Laurel watched for Rowdy until the rodeo started, but she never saw him. She wished she'd had time to explain why she'd told him not to sell the ranch. But how could she tell him that her father was planning to cheat him.

She also felt bad about running off with the banker. She'd panicked and decided the hotel lobby had not been the place or time to cause trouble. There would be enough fireworks Monday morning when her father and Filmore figured out that she was gone. Since they both thought she had little money, they would spend a day, maybe two looking around town for her. Finally, someone was bound to check at the station. Her father would probably send men to bring her back, but she'd be a train ride ahead of them, maybe more. Once she stepped off in a big city, they'd never find her. She could let Rowdy know where to send the rest of her money.

With Rowdy staying in town for a while, no one would suspect him of having anything to do with her disappearance. She knew he'd never tell anyone that he passed half the profit from the sale of the cattle to her.

She wasn't brave enough to stand up to her father face-to-face. She never had been. The only way she could break free was to disappear completely.

The need to give Rowdy a good luck kiss weighed against the possibility of someone seeing them together. The kiss had always brought him luck, but if her father heard about it, he might look for her tonight or suspect Rowdy had something to do with her leaving. To keep him and their partnership safe, she had to be very careful. If that meant not seeing him until after the rodeo, then she could wait.

Her thoughts turned to what would happen when they were alone. It would be easy to tell her father she was riding home with her sisters, then tell her sisters she was going home early on horseback. Neither would check with the other. She would slip into the back of the hotel and Bonnie Lynn would, hopefully, have a room ready. She'd order supper and wait.

Laurel smiled. Women like her didn't have lovers, but tonight, for one night, she would. For one night she'd be desired even if he couldn't love her.

As the sun faded on the last night of the rodeo, Laurel couldn't sit still in the wagon. She had to pace. In a few minutes the rodeo would be over. She knew win or lose her life had changed. She'd never marry Filmore. If Rowdy lost tonight, she'd still be leaving her father's house, even if it took a little more planning.

For the first time she knew her own mind and would not live as a child any longer.

Something else had changed. She'd fallen hard for Rowdy. Not infatuation or a warm kind of cuddly loving feeling, but hard, fast, forever kind of love. For once in her life she'd found something—someone she couldn't resist. If he didn't feel the same, they'd walk away as friends tomorrow, but he'd never leave her heart. She'd have the memory of one night with him forever.

The first saddleback rider didn't make the clock. Three more to ride. Every nerve in her body felt like it was jumping.

Laurel paced. Her father was so wrapped up in what he

was doing he hadn't even noticed the changes in her over the past few days. But others did. She saw one of the cowhands who always followed after her sisters studying her as if seeing her for the first time. A stranger had smiled at her. One of the store clerks had gone out of his way to hold a door open for her. She almost felt like "been kissed" was written on her face. Maybe it was, her lips were swollen slightly from Rowdy's kisses and her cheeks burned each time she remembered the way he touched her.

She laughed suddenly, thinking that after tonight Filmore wouldn't want her anyway. She wouldn't be a virgin. She might spend the rest of her life a very proper old maid, but tonight she'd make a memory. One night with the man she loved was worth more than a lifetime of nights with one she could never give her heart to.

The second rider stayed on, but his horse looked half asleep. The mounts didn't seem as wild and fresh as they had the first night. No one had come close to Rowdy's saddle bronc ride the first night, but the scores for bareback riding were high.

She turned and watched as Rowdy came out of the shoot riding the one horse she'd thought no one would attempt. The animal bucked wildly as if in a death fight. Now Rowdy had no saddle to hang on to. She counted the seconds in her mind. One, two, three.

As she watched him being jerked back and forth she realized he was doing this for her. If she'd stayed out of it, he would have won one event and gone home a winner like Dan had. He wouldn't have put his body through four nights of torture. Her father's men wouldn't have beaten him.

He couldn't say he loved her, but he'd done this for her. He'd risked dying for her.

The crowd began to scream and she realized she'd lost count of the seconds. A moment after she heard a man yell time, Rowdy flew through the air and hit the ground hard. His whole body crumbled as if every bone and muscle liquefied.

Laurel thought of nothing but him. She jumped over the barrier and ran across the field. A rodeo clown and one of the stock cowboys tried to stop her, but she shoved them aside. By the time they had the horse pulled away, she was kneeling at Rowdy's head, tears streaming down her face.

"Rowdy. Dear God, don't let him die! Rowdy." Her hand trembled as she brushed his dark hair aside. "Please don't die on me," she whispered. "Please."

He twisted slightly and rolled to one knee. "You praying over me again, Laurel?"

He'd scared her so badly, anger flashed along with relief. She swung at him, hitting him on the arm.

He stood slowly as if testing bones. Once standing, he offered her a hand. "How about waiting until I find out if I won before you kill me."

She realized everyone in town was watching them. Cheering as he stood. Seeing her cry.

Dan, near the judges' table, gave Rowdy a thumbs-up.

"We won," he whispered. "We won." The joy she'd expected was missing from his tone. "You'll get your money."

She couldn't look up to see what was wrong with him. She'd never made a public scene in her life and she just made one in front of everyone.

When he turned to wave at the crowd, she bolted toward the side of the arena, wishing she could just disappear into the crowd. Trying to think of some way to explain away what she'd done, she moved toward the surrey. Her father looked furious and Filmore, beside him, had turned purple with anger.

"What in the hell were you doing!" Half the crowd heard her father yell when he spotted her coming toward him.

"I thought he was hurt," Laurel yelled. No one seemed to hear her.

He waited until she was five feet away before saying in his low, demeaning tone. "That was not proper behavior, Laurel. I'll be having a few words with you when we get home. I'll not tolerate such a show."

She could hear her sisters laughing and joking.

Laurel realized there would be no controlling the damage she'd done. But, for one moment, Rowdy was all she thought about, not the crowds or her father or the consequences of her action. She could bare her father's anger. She could ignore Filmore. But Rowdy's hard words echoed in her brain.

The crowd was still cheering. Laurel glanced toward the arena, hoping to catch sight of Rowdy. It wasn't hard. He was riding straight toward her at full gallop.

Everyone took a step back when Cinnamon pushed the barrier trying to stop. Laurel stood her ground, letting the horse's powerful shoulder brush against her.

Rowdy didn't look like he saw another person around but her. "I have to know," he said quick and angry. "Are you still my partner or was this all a game?"

She couldn't breathe. She saw hurt and confusion in his dark eyes.

Her father moved toward her, shoving people out of his way.

"I'm still your partner," she answered and lifted her chin.

Rowdy slid his boot out of the stirrup and offered his hand. "Then take the victory ride with me."

She gripped his fingers and stepped into the saddle as he shoved back to make room. A moment later, his arms were around her holding tight.

As her father's hand went out to grab her leg, Rowdy kicked Cinnamon into action. They shot out into the arena.

Laurel closed her eyes and leaned into his warmth. Nothing

mattered but him, not the rodeo or the crowds or even her father. Only Rowdy.

As they circled, she whispered, "I'm sorry. I didn't mean to make a scene."

"That doesn't matter, but it took me a minute to figure out what you'd done. How unlike my shy Laurel to run to me." His fingers circled her waist. "God, I missed the feel of you all day, darling."

Everyone waved and yelled as they rounded the arena, but she didn't care. Rowdy and she had their own private world.

"Stop calling me darling," she said, laughing.

"Why, because you don't love me?"

"No, because *you* don't love me."

"You're wrong there, I do love you. I think I have since the sixth grade. I just didn't know it until that horse knocked the brains out of me."

Dan opened the side gate and Rowdy shot out of it away from the crowds and into the night. He rode for a while until the noise of town was only a whisper behind them, then he slowed.

She relaxed against him trying to let herself believe she'd just heard him say he loved her.

"It took me awhile to figure out why you told me not to sell and why it was so important you acted like I wasn't in the room with you. I spent most of the day mad because you walked away, but then it hit me and you're right."

She started to ask about what, but he twisted her chin and kissed her hard.

"That wasn't my best," he said as he straightened. "But I'll work on it later."

She laughed and he kissed her again.

When he backed an inch away, he whispered against her cheek, "You do love me?"

"Yes." She smiled, watching the last hint of doubt disappear from his eyes.

"Good, then we go with your plan, but you got to promise never to call me dear."

"My plan? What plan?"

He nodded. "I keep the ranch and we don't sell the cattle. In a year we'll have a great place and who cares if no one in town will talk to us. Between the work and the nights together we won't notice."

"We'll be partners?" she said.

He smiled. "We'll be a lot more than that, darling."

Afterword

Rowdy Darnell and Laurel Hayes were married the last night of the 1890 Kasota Springs Rodeo. Within five years the RL Ranch became one of the most profitable spreads in West Texas.

They had three sons and a daughter.

In 1912, Laurel Darnell was elected mayor of Kasota Springs.

Rowdy never rode in another rodeo, but folks talked about his rides for years.

Rowdy and Laurel's partnership lasted fifty-seven years, until she died of a heart attack. Her headstone read, "Beloved wife, mother and partner."

Rowdy didn't mourn her death as his father had mourned his mother. Instead, he passed the ranch along to his children and spent the next two years teaching his eleven grandchildren to ride.

Two years to the day Laurel had died, he passed away in his sleep.

The children were surprised when they learned he'd already ordered his headstone. It was placed next to Laurel's in a small cemetery on their ranch.

His stone read, "Keep praying for me, darling, I'll be there by supper."

THE OUTLAW

Chapter 1

January 15, 1852
Big Bend Country, Texas

Cozette Camanez straightened the pearl-white lace of her wedding gown, hating the dress almost as much as she hated herself. Everything about her life was a lie and it was all about to come crashing down around her.

Two months ago she'd made a mistake. She'd trusted a man she thought she loved and found out one stormy night that he wasn't worth loving, or trusting.

The next morning, she'd thought she could walk away, as he had, but when it was far too late to admit what had happened between them, she'd discovered he'd left her with a reminder of what he'd done to her. A reminder that would cause her father to disown her.

Desperate, she did the only thing she could think to do. She lied. First to herself, then to others, building a world around her as she had as a child. The lies grew so thick, they now walled her in, making escape impossible.

Leaning back on the old wooden church pew of the ranch mission, Cozette wished she could close her eyes to everything and just drift away into nothingness. She took a deep breath, inhaling the musty smell of dust and cobwebs and candle wax.

She'd rushed home with her broken heart to find her father dying. She couldn't tell him the truth then. He was in enough pain already. If he knew she might be pregnant, he'd probably use his last breath to yell at her.

But, as the days passed and he grew weaker, she thought her secret might be safe. She sat beside his bed telling stories of an imaginary love who planned to come for her. She even lied and told her father that they'd already been married by a judge in Austin. As she guessed he would, her father complained that as soon as her love arrived, they'd be married by the priest. Until then, her father had claimed it wasn't a real marriage.

The rafters rattled as the wind blew through the holes in the old mission roof. Cozette looked up into the shadows of the loft thinking how hard it would be for an imaginary groom to appear tonight.

She'd thought she would slip away once her father recovered a little, or passed. Maybe she'd be gone for a few months, or even a year, and return home, an imaginary widow with a real baby. Only she'd gone too far with details, saying her husband planned to meet her at the Grand Hotel in Odessa.

When her father took a turn for the worse, her uncle Raymond told her she had to stay. He took the liberty, without telling Cozette, to send word for the man waiting for her in Odessa to come to the ranch.

From then on, her ball of lies began to unravel amid wedding plans. The house staff took over. They all knew the road to Odessa. A week's journey in a wagon, half that on horseback. As they helped Cozette care for her father, they prepared for the proper wedding. It would have to be as soon as the groom arrived, for her father's days were numbered.

Whispers circled in the hallways. The groom would be

there in a few days, the housekeeper announced to everyone, and the maids began to clean while the cooks cooked. A week at the most, the housekeeper reasoned. Later, everyone except Cozette decided it would be three days if the weather held.

Two days.

Tomorrow.

And finally, last night they all agreed that he'd come before dawn.

Cozette thought she'd go mad worrying about when her imaginary groom would show up. She'd even let them dress her in her mother's dress to wait, though she knew she was waiting for no one.

Then, her father, who'd never forgiven his wife for delivering him with a girl as their only child, did something Cozette never expected. At her uncle's insistence, her father changed his will, leaving the huge ranch not to Cozette, but to her legal husband.

Cozette jumped off the bench and began to pace. Lying on the pew trying not to think wasn't working. She had no one to blame but herself for this mess. She'd piled one lie on top of another and the chaos that was about to start at dawn, when no husband showed up, would be her funeral pyre.

She'd promised her father a hundred times when she was growing up that she'd never lie again. Without her mother to buffer his rage, he'd die hating her, disowning her, demanding she leave and never return. Her father and her uncle weren't men who tempered rage. They didn't just get mad, they got deadly, and at dawn they'd both be furious with her.

Without a husband showing up to claim her and the baby growing inside, her uncle would inherit the only home she'd ever known and kick her out with his dying brother's blessing.

Since she had no hope of an imaginary husband showing up, she had only one path left. She planned to pray herself dead before morning and save everyone else the trouble of murdering her.

There was no other way out.

Better to die now with the priest waiting outside the door. He could perform the funeral. Cooks were baking all night for the wedding breakfast. It would serve as the meal for the wake. More gifts and guests would arrive tomorrow. Everyone would attend her funeral instead of a celebration. After all, they were much the same. All the women cried and everyone would say how nice she looked.

A rustling sounded in the loft. For a second Cozette thought she might be rescued, maybe by a tornado, or a hailstorm, either of which would take everyone's mind off the wedding. Then reality weighed against her heart. A storm wouldn't make the ranch hers. Nothing would. Until a few hours ago her father had wanted the priest to perform the marriage at his bedside when the groom arrived, but he'd finally demanded she marry in the tiny chapel. She'd seen the blood in his handkerchief each time he coughed and guessed the reason.

The rattling above came again. Cozette refused to turn around, thinking the rat in the church must be huge . . . almost big enough to be an uncle. Her father loved the ranch, but Uncle Raymond saw only a fast way to make money. Her beloved San Louise would be sliced up and cannibalized within months, because with no groom, her uncle could chop it into small farms. One of the oldest Mexican land-grant ranches in Texas would vanish.

Shouting came from beyond the chapel walls. Cozette pressed her cheek to the window. She could die in a few minutes when all was quiet, she decided. She saw shadows of men run from one building to another, but she couldn't tell what was happening. Shouts echoed through the foggy night air and she thought she heard gunfire near the barn.

As she pushed away from the window, she became aware of someone behind her. Before she could turn, the barrel of a gun pushed sharply against her back.

"Turn around, pretty lady, and you're dead," came a voice low and rich.

"Who are you?" she demanded, thinking of the old stories she'd heard of outlaws raiding the ranch years ago.

The laughter only inches behind her chilled her blood.

"I'm a bandit come to relieve you of the burden of your wealth. I'll start with that necklace."

She tugged off the heavy gold necklace and handed it to him. "Take it and be gone."

"And the ring." He was so close to her she could feel his warm breath on her bare shoulders.

She jerked off the gold band she'd bought for herself before she left Austin.

"A willing victim?" the robber said. "A change from what I expected." His voice was more educated than she thought a bandit's might be, but the steel of his weapon seemed no less deadly.

"Is that all you want?" she asked as she stared out into the night wishing the gun in his hand would go off and end her misery.

"Oh, we're taking plenty. I checked out the chapel, and my band is loading all your wedding gifts in a wagon."

"Good," she said.

"You don't seem upset that we're taking everything of value."

"I could care less," she answered.

"Don't play games with me, miss. I may not kill you, but my gang wouldn't hesitate."

Cozette placed her hands on the windowsill, fighting to see beyond the thick glass. "Your gang? They wouldn't be three short fat men dressed in black."

"What makes you say that?"

"They're being led away by several of the ranch hands. I don't know how mean they are but one looks like he might be sobbing."

The outlaw pushed her against the window as he looked out. His strong fingers rested on the back of her neck, holding her, but not hurting her. His touch was as warm as the glass was cold.

"That's them." He mumbled an oath. "Great, I leave them for five minutes and look what happens."

"My men will come after you next." She tried to wiggle away. "They're probably already checking every building on the ranch."

For one second his hand slipped against her hair and she twisted to face him. She drew in a quick breath to scream, but his stormy eyes stopped her. He was tall, and darkened by the sun, but his eyes were unlike any she'd ever seen. He was young, maybe only a year or two older than she, yet the sadness in his stare held a hundred years of sorrow.

"Great!" He pulled her from the window. "You've seen my face. Now I have to kill you."

"Good!" she shouted back. "Shoot me!" Heaven had answered her prayer.

She straightened against the wall, bracing herself for the blow. "Shoot me right in the heart." Cozette closed her eyes and waited.

After holding her breath for as long as she could, she let out the air and glared at him. The outlaw was just standing there staring at her.

"What's wrong? All you have to do is pull the trigger."

"I can't just shoot you in cold blood. Not with you ordering me to. In that dress you look like a doll on top of a wedding cake."

"Well, I'm not taking it off, so shoot me."

She took another breath, closed her eyes, and waited. No blow came.

This time when she opened her eyes, he'd lowered his gun to his side. "What's wrong now?"

"I can't, lady. I know it's the outlaw code to shoot anyone who can identify you, but I can't."

All the tension of the day exploded inside Cozette and he was the only one around to take her bottled-up rage. "You are absolutely the worst outlaw I've ever seen. You must have the dumbest gang in creation if they follow you. All you have to do is aim at my heart and shoot me. Then I won't be around to testify and you can go bungle some other job."

"Look, lady, if you want to die so badly, why don't you just take my gun and kill yourself."

"Suicide is a mortal sin. I was schooled by nuns in Austin until a month ago. I know the rules and I always follow them," she corrected him with a bold lie, but then lying seemed to be her main profession of late. "I don't expect a low-down, worthless outlaw to know anything about right or wrong. I'm surprised you aren't lying out somewhere, your dead body feeding the buzzards, or swinging from a tree by rope." She pointed her finger at him. "Now stop wasting time and shoot me!"

He shoved his gun in the holster and stared into her face. "No. Maybe I should tie you up and gag you. I'd enjoy the silence and that should give me time to go spring my three uncles and get out of this place by dawn. I knew this was a bad idea from the start."

"Just shoot me, please." She couldn't believe the answer to her prayers was standing right in front of her refusing to cooperate.

"I can't. Someone will hear the shot." He tried to reason with her.

"Then choke me." She pulled the collar of her gown open, popping several buttons.

He closed the fingers on one hand around her slender neck, but he didn't tighten his grip.

He was so close to her she could feel his heart pounding. "Please, do it," she whispered. "If you don't I'll be forced to watch my father die knowing his only child lied to him. I'll be disgraced and kicked off the ranch by an uncle who hates me."

He studied her with those fascinating, stormy blue eyes that seemed to see all the way to her soul. "Why don't you just tell your father the truth?"

"If I'm not married by the time he wakes up tomorrow, I'll break his heart. He never had much to do with me, thought my mother was a fool for listening to my stories. As soon as she died, he sent me to the nuns and, as far as I know, he's never even read the letters I wrote. He's giving his brother the ranch rather than let me have it unless I marry." Cozette knew she was babbling, but she didn't care. She needed to confess, and an outlaw wasn't likely to judge her.

"Don't you have friends, relatives, the law who will help you?" To her surprise the outlaw actually sounded concerned.

"No one who would stand against my uncle once my father is gone. I'm sure the will is legal." She paused, then tried another angle. "My uncle will kill your gang. He's done it to others who tried to steal from the ranch. They say he beat a cook almost to death for stealing three chickens. My father's a hard man, but his brother twisted one more step into cruelty."

The bandit let go of her neck and backed away. "You've got a mountainload of problems, lady." He handed her back the ring and necklace. "I wish I could help you, but right now I've got my own worries. Those three fat little outlaws in black are all the family I've got, and I'll do anything it takes to save them. I thought if I came along with them tonight, I'd keep them out of trouble, but that plan obviously didn't work."

Cozette stared at the jewelry in her hand. She cared nothing about it or all the wedding gifts. All she wanted was her land, someplace to live, somewhere to raise the child she carried. "Are you sure you won't kill me?"

He smiled, a sad smile as if he was sorry he'd disappointed her. "I can't, lady."

"Then marry me." Cozette covered her mouth, not believing what she'd said, but the logic of it slammed against her. "The priest won't help me. I've lied to him as I did to everyone else. They all believe my husband is coming tonight. But, if I told him you were that man, he'd marry us and my uncle would have to watch the land pass to my husband."

"But I'm not your husband. How's he going to feel when he shows up and finds his wife married to me?"

"He won't show up. I made him up and the land won't really be yours—you'll just hold on to it for a while, then pass it back to me."

The stranger looked confused. "Why?" he asked as if he really didn't want to know the answer.

She glared at him. "Because I may be pregnant." It was the first honest thing she'd said in so long, and it felt good.

"How did that happen? Imaginary men don't get women pregnant." He met her stare, and she swore she saw a bit of a blush flash across the outlaw's face in the candlelight. "Never mind," he corrected. "I don't want to know."

She rushed on, not wanting to remember, much less explain. "I have to marry or lose everything. If you won't kill me, marry me."

"Great plan. What would keep your uncle from just shooting me a minute after the ceremony?"

"The minute we're married, as my husband, you own the land. If you die, it's mine. The ranch hands will stand with whoever is the rightful owner. Some of them don't agree with the way my uncle has been taking over since my father's been sick, but they're afraid to cross him, knowing he could be their boss soon. If they know the ranch will pass to you, they'd stand with you."

A grin lifted one side of his mouth and she thought he looked almost handsome. "What's to keep you from killing me?"

"I'll make you a deal. Marry me and stay with me until my uncle goes back to his place at that gambling hole he calls his town, and then I'll let you take that wagonload of wedding loot out of here." She hesitated, then added, "But if you don't leave when I tell you to, I *will* shoot you, myself."

"How long do I have to stay?"

"Not long. A few days. A week at the most. Just until the guests leave," she lied. "My uncle will suspect a trick. I'll need time to make sure I'm protected. But, while you are here, acting like my husband, you'll have to play the role."

"What about my uncles?"

"If I save them from the rope, will you consider my proposal?"

"Why trust me, lady?"

"You're a thief, I'm a liar. Seems a good match." She thought she saw a bit of hurt flash in his eyes as if she'd insulted him.

When he looked back at her, his blue eyes had turned hard as gray, cold steel. "You've got yourself a deal," he said as if she'd just chosen an impossible task. "Get my uncles freed and I'll play your game. I'll marry you and stay here until the ranch passes to me, and then I'll leave it to you."

"Stay here," she whispered as if afraid to hope. "I'll be right back."

Before he could say a word, she rushed to the tiny side door of the chapel with her wedding dress flowing like a huge white cloud behind her. She tapped twice and a priest opened the door. Then she vanished.

Chapter 2

Michael Hughes walked to the window and stared out into the chilly winter night. She was the most beautiful thing he'd ever seen, and the craziest. The woman made snakes look predictable. He had no hope of her managing to free his three dumb uncles. After all, she was a prisoner herself from all he could tell.

If he had any sense, he'd run. Michael laughed. If he'd had any sense he never would have come back to the Big Ben country. He'd been twelve when his uncles talked him into playing lookout for one of their schemes. They'd failed at robbing a bank and he'd been the only one who got caught. Without parents, Michael had had no one to stand with him before the judge. He'd been sentenced to six years of hard labor.

The first few months had been hell. Then the warden's wife, Mrs. Peters, noticed him and demanded he be assigned to help her. She was six feet tall and as hard as nails, but she was a Quaker on a mission. She ran a school that forced education on every child she managed to catch and draw into her one-room school.

Michael cleaned the schoolroom, built the fires, and stayed with her all day doing whatever chore she yelled for him to do. At night he helped the cook wash up after supper before a guard came to put his chains back on and take him to the huge bay where prisoners slept. When it got warm enough that first spring, he took off his ragged coat to chop wood. Mrs. Peters noticed bruises on his arms and knew he'd been mistreated at night in the cell block. She demanded he be allowed to sleep in the school, and she wasn't a woman even the warden would cross.

With regular meals and a place where he could sleep without fear, Michael began to grow. The animal he'd almost become calmed. In three years he'd read all the books she had and practiced math until he was faster than her with figures. Mrs. Peters never told him so, but he guessed she was proud of what she'd done. Every month she managed to find more books for him to read and she always insisted on calling him Michael, never Mickey or Mike, like his uncles had.

When he was released at eighteen, she gave him the only clothes he'd ever had that weren't hand-me-downs and said she saw great things in his future.

Mrs. Peters told him many times that he was a child never to be loved, but he could manage to be useful if he worked hard. Only, in the two years since he'd seen her, he hadn't managed to be that to anyone. If this crazy bride needed him, he'd do what he could, if for no other reason than to prove Mrs. Peters right.

The Quaker had been wrong about the great things in his future. With men drifting into Texas looking for work by the hundreds, there were no jobs, and even if there had been, no one wanted to hire an ex-con. Michael's years in prison left him unskilled for most manual jobs and the few he got drove him insane with boredom. Finally, he drifted back to the only family he'd ever known. His three uncles.

The three hadn't changed much, but Michael had. He saw

them for what they were, bumbling idiots who loved him simply because he was kin to them.

Uncle Abe couldn't count past seven but liked to cook any meat the others shot or stole.

Uncle Moses followed what he called his laws and believed everything bad that happened in his life was somehow caused by him not adhering to his rules. Of course, the laws included reversing his socks every morning so they'd never wear out and eating all his meals with the same spoon.

Uncle Joseph was the true thief in the family. He stole everything he found not tied down. He even stole from his brothers. They'd long ago given up on trying to talk him out of his habit and now just looked for whatever was missing among his things.

Michael thought he could keep them out of trouble. In the months he'd been back he'd made them clean their shack and clear the plot behind the house for a garden. Then, they convinced him to come along on this one robbery. The people were so rich, they wouldn't notice a few things missing.

Michael's plan was to ride along in case they got in over their heads. He'd thought to hide away in the church for an hour while they wandered around the sleeping ranch collecting all they could carry. Once they made it off the ranch, the uncles would fall asleep and he'd take back their loot.

Even his robbery of the bride had been only a trick. He knew he wouldn't leave with the jewelry. He'd thought she heard him enter and was about to scream when she leaned against the window.

Great job he'd done, Michael thought. Unless he could think of something before the crazy bride got back, he'd be swinging with them from the nearest tree come dawn. She was probably running for help now and laughing that he'd agreed to wait.

The bride, he thought. She was the most beautiful little

thing he'd ever seen, and when he'd touched her neck, he knew he'd never touch anything that soft again. But she had to be nuts if she thought her imaginary husband could have gotten her pregnant.

"Psst," a sound brought him back from his worrying. "Psst, Mr. Outlaw."

She was back. The nutty princess in white.

"The priest has gone to get your uncles. I told him how we were in love and of course in a family way. I said you wanted to marry me but you had to have your family present. Father Timothy also agreed not to wake my father."

Michael stared at her, wondering if he'd ever be able to tell if she was lying or telling the truth.

"The priest agreed to tell whoever is guarding your uncles that they were here for a secret wedding. Once he's got them in his chambers, he'll marry us."

"What about your uncle? He might want to stand in for your father."

She moved out of the shadows and he saw her shy smile. "I told Father Timothy I was embarrassed because of the pregnancy and our hurried wedding without the blessing of the church. I said I preferred to marry now before as few people as possible. He went along with the idea, assuring me that my uncle only wanted me to do what was right and marrying the man I've already bedded would be wise."

Michael watched her closely. "The truth never crosses your shadow, does it?"

"Not often. My mother used to say life is far more interesting when looked at from a different angle."

"Well if we do this I'd like your word that you'll play no games with me. No lies between us from here on out. We'll be honest with each other for the few days the marriage lasts."

"Outlaw honor?"

Michael guessed she'd already figured out he wasn't much of an outlaw. "Outlaw honor."

"Fair enough. We have a deal then?"

"We have a deal."

The priest opened the door and whispered, "Miss Cozette, are you ready? I have the three witnesses."

Michael reached and took her hand. He didn't miss her slight jerk of panic, before she calmed and let him pull her toward the door. "Come along, dear," he said, realizing he'd never used the endearment before. "It's time we married."

"Yes . . ." she whispered.

"Michael," he filled in the blank, guessing, like Mrs. Peters, his short-time wife would call him by his real name.

"Yes, Michael," she confirmed.

They followed the priest into a small room already full of his chubby uncles. The three looked a little the worse for wear and frightened. Uncle Abe wiped his bloody nose with his sleeve. Uncle Moses was shaking his head as if he could wish himself back home. Uncle Joseph ran his fingers over a brass cross as if judging its size before he tried pocketing it.

Michael felt sorry for them. "It's all right," he whispered. "There's not going to be a hanging. I'm getting married and everything will be fine."

Uncle Joseph wrinkled up his face. "You stealing a bride? That ain't right, Mickey boy. It just ain't right."

Michael laughed. He'd finally found something Joseph wouldn't steal.

Chapter 3

"Do you wish to marry this woman of your own free will?" the priest asked.

Michael hesitated, knowing that if they went through with this ceremony, at least one man, her uncle, would want him dead.

The priest huffed with impatience. "Sir, you have already touched this woman?"

"Yes." Michael couldn't lie there. He could still feel the softness of her skin on his fingers. He had touched her, if not in the way the priest was hinting.

"Then in the eyes of the church you are already married."

Michael felt like he was whirling in a storm. Cozette stood close, holding his arm as if she needed support. His uncle Moses started crying and mumbling something about never seeing a wedding up close. The priest glared at him as if he were dirt-rolled evil, which only made Moses cry harder.

All in all, the wedding was worse than first light after a three-day drunk.

They both said what the priest told them to say and did everything he told them to do. When he finished, he looked at Michael and said simply, "You may kiss your bride."

Michael stared down at her and realized she looked as

miserable as he felt. Somehow he found that one fact calming. Touching her chin lightly with his fingertips, he tilted her head and brushed her lips with his own.

She tasted newborn and fresh, nothing like the few saloon girls he'd kissed.

Her lip quivered slightly and he knew this lady might have known a man, but she'd never been loved. She'd never been kissed with tenderness. Deep down, he understood something she might never tell him.

"It's going to be all right, Cozette," he whispered to her. It was the first time he'd said her name and he wished he could believe his own words. "We'll get through this and you will be safe. I swear it."

Her eyes rounded and part of the fear he'd seen there vanished. To his surprise, she believed him.

This time she took his hand and asked, "Will you go with me to my father's bedside? I'd like him to meet you when he wakes."

Michael nodded once and opened the mission door for her. They stepped out into a crowd of men, all with guns raised at him.

The priest hurried out. "Do not worry!" he shouted. "All is well. They are married. This is the man our Cozette picked as her mate."

For a moment, Michael feared those would be the last words he'd hear on earth. None of the cowhands looked like they'd be bothered if his new bride ordered him shot.

Then, surprisingly, the cowboys lowered their weapons and stepped forward to shake his hand.

Cozette's laughter came too loud to sound real. "I know everyone expected us to wait until morning, but I wanted my father to meet Michael as my husband." She waved her hand across the crowd. "I know my uncle plans a wedding breakfast and I'd like you all to wash up and join us at first light."

The wranglers gave a hoot and started toward the bunkhouse.

Michael noticed his three uncles slowly backing into the shadows. "That means you three also." His words froze them in midflight. You'll be joining us for breakfast and you'll behave yourselves."

"There's a well behind the house where you can clean up if you like," Cozette added without venturing any closer to the three outlaws. "I'll have towels and soap set out."

"W-what's going on here?" Uncle Joseph stuttered out his demand. "This don't seem right. W-we ain't never been invited to w-wash or eat nowhere in our lives."

"It's right." Michael knew he couldn't trust them with the details of the marriage. A few drinks and all three would be telling everything they knew about how their nephew found a bride in the middle of a robbery.

While they watched, he kissed Cozette's cheek and motioned for her to go ahead into the front door of the big house. "I'll be with you in a moment, dear."

She glanced at the uncles and broke into a run. Michael had no idea if she feared them or simply got downwind of them.

Once she was out of sight, he turned to his kin. "I need you all. I can only trust family in this matter of life and death."

"W-what can w-we do, get horses, find guns?" Joseph asked. "I'll steal a few. It was just pure luck they caught us the first time. W-we can grab a few bags and be long gone before they notice."

"No." Michael shook his head. Flight seemed always their first thought. "I need the three of you to stay close and keep your eyes open. There are men here who didn't want us to marry. They might mean my new bride harm. I don't want them getting close to Cozette."

"Who's Cozette?" Abe asked.

Michael fought the urge to thump him hard. "My new wife, remember, the woman I just married. The one who told you to wash."

"Oh," he said. "The one in white. I remember now. You called her dear. I never knew you had a dear one, Mickey boy."

"Yes, and we've got to protect her"—Michael stared at them—"with your lives if necessary."

They looked at one another as if he were speaking a language they didn't quite understand. "We're bodyguards?" Moses whispered.

"Yeah, you've been promoted from outlaws." Michael hated to admit it but he did need them. He had no idea what he was stepping into, but it had to be bad if she was willing to die to get away. It offered him no comfort that he was her second choice tonight.

"Now there are three rules you've got to remember. Listen close. One, no drinking. Two, no stealing. You can eat all you want, but rule number three is that one of you is to be armed and standing near my dear wife at all times. I don't want anyone, and I mean anyone, laying a hand on her. She's in danger."

Abe scratched his bald head. "Mind my asking where you got this pretty little wife? You never mentioned her."

Michael said the first thing that came to mind. "We met in church. I didn't know she cared about me, but when she mentioned marriage, I thought it was a good idea."

They all nodded as if he'd explained. Michael had the feeling if any woman had ever mentioned marriage to any one of them she would have been forced to take all three. They came as a set.

"Now, clean up and wait for me inside." He smiled as they hurried around the house, heads down. The food might sound good, but washing had always been treated like a disease.

Michael didn't know what he expected to see when he

walked into the main house on the ranch, but a mansion wasn't it. The place shone grander than the hotels he'd seen in Fort Worth and Austin. It had a long staircase and candles everywhere on tall gold candlesticks.

He straightened, feeling out of place. No way did he belong here. How could he hope to pull this off? He knew nothing about ranching and even less about women.

Cozette waited at the bottom of the stairs talking to an old woman who looked like she might be the housekeeper. He just stood watching Cozette and wondering how he could even be allowed on the same planet with such a creature.

When she noticed him, she moved away from the old woman and walked toward him, her hand out.

"We need to see my father, but the doctor is with him now." Her fingers closed around his. "Maybe we can talk while we wait."

He let her lead him to a long bench outside two massive doors. All his life everywhere he'd been had been small: his uncles' small cabin, the jail cells, the one-room school. For the first time ever, indoors he felt like he could stand tall and breathe without using up too much air.

She sat next to him, almost touching. "We need to get things clear between us. I'm aware that I may have tricked you into this but I want to be fair now. You've done no less than save my life."

He nodded, aware that she was leaning into him. "It seemed the only way out for us both." He didn't bother to add that she hadn't given him much choice in the matter.

She nodded her agreement, then whispered, "My father has consumption. His lungs are filling with blood, so we can't stay long. Only a minute. Last year he moved into his study because the stairs got too much for him." She looked down at Michael's fingers, still laced in hers. "I'm not close to him.

When I was little, he was never around. I thought he hated me. I wasn't much of a consideration in his world."

Michael found it hard to believe she wouldn't be loved. She was rich. She had a grand home. Hell, she even had him for the asking.

She continued, "My mother was French and never really fit in here in Texas. I guess he thought I never would either, because most of the time I was home from school he managed to be somewhere else. When my mother died, it was like he wished I'd disappear. I remember one Christmas at the school he sent me to, he forgot to send someone after me. I ate Christmas dinner with the sisters and, of course, there were no presents allowed."

He closed his hand around hers. He'd never received one gift for birthday or Christmas, but he found himself feeling sorry for her. Little angels in white should have presents to open.

She met his gaze. "Promise me, for the time we're pretending, you'll never be cruel to me."

"I promise," he said, "only we're not pretending. We are married. I'll try to be a good husband, and when I leave, you'll have this place for you and your baby if one grows inside you."

One tear drifted down her cheek. "Thank you," she whispered. "I'll owe you a great debt. Is there nothing you ask?"

He closed his eyes and leaned the back of his head against the wall. Finally, he formed the words. "If you wouldn't mind, I'd like to touch you now and then." He lifted his hand as if showing her an example. "I mean you no harm, but I've never been near anyone so fine."

She frowned. "Are you making fun of me?"

"No," he said, surprised.

She pouted, then shrugged. "I'm a fallen woman about to trick my father, who is on his deathbed. I've been used and tossed away by one man, which makes me worthless, and I never plan to have another. If all you want to do is hold my hand or brush my cheek, I'd say that's a fair enough price for risking your life."

To his surprise, she frowned. "I must tell you, though, I don't like to be touched. It's not something I'm used to. My father never touched me. The nuns never touched me, and the one man who did touch me hurt me. You'd probably be doing me a favor, making me a little less jumpy around men. So touch all you like."

"I'll not hurt you," he added, trying to figure out if she truly meant what she said. "And I've already touched you, when I started to remove your necklace and again when I put my hand around your neck."

She smiled. "For a murder attempt, it was rather gentle."

They both laughed and for the first time he thought this scheme of hers might work. She'd have her land, his uncles would have their loot without fear of jail, and he'd have a memory of a time when he'd been allowed close to perfection.

A few minutes passed before the huge wooden door opened and an old doctor limped out. "You can see him." He shook his head. "I had to ask twice before he'd agree to see you. He doesn't seem to want to use up what little energy he has left."

She stepped past the doctor. Michael followed.

The room was huge and built to impress. Against long windows, a massive desk stood on a platform one step up so that whoever sat behind would be eye level with anyone standing. Books lined the walls into a seating area big enough to hold a full-sized bed. There, a man rested, his dark weathered skin contrasting against the white sheets.

Michael stared at Duke Camanez. Somehow, Michael thought he would have been bigger, but he looked small beneath the covers.

"Father," Cozette whispered as she stepped closer. "Father. I've brought my husband to meet you."

The dying man's eyes opened slowly. He looked at his only child with a cold, uncaring gaze. "You look more like your mother every day, child, and are just as worthless, I'm sure."

Then, without expecting her to respond, he looked at Michael. "So, you married her. She's no more than a bit of a girl, not strong enough to bear many children, I fear." Camanez coughed and blood trailed out of the corner of his mouth. "My condolences. She's made of lies and lace, you know."

"I know." Michael smiled as if he thought Duke Camanez was telling a joke. He'd heard of the rancher—everyone within five hundred miles had heard of the man who ruled his ranch like his own private kingdom.

Michael offered his hand and was surprised when the frail man took it.

"You're a fool who fell for her beauty," Camanez said in a whisper. "I can't blame you, son, I once fell myself." He took time to breathe, then continued, "Keep her pregnant if you can and don't give in to her tricks. Maybe she'll give birth to sons who will run this ranch one day. I pray they get your build and not hers." He coughed, then added as he fought to breathe, "Try not to run the place into the ground before you pass it on to my grandsons."

Michael had no idea what to say. Camanez's hand slipped from his as the old man's body shook from a round of coughing.

A nurse moved from the shadows and put her arm around him as she wiped away blood dripping from his chin.

The doctor mumbled as he pushed them toward the door. "Don't come back until tonight. I'm giving him enough laudanum to let him rest the day away. I fear you've excited him, doing him more harm than good."

As soon as they were outside the door, Cozette straightened

as if she'd been slapped hard and was refusing to cower. "I'll be right back," she said and disappeared down a hallway. A moment later he heard her feet tapping up a wooden staircase just out of sight.

He didn't know if he should follow. Was she upset, hurt, or embarrassed at what her father had said? Or, he reasoned, could it be morning sickness?

Michael returned to the entrance hall, noticing the sunrise shining bright across twenty-foot windows. It crossed his mind that it would take a dozen suns to lighten the sorrow in this house. He'd never considered himself as knowing much about women, but compared to Duke Camanez, he was a knight. If he hadn't heard the words he never would have believed a father could be so cruel to his only child. Apparently, he saw her as only a means to grandsons. His only chance that his blood would continue to own the ranch he called San Louise.

His uncles stood a foot inside the door looking as out of place as pigs in a parade. To their credit, they had tried to clean up. Their faces and hands were washed and they'd slicked back their dirty hair. He thought of Mrs. Peters back at the school near the prison. She probably would have taken one look at these three and had them planted in the dirt in hopes that whatever sprouted might be cleaner.

He joined them as they surveyed the place.

"We could take a dozen of these candleholders and they'd never miss them," Joseph whispered.

Michael glared at all three. "Rule two. Don't take anything," he said softly and all three nodded.

He watched them move around the room, staring at every piece of furniture or painting as if they were appraising its value. Strangers began to come down the stairs and from the hallway where his part-time wife had disappeared. They hung in small groups like travelers at a train station showing little interest in people around them.

Michael guessed some were employees, some might be relatives, but he had no idea if they were holding a death watch or waiting for a wedding. If he had to define their look, it would be curiosity more than sadness or joy.

Five minutes later, they all turned and watched Cozette slowly come down the steps. The feeling that she was too beautiful to be real crossed his mind and he considered the possibility that this was all one long dream. When he'd first begun to read, he'd dreamed that the places and people in books were real, but he'd seen no evidence of it until now.

She played a role before him she must have been born to play. She greeted the sleepy guests who were down the stairs and the cowboys stepping inside, their hats in hand, with the same graceful smiles and comments.

Only one, an older man in black, looked like he hadn't been asleep. He stormed down the stairs glaring at Cozette, then searched the room until his gaze settled on Michael.

Michael knew if looks could kill he'd be dead.

Before being introduced, he had no doubt this was her uncle, Raymond Camanez. The man who would have inherited everything if she hadn't married.

Raymond said something sharp to her as she made the introduction, then glared at Michael as if he knew something was wrong but couldn't quite see the flaw. Then, like a storm breaking, his features cleared. Cozette's uncle Raymond took a step toward Michael, offering his hand.

When Michael took the man's hand, Raymond pulled him close and whispered, "You're a walking dead man for tricking me out of this ranch."

Michael stared as the older man pulled away smiling as if he'd just wished them well.

Cozette had moved away, probably to stay out of reach of

her uncle. Michael could find no words to answer the threat, but he planned to keep watch. He might not know much about women, but he'd seen enough evil men to know one on sight.

The priest arrived and offered a blessing to the house. Then women came from the kitchen with huge trays of food. The ranch hands began to take their seats along a dining table long enough to hold two dozen people.

Cozette moved toward Michael. "You'll sit at the head of the table," she whispered. "I'll sit at the other end."

"No." Michael shook his head. "This is our wedding breakfast. You should stay at my side." He moved to the head of the table and pulled a chair from the wall.

She gave him a puzzled look, then smiled as if proud he was willing to play his part.

As they ate, Cozette introduced him to a few of the hands and they made more introductions. By the time breakfast was over, he could call most of the men by name and, surprisingly, they treated him with respect.

Cozette explained that he'd ridden for four days to get to her and made a joke about how he'd look far better when he got cleaned up.

Michael didn't miss how the men seemed to ignore Raymond Camanez when he stood. He was no longer their boss and every man on the ranch knew it.

The trouble was, Michael wasn't sure he would be up for the job. He could ride and shoot fairly well, but he knew nothing about running a ranch.

He glanced at Cozette and saw a brush of fear shadow her eyes as well. If they didn't pull this off, he didn't want to think about what might happen.

Her hand was icy when he closed his fingers around hers and stood, pulling her up with him. "If you will excuse us, gentlemen, I'd like to take a few minutes to get reacquainted with my wife."

They all laughed and mumbled low comments, but Michael didn't care. "Let's make this believable," he said only for her to hear a moment before he swept her up.

"Good day, gentlemen!" He laughed as they shouted while he started toward the stairs.

She wrapped her arms around his neck and buried her face against his shoulder.

Lowering a kiss on her cheek, he whispered, "Which way?"

"Up," she answered, her lips touching his. "All the way to the back of the hallway."

A cheer went up from the men behind them and Michael paused on the steps long enough to finish the kiss she'd started. The rest of this job he'd signed on for might be frightening, but her lips tasted like heaven.

When he finally let her breathe, her cheeks were rose colored with embarrassment, but she smiled up at him. Without a word he carried her up and set her gently on her feet once they were out of sight of those below.

She moved to the waiting maid and gave instructions in a low tone. The maid nodded and hurried away without looking up at Michael.

When they were alone, Cozette opened the last door on the left of the hallway. "My uncle took the first room when he came here after my father had moved downstairs. It's the biggest bedroom. He didn't know that my parents' rooms were always the last rooms."

She walked into a warm room done in colors of the earth and bathed in sunshine. Michael didn't want to act the fool, but he had a hard time keeping his mouth from dropping. He'd never seen such a room. Books lined two walls, and the view beyond the windowpanes seemed endless.

He glanced back at his uncles thundering up the stairs, Uncle Abe still eating. Before he could say anything, Cozette stepped in front of him and pointed. "Gentlemen, you'll find your rooms being readied in the guesthouses off the garden."

"We get a room?" Abe mumbled. "We'd be fine in the barn."

"No," she insisted. "You're family now. I've asked for baths and fresh clothes to be sent to your rooms."

"But . . ."

Michael didn't know if they were thinking of the rule to never leave her, or dreading the bath, but he said, "I'll watch over my wife, you three do as she says. We all could use a few hours of sleep."

They weren't about to argue with the woman who saved their lives. They all nodded and hurried back down the stairs.

Michael turned to her. "When I'm not close, I want one of them with you at all times. If for any reason I have to be gone, one will be sleeping in this hallway outside your door."

She walked back into what had been her father's room. "That's not necessary."

"I saw the way your uncle looked at us. I insist."

"Already being bossy. I don't like rules."

Michael hesitated, feeling like he might step a foot too far in any direction and be in quicksand. "I'll go along with however you want to play this except where your safety is concerned. Fair enough?"

"Fair enough." She moved to the windows, her black hair shining in the sunlight.

For the first time he thought he saw her relax a bit. She trusted him. It made no sense, but somehow he had the feeling that the only person for miles she believed in was him, the outlaw who tried to frighten her last night.

"This is not your room," he guessed, for there was nothing feminine about the space.

"No," she answered, opening a panel he thought might open into the hall. Only it led to a bathing room larger than most hotel rooms he'd seen. She crossed the tile and opened another door. "This is my room." The end of the hallway had been closed in to connect the rooms.

Michael smiled. It looked exactly like what he would imagine her room would look like. She didn't have the tall windows or the walls of books, but she had a fireplace and comfortable chairs in an alcove, where she could spend quiet mornings. Her colors were in the earthtones of spring.

"I keep both my doors locked whenever I'm in my room and I'll tap on the bathroom door before entering in case you're bathing."

"Fair enough." He tried to act like he understood. The room she'd called the "bathing room" was almost the size of his uncles' entire house.

Three maids banged their way into the bathing room, causing Michael to take one step into her quarters. "What's going on?"

"They're getting your bath ready. I asked them to lay out extra shaving equipment. By the time you've finished, we'll have a few trouser lengths let out and jackets aired. There should be something waiting on your bed that will fit you."

"I have my own clothes." He looked down. His trousers and shirt might have been bought off the shelf at the mercantile, but they were the best he'd ever owned and not more than a week dirty.

"You're my husband. By marrying me you now own one of the biggest ranches in Texas. I can help run the ranch, but you'll need to look the part."

"We need to talk." He began unbuttoning his shirt. "As soon as I've followed your orders and had my bath, I need to know more about this ranch if I'm going to be of any use."

She smiled, her hands on her hips, her eyes watching his hands as they worked the buttons. "I'll be waiting in my room with a hot cup of tea and maps of the ranch when you're ready." She blushed when she noticed he was watching her watch him.

She closed her door and he wasn't surprised to hear the lock click. He kicked the other door closed with his boot and stripped off his clothes. She might think he understood her, but he felt like they were barely speaking the same language.

An hour later, he looked in the mirror and almost didn't recognize himself. His hair was clean and combed back, his clothes probably cost more than he'd ever made in his life all put together, and his boots, though too tight, were fine leather with tooling along the sides. It seemed unbelievable that people kept such clothes around for guests who might need them.

He tapped on her door. After a moment, he heard the lock give and she stood before him in a white blouse and midnight blue riding skirt. If possible, with her hair down and her boots disappearing into her skirt, she looked even more beautiful.

"Come in, sir." She grinned. "You sure do clean up nice. If I didn't know better I'd think you were born to wear those clothes."

He had no idea what to say. He couldn't think of a compliment for her that wouldn't make him sound like a fool.

"How does everything fit?" she asked as she moved to the seating area.

"The boots are too small, but someone came in the bathing room and stole my clothes and boots while I was dressing."

"The maids. They'll bring them back in a few hours, all cleaned and polished. I'll order you new boots by mail tomorrow."

"So, dressing me is part of the bargain." He didn't like the idea, but he did like the clothes.

She shrugged. "I guess so. It seems only fair. After all, I'm the one asking you to play a role."

He almost said, "Any chance undressing you is part of my bargain?" but he feared any boldness might frighten her.

Showing affection downstairs was one thing; being bold here in the silence of her room would be quite another.

She took her seat on one side of a small table set with tea and smiled up at him as if they were old friends.

He gambled and brushed the top of her head with his hand.

As before, she stiffened at his touch, but made no comment. He had a feeling they were both thinking of the bargain they'd made. He'd play the part and she'd let him touch her from time to time.

He took his seat, swearing to himself that before he left her she'd at least not jump when he touched her.

She poured him tea, which he didn't drink as she filled him in on the workings of the ranch. She showed him maps and explained her family history.

He was quiet and polite until she pulled out the monthly expense records. The figures, so carefully kept, interested him. "Mind if I study these?" he finally asked. "If I can follow the income and output, I'll understand the runnings of the ranch better."

"I would say you could talk to our bookkeeper. I don't know his first name. Everyone always calls him Mr. Fiddler." She frowned. "I haven't seen him since I came back. In fact, I haven't even thought to ask about him. He's probably around somewhere."

Michael raised an eyebrow, but said nothing as she continued.

"The past three years' records are on my father's desk downstairs. I saw my uncle looking at them the morning I found out my father's terms for the will. While you're here take as active a part in the running of the ranch as you like." She hesitated a long moment and added, "But never forget our bargain. As soon as the ranch is safely mine, you and your uncles will leave and for your trouble I promise your wagon will be packed."

"I'll hold to my bargain, Cozette, and I'd like to look over the accounts," he said, almost angry that she felt the need to remind him of their pact. He didn't add that since she'd probably be by her father's side the records would give him a reason to stay close.

She opened her mouth as if to question, then reconsidered and nodded in compromise. Last night he'd watched her change from a frightened child to a woman taking control of her life. She'd never be easy to manipulate again and he knew he'd never even try.

He smiled as she fiddled with her tea. He knew he was the only one she had to trust. An outlaw who had threatened to kill her was all that stood beside her now. Michael had seen the look in her uncle's eyes. He wanted the ranch and might just be willing to do anything, including killing them both to get it.

Michael planned to stay by her side until he knew she was safe. He would do so even without the promise of a wagonload of goods.

Chapter 4

The newlyweds came down for lunch late. Cozette didn't miss all the smiles and winks at Michael. He remained the gentleman, never letting on that he knew she'd thrown up her breakfast. He hadn't even raised his head from the book he'd been reading when she forgot to close his connecting door. When she'd visited her father by way of the back stairs, he'd followed and quietly remained at the desk by the window until she'd told him it was time for lunch.

He'd covered his hand over hers a few times during the meal, and when he knew someone was watching, he'd made an effort to brush her cheek with a kiss or lightly circle his arm over her shoulders. Because of her father's illness and the newlyweds' need to be alone, the few guests who'd come quickly made excuses to leave. By afternoon, all the ranch hands had returned to work and the house was quiet.

When she'd excused herself to sit with her father, Michael followed without a word. He'd walked her all the way to the chair by her father's bed, then kissed her hand and said he'd be at the desk across the room.

She'd expected to find her uncle in her father's room and was relieved to see only the nurse.

Shadows were long when Michael excused himself and

left the room. Cozette stood and stretched, then walked around the big desk, noticing that Michael had been studying the records all afternoon. She stopped at the tall windows and stared out at her ranch, loving it so much her heart ached to realize how close she came to losing it.

She brushed her fingers over the slight bulge just above her knee where she'd strapped a gun to her leg. A few months ago she believed everyone to be good and fair. She thought her uncle loved her and only wanted her to be happy when he'd sent a letter introducing the son of a friend.

Fredrick Bates had shown up at her school with flowers and his aunt as chaperone. The nuns had let her go riding with him and to dinner in town as long as the aunt went along. After all, he had the proper family introduction and Cozette was a year older than most girls who left the school. They'd let her stay on another year only because her father had insisted.

Cozette thought she was in love with Fredrick by the fourth outing. He spoke French to her and swore she had angel eyes. When his aunt retired early on the fifth evening, she'd been excited to spend the time alone with a man who pampered her so.

Fredrick had teased her and told her he planned to seduce her as they entered his private quarters. She'd been fool enough to laugh and play along when he kissed her and flirted with her. When the hour grew late, she'd told him she had to go, but he changed. Seduction turned forceful and demanding.

For a moment she thought he was still teasing, and when talk turned to action, she'd been too shocked, too young, too naive to even fight.

It had all been over in a few minutes, and when he pulled away, he'd seemed furious at her. The man who'd spoken his love for her in French stood, straightened his clothes, and said he'd done what he'd been paid to do. He'd left her there, her dress torn, her heart broken as if she were no more than the scraps after a meal.

She'd cried for a while, then walked back to the school and pretended nothing had happened. If she'd said a word she would have been expelled. Her father would have disowned her. Proper young ladies didn't get themselves into compromising positions.

So, she'd held her tongue and come home as soon as she could find a reason to slip away.

Once on the ranch, she'd realized the truth. The letter introducing Fredrick was in Uncle Raymond's handwriting. He had paid a man to dishonor her.

When she said nothing, he must have thought the plan hadn't worked. Then, he'd talked her father into changing his will. He probably figured she'd be too afraid to even talk to another man after her encounter with Fredrick. Uncle Raymond must have thought he'd planned it all out where he would win the ranch without a fight. Half the family wealth had never been enough—he wanted it all.

Her grandfather had fought the Apache for this land, her father had fought outlaws and raiders more than once, and now she knew she'd have to fight her uncle. No one was ever going to stand in her way. The land was hers, paid for with blood and sweat. She would have made a bargain with the devil himself to keep it.

Looking at the chair where Michael had been sitting, she wondered if that hadn't been exactly what she'd done. After all, he was an outlaw. His only three relatives didn't look like they'd completely evolved from animals. Moses snorted like a bull and Joseph smacked when he ate. She couldn't even see Abe clearly for all the dirty hair hanging in his face.

But Michael Hughes looked like he was born to play the role of a rancher. All dressed up, he looked like a perfect gentleman, but he seemed to be holding his cards close to the vest and waiting for her to give him just enough power to take over or run. When the time came, how hard would it be for him to walk away from a ranch this size with only a wagonload of trinkets? By law all her property now belonged to him. Would he give it back when the time came?

She stood and moved to the gun chest. Lifting the false bottom to the shelf, she retrieved two more small Colts. One for beneath her pillow, the other to hide in this room. She'd not be caught unprepared again. The nuns might not have taught her to fight, but they had taught her to reason. She wanted to believe in Michael, but she'd learned the hard way to be prepared.

From the window, she watched her new husband cross through the garden. He didn't turn to the cabins where his relatives stayed but opened a side gate. Taking long strides he walked into the untamed pasture beyond the trimmed and groomed walls of the compound.

He was almost to the trees running along a creek behind the house when he stopped. She watched as he leaned his head back and stared up at the cloudy sky like a man trying to find his bearings.

For the first time, she wondered if he felt as trapped by their bargain as she did. If he hadn't agreed to her crazy scheme he might have been killed last night. Yet, even knowing all she had to do was yell and he'd be trapped, he'd bargained for his uncles' lives. He'd also handled her setting all the rules with more class than she might have in his place. She'd made it plain that he'd play the part of master over all he saw, but she'd make the final decisions on anything pertaining to the ranch. She'd hold all the power. As her father slipped farther and farther from the world, she'd take her place.

One of the ranch hands fell into step with Michael as he walked back to the house. She saw them talking and wished she could hear what they were saying. The ranch hand tipped his hat in salute when he veered off at the garden gate.

Cozette put one of the guns in the pillows by the alcove and noticed he hadn't touched his tea again. Next time they talked, she'd have coffee for him even though he hadn't complained or asked. The least she could do was make him comfortable in his cage.

Chapter 5

Michael walked slowly back onto the house grounds. He was supposed to join her at dinner, but he had no idea when dinner would be. At the prison there were only two meals. One served at dawn, the other an hour before dark. That way men could use daylight to work and everyone would be shackled in by dark and no extra light was needed.

He'd hated those nights. A boy sleeping in among men who yelled and swore and cried. The silence of the classroom was a welcome change. He hadn't minded that he slept on the floor with a single blanket at night. The warden's wife gave him clean clothes every Monday and made him bathe once a week. When he'd finished and dressed, she'd always inspect for dirt under his nails or ears that weren't scrubbed.

If she found nothing, she'd say, "You'll do" and walk away without another word.

He ate his meals on the back porch of the warden's house. Their cook gave him scraps at first. No matter what or how little was on the plate, Michael thanked her every morning and night. Eventually, the meals got better. After a few months, she even gave him a tin with leftover biscuits in it. "You ain't much older than the kids in that school. It ain't fair you don't have no lunch."

Michael thanked her and that night he tasted his first dessert. One scoop of apple cobbler.

When he was growing up with his uncles nothing had an order. Supper or any meal, for that matter, came when the food was done. If nothing was caught and cooked, they ate like chickens scratching around for bits of food.

He passed through the pasture gate and into the courtyard wondering if the San Louise Ranch ever had cobbler.

He saw Abe and Joseph walking out of their small rooms along the row of cabins Cozette had called guesthouses. His uncles were dressed in wool trousers without a single patch and well-made broadcloth shirts.

"Hold up, Mickey!" Abe yelled. "You get a look at our quarters? Real sheets and two blankets each. One of the maids came by to tell us she'd pick up our laundry and sheets every Monday to wash. Imagine that."

Joseph shook his head and stuttered, "They'll w-wear them out w-washing them that often."

Abe took his time chewing his words before he spoke, as he always did when he wasn't sure of something. "How long do you figure we're staying?"

Michael wished he could tell them the bargain, but he'd given his word. "Behave yourselves and you can stay as long as I do."

Abe tried again. "When your pa married our sister, he took her away. The marriage didn't take, I guess, 'cause she was back before all the seasons changed with you in her belly. When she left us she kept saying it was forever. Mickey, you ain't never used that word once."

Michael had heard the story of how his mother left them a hundred times. They did all they could when she went into labor, but she died giving birth to him. Then his uncles stole a goat and somehow kept him alive. He was about seven when he realized his uncles barely had a brain among them.

He tried to make one detail clear to them. "I'll stay awhile but we'll have to leave eventually. This is Cozette's ranch, her land, not mine. Never forget that."

They both nodded and turned toward the bunkhouse.

"Aren't you coming in to dinner?" Michael asked.

"Nope." Abe smiled. "We've been invited to the bunkhouse kitchen for chili."

Joseph grinned. "W-wish we could invite you, boy, but it w-wouldn't be right. You're going to have to eat in the big house w-with all those people w-watching to snatch your plate before you get a chance to lick it clean and more forks than anybody ought to have to put up w-with."

Abe frowned. "One of them fell in my pocket this morning. I guess you'd better take it back before they miss it."

Michael took the fork. "No stealing while you're here, remember?"

Abe's head bobbled, but Michael doubted the message would log.

He walked back to the house. Inside the kitchen, he dropped the fork on a worktable and moved on. The place had more rooms than he could count. There were sitting rooms and proper parlors. Cozette's father's office was bigger than most banks, with closets and doors going off in almost every direction. While they'd looked over the map she'd mentioned her father hadn't smoked in weeks, the area near the desk still smelled of cigars. Michael decided to ask if the bookkeeper smoked. If he did, he couldn't have been away long even though Cozette hadn't seen him.

When Michael finally wandered into the main entry hall, he found Cozette waiting on the third step, her elbows on her knees and her chin in her palms. She still wore her white blouse and riding skirt.

"Am I late?"

"No, you've plenty of time to change for dinner. I laid your clothes out myself."

He frowned. "Why would I change?"

She smiled. "I've wondered that same thing most of my life. All I know is my uncle invited guests again. He's not talking to me directly, but apparently he's not ready to leave and needed a reason to stay. The charade of a wedding dinner with neighbors is as good a reason as any to delay his departure."

"How's your father?"

"The same." She looked up at him, her eyes filled with sadness. "He doesn't squeeze my fingers anymore and he won't open his eyes when I talk to him. I get the feeling he wishes I'd stay away."

Michael took her hand firmly in his grip. He had no idea what to say. The old man was having a hard time dying just as he'd had a hard time living. Cozette had been as starved for love growing up as Michael had been.

He tugged on her hand and pulled her into his arms as she stood. For a moment all he did was hold her against him guessing that the feel of another standing heart to heart was as foreign to her as to him.

She held on tightly for a moment, then smiled her thanks up at him.

"If I dress for dinner," he tried to make light of what had just passed between them, "I'm guessing you will have to also."

She groaned. "Of course, and wear my hair up. After all, I'm not a child any longer. I'm a proper married lady." They moved up the stairs, holding hands.

"I like your hair down." He winked at her. "It brushes your bottom when you walk."

She slapped at his ribs and laughed. "A gentleman never refers to a woman's bottom."

He liked her teasing. This was a side of her he hadn't seen. "I'm sorry, but you know, dear, I'm not a gentleman and I like looking at your bottom as well as your hair." He slowed slightly to take in the view before she pulled him along.

They reached her room, where Moses slept outside her door.

"I slipped past him," she confessed.

"Don't do it again." He hadn't meant his words to roll so hard.

She looked up as if she might argue, then turned and disappeared into her room.

He woke his uncle and told him to go eat chili, that he'd guard his own wife tonight. She didn't like being ordered—he needed to remember that. She expected him to be a gentleman and he wasn't sure how. The one compliment he'd given her apparently wasn't proper. If their marriage lasted beyond dinner tonight, he'd be surprised.

Chapter 6

Cozette jumped at the tap on their connecting door half an hour later.

"Ready?" he said when she shoved the lock free.

She didn't miss his smile, but he looked nervous and somehow that one fact calmed her. With only a slight hesitance, she motioned him into her room.

She couldn't help but stare at him from head to toe. He looked striking in his tailored evening jacket and white shirt hugging his tan throat. "Almost," she whispered. "I can't get the latch of my necklace to hold. Would you do it for me?"

Handing him the jewelry, she turned her back. Her hair was already swept atop her head, so he should have no trouble. Standing very still, she waited.

"Got it," he said.

She felt for the necklace even knowing it wasn't there. "No, you haven't."

He laughed. "No, I meant I figured out how this thing works. Now hold still and I'll rope it around you."

She felt his warm fingers work the lock at the back of her neck. Then his hands drifted down, smoothing the chain along her throat. She didn't move as his long fingers fanned out over her bare shoulders and gently held her still. She could feel his breath against her cheek, but he didn't move.

"Are you finished?" she asked, waiting for him to let go of her shoulders.

"Yes." His voice was oddly low. "I'm just enjoying the view from here. I think I like it better than I do the one of you walking away. You seem very nicely rounded in several places."

She turned preparing to snap at him, but he was even closer than she thought. They were almost touching. The warmth in his eyes shocked her, as did the honesty. He wasn't flattering or playing with her, he was simply telling her how he felt. He had no reason to play games with her. They both knew the bargain between them was already set.

She raised her chin slightly. "It's time to go downstairs."

He took her hand and put it in the bend of his elbow, then led her down the steps to a dozen people waiting to see the newlyweds.

Cozette smiled when she saw them. Most of the women had been friends of her mother's from years ago. She remembered them coming to visit when she was little, but they'd stopped dropping by after her mother died. Uncle Raymond would have to be on his best behavior. Even if he was furious about the marriage, he couldn't afford to let on in front of them or the powerful husbands who stood at their wives' sides.

Michael remained near, smiling but saying little. He asked where each guest's land was and if it bordered San Louise, then talked of the weather, but little else.

Her mother's friends seemed to tolerate Raymond more than like him. By the time dinner was served it was plain they came to see her and the man she'd picked to marry. Judging by their smiles, the neighbors liked her new husband just fine.

The only thing Michael did out of order was pull up her chair beside his when they walked in to dinner. The guests laughed and kidded him about being a new husband. One lady even commented that it was the dearest thing she'd ever seen.

About the time the main course was served the talk turned to books. Cozette tried to shield questions meant for Michael. She wasn't sure he was well read and she didn't want these people to hurt his feelings. But, after a few moments, she realized they were united in their mission to get to know him.

When she glanced at her uncle she knew that somehow he was behind their curiosity. He must have planted a seed that her new husband was not good enough for the princess of San Louise.

Finally, a man on their left asked Michael, point-blank, what he thought of *Moby Dick*.

Michael set down his fork and said simply, "I think it's a wonderful study on social status and it makes you speculate on your own personal beliefs as well as your individual place in the universe." He fought down a smile, probably proud of himself for remembering most of a review he'd read. "I also think, at over eight hundred pages, it's a bit longer than it needed to be."

The room was silent for a moment, and then everyone talked at once. He'd somehow passed the test and been accepted. For the rest of the meal, no one bothered even to look at Uncle Raymond.

"You read," she whispered near Michael's ear when she got a chance.

"Yes, dear." His hand moved over her skirt and brushed her leg. Then, without hesitation, he kissed her lightly.

Cozette blushed and pushed his hand off her skirts. He might read, but as far as his manners, he would barely be considered housebroken. No man, not even a husband, would touch his wife's leg in public. Thank goodness they were at the end of the table, where no one could see.

The table roared with approval over the kiss as she slipped her hand beneath the table and pushed his hand away a second time.

"Do it again! We missed the wedding!" someone yelled. "At least we should be allowed to see a real kiss."

Michael waited until she turned in his direction. This time his hand gripped her leg with determination and she felt the heat of his fingers through the layers of her gown. With his free hand, he lifted her chin and lowered his mouth over hers.

The kiss was sweet, tender, but his hand moved purposefully up her leg with shocking familiarity. After a few moments she pulled away. Anger flashed before she realized they were on the same side. His bold actions made everyone believe they were in love, and her shocked hesitance only led them to believe that the girl was becoming a woman.

Michael smiled down at her as his hand beneath the table moved back to her knee, straightening the silk gown as he went, as though he could somehow erase the feel of his hand.

The crowd clapped and yelled. "Look," someone shouted, "she blushes with just a mere kiss!"

Cozette wanted to jab him hard in the ribs but he was playing the game they'd agreed to play. No one in the room would suspect they'd married for anything but love or maybe passion.

All evening he kept her close. He played with her hand while someone read poetry, and when the evening progressed and the wine flowed, and they no longer became the center of attention, he remained close, always touching her hand or arm, or brushing his leg lightly against hers.

She considered the fact that he might be trying to drive her mad. After all, he'd have everything if she went crazy. Each touch seemed a fraction bolder than the last. She found herself warming to each, waiting for the next.

People grouped together to sing around her mother's

piano. Two old men were sound asleep near the door, their brandy still in their hands. To her surprise, Michael moved even closer to her after her uncle retired.

Cozette felt the length of the day. With no sleep the night before, she couldn't remember when she'd last had any rest. She'd tried for an hour in the afternoon, but there was far too much to do. Now, with the warmth of him beside her, she melted against him, no longer worrying about what was proper.

He seemed to understand, putting his arm around her and pulling her close, then brushing her cheek as he encouraged her to rest her head on his chest.

She didn't protest, surprised at how good it felt to have someone watching over her. The guests fell away, their good-nights little more than buzzing around her. Even the doctor's report that her father was resting comfortably hardly registered.

When they were alone, Michael pulled her onto his lap and cradled her against the soft arm of the settee. "Sleep, my dear. I'm right here to watch over you."

She felt his hands brush along her side and his lips kiss her temple, and then she drifted deep into sleep.

When she awoke, he was carrying her up the stairs. Embarrassed at being carried to bed like a child, she didn't move or open her eyes.

He went to his room and crossed the space between to hers. Without a word, he gently laid her down on the bed. She didn't move as he unlatched her heavy necklace. His fingers drifted down and brushed lightly over the rise of her breast, and then he moved to her feet and removed her shoes. His hand glided up her leg to just above her knee where a strap held her gun in place. He didn't seem surprised by the weapon but simply removed it and pulled her skirt back down.

The thought crossed her mind that if he went any farther

she'd scream, but she knew no one would come to stand between a husband and a wife on their first night together.

His hands slid along her sides from knee to shoulder, and then he tugged the covers to her chin and moved off the bed.

She expected him to cross back into his room, but he didn't. He locked her door, pulled the curtain across the alcove, stoked the fire, and removed his boots and jacket.

Then, very carefully, he lay down atop the covers at her side.

With her eyes closed, she tried to breathe slowly as if asleep as his hand moved across her waist. He stretched, then was still and his breathing calmed.

She risked a glance as she turned to face him.

He was sound asleep.

Chapter 7

When Cozette woke the next morning, Michael was gone but his new boots and coat remained in her room, looking very much like he'd tossed them there before taking his bride to bed.

She stood, removed her wrinkled dress, and hurried into her morning clothes. She wanted to check on her father before the rest of the house came awake.

The doors between her room and Michael's were open. His room was empty and for a moment she thought her part-time husband might be gone. She stared out the window until she spotted him in a corral near the main barn. He was on horseback, circling the corral as if testing one of her father's horses. He wore the tailored trousers and starched shirt she'd left for him along with the leather vest. He looked the part of a rancher.

Two of her three uncles-in-law were hanging on the fence watching Michael. She had no doubt the third little round man was outside her door on guard.

The two on the fence both had on the clothes she'd sent down for them to wear. She'd picked the largest clothes from their stock of work trousers and flannel shirts and asked one of the girls to hem all the pants up at least six inches.

How could Michael be so tall and lean and have three relatives who looked like tree stumps?

As she watched, one of the uncles opened the gate and Michael bolted out across open land at full gallop. He could ride. Not like a gentleman from the East might ride, but like a cowhand used to living in the saddle.

After a few minutes, he turned the horse and raised his hand. Several riders joined him. Within minutes they were galloping at full speed toward the open range. Just before they crossed the ridge, he turned his head toward the house . . . toward her.

Cozette stepped back as if she'd been caught spying. She darted out the bedroom door and headed down the back stairs to the kitchen. The sound of her chubby bodyguard rattled along behind her.

In the kitchen she sat Uncle Moses down at one of the worktables and promised not to try to slip away. "Stay here and have your breakfast. I'm going to check on my father. You can watch the door to his office while you eat."

Moses nodded, liking the idea of being able to stand his guard while sitting at a table eating.

Cozette hurried down the hall wishing she'd checked on her father before she'd gone to bed. She knew there was nothing she could do for him, but still she needed to know when anything changed.

The doctor was sitting beside the bed when she entered the office. A stack of bloody towels nearby was almost as high as the mattress.

The doctor shook his head slowly. "No change and I don't think we could wake him this morning if we tried."

She moved to the other side of the bed and took her father's hand. His fingers were colder than they had been the first day she'd returned home. He no longer opened his eyes, or spoke to anyone. He might not be in pain, but he was less with the living than he'd been yesterday.

"I've made him as comfortable as I can," the doctor whispered. "His heart grows so weak I'm not sure I hear the beat sometimes."

She looked up at the doctor and he added in a voice so low he almost mouthed the words, "I'll be surprised if he's here much longer."

Cozette nodded and took her place beside the bed. A few hours later she was aware of the doctor leaving and of Michael coming in. He walked to her side and kissed her cheek without saying a word. She watched as he moved to the massive desk and began looking over the accounts. His trousers were stained, his shirt was sweaty, and his old boots were dusty. Her husband was looking more and more like the rancher she'd asked him to become.

When the housekeeper brought lunch, he stopped long enough to sit across from Cozette by the window. She ate only a few bites. When she smiled her thank-you to him for not trying to talk to her, he seemed to understand.

As they finished and stood, he pulled her to him for a tight hug, and then she tugged away and went back to her watch. He followed as if she'd need him to hold her chair. When she was seated once more, Michael brushed his hand over one lock of her hair.

"When there is time," he said as he rested his hand gently on her shoulder, "I'd like to talk to you about the books."

She nodded, thinking more about how she liked this man's gentle touch . . . almost comforting, almost loving. "I don't know much. Mr. Fiddler can answer your questions."

"I've asked about him," Michael said as he brushed her shoulder. "No one has seen him in days."

"I'll worry about it later," she said as she stared down at

the man who liked being called Duke but never took to the name Father.

He had never been there for her, or her mother if the stories were true, but she had to sit beside him now in his last hours. Maybe she just wanted to show that she was a better person, or maybe she didn't want even him to be alone. All his life he'd considered his only daughter worthless, yet she was the only one to stand near in his final hours.

She listened to the shallow intake of breath after breath . . . until there was none. The late sun shone golden across the windows as she realized he'd passed.

"Michael," she whispered, knowing that he'd come to her side.

When she felt his arm circle around her, she collapsed into his embrace wanting nothing more than to step away from the world for a moment.

She was barely aware of him taking her upstairs. When he laid her beneath the covers, she curled into a ball and cried softly. For a while she was alone, but then she felt his weight move the bed and he was at her side again. He pulled her into his arms and held her without saying a word. As always, his hands moved over her, only tonight she found comfort in his touch.

The next morning Cozette moved as if in a dream through the funeral of her father and the reading of his will. She ignored the angry looks from her uncle, knowing he wouldn't dare say a word with people filling the house and spilling out onto the yard. To no one's surprise, her father's will was short, leaving everything, not to family or kin, but to his only daughter's husband with the request that he always treat her fairly.

She slipped up the back stairs as Michael saw the lawyer out. Cozette needed a few moments alone. She'd lived in the eye of a tornado for weeks and, finally, the storm was settling.

After refusing to let a single tear fall in front of others, she washed her face in cold water and went to greet those who came to pay their last respects to a hardworking but never-loving man.

She noticed Joseph watching her from his chair near the back stairs as she stepped into the hallway. Reluctantly, he abandoned his breakfast and downed the last of his coffee before following.

From the other direction, Uncle Raymond appeared suddenly in her path and stopped her progress with an iron grip around her arm. He twisted cruelly, slamming her against the wall. "We need to talk." Anger flowed like hot lava around her. "You think you got away with something here, but . . ."

Uncle Joseph bumped into Raymond like a blind bull, knocking her uncle a few feet down the passage and away from her.

"Oh, s-sorry," Joseph said. "I was so busy eating I didn't even notice you blocking the w-way." He smeared sticky fingers covered in warm cinnamon and sugar along Raymond's buckskin vest. "You really should go get you one of those rolls w-while they're hot."

Raymond hissed, "You'll be as sorry as your nephew."

"Oh, I am," Joseph whined. "There w-was still some g-good finger licking on that hand when I touched you. I'll miss those few b-bites."

Raymond swore.

Joseph straightened. "I don't think it's right to talk that w-way in front of Mickey's dear one."

For once Raymond was too upset to form words. He decided to storm off.

Cozette smiled at Uncle Joseph, seeing for the first time how her husband could love such a man.

"Thanks," she said, realizing that Michael might have been right to enlist three bodyguards for her.

"I d-do my best," Joseph said simply. "You're Michael's pretty little bride. I can't let anything happen to you on my w-watch."

He followed her into the huge dining room and stood in the corner looking about as invisible as a two hundred–pound frog, but she didn't care. This morning he was her knight in shining armor.

She greeted her guests, offered them food and coffee. The room was almost full when Michael walked in. He didn't seem to see anyone in the room but her. He walked right up to her, circled her waist, and kissed her forehead with tenderness.

Two wranglers she recognized as having worked for her father for years followed a step behind Michael like war lieutenants storming into battle.

"It will all be over soon," he whispered to her. "Until we have time to talk, these men will be on watch."

She looked into his blue-gray eyes and saw worry. Something had changed, but her father's funeral was no time to talk.

"It'll be all right," he said, brushing his hand over her arm.

She had no idea what he was talking about, but she believed he'd keep her safe. She'd picked an outlaw to trust, and somehow, he'd proved worth the loving.

She remembered the way he'd readied her for bed last night. He'd carried her to her room, tugged off her shoes, and pulled the pins from her hair. He'd even slid his hand beneath her skirts and removed the small Colt strapped to her leg just as he had the night before. Only last night she thought she remembered his fingers lingering longer along the soft flesh above her knee. When he'd unbuttoned a few buttons of her blouse, his knuckles had traveled down the valley between her breasts.

She'd moaned softly meaning to pull away, but his gentle

touch calmed her. The next time his hand moved between her breasts, he'd caught her moan in his kiss.

He'd done everything almost exactly like he'd done the night before, only last night he hadn't slept on top of the covers. They both might have been fully clothed, but they'd slept with their bodies pressed together.

As before, when she'd awoke, he was gone. She'd found him downstairs making all the plans for the funeral.

Now, as people passed by to tell her of their sadness over the death of her father, Michael did exactly what he'd signed on to do. He acted the part of the perfect husband.

He even walked her to her room when all had left. She was surprised he'd ordered tea and sandwiches for her. With one kiss, he ordered her to rest. When he left, she had no doubt one of his uncles was just outside the door.

Chapter 8

As the day passed, Michael checked on his sleeping wife several times before he finally settled in the study to work. A few of the ranch hands he'd become friends with dropped by to offer suggestions on what needed to be done on the ranch. With the Duke's illness and Raymond only doing what had to be done, much had been neglected.

Michael took the men's advice but knew he'd have to check the books himself. No one could find the bookkeeper named Fiddler or remember exactly when he'd left. Michael noticed there were slight changes in the printing of numbers starting about four weeks ago. The handwriting was close, but whoever had started keeping the books had a heavier hand.

The nurse passed in front of the desk at dusk and lit the lamps. Michael barely noticed. What he was discovering in the accounts of the ranch was shocking. For the last six months, since Uncle Raymond had been helping run the place, small amounts of money had gone missing. Sometimes bills were double paid while others went weeks on the books without any payment. Each month the amount disappearing off the books grew.

Then, the last month, the month before Duke Camanez

died, nothing went missing. Apparently, Raymond was so sure he would inherit, he'd stopped stealing.

Michael frowned, wondering if the answer more likely might be that whoever was stealing feared being caught.

"Sir?" the nurse said softly as she lifted her bag.

Michael glanced up unsure whom she was talking to, but she was looking straight at him. "Yes?" he managed.

"If you don't mind I'll leave now. I've packed up all the doctor's things."

"Thank you," Michael said. "Thank you for being so kind."

She hesitated, then added, "If you and the missus need me when the baby births, I'll be happy to come."

"You know about the baby?" He couldn't believe Cozette would tell anyone.

"I've seen the signs, but don't you worry about me saying anything. The first one sometimes comes early. Nobody will count the months. You just send word if you need me."

He managed a nod without raising his head as she closed the door behind her.

He tried to go back to the books, but he couldn't focus. He'd seen the signs too. His bride hadn't been lying when she'd said she might be pregnant. She was pregnant.

Forcing himself to concentrate, he decided to work on one problem at a time, knowing deep down that if she was truly with child, he wouldn't be able to keep his word and leave her.

He wasn't aware of anything but the books for a while, then, out of the corner of his eye, he saw Cozette slipping through the door.

With her puffy eyes and red nose, he had no doubt she had been crying. She smiled as she neared. "Thanks for handling everything today," she said as she moved closer. "I don't know what is the matter with me. I thought to only nap and ended up sleeping the day away."

"You're welcome," he answered, wishing he could read her mind as she walked closer. "There was no need to wake you. You needed the rest."

When her hand brushed over his head, he jerked in surprise. He hadn't expected her to touch him. That hadn't been part of the bargain. A few times she'd taken his hand or put her fingers on his arm, but nothing like this—almost a caress.

"You look like you belong in that chair, Michael. The housekeeper told me you've had the men do more work today than they've done in a month."

He pushed his chair back. "Come closer," he ordered gently, loving the easy way she came to him as if they were lovers.

She slowly moved against his side and he handed her his handkerchief. As she blew her nose, he pulled her onto his lap. As always, she hesitated like she might refuse his closeness, then relaxed against his arm.

"Are you all right?" he asked, playing with a curl of her hair.

"Everyone has been so nice," she said, then laughed that little giggle she had that wasn't really a laugh at all. "Well, everyone except Uncle Raymond, who is, at present, eating his dinner surrounded by your uncles because he keeps trying to get close to me."

Michael brushed his hand over her shoulder and along her arm. The need to touch her grew stronger every hour. He'd learned that once he was close to her, she quickly grew accustomed to his touch and no longer tightened her muscles as if expecting a blow. Either she was learning to trust him, or she saw him as no more than a bothersome gnat to be ignored.

As Cozette talked about the guests and all they'd said, he slowly moved her hair away from her neck and leaned close enough to brush his mouth along her throat.

When she didn't react to his light kisses, he opened his mouth and tasted her skin. He could feel her pulse beneath his lips. Curling his fingers into the collar of her dress, he tugged to reveal more of her neck. The material gave to his demand, showing the rise of her breasts against the black of her dress.

"Are you listening?" she said, tugging away so that she could look him in the eyes.

"Yes, dear," he lied. So she wouldn't consider standing, he circled her waist as he pushed the chair closer to the desk. He wanted her close enough to feel her breathing. "But before you continue I need to show you something I've found." His hand rested just below her breast and he almost forgot what he was saying. She was perfection in his arms.

She leaned over the books unaware that he now cupped the bottom of one breast in his hand.

He pulled her back and whispered against her ear. "I love touching you." His fingers closed gently over her breasts. "Am I hurting you?"

She shook her head. "I think I like the feel of you touching me." She took a breath, letting the front of her dress press lightly against his hand. "It seemed a strange request but I've found it comforting."

He moved his fingers over her, needing to feel all of her. "And pleasurable," he whispered.

She stopped breathing for a moment, then took a deep breath and sat perfectly still while his fingers tightened once more. "And pleasurable," she admitted.

He watched her face for any sign that she wanted him to stop. He saw none.

He kissed her ear. "I love being near you. The best part of the bargain we made was you agreeing to let me hold you."

She giggled. "I had a feeling you'd say that. You're an easy man to get used to." She gently pushed his hand away. "Now, tell me about the books."

He smiled in agreement to her suggestion, knowing he'd

never be able to concentrate if he didn't. As his hand brushed over her one last time, he promised, "Later."

She managed a shy smile. "Later."

They pored over the books for half an hour with her questioning and recalculating every step and him fighting the urge to touch her as he answered her questions.

When she took extra time refiguring what he'd already checked, he didn't mind at all. As she studied the books one last time, he lightly began to brush his fingers over her gown. He'd gone long enough without the feel of her in his hand.

She'd grown used to him and except for now and then absently pushing his hand away she didn't seem to mind his attentions. He kept his touch light, a promise between them.

Finally, when he thought he might go mad, she turned to him and smiled. "You're brilliant. Now I have a reason to demand my uncle leave. It's obvious he's been robbing my father for months."

To his shock, she leaned close and kissed him quickly on the mouth.

When she started to pull away, he whispered against her ear, "Do that again."

And she did. Soft, light kisses that turned to fire as they lengthened. When she'd pull away her eyes were huge with wonder and her mouth pouty. Then, she'd smile and he'd ask for more.

They played the game until the housekeeper tapped on the door to remind them that it was well past dinnertime.

When they sat down to a late meal, neither seemed to want to talk. They both knew the bargain they'd set. As soon as Raymond left, there would be no reason for Michael to stay. Their time together was coming to an end and neither wanted to waste a minute of what they had left.

Finally, when they moved to the parlor with their cobbler,

Cozette smiled. "You played your part of loving husband well. I'm growing very used to your kisses, sir."

"You're an easy woman to kiss, to cherish. That first man you knew, who hurt you and left you, was a fool."

"How do you know he was the first man? Maybe I've had many lovers before."

Michael shook his head. "In the study you were learning to kiss. If you'd had a lover, you would already have known." He winked at her. "By the way, you're learning very well."

She blushed as she winked back. "I think I need a little more practice if you don't mind."

"I don't mind at all. A woman with child should already have learned such things."

He watched her carefully, guessing she was about to lie. "The truth, remember. Always the truth between us."

She looked down at her bowl. "It's worse than you think. He didn't just hurt me and leave me with a child, he was paid to do so. Paid to dishonor me." She gulped down a sob. "And somehow it is all my fault. I should have fought harder or killed him. I should have . . ."

"It's not your fault."

She shook her head. "My father said I have my mother's blood. Several times I heard him tell my uncle that it was just a matter of time before I disgraced the family."

He cupped her face in his hands. "I didn't know your mother, but if you are like her, she must have been a wonder." He moved his thumbs across her cheek. "Tell me about her."

In the shadows of a dying fire she told him all she remembered of a loving mother. When she could think of nothing more, they sat side by side.

Finally, she patted his leg. "Thank you. I needed to remember. No one mourned my father's passing but I remember how it was when she died. I think I cried today because I'm alone, not because I'll miss my father."

"You're welcome." He covered his hand over hers for a moment. "And you are not alone. I'm right here beside you."

Standing, he pulled her gently up and kissed her cheek. "It's time we called it a night. Do you think you can undress yourself tonight? I've work still to do on the books." He didn't add that he wanted to hide the records while Raymond was still in the house. If the books were lost, it would only be his word against Raymond's.

She looked up at him. "Of course. You're right. It is late. Will you be sleeping in my bed?" It was such an innocent question, but there could be only honesty in the answer.

"Do you mind? I enjoy holding you while you sleep. I know you're safe."

"I don't mind," she whispered. "Just don't wake me when you finally come to bed."

He knew they were both adults, but there was something almost childlike in the way they trusted without reason. He wasn't sure what she thought. Maybe she believed nothing would happen. Maybe she was simply living up to the bargain he'd requested.

But there was nothing childlike in the way he felt about her. Each brush of her arm or taste of her lips only left him wanting more. Two days ago he thought he'd be happy just to be able to be near her, but now he wanted more, much more.

In the eyes of God and by law they were man and wife, but in her eyes, he was no more than an outlaw she'd made a bargain with to hold on to her ranch. He had a feeling she would have found another way if he hadn't been near.

If he took advantage of her, he'd never forgive himself, but if he walked away without loving her, he'd regret it until he died.

He walked her to the stairs. After she took the first step she turned and said good night.

He didn't turn her hand loose. "Kiss me good night," he whispered with more need than demand.

Slowly, she leaned forward. "Yes, dear," she answered as she pressed her lips to his.

He closed the distance between them as if he were starving for what she offered.

When she finally ended the kiss, she was breathless.

"That was . . ." She couldn't find the words.

"Perfection," he helped. "Good night, dear. When I come to bed I'll not wake you, but I make no promises not to touch you."

Her eyebrows lifted and she whispered, "Oh."

He smiled. "Would you like another kiss, my wife, or can you wait until I'm beside you?"

"No." She stumbled up the next step. "Though I've no complaints about the one."

He fought the urge to follow her up the steps. "You might think of wearing a gown tonight. I'm sure you're tired of my wrinkling your clothes. I'll kiss you again when I come to bed."

"I'll be asleep," she said, her eyes wide awake.

He grinned. "I won't mind."

She turned before he could say more and disappeared up the stairs.

It took every ounce of his willpower to make himself walk to the office. His time was limited but he wanted to give Cozette something and the proof of her uncle's embezzlement might keep her and her child safe. She might like flirting with him but that didn't mean she wanted to give him half the ranch. He'd learned a long time ago to expect nothing.

Michael worked late into the night, forcing all his energy into his work so he wouldn't think of the woman upstairs waiting for him to share her bed, but not her life.

Finally, when the numbers started to blur on the page, he hid the books beneath the sickbed, blew out the lamp, and climbed the stairs. He walked through his room, removed his shirt and old boots, and tossed them on the floor. A new pair of boots stood at the end of his bed along with a clean set of clothes he knew would fit him perfectly. She might not want him around long, but while he was there she treated him with more kindness than anyone ever had. He would miss the coffee served to him every morning and the cobbler every night.

When he lowered onto her bed, she was asleep, as she'd promised she would be. For a while, he just watched her, wondering what life would be like if she really belonged to him.

His hand moved beneath the covers. Only one layer of soft cotton separated his touch from her body. He moved near her soft breath and touched her lips with his as his hand began to explore.

The feel of her washed away all the exhaustion. He traced the outline of her breasts and slid his hand over her slightly rounded tummy, wishing it were his child growing inside her. When he moved her head onto his shoulder she made a little sound in her sleep, but she came to him willingly.

He began at her ear with his light kisses. When he reached her mouth, slightly open and waiting, he couldn't resist.

He felt her come awake slowly, one sense at a time. She shyly kissed him back. He ran his hands into her loose hair and pulled her head off the pillow as he rolled and brought her on top of him.

In the shadows he watched her look down at him with sleepy eyes. "Kiss me again," he whispered.

She smiled and did as he requested.

Before her lips pulled away, he whispered, "Again."

She giggled and wrapped her arms around his neck.

The kiss exploded with passion. She was fully awake now and wanting his nearness as much as he wanted her.

When they finally had to stop to breathe, he rolled her on her back. "Now again, if you don't mind."

"You don't have to keep asking. I've no plan to stop until you beg me to."

"I'll take that challenge."

This time, as their lips touched, he cupped her breast and brushed his thumb across the peak. She reacted as he hoped she would, by pulling him close.

"I want you so much," he whispered between hurried kisses.

He told himself they were married. He had every right, but he knew he'd make love to her only when she said she wanted him. He knew if he ever took her as his real wife, he'd never leave. Not her, or the ranch, or the child she carried. There were some things a part-time husband could never do as part of a bargain.

He broke the kiss and looked down at her. In the pale light of the fire her lips were swollen, her hair was spilled across the pillows, and her eyes shone bright with unshed tears.

He rolled away, onto his back. Her silence had told him all he needed to know. He might want her, but she didn't want him . . . not in the way he needed her. If she had she would have said something.

Mrs. Peters's words came back to him. *You'll never be loved, but maybe you'll make yourself useful.* That was all he was to her. Useful.

He'd fallen for a woman who didn't or wouldn't love him. He'd fallen into hell.

Chapter 9

Cozette pretended to sleep the rest of the night. Until he'd told her he wanted her she'd thought they were simply playing a game. He was touching her, she was enjoying it. When he'd said he wanted her, she knew he was no longer playing. He hadn't said he loved her or wanted to stay forever. He simply wanted her, and she'd already had one man in her life who'd simply wanted her.

She felt him slip from her bed long before dawn. He hadn't touched her since he'd rolled away from her, so she had no warmth to miss.

Maybe she should have said she wanted him, but she wasn't sure she'd ever want a man in that way again. It hadn't been a pleasant experience. In fact, the mating had hurt when she'd been forced down without warning.

Michael might be gentle and kind, but she wasn't sure the act wouldn't still hurt.

She had loved his kisses, though, and the way his hands touched her as if they were worshipping her. She'd even thought of asking him to touch her again, but she didn't know how. That kind of honesty had never circled so near before.

She slipped from the bed and crossed the bathing room to his bedroom. He'd pulled on clean trousers and was sitting by the open windows tugging on his old boots. The cold air blew her gown as if pushing her back, but she tiptoed toward him.

He didn't look up but she had a feeling he knew she was there.

"Your new boots should fit far better," she said calmly.

When he didn't look up, she took one step more. "Are you mad at me?"

"No," he answered too quickly.

"Good," she played along as she moved closer. "Then, you'd have no objection to a good-morning kiss."

"It's a long time until morning," he mumbled before looking up at her, and a moment later she was running into his arms. He was her only friend. The only one she could trust. She couldn't stand to see hurt in his wonderful blue eyes and know that she'd caused it.

"You promised you'd never be cruel to me," she whispered. "Don't turn away from me now."

He buried his head in her chest and let out a long sigh, then kissed her wildly as if a hunger for her had almost killed him.

She laughed as he stood, holding her in his arms, and walked over to his bed. He tossed her atop the covers and stared down at her for a long moment before joining her. "It's cold in here. You should be under the covers, dear."

As the first light shone through the open windows, he tugged the front of her gown open. "If you just want to be touched and nothing more, then touch you I will."

His fingers shoved the cotton aside a moment before his warm hands covered her breasts. "But I plan to do so all over."

When she gasped, he kissed her deep as his hands made his promise true.

After awhile, he rose his head to look into her eyes. The pain she'd seen was gone, and passion had taken its place. She whispered between gulps for air. "Again, Michael. Touch me again."

He pushed the gown off and lowered his mouth to her peak.

Crying out from the pleasure, she rocked back and forth. He moved back to her mouth, holding her face in his hands as he kissed her.

"Is this what you want, my love?" His words whispered against her mouth.

"Yes," she answered.

Slowly, he gentled as he removed her gown and lightly brushed over her body with his fingertips. When she shivered, he rolled her onto her stomach and stroked her back, dipping lower until his hand covered her bottom.

He didn't say anything as he explored her body with bold strokes that warmed her skin.

Part of her couldn't believe she was letting him. Knowing he wanted her wasn't the same as loving her, but it was close. Reason told her she never wanted another man, but emotions warring in her wouldn't allow her to stop him. Just seeing the pleasure in his face made her happy. He was a good man who'd had very little pleasure in his life, and it pleased her greatly to know that she could offer him something in return for all he'd given her.

She finally curled next to him and he pulled a blanket over them both. They fell asleep with her head on his shoulder and his hand spread across her stomach.

When the household began to wake, Cozette stirred, loving the warmth of him near.

He opened one eye and looked at her.

"Can I have my good-morning kiss, please?" she pouted.

"Of course," he said, "but only one."

He kissed her soundly and pulled away. "Tonight I think

maybe you should forget the gown. It will only get ripped. I plan to repeat our early morning activity."

"I'll keep that in mind," she smiled.

"Don't worry. If you forget, we might have to do it twice."

She blushed. "Oh, I see. I should probably warn you my memory's never been good."

"Don't worry. I'm here to help."

They both laughed, but she didn't miss the warm fire in his stormy blue-gray eyes.

She tugged the covers around her as she watched him dress. She wanted to ask him if he'd be happy just touching her and nothing more, but she wasn't sure she wanted to hear the answer. When he left she'd keep the memories of their nights together close to her heart. She might not have a real husband, but she'd know that once, for a few short nights, she'd been touched completely and lovingly.

After he strapped on his gun belt and lifted his hat, he crossed to the bed and kissed her on the head. "All day, I'll think of you here like this and long for the night."

He was gone before she could answer. Without giving any thought of what was proper, she curled back under the covers and went to sleep in his bed.

Her day could wait a little longer to begin.

Chapter 10

By the time Michael reached the barn, he'd calmed some. Another night of touching his wife without making love to her would surely kill him, but he'd gladly die. He'd known she wasn't sleeping after he'd pulled away in the night. He'd lain awake angry at how she'd reacted when he'd told her he wanted her. Surely she wasn't so young to believe that all they were playing was a game.

When he'd left her bed and gone back into his room, he'd still been angry and hurt. She was spoiled and he appeared to be no more than a puppet husband. She'd hardly noticed how he'd been organizing the ranch and getting it running back on track.

Then, she'd come to his room, tiptoeing like a child and looking every ounce a woman in her thin gown that hid little from view. For a moment he'd thought of telling her how impossible her request was. To touch her and not love her was ridiculous. But then, she'd ran to his arms and he'd known he'd have to try.

He knew he hadn't been as gentle as he should have been when he'd tossed her onto his bed, but she hadn't complained, hadn't protested or pulled away. And, once he'd gentled his touch, she'd let him handle her body, exploring, caressing, tasting wherever he liked. She'd given herself to him in every way but one. The one way only a woman can give herself completely.

He knew without thought that no other woman would ever satisfy him. If he didn't have her, he'd be unfulfilled for the rest of his life.

He walked to the corral, tossed a lead rope around his horse, and entered through the back of the barn, his mind still filled with thoughts of Cozette.

Two hands were at the front of the barn looking out toward the house as he neared. Neither noticed him.

The tallest one complained, "Raymond promised us all a bonus after he got rid of the brat of a girl. But she married, so who knows how long a bonus will be coming, if ever."

The other added, "We won't have to wait more than a few days, I'm guessing. I heard one of the men say Raymond plans to get rid of them both."

"Run them off or kill them?" the tall man questioned.

"Probably make it look like an accident, or better yet make it look like those three bumbling uncles of his killed them. The sheriff will take one look at those three and start looping a rope."

"Well, I'm not waiting around to be thought of as part of a killing. I hear there's work up north. I think I'll head out before something happens."

"You'd better stop complaining or the same thing will happen to you that happened to Fiddler."

Michael released the strap on his Colt and moved forward. "What happened to Fiddler?" he asked slowly.

Both men jumped and reached for their guns, but Michael cleared leather first.

"We don't know, boss," the tall one said as he lifted his hands. "We was just talking."

"There will be no bonus from Raymond. He got his inheritance forty years ago and squandered it if rumors are true. His brother built this ranch without any help."

Michael lowered his gun as he continued, "Raymond has no right to the ranch, gentlemen. My wife is not leaving and there will be no accident."

He thought of firing them but reconsidered. He couldn't afford to make enemies too quickly. "I'd like you men to decide if you want to work for me for a fair wage or pack your gear. But, understand, if you stay, you stand with me, not Raymond Camanez."

The two men glared at each other. They were hard men, but not fools. Jobs with good wages and regular food were hard to come by. "We stay," one said and the other nodded agreement. "None of us believed Raymond anyway when he talked of bonuses when he took over. He's all talk."

Michael holstered his Colt. "All right. I've an assignment for you both. See if you can find out what happened to Fiddler and do it without Raymond, or anyone you think might be with him, aware that you're looking. We need to find the bookkeeper if he's still alive."

Both men nodded.

Michael eyed the shorter of the two. "Smith, right?"

"Yes, sir. Ace Smith." The man seemed surprised Michael remembered his name.

"I'll expect that report tonight. I'll meet you in the chapel after supper."

Both men tipped their hats. "We'll do our best," Smith said.

Michael moved away to saddle his horse. It crossed his mind that he could have passed the job along to someone else, but he believed a man should always take care of his own mount. Besides, if accidents were predicted, he wanted to make sure no one got close.

He saw Smith and his friend saddling up. The tall man walked over to Michael while his friend waited in the morning sun. After a few moments of just standing, the man said, "Mind my asking why you didn't fire us on the spot, Mr. Hughes?"

"No, I don't mind." Michael climbed on his horse. "I knew a lot of men once who no one gave a second chance to. Some were worthless, but others might have made better men if anyone had let them try."

"Fair enough. We want you to know, we don't hold nothing against your little wife. Thanks for giving us a shot." The man turned to move away.

"You're welcome, Phil." Michael finally thought of the second man's name.

He rode out knowing Cozette would be safe with his uncles watching over her. He needed to make sure the ranch hands were with him and the only way was to spend the day in the saddle. When he reached the cattle he was glad to see two dozen hands already hard at work.

Michael took the time to talk to each man. He mostly asked questions, unafraid to let them see how little he knew. By the end of the day he knew every man and that they were his men.

When he rode home he was tired but satisfied. Part of him couldn't believe that Cozette's uncle would think of killing her, but he might not feel the same about Michael.

He wanted time to look over the accounts one last time. They'd agreed they'd confront Raymond tomorrow. It seemed cruel to kick him off the land the day after they buried his brother.

Michael had told his uncles to guard his wife and that at least one of them should always keep Raymond in sight. He smiled as he walked into the office guessing that Cozette's uncle probably had had a horrible day with one of them tailing him.

An hour later, he looked up from the books to find rain splattering softly against the huge windows of what he thought of as his study.

"My study?" Michael whispered, knowing that this wasn't and would never be his study, or his ranch. He'd been playing a game of make-believe.

The woman upstairs would never be his wife. It was all pretend. Somehow he'd gotten caught up in her fantasies. The pretty little liar had taken down the outlaw without one shot. When he left this place he knew his heart would be staying behind.

Thunder rattled the night and lightning flashed. Michael closed the books, no longer able to stay away from Cozette.

He was at a run when he reached the stairs and almost collided with the housekeeper.

"Sorry," he managed, trying to look respectable and not like the wild kid he was.

She smiled. "The missus said you'd be home late. She asked that I bring supper up to her room tonight."

He nodded as if he wasn't surprised. "What about her uncle?" Michael didn't want to sleep without knowing where Raymond was.

"He left a few hours ago."

"For good?" Michael hoped.

"No." The housekeeper frowned. "For a ride, I think. He said he wouldn't be back for dinner this evening and I heard him say he'd shoot anyone who tried to follow him."

"My uncles?" Michael asked, worried that one of them might have tried.

"They're all three in the hallway. Said they wouldn't leave your dear one until you got home." The housekeeper smiled.

"I had a meal sent up to them and the cook is baking cookies for them now. Dear little men, all three."

Michael wasn't sure she didn't have them mixed up with some other three short fat men. He'd never heard anyone pay them a compliment.

When he reached the top of the stairs, there they were, all on guard. "You watch over my wife today?" he said sharply bringing them all to attention, or as much to attention as they could get.

"We did," Abe said. "Had to quit watching Raymond, though. None of us can ride well enough to trail him, so we decided to all guard her."

"Plus, here w-we don't miss meals. That's something to c-consider." Joseph pulled two forks from his pocket and placed them on the hallway table. "I w-wasn't going to take them, Mickey, I w-was just keeping them in case more food w-wandered by. Food comes along here as regular as a train. I ain't never s-seen the like of it."

Michael said good night to them and reminded them that hot cookies were waiting. He realized that for the first time in his life he was proud of them and, more important, they were proud of themselves.

He opened the door to his room and walked across to the bathing room separating him from Cozette.

The door was closed, but not locked. When he pushed it slowly open, he swore his heart stopped. She must have just stepped from the tub, her body still dripping as she reached for the towel.

He saw her completely. Her beautiful face, her long damp hair, her rounded breasts and pleasing bottom. She took his breath away along with the power to speak or think.

When she turned and smiled at him, he couldn't move.

"Good evening, Michael," she said shyly. She lifted the

towel and put it around her back, leaving her front still open to his view. "I thought we'd have a quiet dinner and talk."

She began to wrap the towel around her, but his hand shot out to stop her. "Later," he said, staring into her eyes. "First, I have to hold you."

She tugged away from him and crossed the towel over her. "No, first you have to take a bath. Like all ranchers, you smell like a horse."

He would have argued, but she began unbuttoning his shirt. He just stood as if stone while she removed his shirt and gun belt. When she began unbuttoning his trousers, he stopped her. "I'll bathe," he said. "Alone."

The pouty lip he'd spent hours thinking about came out, but she turned and headed to the door.

He had stripped and slid into the tub and was already thinking of what he wanted to do with her when the door to her room opened. She was still wrapped in her towel, but she was dragging a stool behind her.

"What do you think you are doing?" he asked with a smile.

"Watching," she answered.

"I should have locked the door." He blew out all but one of the candles beside the bath.

"There's no lock on your side, only on mine." She sat down as if waiting for the play to start.

He gave up. He scrubbed off a layer of dirt as fast as he could and then asked for a towel.

She pointed to one three feet away and didn't make a sound when he stood and grabbed it. Looking at her was one thing, but having her stare at him was quite another. He planned to tell her so over breakfast.

"What's all this about?" he asked as he dried.

"I've decided to change the rules a little. You seem to be having so much fun touching me, I thought I'd touch you tonight, if you don't mind."

He studied her trying to figure out what she was up to. They both knew that tonight might be their last night together. Tomorrow they'd confront Raymond and run him off the ranch. Michael knew several men working for her who would be great bodyguards just in case Raymond decided to come back.

When he left her, he'd leave her well protected.

It occurred to him that she must want tonight to be a memory they'd both take with them.

He crossed the room and stood above her, his towel now draped low around his hips.

She looked up at him without fear. She might never learn to love him, but she'd learned to trust him.

His fingers slid along her slender throat as they had when they'd first met. For a moment, he tightened his grip as he had in the chapel, holding her firmly, but not hurting her. Then he lowered his mouth and kissed her.

It wasn't a hungry kiss, but a slow, loving kiss that warmed them both. His fingers moved down her throat and over her shoulders, then shoved her towel away. "I love the way your skin feels," he whispered into her mouth as he pulled her up and kissed her again. "I don't think I could ever get enough of you."

Every moment, every move, he expected her to tell him to stop, but she didn't and he couldn't shake the feeling that tonight he was a part of her fantasy.

She didn't say a word. She opened her mouth, welcoming him as his hands branded across her body. Timidly she brushed her finger over his chest and along his arms. Her touch was so tender it was almost painful. He knew he was lean with a few too many scars across his body, but she didn't seem to notice as she touched him.

He turned her toward a long mirror, pressing his body

against hers as he watched his hands move over her. She leaned her head back and kissed his throat as her hair tickled across his chest.

He had to try one more time. "Love me, tonight," he whispered in her hair. "Be mine for one night."

She turned in his arms and kissed him as she pressed against him silently, giving him the answer he'd waited for.

When he rubbed his chin against her cheek, he felt her tears and pulled away enough to meet her gaze. "What's wrong?"

"Nothing. I just didn't think it could be like this. I didn't expect it . . ."

He understood and pulled her close. Both their towels were forgotten as they moved to her bed and he pulled the covers back. She lay down and waited, looking unsure.

"I promise I won't hurt you, but if you'll let me, I want to make love to you."

She didn't answer. This time he didn't pull away. He saw all he needed to see in her warm eyes as her soft hands trailed along his body and she tugged him closer.

He kissed his way down her until he came to the slight rise at her middle. "I love you," he whispered, "and I'd love this baby growing inside you if you'd let me. I want it to be my baby. After tonight. After we've made love. There will be no other past but me and tonight."

He hadn't planned the words. He wasn't sure if he'd said them aloud or not, but when he kissed her where the baby grew, her hands moved into his hair and held him to her.

The storm rattled outside as they made love slow and easy. She was shy and he was uncertain, but passion washed over them smoothing everything into mindless perfection. They floated in the warmth of each other unaware that time existed. For two young lovers there was no past or future, only this moment.

When he held her to him afterward, he kissed away her tears. She hadn't said a word and he wasn't experienced enough with women to know whether her tears were tears of joy.

He just held her close and whispered his love for her, wondering if there was any chance she'd believe him . . . wishing he had a lifetime ahead to tell her how he felt. But tonight, this time, this place, would have to be his lifetime. All before, all after, didn't matter.

When Cozette was sound asleep, Michael slipped from her bed and dressed, already missing her before he left her room. He had a meeting in the chapel tonight, and then he'd be back to wake her.

Tonight, he'd know the truth about Raymond. He'd know how to keep her safe.

He walked from her room and put his boots on in the hallway. They were a perfect fit. Within a few minutes he let himself into the chapel.

Smith and the tall man named Phil were waiting for him. They both looked tired and wore dusters soaked in rain.

"What news do you have?" he asked, in a hurry to be done with the meeting and get back to Cozette.

"A farmer north of here found Fiddler's body two days ago. The farmer didn't recognize him, being most of his face was shot off, so he took the body into town."

Phil stopped talking and his partner continued, "Sheriff said he knew at once who it was. Said he'd noticed the ink stains on Fiddler's hands once. The sheriff also noticed once that the bookkeeper had the longest fingers—piano hands he called them—with ink spotting heavy across his knuckles."

"Any idea who killed him?" Michael asked.

"No. He'd been dead for a while. Folks claimed they could smell him an acre away. Sheriff had him buried."

Michael thanked the men. They talked as they walked back

to the house. Both were convinced Raymond had something to do with the killing, but with a body already in the ground and any clues washed away by the rain, they weren't likely to prove it.

Michael noticed the study's lamps were lit, burning low, when he walked into the house. He remembered blowing them both out just before he hid the ranch records under the bed. Caution set his nerves on edge as he walked into the study.

Cozette sat very still in the chair behind the desk. Her hair was down and wild around the heavy robe she wore. When she looked up at him, he saw terror in her eyes.

He took two steps toward her before he realized someone was standing behind the door waiting. He'd stepped into a trap.

"Come on in," Raymond said from behind him. "Your bride and I have been waiting for you to come back."

Michael faced the gun as he backed toward the windows and away from his wife.

"I know you two thought you could get away with this trick you played on my brother, but I've finally decided to put a stop to it." He moved to the center of the room so he could keep an eye on both of them. "So, the only question is, which one should I kill first? With this storm no one will even notice the shots."

"Kill me!" Michael shouted with enough anger to rattle the windows. "Because if you don't, I swear I'll kill you if you harm her."

Raymond must have found his power over them amusing. "Oh, so you've fallen in love with the family tramp. Did she tell you she's already been with a man and she's barely out of school?"

Cozette let out a yelp and Raymond turned his gun on her.

He smiled. "I've even heard the house rumor that you're

with child. What would your father say? He'd shoot you himself rather than let you disgrace this family."

"It's my child!" Michael shouted. "And she's my wife. She's had no other lover but me."

Raymond pointed the gun at him. "Then you are a bigger fool than I, for she's tricked you. I've had enough of you both. It's time to—"

Something short and round barreled into Raymond like a freight train, knocking him off his feet.

The gun fired, clipping Michael in the shoulder as three men jumped on Raymond like hungry dogs on a fat rabbit.

Pain shot through Michael's body as he watched his wife scream and rush toward him. He could hear his uncles pounding away on Raymond but nothing seemed real. All seemed part of a dream, even Cozette.

Then, all went quiet in his world. All went black and he circled in midnight water until he could see or hear nothing, not even his own heartbeat.

When he awoke, he was spread out on one of the couches along the wall and the doctor was smiling down at him.

"'Bout time you decided to wake up and join us. You're a lucky man, son. The bullet hit only muscle and I dug it out without much trouble."

Michael sat up slowly and looked around. "Where's my wife?"

"She'll be back in a minute. I made her go get dressed if she was going to insist on sitting with you. She told me she was in a family way and planned to stay close to you."

"Raymond?" Michael asked.

"He's on his way to town. Sheriff said he'll have charges filed in the morning for attempted murder of you and the murder of a man named Fiddler. Seems Fiddler told my nurse one afternoon while she was with the old man and Fiddler was doing the records that if he ever showed up dead they should look in the books for the murderer. Your wife showed us where her uncle had been stealing for months. We may never know if Fiddler was part of the theft and just got scared or if he found out the truth and confronted Raymond. Don't guess it matters much, he's dead either way."

Michael's head pounded. It was over. Cozette was safe. She'd never be bothered again. He leaned back and rested until he heard her come in with his three uncles right behind her.

"How is he?" she asked the doctor as if Michael weren't staring right at her.

"He's fine. A good night's rest and he can be back in the saddle tomorrow." The doctor began packing up his bag.

"I'll be heading out tomorrow," Michael said. He'd keep his promise to her.

To his surprise anger flashed in her eyes and she stood. "You're not walking out on me and the baby."

All three uncles said, "*Baby?*" at the same time.

She nodded toward them. "That's right. The doctor just confirmed I'm pregnant. Right?"

"Right," the doctor mumbled, obviously trying to stay out of the argument.

Cozette stared down at Michael. "Am I or am I not your wife?"

"I'm not deaf, dear. Of course you're my wife."

"And is this your baby growing inside me?"

He stared at her remembering his wish. Remembering how he told her there was no time, no one before him. "It's my baby."

"Then, Michael, you are not going anywhere." She whirled to the doctor. "You might not want to leave yet. I may have to shoot him in the leg to convince him to stay."

To his surprise the uncles looked like they were on her side. They all stood behind her, their knuckles white and ready to beat him to a pulp.

"It ain't right," Uncle Moses said. "Getting her pregnant and talking of leaving. It ain't right, Mickey."

Cozette pulled a pistol from behind one of the pillows. "I may be a widow, but I don't plan on being left."

She pointed the gun at him and all three uncles folded their arms and waited.

"Don't shoot." He smiled. "I'll stay, dear."

"How long?" she asked without lowering the gun.

"Forever if you'll say you love me."

She grinned. "Then I won't shoot you, because I do love you."

All three uncles nodded as if they understood what was going on. The doctor shook his head, totally lost.

Michael raised an eyebrow, wondering if he'd ever be able to tell if she was telling the truth. He guessed he'd just have to stay about forty or fifty years and find out.

He might not be much of an outlaw but somehow he'd managed to steal the lady's love.

Holding his side, he stood. "I think it's time we said good night, dear."

She smiled and moved beneath his arm as if they were now an old, settled married couple.

He pulled her close, knowing that in the future he'd be whatever she wanted him to be, but he'd be beside her.

Once the couple was halfway up the stairs, Uncle Abe shouted, "Mickey! How long you figure we're staying?"

He glanced down at the three men who'd done their best to raise him.

"Forever," he said.

"Forever," she whispered beside him.

THE RANGER'S ANGEL

Chapter 1

Texas
April 1870

Annalane Barkley pulled her knees to her chin and lowered her head. Her ruined navy blue hat flopped forward like a gaudy curtain hiding her from the world.

She would give anything if she could go backward in time three weeks to the moment she decided to make the trip to Texas. She should have ripped her brother's letter into tiny pieces and stomped on it. Since the day Devin realized he'd never be as tall as his sister, he'd hated her. Why had Annalane thought two years apart would have changed anything? If he wanted her with him at Camp Supply it was for his benefit, not hers.

She vowed that if she lived through tonight, she'd demand he send her back to Washington, D.C. If she had to, she'd live with their great aunt Fretta, who dripped snuff from the left side of her mouth and had eleven cats, but she'd never come west again.

However, from the looks of things her brother, Devin, wouldn't have to pay for the ticket back. Her chances of surviving the night were growing slimmer by the hour.

Rain pounded on the roof of the one-room hut these Texans called a stagecoach station. Normally she loved the rain, but not this hard, fast downpour that thundered in rage. It shook the dust from the rafters, causing tiny bits of dirt to filter down through the damp air and turn into almost invisible mud balls on her skin.

Annalane raised her head enough to watch the four men trapped inside like her.

The driver of the coach was a little old man with nervous movements and a half-empty bottle sitting next to him for comfort. His bloodshot gaze darted around now and then like a rat waiting for a secret tunnel of escape to open up.

The station manager moved around in the corner that served as a kitchen. He was a beefy German who appeared to be multilingual only when he swore, which had been a constant rumble since their stage pulled in at full speed with outlaws in close pursuit. He'd had a meal of mud-colored stew waiting for them, but no one had ordered food.

The third man—a gambler she guessed—had a dull kind of politeness that was born more of habit than purpose. His dreary brown eyes reflected the look of a man who didn't much care if he lived or died. His collar and cuffs were stained with sweat and dirt, but a polished gold watch chain hung from his vest. She'd never seen him check his watch, not once since he'd joined the stage at dawn.

What kind of man wears a watch and never looks at it? She smiled to herself, figuring out the riddle. The kind of man who owns only the chain.

Annalane moved slightly so she could study the fourth guest, a Texas Ranger, who'd got them to this shelter alive when the shooting started. He was long and lean, with a thin scar along his left cheek that had ended what once must have been a handsome face. His clothes were worn but well made, and his boots, though mud-covered, looked hand-tooled. He had twin Colts strapped to powerful legs. The sun had baked his face until she couldn't tell if he was in his twenties or forties. Not that it mattered; she'd seen more talkative hitching posts.

Annalane sensed things in the way men moved that most people didn't notice. All those in the room knew of hard times, but this one, this Ranger, was battle-worn. From the way he folded his muddy gloves into his belt, to the way he watched the window for trouble, hinted to her about his past. He'd fought, and killed, and survived many times.

Now, the Ranger was on guard. The others, including her, were just observers, or maybe future victims. The driver's hands weren't steady enough to fire a weapon. The station manager's apron was still wrapped around his waist, proving he wanted no part of any fight. Neither man could move fast enough to be of any help if trouble barreled through the door. The gambler didn't look like he cared enough even to defend his own life. Only the Ranger seemed ready.

Annalane cut her eyes back to the gambler. A coward, she thought, as she watched him flip cards onto the table. He'd run, or bargain his way through life, but never fight.

She looked back at the Ranger, who'd introduced himself as Wynn McCord when he'd climbed into the coach in Dodge. Like her, he carried a paper allowing him into the Indian Territory. Her letter said "visiting relative at Camp Supply." She had no idea what his said, but she guessed he hadn't come for a visit.

To her surprise, he glanced up and stared at her from across the room, with stormy blue eyes so piercing she had the feeling she'd been touched. His unnerving stare seemed to tell him all he needed to know in seconds. He shifted his attention back to the night beyond the window.

She stood, straightened the pleats of her traveling dress, and walked toward the Ranger.

As she stepped into the square of watery moonlight glowing on the dirt floor, the Ranger's arm shot out toward her. His fingers dug into her waist. He tugged her almost violently toward him and away from the light.

Before she could make a sound, her back hit the solid wall that framed the left side of the window and the Ranger's body held her in place.

"Thinking about suicide, lady?"

Annalane fought for breath.

"You stand in the light for long, a bullet's bound to find you." His voice was so low she doubted the others heard him.

Annalane pushed at his chest. She wasn't used to anyone being so close to her and this man towered over her as few could.

He moved back an inch. She could still feel the heat of his body and the dusty smell of leather and gunpowder that seemed to linger around him.

She straightened, deciding not to yell at him. She needed this Ranger if she planned to stay alive long enough to reach her brother at Camp Supply.

"I'd like to ask you a few questions." There was no need to do more than whisper. The man still stood so close she wouldn't have been surprised if he could read her thoughts.

As if she weren't there, he went back on watch. "I'm all out of answers. Ask someone else."

"I'm asking you." She knew she didn't have to voice the questions. He knew what she wanted to know. "And I want the truth," she added in her head-nurse tone, just to let him know he wasn't dealing with a frightened girl.

He looked at her then and smiled. "All right. The truth. Proper ladies like yourself should stay back East, where it's safe and your husband can take care of you just by locking the door at night."

He glanced at the broken parasol by the door, which she'd

thought would protect her from the rain, then at her very proper shoes now muddy and ruined.

She jerked off her worthless hat before he had time to glare at it and thought of telling him that she'd used most of her savings to buy this outfit. She wanted to make a good impression when she arrived at the camp that would soon become a fort.

When she'd dressed this morning she'd thought she would be meeting her brother by nightfall. He'd written that they would have dinner with the fort's officers. She had hoped to look more than just presentable. She wanted to look, if not pretty, at least able to fit the definition of "a fine woman." But obviously, even in this Ranger's eyes, she hadn't measured up.

This morning she'd thought she was still in a civilized world. Tonight she knew different. If anyone in this territory had an ounce of brains, they'd give the horrible place to the Indians and leave. If they did need a camp to keep some kind of order, they should have crossed the Red River and set it up in Texas.

She told herself she didn't care what Ranger Wynn McCord thought of her or her clothes; he'd been nothing but rude to her all day. When the firing started he'd shoved her to the muddy floor of the coach and demanded she stay there. When they'd pulled up at the station, he'd almost ripped her arm off, jerking her from the stage and telling her to run. When she'd turned to grab her small carpetbag, she swore she had heard him growl at her.

As Annalane opened her mouth to finally point out a few of his faults, she froze, seeing only cold steel across the depth of his winter blue eyes, and she knew he wouldn't care. For one second, she wished he'd let down his guard and she could see what was inside this hard shell of a man. Surely something lay beneath.

Had he ever wanted to belong somewhere, just for one

moment in time? Wanted it so badly he would believe a lie to think he was needed? Wanted it so desperately that he tried to mold himself into something he wasn't?

For one blink, she thought she recognized a loneliness that matched her own, but she doubted he had the hunger to belong somewhere as she'd had for ten years. The need to belong to someone ached in her sometimes like an open wound, but need and dreams had no place in her life.

She'd held to a dream once, then it had been shattered by one bullet. Annalane guessed this Ranger had never known love, not even for one minute. McCord had probably been born to this land and hard times. She'd not reach him with sentiment and crying.

Honesty was her only weapon and she prayed it would work.

"I have no husband to lock the door at night. I was married once for an hour before he left for the war. When he returned, his body was nailed into a box. I joined the army of nurses needed, and for four years moved between hospitals and battlegrounds." She knew she was rattling on, but she had to reach McCord. "I was baptized into battle medicine at First Bull Run, Virginia, in '61 and was there at the last in Bentonville, North Carolina, in '65. There were dozens of other places where blood soaked the earth. Until last month, I worked at the Armory Square Hospital."

Something changed in the Ranger. He shifted. "I was at First Bull Run with Terry's Rangers. Hell of a battle."

She almost commented that a few of the bullets she dug out of Northern soldiers were probably his, but she remained silent. The war was over, had been for five years, even if the nightmares still remained.

"What do you want to know?" His voice was as low as the rumble of thunder outside.

"What are our chances? What options?"

The corner of his mouth lifted slightly and she had the feeling he hadn't smiled in a long time. "Spoken like a soldier."

She accepted the compliment. "One thing, remember." She held his stare. "The truth."

"I'm not in the habit of lying, Mrs. Barkley."

"No sugarcoating. Nothing left out." She'd been lied to enough to last two lifetimes. Even as she'd packed, she'd known her brother wanted her help for something other than to set up his medical practice. The silver lining in her predicament was that she'd spoiled whatever plan he had for her tonight by being late.

"Fair enough." She felt the Ranger's words against her cheek more than heard them. "I guess for what you did during the war and afterward, you deserve my respect. I saw nurses handling chaos that would bring most men to their knees. One angel in blue stopped by me in the shadows of a battle once. She wrapped my leg tight and whispered for me to hold on." The side of his mouth twitched in almost a smile. "I'm not sure I would have made it if that woman hadn't been so determined I would."

He looked at her and raised one eyebrow, as if wondering if she could have been that angel.

Annalane didn't answer. She'd done such a thing many times, as had all the other nurses. When they moved among the blood of battle they didn't think of sides, only of helping.

McCord shrugged. "I don't guess it matters now. You wore blue and I wore gray, but I figure we were in the same hell. You'll have your whole truth and my help if you want it."

She nodded, accepting his offer.

The German station manager passed around cups and offered coffee. The stage driver doctored his with whiskey. The gambler stared into the empty cup as if inspecting it for bugs before he allowed the station manager to pour coffee.

"Our chances?" Annalane whispered.

"The men waiting out there for this rain to let up before they attack are a mixture of the worst men in Texas, led by a devil who calls himself Randolph Thorn. I've been chasing them for four months. I got a tip that they planned to rob the stage for the mailbag. They think there's something in it worth crossing into Indian Territory and risking their lives for."

"Is there?"

He hesitated, then, as if remembering his promise, answered, "Yes, but I wouldn't be worried about that if I were you. The problem you face is that Thorn and his men tend not to leave witnesses."

She saw his jaw tighten, but he forced out the truth. "If you got a gun with you and they get past me, you might want to use it. I've seen the way this gang treats women. If they find you here, you'll be wishing you were dead long before they kill you. Someone told me once that he heard Thorn brag that he kept a woman alive for four days just to hear her scream. When she was finally too weak to react no matter what he did, he left her bleeding and helpless for the coyotes."

She swayed.

The Ranger's hand brushed her waist to steady her.

"Options?" she whispered, forcing her back to stiffen.

"If we could put a gunman at each window, the firing would keep them away, maybe even kill enough that they'd leave."

She looked across the room. Not one of the others looked like he could protect himself, much less her.

He read her mind. "Can you handle a gun?"

"A rifle fairly well, but I've dedicated my life to saving others, not killing them."

He set his cup down and gripped her shoulder hard. "I need to know, Mrs. Barkley. Can you handle a rifle and fire to kill if you have to? Not to protect some mailbag, but to protect yourself."

All the hundreds of men she'd bandaged and held while they cried for their mothers or wives before they died filled her mind. All the men left broken and amputated who'd stared at her with hollow eyes, as if wishing she'd left them to die in battle.

She wasn't a coward. She faced the Ranger directly when she whispered, "I'm not sure."

She'd expected to see disappointment in his eyes, but instead she saw understanding.

As Annalane had all her life, she made up her mind and acted. "Whatever you plan, I'm going with you."

"It won't be safe. I could travel faster alone, maybe bring back help."

"It isn't safe here." She glanced at the other men. None of the three looked like they would hesitate to use her as a shield. "I won't slow you down. I promise."

The Ranger nodded once. "One condition. You follow orders."

"Agreed." She saw something in his gaze. "What else? What have you not told me?"

He bit the corner of his mouth, hesitating, then leaned so close his chin brushed her hair. With his breath against her ear, he whispered, "I think one of the men in this room usually rides with the outlaws. Problem is, I don't know which one."

Annalane would have fallen if his lean body hadn't shifted slightly to hold her up.

Chapter 2

Ranger Wynn McCord tried to tell himself he was just helping the lady out—being polite, that was all—but he knew the truth. From the moment he'd seen her in the coach, all prim and proper, he'd thought about what she'd feel like to touch. He didn't want to just help her; he wanted to hold her close. It had been a long time since he'd felt that way about any woman. He'd probably lost the ability to even talk to a woman like this one, but that didn't stop him from thinking about what they might do besides talk.

Now she was pressed against him from knee to chin and he didn't want to step back. She had that never-been-touched look about her and he wondered if, beneath all those pleats and buttons, a man had ever thrown a rope around her. She said she'd been married for an hour before her husband left. It would take a great deal longer than that to convince her she was desired.

He'd watched her all day while the others thought he slept. There was a grace about her that fascinated him. She'd talked to the gambler a few times after Frank Sanders told her he'd lived in Washington, D.C., but mostly she read from a little book she kept in her purse. Since she was careful not to turn it where anyone could see the cover, McCord guessed it was one of those adventure/romance dime novels he'd seen around, written for people who wanted to experience the Wild West secondhand.

"Mr. McCord." Annalane Barkley's hand pushed against his chest, making him very much aware of just how close they were. "I'll have to ask you to . . ."

"If you're going with me, we need a reason to step outside, Mrs. Barkley. Time's running out," he whispered without giving an inch. "So, shall we give them that reason, that we might need a little privacy?"

He moved his hand against the back of her head and pulled her to him. "Make it look like you can't keep your hands off me." Grinning, he had no doubt the proper Mrs. Barkley wouldn't have a clue about what to do. "We need to make it to the barn before the moon's free of clouds again."

She let out a tiny cry of surprise as his mouth lowered to hers. A moment later, her hand stopped trying to shove him away. She was frozen stiff in his arms, but she didn't break the kiss.

McCord had meant only to brush her lips. They were in far too much danger to take time for a real kiss, but he couldn't pull away. Her bottom lip quivered slightly as he parted her lips and deepened the kiss. She tasted far better than he'd let himself imagine in the hours he'd spent daydreaming about her.

"Hey!" the drunk driver yelled. "What's going on?"

McCord broke the kiss with an oath, but his hand still held her head in place. "Shut up, old man. Nothing that's any business of yours is happening. The lady and I have just found a way to pass the time."

He slowly turned toward the three men, staring at each one in turn. Daring them to say more.

When they were silent, he added, "Come on, Anna, let's find someplace without an audience."

"And where would that be?" The gambler shrugged, seeming to be enjoying the show they'd put on.

McCord wrapped his arm around the tall woman's waist and pulled her toward the door. "With this rain, no one is going to storm the place. We'll be in the barn." He glared at the men. "And don't come looking for us unless you're ready to die."

He grabbed his leather coat from the peg by the door and tossed it over Anna's head, then lifted her in his arms and headed out. She kicked and yelled and screamed, but the rain and the coat muffled all sound.

When he made it to the dry silence of the barn, he checked to make sure no one lurked in the shadows before pulling the coat off Annalane and laughing. This very proper lady looked madder than hell. Maybe he should have taken a little more time to explain his plan.

"How dare you!" She poked her finger into his chest as if it were a knife. "Do you know what they all think we are doing right now?"

"I don't care, lady. I just wanted out of there, and you said you wanted to come with me." He frowned at her. "If you want to go back just tell me, because where we're headed isn't going to be easy, and I can make better time without you. I left the mailbag inside. They can bargain for their lives with it, but I don't think any one of them would worry about you."

The woman proved she was not a fool. She said simply, "I want to stay with you."

He tugged his coat around her shoulders. "We got an hour, maybe more if this rain doesn't let up. We need to get as far away from here as possible before they notice we're gone."

She nodded.

"Any way you can shed a few of those skirts? They're going to get heavy once they get wet."

He'd expected her to argue, but she said, "Turn around."

The petticoats rustled as they fell to the floor. He fought the urge to glance back.

"I've practical shoes in my carpetbag," she said, pointing at the stage, halfway between the barn and the station.

He thought of telling her they didn't have time, but a minute probably wouldn't matter. Their chances of making it away were so slight, the odds wouldn't change much just because she switched shoes. He trudged out to the coach and grabbed her bag along with the extra Winchester the driver must have forgotten. He thought of taking a horse, but the animals were exhausted and someone from the station might notice a horse being unhitched and led away.

When he got back, she had pulled her wild hair down out of a ridiculous nest of curls and was braiding it in one long, midnight braid. The woman was practical.

"Ready, Anna?"

As she shoved her feet into lace-up leather boots, she said, "My name is Annalane."

"All right." He watched her, thinking he liked looking at her more than listening to her. The quick Northern accent grated on him. "If you can't keep up . . ."

"I'll keep up," she said. She didn't seem one inch shorter. The woman reminded him of a willow. He smiled, remembering how he didn't have to lean down to kiss her; he only had to turn his head to cover her mouth with his.

McCord tossed her worthless hat in the hay. "I won't leave you, Anna, don't worry. But tell me if you need to slow down."

"I'll keep up," she repeated without commenting on how he'd just thrown away the only hat she'd ever thought looked good on her. She packed up her carpetbag and moved it behind her as if she thought he might toss it as well.

He smiled. The woman wasn't far from wrong. He might have tried if he'd had the chance.

They walked out the back of the little barn and headed into a stand of trees that wound along a stream now busting its banks. Anyone watching the station would have had to be within three feet of them to notice them passing.

He'd expected her to slow him down, but she matched his steps. They moved for two hours, with her never more than a few steps behind him. When he climbed, he'd turn and offer his hand. She'd accept the help only as long as needed, then let go. She never complained.

The rain now became their ally, blanketing the sounds, erasing footprints.

He left the stream reluctantly and moved into the rocky hills. If he remembered correctly, they could cross over on foot and save a few miles. The boulders also offered some protection. The outlaws would have to leave their horses if they decided to follow on the uneven ground.

She bumped into him from behind. "Sorry," she said, sounding out of breath.

McCord turned. "How about we stop for a few minutes." It had been almost twenty-four hours since either of them had slept.

"I'm fine." She lifted her chin.

He grinned. "I know, but I'm a little tired. Ten minutes' rest and then we'll climb some more."

They moved between two huge stones and found enough shelter to avoid the rain. It was so dark he could barely make out her outline, huddled on a rock a few feet off the ground, but he could hear her teeth rattling. Pulling his flask from his pocket, he offered her a drink and was surprised when she took it.

When she handed the flask back, he told her to turn around

and lift her feet out of the tiny trickle of water that streamed between the boulders. When she followed orders without speaking, he straddled the rock she sat on and pulled her back against his chest. "I'll rest on the rock, you rest on me. We won't be very comfortable, but we won't be as cold."

She hesitated, then leaned back against him. He propped the rifle at his side and circled her with his arms. She felt as stiff as stone.

"Relax, Anna, I'm not going to attack you."

"I know," she said without relaxing.

"How do you know?" He smiled at her in the dark. "I've already done it once tonight."

"You had to do that to plan our escape. I shouldn't have taken offense." She leaned into him just a little. "I'm surprised it worked. I'm not the kind of woman men lose their heads over. You'd think one of those three would have noticed."

It took his tired brain awhile to figure out what she was saying. She didn't think of herself as attractive.

He wanted to argue, but he had a feeling she wouldn't believe him. Slowly she warmed in his arms, and he felt the moment she relaxed into sleep. Her body seemed to melt against him. He shifted so that her head rested on his shoulder, then ran his hand down her leg from hip to calf. He told himself he was just seeing how wet her clothes were, but he knew something else drove him. He liked the nearness of this woman more than he'd ever liked any of the saloon girls who'd wiggled up to him wearing only their underwear.

"Sleep, Anna," he said against her hair. "I'll watch over you." He tightened his arms and she cuddled closer.

After holding her for a long while, he tilted her head up. It was time they moved on. The rain had stopped and it would be light before long. They needed to be on the other side of the hill before then.

McCord looked down, wondering how to wake a woman who'd spent the night resting next to him. Her mouth was slightly open. Her warm breath fanned across his face.

He didn't even think of resisting the urge to taste her. He pulled her close and nibbled her bottom lip.

One taste was not enough.

Chapter 3

Annalane came awake one sense at a time—the warmth of someone close, the smell of rain, the feel of someone kissing her the way she'd always longed to be kissed.

Her body jerked as reality shot through her. The taste of whiskey blended in with the kiss that demanded she respond. His hands were beneath her arms, as if he'd pulled her up over his body, and his palms pushed against the sides of her breasts when she tried to breathe. He shifted his mouth and she felt the stubble of the beginnings of a beard as his tongue parted her lips, demanding entry.

Opening her eyes, she saw nothing but midnight shadows and the dark outline of the Ranger. She lifted her hand to shove him away, but he circled his arm and caught it, tucking it behind her back as he pulled her closer still.

"Not yet," he whispered against her tender lips. "I can't let you go yet." His arms were iron around her. "I haven't had near enough."

She knew she should pull away and demand he stop, but no one had ever kissed her with such desire, with such need, with such passion. Relaxing, she let the fire of it sweep over her.

He felt her surrender and slowed. The kiss went from demanding to teaching, as he silently showed her what he wanted and rewarded her with bold strokes of his hands along her body as she learned each lesson.

For the first time in her life, she was mindless, floating in gentle waves of pleasure. The way he tugged at her bottom lip with his teeth, the way he held her so close and kissed her throat when he gave her time to catch her breath, then pulled her mouth back to his as if starving once more.

When his hand finally passed over the fabric covering her breast, she arched and cried out. He laughed against her mouth, then kissed her deep and long, not giving her time to react or even think.

"You taste so good," he whispered with his mouth still on hers. "It'll take me a long time to get enough of you, Anna."

Before she could answer he was kissing her again and she was welcoming his touch. Somehow in the nowhere of this land she could let down her guard and just react.

The sound of a horse, ridden fast, drifted into their world.

McCord groaned and pulled away. "Stay here," he ordered as he shoved her farther into the shadows and disappeared.

Annalane sat perfectly still, listening to her own heart pound. What had she just done? She could still taste him on her lips, still feel his warmth against her body. The grip of his fingers over her breast now burned through the layers of cloth. What had she done?

The fear of being killed by a band of outlaws no longer frightened her near as dearly as the fear of facing the Ranger when daylight came. She'd behaved like a wanton woman and he'd . . . he'd patted her on the bottom as he'd left her. No man had ever done that! All her life she'd never allowed anything so wild to happen. He had no right to . . .

"Are you all right?" His words drifted in the night. He sounded almost angry, as if in a hurry for an answer.

She nodded, then realized he probably couldn't see her.

"I'm fine," she lied, wishing she could crawl back under the rock for a few minutes, or days, or maybe years.

His hand brushed her arm, then found her fingers and gripped tightly. "We have to move fast, Anna. We need to be over the ridge by dawn. I couldn't tell who was on that horse riding by below, but I don't think it will be long before more follow."

He didn't give her time to answer; he just tugged her out of the shadow of the boulder and began climbing. The rain had turned to a mist making her feel like she was moving in a dream.

She kept moving, trying not to think. Maybe she'd get lucky and they wouldn't make the ridge, and the outlaws would shoot them down. At least then she wouldn't have to face him. Never, never, never had she allowed a man to touch her the way he had. The only other kiss she'd truly received had been at her wedding. There had been no time or privacy for more.

She thought of how hard the Ranger's face had looked, even when he'd slept in the stagecoach, chiseled like weathered granite. How cold his eyes were.

How demanding his kiss. How bold his hands. She mentally slapped herself for letting her mind wander.

He'd advanced so fast she hadn't been able to think about how to reject him. This was all his fault. She should have nothing to be ashamed of.

If the man would slow down now, Annalane swore she would kill him. What right did he think he had to kiss her like that? To touch her. To wake her up to something she told herself she had been perfectly happy not knowing about.

Her anger stewed as she climbed. She barely noticed the eastern sky lighten. They were at the ridge by the time dawn washed over the rocks.

McCord jumped down off a rock and turned, lifting his arms to catch her. He swung her around. "We made it."

A smile lit his face, making him look younger—closer to thirty, not forty as she'd first guessed. Despite her anger and exhaustion, she smiled. They were safe, at least for now.

He set her on her feet, took her hand as if he'd done so a thousand times, and started down the shadowy side of the hill.

Halfway down, he stopped to allow her to catch her breath. While she rested against a cold rock, he searched the valley below.

"The driver told me you were going to meet your brother at Camp Supply."

She nodded as she fought exhaustion.

"He'll know the stage didn't make it in last night, and I'm guessing troops will be headed this way. If I'd been waiting for you, I'd be an hour in the saddle by now, maybe more."

If Devin hadn't planned to introduce her at dinner last night, she doubted he'd even notice she was missing. He was more likely to wait and blame her for being late than come after her, but Annalane didn't want to admit that to McCord.

The Ranger kept watching. "On horseback they could cut some time off the stage trail and be here in an hour, two at the most."

Annalane closed her eyes, wishing the driver hadn't been so nosy, but a woman traveling alone was a rare sight in these parts, and she thought it would help if he knew she had someone waiting to meet her. It might make her sound not quite so like an old maid. At least she hadn't told the driver more. She never told anyone the truth. What would people say, or believe, if she told them that her brother never contacted her unless he needed something from her? She swore that ever since he could talk he'd manipulated everyone around him. Life was some kind of game and people just cards to play to him.

She sniffed, thinking she was really pathetic. Even knowing what he was like, she'd traveled half a continent hoping that this time he'd act like a real brother. Maybe for once he was thinking of her, alone in Washington, and not just himself.

I will not cry, she silently vowed. *I will not cry.*

McCord startled her when he stomped back to where she stood. All she could manage was to glare at him when he cleared his throat.

"About last night . . ." he started, forcing out the words as if he were reading his own obituary.

"I don't want to talk about last night," she hissed through her teeth to keep from screaming.

"Good." He slapped his gloves against his hand. "'Cause I don't want to hear you talk about it. Never could tolerate the Northern accent. How about we just agree to talk as little as possible?"

She didn't need a weapon, she decided. She'd kill him with her bare hands. She'd just grab his throat and bite him, then she'd watch the blood pump out of his long, hard body and say sweetly, in her most proper Northern accent, that she was wrong about not having the killer instinct. It appeared she did.

Before she could pounce, he plopped his hat on her head and dropped his gloves in her hand. "Put these on, Anna. There's brush the rest of the way down that'll cut you if you grab for a handhold, and the sun's going to turn hot enough to put that blush permanently on those cheeks."

He'd never know how close he came to dying, she thought. She'd let him live awhile longer. Not because he'd said something nice to her. A nice word would probably choke the man. But he had shown a degree of thoughtfulness. The dirty hat and the worn gloves couldn't make her look worse.

She sniffed again, deciding that on top of everything else,

she'd caught a cold. The only silver lining to it lay in the hope that she'd passed it along to the Ranger while he'd kissed her.

"You getting sick?" he asked, already ten feet ahead of her.

"No." She picked up her bag and followed.

"Well, then hurry up. We want to be off this hill by the time they ride by here."

She almost laughed. Her brother was probably having his second cup of coffee and telling everyone about how his sister couldn't manage to do anything right, including get to him.

Two hours later, when they were almost to the trail that served as the stage road, she collapsed. Her legs simply folded. Three days with nothing to eat and little to drink. More hours than she could count without sleep. Like a clock running down, she stopped.

As she lay in the dirt, she heard the Ranger backtracking to her. She half expected him to yell at her to get up, but he simply leaned down, picked up his hat and her bag, then lifted her into his arms.

Without a word, he began walking, carrying her like she was a child and not a woman almost his height.

Annalane closed her eyes. She'd have to kill him later. Right now all she wanted to do was sleep.

Chapter 4

McCord walked half a mile before he found an old cottonwood tree with branches almost touching the ground. He pulled Anna into the cool shade where roots bowed from the earth, making a natural cradle for her.

Anna's eyes fluttered open. She watched him, a mixture of fear and panic in her exhausted gaze, but she didn't say a word.

"You all right?" he asked, feeling her face to see if she had a fever. "We about froze last night in the rain, and now it's hot. I swear, Texas is the only place I know of where you can experience all four seasons within twenty-four hours."

She didn't act like she could hear him. McCord pulled his leather coat off her shoulders and spread it out on the ground, saying, "You'll be safe in no time, Anna. I promise." He tugged her arm, leaning her down atop his coat, with her head on her bag for her pillow. She didn't fight him, but the stiffness in her movements told him she didn't believe him.

"That's better." He patted her hip, liking the roundness of it on her slender frame. "Rest." There was no telling how long it had been since she'd eaten. He'd seen her shoving food around on the tin plates when they stopped yesterday, but he hadn't seen her lift a bite to her mouth.

He laid the back of his hand against her cheek. She was warm, but not burning with fever. When he began unbuttoning her traveling jacket, she moaned and shook her head.

"Easy now," he said, thinking that was probably more something he should say to a horse rather than a woman. "I'm just going to make you comfortable, then I'll watch the road for your brother."

Her fitted jacket was tight across her ribs and he wondered how she'd stood it all night when they'd been climbing in the rocks. When he finished undoing the last button, she let out a sigh and closed her eyes. He couldn't resist sliding his finger beneath the wool and feeling the warmth of her covered only by a layer of wrinkled cotton.

He brushed a few stray strands of hair away from her face. "You're quite a woman, Anna. You collapsed before you complained once." He pressed his lips against her cheek. "Sleep now, but remember that we're not finished, me and you. Not by a long shot."

She moaned something in her sleep and McCord brushed his fingers over her ribs. He liked the feel of her, the look of her; but most of all, he liked her spirit.

When he was sure she was sound asleep, he moved to where he could see down the road in both directions. If the army didn't come soon, looking for the coach, the outlaws would be finished with the men at the station and realize what they were looking for was not in the mailbag. Thorn, the leader of the worthless gang, would be madder than hell and heading toward them.

McCord tugged the envelope from a slit in the lining of his boot. The letter Thorn was fighting so hard to get wasn't in the mailbag. It never had been. The governor had trusted it to one Ranger. McCord had orders to burn it before letting it fall into the wrong hands. There'd been no need to ask—he knew he was expected to protect it with his life and deliver it to a Quaker who served as an Indian agent in this part of the world. This one document could change history, maybe end the Indian fighting years early and allow settlers and Indians to live in peace.

McCord knew without any doubt that he'd die before he'd fail. For the first time in longer than he could remember, his actions might save lives. He smiled, thinking he would do just that, even if he had to kill Thorn and all his gang to do it.

He moved away from Anna, fighting the need to lie down beside her, fearing that if he did, he'd frighten her even more than he had. He wanted her, but not tired and half asleep, at least not the first time. He wanted her awake and willing in his arms, and to reach that goal he knew he'd have to go slow, very slow.

Problem was, he had no idea how.

McCord frowned and turned his back to her, hoping his need for her would ease. For a man who'd counted his life in days and never looked too far in the future, going slow toward anything was not his nature. He'd been seventeen when he'd ridden with a posse that tracked raiders who'd burned a farm near his parents' place. He'd killed his first man that night, seeing the bodies of the family they'd pulled from the fire and not the outlaw he'd killed. From that night on, McCord had always felt he'd been playing cards with the Grim Reaper, and one of these times he'd draw the short hand.

He glanced back at Anna curled in among the cottonwood roots. "Slow and easy," he promised, proud of himself for taking the time to talk to her a little and not just leave her among the branches. It had been a long time since he'd comforted a woman.

An hour later, he heard riders coming and watched until he recognized the blue uniforms of the cavalry.

McCord stepped in the trail, his hand up, his gun pointed down.

One rider stood out among the soldiers. A young officer on the short side who sat a horse like a greenhorn. He had to be Anna's brother, same black hair and dark eyes. Wynn remembered her telling the gambler on the stage that her brother was a new doctor who'd just been transferred to Texas before being sent to Camp Supply.

The Ranger decided he disliked the man on sight.

The short doctor, in a uniform that didn't quite fit, half climbed, half tumbled from his mount and hurried to catch up to a sergeant heading toward McCord.

"Ranger McCord." Sergeant Dirk Cunningham smiled and offered a friendly salute. "When we heard the stage was late and you might be on it, I headed out just in case you needed help." He laughed. "You know, burying the bodies or hanging the outlaws. I've known you long enough to know if there's trouble you'll be the last one standing."

McCord touched his hat in a two-finger return salute to a man he'd crossed paths with so many times over the years they'd become friends. "I thought you might be worried about me, Cunningham."

The sergeant shook his head. "Not you. I followed you when we was dodging Sherman in the war. You'd fight a twenty-gun man-of-war with a tug boat and still come out ahead."

The doctor finally reached them. Anna's brother pushed his way forward. "If you were on the stage, where are the others? My sister should have been with the stage, unless she missed her connection. I swear, if there was a dog in the road, she'd stop to help it even if it meant missing the stage." When both men just stared at him, the doctor added, "Was there trouble? Is anyone hurt?"

Cunningham took the lead. "Ranger Wynn McCord, this

is Doctor Devin Woodward. You'll have to excuse his manners—he's worried about his sister."

Wynn faced Dr. Woodward. "Your sister is all right, sir." He turned back to his friend. "We were attacked by what looked like Thorn and about a dozen men, but we managed to make it to the station just as the rain hit." Wynn met the sergeant's gaze and they both knew they'd talk details later when they were alone.

"Oh, my God," Dr. Woodward yelled. "Was my sister hurt? If she's back at the station in pain, I'll hold someone accountable. We have to hurry!"

"No." Wynn turned back to the doc. "She's asleep right now. I brought her with me when I escaped in the rain. I figured her chances would be better than at the station once the rain stopped. We followed the stream behind the station for a few miles, then climbed over those hills."

Devin Woodward didn't look like he believed the Ranger.

McCord added, "She's quite a little soldier."

"You let her leave with you!" Dr. Woodward turned his anger on the Ranger. "You dragged a woman out in a storm and across those hills? Good God, man, you could have killed her."

McCord's jaw tightened. "I didn't drag her anywhere. Your sister is a strong woman who knows her own mind."

"My sister is an idiot. If she'd had any brains, she would have married and not taken on nursing as her cause. She's wasted her youth running from battle to battle during the war, and now will probably be my burden to bear for the rest of her life."

McCord thought of hitting the doc. One good punch should put him out for a while. Anna looked to be almost in her thirties and Woodward appeared to be just past twenty. He'd been too young to fight. He couldn't know how many men lived because of nurses who worked round the clock in roofless field hospitals and old barns turned into surgery stations. The doctors might have done the cutting and the patching, but it had been the nurses who bandaged and fought fevers and held men as they faced death.

Wynn looked toward the cottonwood and silently swore.

Anna, her back straight and his coat folded over her arm, walked slowly toward the men. The face that had shown such fire when she'd been mad at him, which was most of the time he'd known her, now looked stone cold, as if no emotion would ever reflect in her features. Only her eyes looked tired and sad, very sad.

"There you are!" Woodward shouted. "You had us all worried to death." He didn't move toward her but waited for her to join them. "I'd hoped to start setting up the infirmary today, but from the looks of you, we'll have to put it off until tomorrow."

McCord balled his fists. Just two punches. One to the doc's face, leaving him unwilling to talk around a busted lip and a few missing teeth, and one to his gut to knock some of the wind out of him. Couldn't he see that his sister had just walked through hell to get to him? Couldn't he imagine how frightened she must have been, and how brave?

The sergeant stepped past McCord and moved to Anna. "Are you all right, ma'am? Ranger McCord told me what an ordeal you had last night and I'm surprised you're still standing. May I be of some service to you?"

McCord saw her glance at the stripes on Dirk's sleeve before answering, "Thank you, Sergeant. You are kind."

Dirk Cunningham might be an old fighter, but there was enough Southern gentleman in him to know how to treat a lady. They left the doc standing in the trail as they moved to the troops still in their saddles.

"I need three good men to go with me back to the station and check on things." McCord fell into step on the other side of Anna. He could hear the doc following, asking questions and demanding answers, but no one listened.

The sergeant nodded. "I got two good boys you'll know, and a Yank who can shoot a flea off a rabbit's ear at a hundred yards. He's just a kid, so keep him out of any close scraps if you can, but he'd be good at lying low and covering your back."

McCord understood what Dirk wasn't saying as much as what he was. The "good boys" were Texans, probably ex-rebs, who could take care of themselves. The kid, a Private Clark, was green, but his skill could come in handy.

Cunningham helped Anna onto one of the extra horses the men had brought along. There was no time to say anything to her as McCord closed his hand over hers when he handed her the reins. He'd have to do his talking to the sergeant. "Take care of her, Dirk. She's a real trooper."

The sergeant nodded, understanding the Ranger's compliment. He turned to the doctor. "Awaiting your order to ride, sir."

Dr. Woodward straightened as if just remembering that he was the one in charge. "Go ahead, Sergeant. Start back. I'll have a word with the Ranger first and join you." When he faced McCord, the Ranger was already moving toward an extra horse and the three men waiting for him.

"I have a few questions," Woodward demanded.

McCord swung up on his mount. "Well, I'm all out of answers." He did wonder why so many folks seemed to be starting conversations with him lately with that statement. "Why don't you ride back to the stage station with us and maybe you'll find your answers?"

"I think I'll just do that." Dr. Woodward climbed on his horse. "I plan to ask the other passengers if you forced my sister to go with you, and if you did, sir, I'll have you know, I plan . . ."

McCord didn't listen to more. He and the three soldiers were a hundred yards ahead of the doctor before he could get his horse moving. The soldiers stayed right with Wynn, enjoying the entertainment of watching the little doctor try to keep up with them.

When they reached the station, McCord could read all the answers in the tracks, but he said nothing. He waved Clark, the sharpshooter, in from where he'd been hiding in case they'd been riding into a trap, and they all waited for the doctor.

The soldiers stayed on guard while McCord let Dr. Woodward storm into the stage station first. Two minutes later, he ran out and threw up at the side of the porch. "They're both dead!" the doctor said.

One of the soldiers swung from his horse and read the ground as easily as he might a headline in the paper. "Looks like there were ten or more of them. I'm guessing they came in fast." He scratched his head. "No shells in the mud, so they didn't come in firing."

McCord stood at the door and looked in. "The driver and station manager were already dead by the time Thorn and his men rode in."

"How do you know that?"

"There's half a dozen spent shells scattered among the cards by the table. One man who was here last night is missing. A gambler who called himself Frank Sanders. My guess is he shot the others, waited for a while to make sure I didn't come running from the barn, then lit out with the mailbag. I heard a horse traveling fast sometime before dawn."

Dr. Woodward wiped his mouth. "If this gambler killed those two, why did the gang ride in?"

McCord shrugged. "Maybe they thought the gambler left

something behind. Maybe he took something they wanted. If so, they're after him and not us."

"So if we go after the gambler, we might just find this Thorn bandit everyone talks about."

McCord nodded.

Dr. Woodward straightened and tried to pull himself together. "The flaw in your plan, Ranger, seems to be we have no idea where this gambler went."

"I don't have to go after him," McCord answered. "I know where he's headed."

Woodward frowned. "And where might that be, Ranger McCord?"

"Camp Supply. Two people saw him and now know he's part of Thorn's gang. He'll be heading to try to permanently silence me and your sister."

Chapter 5

Annalane fought to keep awake enough to stay in the saddle as she rode, surrounded by soldiers, toward Camp Supply. The land rolled over low hills covered in the green of early spring, and she wondered how such beauty could ever hold danger.

Sergeant Cunningham fussed over her. When they reached the camp, he showed her to her brother's quarters, ordered men to bring a bath and a hot meal, then stood guard outside her door so she'd have privacy.

Devin's quarters were minimal. The room had been set up for four officers to sleep in a room, but the sergeant said all the officers had not arrived yet, so her brother had the room to himself. She managed to find everything she needed in either his supplies or her dusty bag. Soap, a brush, towels, clean underclothes.

She soaked in the tub until the water turned cold, then washed her hair. Pulling her undergarments from her bag, she put them on before wrapping herself in one of Devin's extra bedsheets. The food was simple: milk, cheese, biscuits with jelly inside, and creamy chicken soup. It all tasted wonderful. When she finished, she curled up on one of the bunks and slept soundly.

The late afternoon sun shone through high west windows when someone tapped on her door.

"Begging your pardon, ma'am," the sergeant yelled, "but one of the men who went to the stage station just delivered your trunk. He says to tell you that if you're able your brother would like you to dress and join the officers for dinner in an hour."

Annalane pulled the sheet tightly around her and opened the door.

The sergeant kept his eyes low as he set the luggage inside. He didn't look up until she asked if McCord had made it in with her brother.

Cunningham smiled. "Yes, ma'am. He checked to see if I was on guard, then went over to the barracks to clean up. The Ranger always eats with the officers the first night when he's in camp, just to pay his respects, but he'll be having breakfast with us come morning."

She understood. "He's more comfortable. I see."

Cunningham shook his head. "I don't think McCord is comfortable anywhere. It wouldn't surprise me if he sleeps wearing them twin Colts fully loaded and strapped on. But maybe he feels a little less uncomfortable around his own kind. I've heard that his family all died while he was off fighting. Haven't seen him care about anyone or anything in years, until this morning."

Before she could ask, he added, "The look he gave me when he told me to take care of you left no doubt about how he feels about you, ma'am."

She thought the sergeant must have read something more into McCord's order than was there. Maybe the sergeant was just hoping his friend had changed. All she had to do was listen to know that Cunningham and McCord had the same accent. Not Southern exactly, but uniquely Texas.

She thanked the sergeant as she closed the door, and

dressed in one of her plain navy suits she'd worn as a nurse. There had been only enough time and money to buy one good traveling dress. All the rest of her clothes were uniforms or housedresses. Years ago she'd had a few evening dresses and two Sunday dresses, but they'd long been packed away. There never seemed time for such things, and she always worked on Sundays when the nurses with families liked to take off.

Annalane hoped her brother would come to walk her over to dinner, but when she opened the door only Cunningham waited for her outside. He offered his arm and she accepted the gesture kindly. He filled her in on what her brother and the Ranger had found at the station. She knew there would have been one more body on the dirt floor of the shack if she hadn't left with McCord. The thought chilled her.

Four officers and one Ranger stood as she stepped into the small dining room. Her brother introduced her to each officer. They were all polite, but as usual none gave her more than a passing glance. She was not the kind of woman who drew a man's attention.

To her surprise, McCord didn't meet her eyes when he took her hand in greeting.

Devin hadn't introduced her to him, but the Ranger stepped forward and paid his respects just like the others. He'd cleaned up and had on clothes that looked free of dirt. If he hadn't been frowning, she would have almost thought him handsome. How could this man of granite, with his cold winter eyes that missed nothing, be the same man who'd kissed her so wildly in the darkness?

She didn't waste time with nothing words. "Thank you for saving my life."

"You are welcome." He finally looked up, staring at her as if he saw no one else in the room. "As I remember, you insisted on going."

"You could have left anytime after the rain started. Why did you wait?"

He lowered his voice. "I wouldn't have left without you. If you hadn't wanted to go with me, I would have remained and fought."

Annalane stared, knowing he meant every word.

Her brother tugged at her arm, insisting she sit between the captain and a tired-looking man with thinning hair named Lieutenant Dodson.

As Devin tucked in her chair, he said, "I asked one of the men to move your things out of my room and into the new infirmary. You can stay there. It wouldn't be proper for you to stay in the officers' quarters. I'm an officer so I belong there, and even though you're my sister, you are still only a nurse."

When she raised an eyebrow, he added, as if she'd asked, "The three-room infirmary is finished, at least on the outside. One wide front room that will serve as an office and examining room, one smaller storage room, and a large room to be set up as a small sick ward. Once we get everything out of crates, I'm sure you'll find plenty of room for a bed in the storage room."

"Nothing is set up?" She knew her brother had been at the camp over a month—surely he'd done something. It occurred to her that he might not know how. Surely any graduate from a medical school would know how to set up at least an office and examining room.

"I've been busy," he answered. "It's not my top priority right now. I'm not just the camp doctor, I'm also an officer."

She nodded, telling herself he was lazy, just waiting for her to do the work. He'd been that way as a child, and no uniform had changed his habits. Pushing aside a nagging worry that he might not have spent all his time away in medical school, she resigned herself to sleeping among crates tonight.

She glanced around at the proper table service and wished

McCord were not a table away. He was the only one she felt safe with. He was the only one she wanted to talk to. She smiled. In truth neither of them probably had enough skills to keep a conversation going throughout an entire meal.

It made little sense—the man had barely talked to her—but in a deep, primal way she needed to be near McCord.

The captain was formal and polite, but not interested in talking to a woman. Her brother never spoke to her, except to tell her to answer the questions. Lieutenant Dodson, on her left, was a few years older than she was, thin and pale among the other men tanned by the sun. He told her he was the paymaster. The man reminded her of a hawk, and had the habit of blurting out questions in random order. Her answers quickly shortened to simply yes or no, since she had the strong suspicion he wasn't listening but trying to think of what to ask next.

By the time the meal was served, she'd formed a shell around herself. The men talked around her as if she were invisible. Her brother related his trip to the stagecoach station, including how the bodies looked on the floor and how many times each had been shot.

When one of the young officers suggested that such talk might not be proper in front of a lady, Dr. Woodward announced that his sister loved blood and gore. She'd been at half the battles during the Civil War and came home to work in a hospital for dying veterans when the war was over, as if she hadn't had enough after over four years.

When dessert was brought in, Annalane excused herself, saying she knew the men would want to enjoy their cigars with coffee and she was still very tired. They all stood and bid her good night, but she had the feeling that only Ranger McCord's gaze followed her out.

Sergeant Cunningham waited on the steps to see her to the infirmary. "The boys have been scrambling while you were at dinner, ma'am, trying to clean up at least one of the rooms for you. I'm not sure where your brother thought you'd be sleeping when he ordered your things sent to a half-finished building with boxes everywhere."

Annalane thought of saying she doubted Devin cared, but she tried to smile as she said, "I'm sure it will be fine."

When she entered the building, she was met by the three men who had gone with McCord to the station. One looked barely old enough to shave and the other two were like Cunningham—they'd fought for the South. They were all smiling at her.

As the men stepped aside, she glanced into the larger room that would become the hospital bay and she laughed. They'd put a tent in the middle of a room lined with boxes. One of the privates stepped forward. "We figured we didn't have time to clean the place so we put up a new tent for you, ma'am, with supplies we found in some of these boxes."

Another added, "You got a lock on the door to the room, so you'll be safe, but you'll have your own apartment once you're in the building." He lifted the flap. "We put some coals on the grate so you'll be snug as a bug in here tonight."

Annalane laughed and clapped her hands. "Thank you, gentlemen. I've never had something so grand." They'd even put a little white tea set by the grate and a rug made from blankets on the floor.

They all smiled and would have watched her move in if Cunningham hadn't shoved them along. "Lock the door behind us, ma'am. We'll take turns tonight guarding outside, so all you have to do is yell if you need anything."

Annalane thanked them each again, locked the door, and stepped inside her very own playhouse tent. She had the feeling a few of the items had been stolen from her brother's room, but tonight she didn't care. She was in heaven.

First, as she'd done for years traveling with the supply

wagons and medical tents, she unpacked her few belongings and laid them out so they'd be in easy reach when she was called to work. Then she dressed in her white nightgown and warm robe that tied empire style. The hem might be frayed and the lace threadbare in a few places along the collar, but she always felt elegant in her robe.

She sat in front of a little mirror and brushed her hair, then braided it in a long braid. Smiling, she remembered how her mother used to tell her that she might never be a beauty, but she had pretty hair.

Her parents had both died two years ago when a flu hit the city hard that winter. Devin had been in his first year of medical school and couldn't come home. She'd tried to keep working and deal with the debts. One by one she'd sold off everything they'd had, to pay bills and keep Devin in school. He resented having to join the army because there was no money to help set up his practice, but deep down Annalane had thought it would be good for him.

A knock sounded at the door just beyond the folds of her tent.

She checked her robe, slipped from her warm tent and opened the door.

McCord stepped inside, frowning. "Don't unlock the door unless you know who is on the other side."

"All right. Go out and knock. I'll pretend I don't know you." He'd been nothing but cold to her all evening. If she didn't know better she'd swear someone else had been in the shadows with her last night. Someone else had kissed her. Not this man who hadn't looked at her once during dinner.

He ignored her suggestion and raised an eyebrow at the tent.

She was thankful for the distraction. "The boys put it up for me. Isn't it great?"

He didn't smile, but at least he stopped frowning. "Yeah, it is."

"What did you need, Ranger McCord? It's a little late for a social call and I do have a guard outside."

McCord reached behind her and shoved the bolt. "I told that Clark kid, who's guarding this place like it's the national bank, to go eat some supper. I need to talk to you."

"About what?" He'd had an hour to talk to her at dinner and never said a word.

"About this." He leaned closer, backing her against the door, and hesitated a few inches from her mouth. "I'm going to kiss you again, Anna. If you have objections, you'd better voice them now. All you have to say is stop. Just say the word and I back away." The words were snapped like orders he'd rehearsed. "But if you don't . . ."

She could feel her breathing quicken but she faced him squarely. This was probably his idea of having a conversation with a lady. The man had the social skills of a turtle. "Well, first of all, my name is Annalane, not Anna, and I'll not tolerate being manhandled or talked to like I'm . . ."

He closed the distance between them and covered her mouth with his. She pushed on his chest and tried to turn her head away, but he held her with his body pressed hard against hers and his hand cupped around the back of her head. Evidently the conversation part of his visit was over.

This was no gentle kiss of hello, but a demanding, searching advance based on need and longing. He slid his hand to her jaw and urged her mouth open so he could taste and smother her complaint.

As she knew he would, he gentled when she kissed him back. He moaned low and twisted his fingers through her hair as he took her through the lessons he'd taught her the night before in the blackness.

Finally, when he moved his mouth to her throat, she

breathed in deeply as he whispered, "That's the way, Anna. I knew you'd feel this good, taste this good. I couldn't have imagined last night when you were lying against me."

He brushed the tips of his fingers along her chin. "I think I might have died if I'd had to sit across the room much longer without touching you." He held her cheek as he kissed her again and again while he mumbled something about going slow.

The thought of saying stop never occurred to her. She wanted a man who was gentle and caring, maybe even hesitant as a lover, but she'd not tell McCord to stop. She felt her body melting against his, needing his nearness, his touch, his kiss, as deeply as he seemed to need her.

Finally, he leaned away and studied her, drinking her in with his stormy gaze.

She knew he'd kiss her again if she tried to talk to him, so she lifted her arms to his shoulders and let her breasts rise and fall against his chest with each breath.

He raised his head and smiled at her as if he could read her mind. His hand circled round her braid and he tugged until she leaned her head back, offering him her throat.

He unbuttoned the first few buttons of her high-collared gown and began nibbling along her throat. He stopped where her heart pounded just below the surface of her skin and kissed just there. Then, as if in thanks for her offering, he returned to her mouth and kissed her lightly, playing with her tongue. He didn't have to say he missed her—he was showing her. There'd been no need to tell her he had to touch her—she knew.

When she pulled him closer, she felt his low moan more than heard it. "I know, Anna," he whispered against her ear. "I know."

Slowly, the kiss grew deeper. Her whole body felt like it was on fire. He stepped back and tugged at the ribbons holding her robe. When she protested, he pushed her hands away. When she tried again to hold her robe closed, he placed both of her hands behind her with one strong grip and he opened the robe with his free hand.

She wiggled, trying to get free. He was going too fast, being too bold. She wanted a gentle lover, a slow lover, a hesitant . . . the feel of his hands tugging her robe free made her forget her list of wants.

She wouldn't stop him and he smiled down at her, knowing what they were doing was new and frightening to her.

"Easy now, Anna. Just relax against me. I wish there was time to go slower," he whispered as he kissed his way from her ear to her lips. "You know I'm not going to hurt you, don't you?"

She nodded and moved her hands to his shoulders, barely aware of when he'd released her.

"I'm going to touch you, if you've no objection. This will be no light brush over your clothes, like before. When I'm finished there will be no doubt you've been handled a bit." He kissed the corner of her mouth. "And, darling, you're going to love every minute."

When she opened her mouth to question this, his kiss stopped the words and his hand moved over the cotton of her gown to grip her breast boldly while his strong arm circled her. She jerked and twisted, but he didn't let go. Her breast filled his hand. His grip was strong, almost hurting her, but he didn't turn loose or let her free.

When she pulled her mouth from his, he let her turn and gulp air. His fingers spread out, pressing her breast against her pounding heart. She saw fire in his eyes, but she felt no fear of him, only of herself and what he might awaken in her.

She tried to turn away, but he didn't move. They both knew she could stop him with a word. She was fighting years of closing herself off from any tenderness, any loving touch, any passion. This cold, hard man seemed to understand her when no one else had even tried.

"Kiss me, Anna," he whispered, almost angry. "Kiss me."

She turned toward him, seeing the need in his eyes, and then the surprise as she raised her chin and moved her mouth to his. After a moment of hesitation, he took her offering fully.

When she finally calmed and stilled in his arms, he kissed a tear from her cheek and loosened his grip around her. "There now, that wasn't so bad, was it, darlin'. You're more afraid of something new than of me."

It crossed her mind that he was mad. She was with a madman. Who bossed her around. Who saved her life. Who kissed her with a passion that would probably set them both on fire any minute. He thought he could kiss her and handle her just because he wanted to. He treated her like a treasure. Like a woman. Like a passion too deep for either of them to understand.

His hand gently brushed over the thin layer of material covering her shoulder.

When he leaned down to take a first taste of her throat, she pushed away and moved into her tent.

He followed, knowing that he'd be welcomed as he moved up behind her, circling her waist and pulling her back against him. He wasn't imprisoning her now—she could have stepped away, but she leaned into him and sighed at the whirlwind of feelings circling through her body.

He kissed her ear and she heard his breathing, fast and heavy like her own. "Unbutton your gown." He spread his hands out wide at her sides.

"No," she whispered.

"Unbutton your gown." His order was muffled as his mouth moved down her throat.

"Only a few," she whispered back in compromise.

Her fingers fumbled, opening the buttons as he kissed his

way to the hollow of her throat. There was something raw and hungry in his touch, as though he'd waited a lifetime to hold her.

She was beyond thought and full into pleasure. Slowly, hesitantly, she began unbuttoning more tiny buttons. He rewarded her with kisses along her neck and his fingers moving over her body.

When she reached the buttons between her breasts, he whispered again, "Now, pull the gown down off your shoulders."

He watched her slow progress. First one shoulder, then the other. The robe dropped to the floor but the soft gown hung at the tips of her breasts.

"You're so beautiful," he whispered.

She wondered if he was aware that he said the words aloud.

His hands moved to her shoulders and began to slowly slide down. He played with the material hiding her from him. He hadn't pushed her in this, he hadn't forced her. He'd simply asked and she'd done what he wanted. He could not possibly be as surprised as she was.

She closed her eyes, expecting him to shove the cotton down and stare at her, but he didn't. He turned her slowly in his arms and drew her against him and held her for a while. She'd never felt so treasured.

Anna cried softly against his shoulder without knowing why. All her life she'd discouraged men with a turn of her head or a frown. She'd been in mourning, or too busy, or thought herself too old. But there was nothing hesitant in this man's advance. Nothing shy.

She shook, aware of just how close he stood and how unbelievably natural it felt to press her body so close to his she could feel his heart pounding.

When his mouth found hers once more, he was giving, not

taking. The kiss was long and pure. Her bruised lips took the pleasure of it like cool water.

Finally, he broke the kiss and pressed his forehead against hers. "We have to talk. I haven't got much time even for this heaven."

"I thought you didn't like to talk."

He grinned. "Believe me, there are a million things I'd rather do with you than talk, but this time it's important that you follow orders."

"Your orders?"

"Yes, my orders. That gambler back at the stage station, Frank Sanders, is part of a gang led by a man named Thorn. We've both seen Sanders and therefore can identify him. Which means Sanders, and maybe Thorn, will want us dead as soon as possible. I want you to promise to stay in the camp until I get back. Trust no one that Sergeant Cunningham doesn't trust."

He squeezed her shoulders. "Do I make myself clear?"

"I'm not in the habit of being bossed around, McCord."

"Well, I'm not in the habit of caring about anyone." He swore and added, "There is nothing I'd like more than to bed you right now and we both know I could, without you stopping me."

"Would you have stopped if I'd said the word?"

"I would. I will." He set his jaw as if testifying in court. "I said the words and I meant them. I had to let you know you had control. I know I came on a little fast and strong, but on my honor I would have stepped away if you'd ordered me to."

"A *little* fast," she mumbled, knowing her lips were bruised from his kisses and her throat probably black and blue from where he'd taken the time to nibble on her flesh.

He kissed her forehead. "I've a mission to finish and if I bed you tonight, I might end up leaving you alone with child. I'll not do that, Anna." While hugging her, he let his honest words flow over her. "I have a hunger for you, like I've never felt before. I don't know if it's that I want to believe you could belong to me, or if part of me already belongs to you. This doesn't feel like something we can cure in one night."

She was shocked by his caring. She had no doubt that he wanted her, but now she knew he cared. "You might get killed on this mission? Is that what you're telling me?"

"The odds aren't with me this time. I feel it so strong I'd already decided before I climbed on that stage that this would be my last ride as a Ranger." He lowered his head and kissed her bare shoulder. "If I make it through the next few days, will you be waiting for me? I'm not asking for any promises, I'm just asking that when I knock on that door again you'll throw the bolt and let me in."

She stepped away, shaking. He hadn't asked her to let him *stay*. This wasn't a marriage proposal or even a promise of one, but it was as close as she'd ever come to one again. She had always been a proper lady. What he was asking was that she'd welcome him in. Not just to her house, or room, but to her bed.

She fought back a sob, longing for him to whisper "forever" between them, but knowing she'd not ask for so much. She might never have him stay. Without a single doubt she knew it would take all the strength she had to take only what this Ranger could offer and then watch him leave when their time was over.

"Anna," he snapped. "Stop breathing so fast. You're driving me crazy."

She looked at him and then down at the gown almost falling off her breasts with each breath. Crossing her arms over her, she began to pull up her gown.

His hands shot out to grip her wrists.

She met his eyes, no longer cold, but stormy with anger and need.

"Don't," he said, gritting his teeth.

He hesitated as if refusing to explain why.

"Let go of me," she said. "Stop." She felt like she was bending him to the breaking point. She guessed there were very few things in his life he wanted or needed. Apparently she was one of them, but if he didn't let go right here, right now, they would never be equals, and for her there could be no other way.

"Stop," she said again, almost calmly. "Turn loose of me."

She saw the blink of his eye and knew she'd stood down a fighter who'd never backed away.

His grip loosened and gave. He stepped away and raised his hands in silent surrender.

She'd broken him, but passion still fired in his gaze like a fever out of control. "Sit down." She pointed to her traveling trunk.

He raised an eyebrow, but did as he was told. The trunk was too high to be a chair, but made a good bench and put her a head above him.

She walked over to stand directly in front of him. "You'll never take anything from me, Wynn McCord. Not one thing," she said. "Get that clear. You'll never take me. I think you'll have to learn to come toward me some other way than at full charge. If there is to be anything between us, there will be no orders." She'd give him everything, if he asked, but nothing if he demanded.

She sensed he was in uncharted territory, but he was a strong man and his face showed nothing of how he felt. His glare was so strong she swore she could feel it on her skin.

Slowly, she lowered her crossed arms and her gown slipped back to where it had been, barely covering the peaks of her breasts.

He glanced from her chest to her face, trying to read what she was offering. "I know no words, Anna. I'll never come a'courting. I'll never know what to say or how to tell you the things women want to hear."

"I don't expect such things," she said. "But I do expect honesty."

"You've told me that before, Anna."

She smiled. "And next time taking it a little slower wouldn't hurt."

Carefully, he raised his hands to her waist and tugged her toward him. Then he lowered his mouth and planted a feather kiss on the top of each breast before he looked directly into her eyes and said, "I'll work on it if you're willing to put up with me." He lowered his head and she felt his smile against her skin.

Anna began to shiver as he moved over her flesh. Her hands rested on his shoulders as he drew her to him and nuzzled between her breasts, then turned slowly from one to the other, breathing her in as if she were a flower.

When he straightened, he grinned at her as his hand moved up her ribs and tugged her gown down.

For a while he just looked and moved the tips of his fingers over her gift to him. "You are so beautiful," he said again as he lifted the weight of one breast and brushed his finger over her skin.

She would have fallen with pleasure if his arm hadn't held her up.

He stood and carried her to her cot. When he lay her atop the quilt, he knelt beside her. "Don't worry," he whispered. "I don't want to frighten you."

"I know," she whispered.

Part of her wanted to fight, to break away and run, not from him, but from herself. From feelings so long denied she'd forgotten how to live.

His big hand stroked over her bare body, pushing the gown lower until it barely covered her hips. She closed her eyes and moaned softly as he kissed her. Again and again, he moved up to her lips, his kiss deep with need as his hands branded her.

She relaxed, giving over to the pleasure of his touch. When he stopped, she opened her eyes, wondering how this man could have gotten so close, not with tender words and soft touches, but with honesty in his longing for her.

His hand spread out across her abdomen. "I have to go." He said the words slowly, as if forcing them out. "But I'll have your word you'll stay in camp before I go. Nowhere is totally safe, but you'll be surrounded here."

She didn't trust her voice. She simply nodded. He'd just shown her how much he wanted her. With his words he was telling her how much he cared for her.

She'd thought he would continue touching her, but he stepped away and picked up her robe. Silently she stood, barely aware of the gown falling away as she stepped into the robe he offered.

He tied it above her waist and took one of her hands, kissed it, and then pulled her to the door.

"Hell's fires won't keep me from coming back," he whispered as he pulled her to him one last time.

They held each other tightly for a minute, then he patted her on the bottom and pushed away from her.

A moment later, he was gone. Anna shoved the bolt closed and went back to the cot where she cried herself to sleep, knowing when he came back she would let him in . . . whether he stayed a night, or forever.

Chapter 6

McCord rode for half the night before he stopped to water his horse. The hardest thing he'd ever done was leave Anna, but deep down he knew leaving her was the only way he'd keep her alive.

The gambler was hunting them both, and McCord knew men like Frank Sanders would come after him first. He'd consider the woman easy pickings, not near the challenge a Ranger would be to kill. He'd want McCord out of the way so he could take his time with the woman. McCord doubted Sanders or Thorn had put the pieces together and figured out that the letter they wanted so desperately to stop from being delivered had been with a Ranger, and not in the mailbag on the stage.

McCord had to draw Frank Sanders away from Anna, and he had a mission he had to finish. If he had a choice, he'd meet the outlaws out in the open so Anna wouldn't be in danger. Then, when they were dead or in jail, he'd ride back and linger for a week in that funny little tent inside a building.

It was almost dawn, but he could still feel her against him. The woman had climbed into his blood and was pumping through every part of his body. He didn't want to marry her and have kids and settle down. He wanted to make love to her until they both died of hunger. He wanted to touch her all night long and wake her again and again with passion. He wanted to be so deep inside her he stepped out of this world.

McCord was so lost in his thoughts he almost missed the glint of sunlight off a rifle. The bullet came within a foot of his head as he dove off his horse.

He rolled into the brush, both guns ready and waiting.

Nothing.

An hour passed. Not a sound. Frank Sanders was playing with him. The idea that McCord had escaped and taken another witness with him must have infuriated the gambler. Thorn and Sanders planned to pay him back by making him sweat awhile before they killed him. McCord wondered if the horse he'd heard riding past while he and Anna hid in the rocks that first night had been ridden by Frank. After he killed the others at the station, the gambler might have raced after them, knowing he'd be in real trouble if he failed Thorn by not finding the letter *and* by letting witnesses live.

McCord burrowed in and waited out the day, determined not to give the gambler any chance to fire again.

At dusk, he climbed on his horse and rode out before even the stars offered light. He'd have to be more careful, but when his job was done, he would track the gambler down.

By sunup McCord and his horse were safely away, miles to the north of where he'd been shot at. The Ranger needed a few hours' sleep and then he had to think. The letter in his boot was due by the end of the week to an Indian agent deep in the territory. He could make the ride in two days on a good horse. The question was, did he deliver it first, then find Frank, or try to find the gambler first, then burn leather to make it to the agent in time?

Only one answer came to mind. The outlaw could wait a few days to be arrested; the letter had to be delivered. Hundreds of lives might be saved if the agent could put the governor's plan into action.

Splashing across the Cimarron River, he entered the rolling hills of Indian Territory. The outlaws wouldn't follow him this far. Once he was out of Thorn and his mens' rifle range, he could ride hard toward Medicine Lodge on the Salt Fork, where the agent was reportedly staying.

Anna was safe at the camp, surrounded by a hundred armed men, and with luck he'd be back in time to catch Thorn's whole gang before they caused any more harm.

Chapter 7

Annalane spent her first few days in camp setting up the long, narrow room at the front of the infirmary to serve as a doctor's office and operating room. She wasn't sure if it was curiosity, or the long absence of an infirmary in camp, but people dropped by to help and to complain about small ailments. Two of the three women in camp were pregnant and happy to see someone they could talk to.

Her brother walked in on the third day to nod his approval at the job she was doing. Shelves filled with organized and labeled supplies lined the wall. He talked of his excitement at being posted at his first fort, but said little about medicine. When she asked a few questions about where to put tools, he seemed unsure. She knew medical school was mostly two terms of lectures and some work on cadavers if students could afford them, but she was shocked at his lack of knowledge. A nurse, a week into training knew the names of medical supplies.

Before she could begin to ask more questions or suggest he might help set up his own office, Devin announced, "I'll be riding back along the stage line to inform the owners of their loss of employees. Not that it's the army's fault—we warned them not to try a run this far north. Teamster wagon trains a hundred long were safe enough to move from fort to fort, but it is far too early to even think about establishing a stage line." He pointed at her. "You were a fool to take a stage. You should have waited at Dodge until supply wagons with guards could have delivered you."

She hated the way he talked down to her, never thinking to ask if she'd had enough money to wait in Dodge. Before she could fire back, he stormed toward the door.

Glancing back, he added, "I'm assuming you can handle everything here while I'm gone."

"How long will that be?" Annalane asked, thinking one, maybe two days there and the same back should do it. What if the camp needed a doctor while he was gone? She wondered if her little brother had yet had his hands covered in warm blood. She doubted it. Being a doctor to him was more theory and grandeur than reality.

"I'll be gone a week," he said without meeting her gaze. "Maybe more. I have army business to take care of that doesn't concern you."

She straightened. "Devin, I'm here to help you, not do all the work. Don't you dare treat me like your servant."

He frowned. "Or what? Or you'll pack up and leave? Go ahead. You've never been much good at staying around. I doubt if it ever occurred to you that all those years during the war your family might have needed you around. Times were hard then, you know." For a moment he looked like the boy she remembered and not the man before her.

Annalane fought down words she knew she'd regret saying. She didn't have the funds to go anywhere and he was well aware of the fact. She might be able to make it back to Fort Worth, or even Austin, but then she'd be penniless, looking for a job. She wanted to also point out that if he thought it was hard at home, he should have tried being at the battles.

But she wouldn't tell him. That was the past. Hopefully he'd never know war, and in time her memories would fade.

When she didn't snap back, he softened slightly. "Look, sis, I know it's hard on you, but you're used to hard times. I want to help you, I really do. My plan is simple. Help me set up this place and get it started, then maybe one of the single officers will see how useful you are to have around. Lieutenant Dodson is a widower with three kids and having a hell of a time. If you play your cards right, you could be married to him by Christmas and have a man to take care of you."

"You're delusional." Who would take care of Dodson . . . and the three children . . . and the house . . . and . . . She frowned, knowing her brother would never understand that marriage is *not* a ticket out of work.

Devin laughed. "Come on, Annalane, you need a husband and Dodson can't afford to be too picky. It might not be a marriage of love like you and your first love thought you had nine years ago, but it would be practical. He's been in the army for over ten years, so he's made of sturdier stuff than the kid you called husband for an hour."

Annalane fought the urge to slap her only kin. If Sergeant Cunningham hadn't walked through the door, she might have. Devin had always been spoiled as a child and he hadn't changed much.

Cunningham saluted Devin, then addressed her. "I'm sorry to bother you this early, but I've been sent to tell you or the doctor that Private Price's wife is going into labor and everyone in camp knows Victoria is a screamer when she's not happy."

Devin headed for the door. "Take care of it, Annalane. I've got men waiting for me. Surely even you can handle a birthing." He was gone before she could answer.

Annalane grabbed a basket she'd put supplies in and shoved it toward the sergeant. "Let's go. Babies don't wait."

Cunningham led the way. "Did your brother ever deliver a baby?"

"Not that I know of," she answered, aware that most of Devin's experience had probably been on corpses.

"That's what I figured. He looked a might pale. How about you?"

"I've delivered a dozen or more near battlefields. Wives wanting to see their men one more time before the baby came." They moved through the tents and corrals along the outside of a wooden stockade that held supplies, as she added, "The hospital where I worked only treated veterans, but some women didn't know that until they arrived, already in hard labor. We kept a room ready for emergencies like that. Over the four years I was there, I welcomed many a life into this world and helped the mother mourn the passing of a few wee ones who didn't make the crossing."

The sergeant smiled. "Mrs. Price will be real happy you're here. She didn't much like the idea of having the doc come. She tried to talk to your brother last week about how to prepare, her being still two years from twenty and all. He told her she had no business following her man into unsettled territory and should try to make it home before she went into labor."

Annalane thought that sounded exactly like what Devin would say. She stepped into one of the new two-room cabins built for married men. The smell of fresh-cut wood greeted her, along with the sound of a woman crying for help. She sounded far more frightened than in pain.

"Set the supplies down, please, Sergeant. I'll need a stack of towels and a large washtub, cleaned and scrubbed with soap and hot water." She passed a man standing at the bedroom door, looking like he might pass out at any moment. "And, Sergeant, take Private Price with you."

Sergeant Cunningham followed orders.

Annalane moved to the bed already stained with blood.

"I'm here to help, Victoria, so don't you worry. Together we're going to deliver this baby."

A girl not out of her teens looked up, wide-eyed and near panic. "I don't know what to do," she shouted, as if Annalane might be deaf.

"I do," Annalane answered. "You can call me Anna. I'll help you through each step. We're going to climb this mountain one step at a time." She pulled a small pair of scissors from her apron pocket. "First, I'm going to place these under the bed right below you. My grandmother used to tell me they will cut the pain in half for the rest of your labor." Annalane smiled, realizing the girl believed her. "And when the baby comes, I'll know right where the scissors are when it's time to cut the cord. Now, Victoria, the first thing I want you to do is lean back and relax. When the next contraction comes take deep, slow breaths and let the tightness roll over you, knowing that it's not pain, but just your body practicing for the job it's got to do."

The girl followed orders and Annalane did her job. Nine hours later, she carried a newborn son to the private, who still looked like he might pass out. He kissed the top of his son's head, then walked into the bedroom.

"You did a fine job, Anna." Sergeant Cunningham smiled.

She collected the stained towels and sheets. "She did all the work. I only helped."

When Anna got back to the infirmary, a meal was waiting for her. She hadn't expected her first duty to be delivering a baby, but she was glad. It reminded her of why she loved nursing. Not the dying and hurting, but the healing and helping.

She was almost asleep in her chair when someone stepped into the little clinic.

"I beg your pardon. Is it too late to call?"

Anna stood. "Lieutenant Dodson?" He was not a big man, in size or manner. She would have had to slump to be eye to eye with him, and Anna refused to slump. Despite what her brother thought, she wasn't interested in a man who planned to consider her because he "couldn't afford to be picky." "Is there something I can do for you, sir?"

His gaze darted over her as if taking her measure. She saw intelligence, but not kindness.

"I heard what you did today and I commend you," he began formally, then rolled his shoulders, forcing himself to relax. "I lost my wife to childbirth last year, so I know what a trial it is. My children are in Kansas City with her folks while I finish this tour, then I hope to have them back with me."

"You must miss them," Anna said, watching him closely, wondering why he'd come so late.

"It's not that, ma'am. It's the fact that they belong with me. I'm their father." He frowned. "I know I'm a military man, but I've always believed a wife belongs with her husband, and the children should be raised and disciplined by their parents. There is an order to things, in and out of the army."

"I see," she said, then waited for him to explain why he'd dropped by.

He glanced around the office, frowning at the piles of supplies still remaining to be organized, then continued. "I planned to ask you to dine with the officers tonight, but I see you've already eaten."

"Thank you, Lieutenant, but you needn't worry about me. I'll be fine here." She'd found the officers' dinner boring. "I prefer to eat my evening meal in silence. It's become my habit over the years."

"You are a woman too long alone." He said the words slowly, as if he thought they might frighten her. "And this is not a country for women alone. It's the nature of things that men and women should be married. If not for love, then for convenience."

"I've been on my own since I was nineteen." She met his

stare. If he expected her to be helpless and needy, he was about to be disappointed. "Now if you'll excuse me, I think I'll turn in."

He puffed up slightly, as if not used to anyone dismissing him. Then he nodded once and mumbled good night.

Anna stood in the doorway watching him walk away, but her thoughts were on Ranger McCord, not the lieutenant. If Wynn had stepped into her quarters, he would not have left without touching her, and one touch would have made all her exhaustion vanish. He'd told her that what was between them was not finished, and she agreed. He might bruise her lips with his kisses and hold her so close to him she couldn't breathe, but she knew he was attracted to her, he wanted her, needed her. There was no "convenience" in his passionate touch.

Dodson seemed about to propose a business arrangement. He hadn't even taken the time to get to know her. Anna had the feeling that, in his mind, any woman would do.

Anna would never settle for so little. She'd rather have one honest day with Wynn McCord than a lifetime of convenience.

"Miss Anna?" Private Clark's voice sounded from the other side of the porch. "Just wanted you to know that I'm on guard tonight. I'll put my bedroll in front of your door once you're inside so you won't have to worry about anyone else coming along just to visit."

She smiled. Clark was a good kid. He would have to be, for all the Texans to accept him. "Thanks," she answered. "I'm going to turn in soon, but thought I might circle the camp once to get some air." The smell of blood still lingered in her lungs. "Would you mind walking with me?"

"I'd be honored," he answered as he set his rifle just inside her door threshold before offering his elbow. He didn't seem to notice that her hair was a mess and she still wore the stained apron she'd had on all day.

She tucked her hand on his arm and they walked, talking quietly as the sun set. The camp was like an ant bed of activity with movement tonight. Someday, if the camp grew into a fort, the place would be surrounded by walls, but now most of the buildings and tents circled the stockade of supplies. Teamsters had brought in a line of wagons and everyone seemed to be helping with the unloading.

She watched the movements but spoke low to Clark. "You were listening to what the lieutenant said to me." It was a statement, not a question.

"It was hard not to. The door was open," Clark said, defending himself.

Anna smiled. "I got the feeling he'd come to ask me something."

Clark laughed. "I swore I heard the trap door about to fall, but you played it smart."

"Maybe we're just guessing what he wanted. Maybe he just came to thank me for helping with the birthing."

"Maybe," Clark answered. "My guess is he didn't know about McCord or he wouldn't have even been hinting."

She stopped walking and looked at the kid. "What about McCord?"

"He's your man. All the enlisted men know it. I'm surprised the officers don't."

Anna had to ask. "How do they know it?" She couldn't imagine McCord talking about their time together.

"McCord told us before he left. He said every one of us better keep an eye on his Anna or there'd be hell to pay when he got back."

Anna started walking again, pulling the private along beside her. "I'm not his Anna and he's not my man."

"Yes, ma'am," Clark said as he fell into step beside her.

"He also said not to argue with you no matter what crazy thing you said."

"Oh, he did," Anna said, more to herself than the kid. She wanted to get home and think about what Clark had told her, then decide whether to kill McCord when he came back. A few kisses and touches did not define ownership, even if those kisses still filled her dreams at night and the memory of his touch still warmed her each time she thought of it.

When they stepped back into the infirmary, she noticed Clark's rifle was missing beside the door, a moment before she saw two men standing in the shadows. Clark's muscles beneath her hand tightened, and she prayed the kid wouldn't go for his Colt. Maybe they should have locked the door before leaving, but they'd both felt safe inside the circle of the military.

"Evening," one stranger said as he stepped forward, a rifle pointed at Clark's chest. "We've come to ask you, lady, if you'd like to take a ride with us." He smiled, showing rotting teeth in a face weeks past needing washing. "There's a gambler who says he has a little game to finish with you. He says you ran out on him before all the cards were on the table."

The stranger laughed as if pleased with his politeness, then glared at Clark. "I guess you're coming too. If we kill you it'll draw attention, and I'd like to ride out of here the same way I rode in. Unnoticed. A soldier riding along with us will make us look all the more legal."

Anna panicked. "No. Tie him up and I'll go with you without a sound." She guessed they'd kill Clark when they were far enough away from the camp that no one would hear the shot.

"No," Clark answered calmly, his eyes staring at the man without any fear showing. "I go with her. I'm her guard. If I'm not outside someone will come check on her, but if we're both missing they'll think we're somewhere in camp."

Anna closed her eyes, wishing he wouldn't be so logical. He was signing his own death warrant.

The second stranger, a bookend of the first outlaw, moved out from the shadows. He had the same wide-rimmed hat that his partner wore, but his clothes were buckskin, not wool. If possible, he looked even meaner than the first, with a touch of insanity flickering in his whiskey-colored eyes. Both were men who would not be welcome in anyone's home. Something about them seemed more animal than human.

Clark raised his hands as the men took the Colt at his side and tied his hands.

"That's the way, boy," the first outlaw whispered. "Come with us nice and easy and we'll make the end quick for you."

The mad twin tied her, spitting out a giggle when his hand kept slipping to brush against her. He was having so much fun, he didn't notice when she twisted her wrist wide as he pulled the knot.

"Where are you taking us?" Anna demanded.

"Luther and me ain't got no orders to kill you, if that's what you're asking. We're just planning on delivering you."

Anna decided the smart one was dumb as a cow patty and his partner, Luther, smelled worse than one. When she opened her mouth to ask more, Luther wrapped a dirty bandanna across it.

"Make a sound," the leader added, "and we kill your bodyguard. We weren't told to bring him along anyway, so if one of our knives happens to slip between his ribs we know it won't matter one way or the other to the boss."

Anna had no doubt he meant what he said. Luther pulled a long knife and began poking them with it.

While the leader waited and watched for full dark, Luther pressed the point of the knife against her throat and giggled when he drew a drop of blood.

Anna stood perfectly still, refusing to move or cry out. She knew she couldn't get away if he wanted to kill her, but she wouldn't play his game.

Each cut drew one bubble of blood. Two, three, four pricks. Luther watched each drop slide down her throat and melt into the lace of her collar.

"It's dark enough," the leader whispered as he shoved Clark and her out of the infirmary and around to the back where they'd left horses tied. A small wagon train of settlers had been picking up supplies before dark and the outlaws had no problem blending in among the other visitors.

Anna forced her mind to notice every detail as she dug her heel hard into the ground before they lifted her onto the horse. The outlaws had brought two extra horses. She knew they hadn't planned on Clark, so the other mount would have been for McCord.

She smiled. It had been three days since McCord left. If they expected to pick him up here, then they hadn't caught, or killed him. He was alive and she had no doubt he'd be coming after her.

All she had to do was stay alive until he reached her.

Chapter 8

Ranger McCord delivered the letter to the Quaker in charge of the territory. He stood, forgotten, as the man read suggestions from the governor of Texas. McCord could tell by the way he folded the letter away that the Indian agent didn't plan to put any new policies into action. The Indian Wars, which had been raging for thirty years in Texas, Kansas, and New Mexico, would continue. He'd ridden all this way and risked his life for nothing.

Thorn and his men wanted the trouble to continue, so they could play off both sides. Now they had won, not by interfering, but by the indifference of one man.

The Quaker looked up as if just remembering Wynn was in the room. "Thank you for delivering this," he said in a tired voice. "I have no reply."

Wynn backed out of the office and walked to his horse. He'd planned to find a meal and a bed for the night, but all he wanted to do was get back to Anna. She'd never left his thoughts. The possibility of asking her to marry him crossed his mind more often than he wanted to admit. He had a good-sized spread from a land grant his father bought fifty years ago. They could settle down in south Texas where things were calm and be hundreds of miles away from the fort line where trouble blew in with every new wind. Behind the line of forts a man could raise his family and worry about crops but here life was never easy.

He didn't want her to just let him in when he came back. He felt a hunger for something that might fill a hole in his heart that he'd been ignoring since the war. For the first time in more years than he could remember, Wynn wanted to stay.

Smiling, he wondered if she wouldn't mind wearing a ring and a gag. He'd never get used to that accent of hers. If he could just keep the woman quiet, she'd be darn near perfect. He didn't even care if she could cook. Hell, he'd been eating his own grub for so long, any food that didn't crawl off the plate looked good to him.

McCord swung into the saddle. He'd trade mounts at the edge of camp and make a few hours of hard riding before he slept. With luck he'd be back to Anna in two days.

As he always did, his mind focused on his goal and he rode hard with little food or sleep. Only this time he didn't feel like he was running away from something. This time he was riding toward her.

He was three hours out of Camp Supply when he saw soldiers riding fast. Wynn knew who they were by the way they sat their saddles. Seasoned soldiers, Cunningham and the two other Texans.

The men pulled their mounts up when they reached McCord, but only Sergeant Cunningham stepped down.

McCord slowly swung from the saddle, knowing something was wrong when his friend didn't smile. "What is it, Dirk?"

Cunningham didn't waste words. "From the markings, two men, probably part of Thorn's gang, took Anna and Private Clark at gunpoint two nights ago. We've been trailing them since dawn yesterday."

McCord didn't move, but inside he felt his entire body take the news like a blow.

"Captain's had every man out on patrol looking. We got lucky and picked up fresh signs this morning. Spotted a woman's footprint out back behind the infirmary yesterday as we left. About the time we figured we'd lost them for good, we spotted her print again near a creek bank. From there it was easy to follow the trail of four horses. Every time they stop, your Anna must be stomping around leaving footprints everywhere." He stared at his friend as he told the whole truth. "Along with fresh blood. They're heading due south."

"No body?" McCord said as he checked the cinch on his horse. "Clark's still alive."

Cunningham nodded. "That's my guess."

"Then we'd better get to them fast. Clark's not the one they want, so they'll kill him as soon as possible. I'm surprised he's lasted two days."

"I figure the men who kidnapped them don't do much without orders. So we've got till they get to camp, where the boss is." Cunningham reached for his saddle horn. "Looks like they're heading toward Red Rock Canyon. Once they're there, we'll never find them."

Both men mounted and rode without another word.

It had been a long time since McCord had felt anything, including hate, but he felt it now. He'd kill every one of the outlaws if even one touched Anna. He might have given up on ever being able to love anyone or anything in this lifetime, but he could still hate.

They rode until almost dark before they spotted movement ahead of them. Then, without a word, Cunningham signaled and the four men spread out, leaving no trail of dust big enough to notice if one of the outlaws glanced back.

McCord took the center, riding in the open, daring them to look back. He rode fast, but not full-out; he had to give the others time to move into place. As he climbed, he closed in on four riders, one in what looked like a blue dress. Anna, he thought. His Anna.

One outlaw led the line, pulling the two captives behind him. The other outlaw rode drag, but he wasn't on guard like he should have been. Not once did he look back, and from what McCord could see he held no weapon at the ready.

The captive next to Anna slumped in his saddle. It had to be Clark, but he was either asleep or hurt.

When they crossed over a ridge, McCord saw that the outlaws were moving toward two men camped out near a stream in the bottom of a shallow canyon. Both men were waiting, watching the riders approach. If they'd looked beyond the riders, they might have seen McCord in the long shadows, following.

He waited as the day aged and the outlaws slowly wound their way around rocks and streams toward the camp.

In the campfire light McCord swore one of the men had to be the gambler. He even noticed the flicker of gold from the watch chain on the gambler's vest. The other man in camp was tall and dressed in black. If this was an outlaw camp there would be one, maybe two men in the shadows on guard, but the Ranger had no time to worry about them now. Anna's and Clark's lives might be measured in minutes.

McCord knew his part. He could go no closer without the men in camp seeing him, and when they did he needed to be ready. He drew both his Colts, not bothering with the rifle, circled the reins around his saddle horn, and kicked the tired horse into a full run. With Anna and Clark halfway between him and the camp, Wynn knew he'd reach her long before the outlaws could make it to the others watching from the shadows.

The minute the outlaws, with their captives in tow, spotted him, McCord opened fire. He hit the man leading the two prisoners with his first shot. The other outlaw grabbed at the rope on Anna's horse. Clark shouted something as he tumbled off his horse, hands still tied behind his back. A second later, Anna also tumbled and rolled from a horse gone wild from the noise.

The outlaw with Anna was so busy fighting to control the horses he didn't notice that he'd lost his captives. Both men at the camp grabbed their weapons and shouted orders.

Suddenly, shots exploded from every direction. The men standing at the camp jerked in a fatal dance with bullets. The outlaw on horseback tried to ride away.

A dozen more shots rattled across the sky and then the night fell silent. Both men at the campsite lay dead. The mounted outlaw screamed as his horse bolted, and tumbled. One of his feet remained in the stirrup dragging him behind his horse. One shot from somewhere left of McCord silenced the screams, but the outlaw's body still bounced over rocks as the horse ran.

The screams and the last shot echoed into the canyon until they were only whispers on the wind. McCord took a deep breath. He'd felt the peace after a battle many times. One more time he'd survived, but tonight his thoughts were for another.

McCord holstered his guns and headed toward Anna. He found her sitting beside Clark, wrapping what was left of her apron around the kid's arm. Both of them smiled as he neared.

"She said you'd come," Clark groaned. "Drove the two fellows crazy with her threats of what you'd do to them when you came."

McCord didn't look at her; he couldn't, not yet, not till he knew it was over. "You all right, kid?"

"I'm fine. They shot me in the right arm this morning because I told them I was a crack shot. But Anna made them let her bandage it. She says I'm lucky the bullet went right through."

McCord saw Cunningham and his men moving into the campsite, making sure the others were dead.

Clark's voice shook a little. "They told us they were going to hang us tonight, then gut us like we was fresh game. They knew you'd be coming and they figured when you found our bodies, you'd be foolish enough to do something stupid."

Anna stood. "Which you did." Fists on her hips, she faced him. "You rode straight in here like a madman. It's a wonder you don't have four bullets in your chest." Her voice was fired with anger. "When I saw you barreling straight toward us, Wynn McCord, I almost had a heart attack."

McCord finally looked at her. "Startled men don't take the time to aim. I knew I could kill one, maybe two before they'd get a shot close to me. I was giving the sergeant and his men time to step out and open fire from other directions." He hesitated, fighting down a smile over her finally using his first name. Damn, if she wasn't adorable all covered in dirt and twigs. "Glad to see you, Anna."

When she straightened up as if planning to give him a lecture on being careful, he raised his hands in surrender and closed the distance between them. He couldn't very well grab her and kiss her in front of the other men, but he could at least get close.

The click of a rifle cocking sounded from somewhere in the night. It had to be the lookout the outlaws posted. The outlaw McCord had forgotten might be hidden in the night.

He dove at Anna, knocking her down a second before the bullet meant for her blasted into his back. He felt her beneath him, then pain exploded all other thought. The last thing he heard was another round being fired. He waited for the second bullet to hit, but before he realized it hadn't been meant for him, blackness washed over him, carrying him under like a huge wave.

In the silence of dying, he drifted back to the battlefield years ago when he'd fallen. The arms of the nurse who'd stopped to help him circled him and whispered, "You're going to be all right, soldier. You're not going to die."

Only this time McCord knew she was wrong. He'd finally drawn the short card.

Chapter 9

Anna frantically bandaged the Ranger, trying to slow the bleeding as the others built a travois to pull him home.

"Don't you die on me, Wynn. Don't you dare die on me."

He didn't respond.

Angry, she continued. "I don't care if my voice irritates you. You're not going to die. Do you hear me? You're not going to die."

Blood soaked the strips of cotton that had once been her underskirt. She pulled the bandage tighter, hoping to keep the blood from flowing out the hole in his back. When the men came to lift him onto the travois, she followed a step behind, giving unneeded orders for them to be careful.

Once they were moving, Sergeant Cunningham ordered one of his men to ride ahead with her and Clark. With luck they could be back in camp by dawn.

She didn't want to leave her Ranger, but Anna saw the logic. She hadn't sat a horse since her days as an army nurse, but she hadn't forgotten how to ride hard, and Clark, despite his wound, rode as easy as he walked. McCord's wound was too deep to risk traveling fast, and Clark's arm still needed proper care or the infection could kill him. The practical side of her she'd always depended on overruled her heart.

Clark signaled that he was ready and they were off. They rode fast across flat land, with only the moon for light, and reached the camp at first light. Anna swore half the garrison turned out to help.

While she cleaned up, three men washed a few layers of dirt off Clark. Another lit a fire in the examining room and spread out a buffalo hide on the table for the Ranger.

Anna doctored and bandaged Clark's arm with the roomful of men watching. They groaned with the kid, like midwives at their first birthing. Anna grinned at Clark, guessing he was complaining more than necessary just to hear the echo.

As she wrapped the wound, one of the men who'd ridden with Cunningham asked Clark, "How'd you shoot that one hiding in the shadows without your firing arm?"

Clark thought for a moment, then started slowly into a story he knew he'd tell more than once. "When I heard the shot coming out of the night, I grabbed a rifle lying in the dust. The bandit, who'd been riding behind us all day yelling obscenities, must have dropped it when he was knocked out of the saddle. I raised it toward where I'd seen the flash of fire. It was so black I couldn't see anything but his eyes. I just shot between them."

"With your left hand?"

"My father always said, 'You got two, might as well learn to shoot with them both.'" Clark smiled. "I didn't want to mention that to the outlaws earlier. Thought they might decide to blast away at my left arm as well."

Anna smiled, doubting any of the men would call Clark a boy again. He had a wound he'd heal from and a story he might live to tell his grandchildren. He'd not only killed an outlaw, he'd saved other lives. If he hadn't fired when he did, the outlaw would have picked them off one by one.

Everyone fell silent as Sergeant Cunningham and one of

his men arrived with the Ranger. There would be no laughter, no telling of stories now. A Texas Ranger was down.

They placed him on the buffalo hide, facedown. He didn't make a sound. Then the men stepped back and watched as Anna cut off his shirt with shaking hands. Blood seemed to be everywhere.

Cunningham and one of the others she didn't know stepped up to help. Both took orders from her as if she were a general. They could make him comfortable, clean him up a little, but then it would be up to her.

When the Ranger's star hit the floor, everyone froze.

Anna took a step and picked it up. She shoved it into her apron pocket. "I'll keep this safe for McCord until he needs it again."

No one believed he ever would, but they all nodded as if agreeing that she should be the one to keep it safe.

When Anna had the wound cleaned, Cunningham seemed to think it was time for the audience to leave. He ordered everyone out except Clark, who'd fallen asleep in the corner.

Anna set to work, doing what she knew best. Years of working under all kinds of conditions kept her hands steady. She'd done her job when cannon fire still filled the air, when it was so cold that bloody bandages froze on the wounds, when sleep was a luxury she couldn't afford. She could do what had to be done now.

"Listen to me," she whispered to McCord as she worked. "You're going to live. You're going to come back. I don't care if you like my accent or not, you've got to hear me. You've got to come back to me."

Sergeant Cunningham returned with whiskey he claimed was for McCord when he woke up. Anna hardly noticed the sergeant moving around the room trying to find a comfortable spot. She talked only to Wynn as she worked, telling him everything she was doing and what kind of scar he'd have when she was finished. Over and over, she said, "You're going to make it through this. Hang in there. You're going to be good as new once you heal."

Finally, when she leaned back to rest her back a moment, the sergeant placed his hand on her shoulder. "He'll come back to you, Anna." He barked out a laugh. "Hell, if a fine woman like you ordered me to, I'd come back from hell itself, and I reckon McCord feels the same way."

An hour passed. Cunningham began sampling the whiskey. Clark slept on a cot in the corner, snoring away. Anna worked, with memories of a hundred hospital camps after a hundred battles floating in her mind. All of the horror she'd worked through, all the exhaustion, all of the skills she'd learned, all boiled down to this day, this time, this man.

If she could save him, all the years would be worth it.

"I'm never giving up on you, Wynn, so you might as well decide to live because I'm not letting you die," she whispered. "I hear Rangers are made of iron. Well, you'd better be. You're going to come out of this. Hear me good."

Finally she finished and wrapped the wound where a bullet had dug its way across Wynn's back. He'd lost so much blood she was surprised he was still breathing, but she could feel the slow rise and fall of his chest and the warmth of his skin against her touch.

Exhausted, she pulled a stool beside the table and leaned her face near his. "You're going to be all right, soldier. Hang on. I'm not going to let you die." Her fingers dug into his hair and made a fist. "I'm expecting you to come knocking on my door one day, and when you do you might as well plan on staying because I don't think I can let you go."

She fell asleep in the middle of a sentence, with McCord's shallow breath brushing her cheek.

In what seemed like minutes, someone woke her to tell her breakfast was ready. It took her a minute to realize that twenty-four hours had passed since they'd brought McCord in.

Anna left her meal untouched as she walked around Wynn, checking the wound, feeling his skin for fever. Wishing he'd open his eyes.

Finally, at Cunningham's insistence, she ate a few bites and drank a cup of tea. Clark ate everything in sight. Men took over the sergeant's watch by the door so he could get some sleep, and the day passed in silence.

Lieutenant Dodson tapped on the open door to the office just before dark. He waited until she nodded for him to enter, then removed his hat. She had no doubt he'd heard about what had happened, probably including small details like how she'd stabbed one of the outlaws with her scissors when he'd tried to tie her hands after she'd pulled free. Hopefully Clark had left out the ways the outlaw called Luther had threatened to rape her before they killed her. The words he'd used still made her cheeks burn.

Pushing aside the memory, she stared at the pale officer her brother had said couldn't afford to be too picky in finding a wife. That dinner her first night in camp seemed more like a hundred years ago rather than just a week.

Lieutenant Dodson began talking as if giving a speech. Anna barely followed along. The man liked to hear his own voice.

Anna didn't say much. Dodson had been politely cold to her both times they'd met and had obviously seen her only as a possible solution to *his* problem. Now he seemed to look at her quite differently. He even told her he had always admired tall women who could carry themselves well. It appeared, since she'd survived a kidnapping, her value had gone up in his eyes.

The change in the lieutenant bothered Anna far more than his flattery did. She was glad when the sergeant showed up for his nightly guard duty before Dodson lied and said that she was pretty. Anna had always known she was simply plain.

She didn't want to hear words she knew weren't sincere; she wanted to see the way a man felt in his face, and read the truth of his compliments in a touch.

All in all, she'd been lucky: two men in her life had been blind enough to see her as beautiful. One had been young and in love with love. The other lay on the table before her. She had no doubt, despite their shortsightedness, that both men had believed every word they said.

The lieutenant invited her to dine with him and Anna declined. She didn't even give a reason. She just said, "No, thank you."

The moment he'd gone, Cunningham closed the door. "Anna," he began in his slow, polite way that hinted they'd been friends for years and not days. "You need to get some sleep. I'll stay awake tonight and if McCord so much as twitches, I'll yell out for you. With the tent so close you'll probably hear him anyway."

Anna shook her head. "I'd like to have a proper bath and a clean change of clothes, but after that, I'll be back."

Cunningham looked like he thought it would be a waste of time to argue.

Chapter 10

McCord felt his body moving through layers of muddy water, floating slowly to the surface. He forced himself to take a deep breath and swore he smelled buffalo. He hated buffalo. Orneriest creatures God ever made. The only thing worse than having them roam over the plains, eating every blade of grass for miles, was seeing the thousands of carcasses rotting after the hunters shot them.

He tried to swallow, but couldn't. His mouth felt like it was packed with sand.

Opening one eye, he noticed he was lying on what looked like a buffalo hide, and just beyond that was a mass of midnight hair. "Anna," he whispered.

She raised her head and looked at him with eyes heavy with sleep. Her mouth opened slightly in surprise. "Wynn," she whispered, as if she'd just been dreaming of him.

She looked delicious. He moved to kiss her and felt the stab of a dozen knives in his back.

"Don't move," she ordered, her hand on his shoulder.

Memories came back with the pain. The feel of her beneath him a moment before fire crossed his back. Floating in darkness, unable to open his eyes. The sound of her voice constantly talking to him, pulling him closer to shore, not letting him sink away from the pain . . . away from life.

He closed his eyes and tried to think. Maybe he had died. It would be just his luck that hell would be full of Yankees and they'd all be talking.

He opened one eye again. No. He was alive and Anna was sitting beside him. He caught her fingers when she touched his hand, gripping tight, needing to know that she was real. Almost losing her had tortured his mind for days, and when he'd watched her fall off the horse he swore his heart stopped until he saw her rolling on the ground.

The fingers of her free hand brushed through his hair. "You're going to be all right, Wynn. Just rest. You've lost a lot of blood. Sleep now."

He smiled and closed his eyes, thinking of how he liked the way she said his first name. He hadn't heard a woman say his name in years.

When he woke again, morning shone through the windows, but the face in front of him was Dirk Cunningham's. The sergeant looked tired, but a smile spread from ear to ear.

"'Morning," the sergeant said. "You look terrible."

McCord groaned. "Where's Anna?"

Cunningham laughed. "She'll be back. I'm not surprised that my face wasn't the one you wanted to wake up to, but you could at least act like you're glad to see me. Anna said if you wake I'm to roll you over like you was a newborn and prop you up."

McCord swore as Dirk lifted his shoulders off the buffalo hide.

"Stop your complaining. I ain't never said I was a nurse."

"That's an understatement," McCord managed as soon as the pain subsided enough for him to breathe. "Where is Anna?" Somewhere in his dreams he'd thought he heard someone ask her to dinner.

"She went to tell the cook how to make broth for you. He sent some over that Clark and me thought was fine, but she said it wasn't near thick enough." Cunningham shook his head. "That woman's been giving more orders than the captain and, unlike the orders we usually get from him, every man on the place does what she asks."

McCord wasn't surprised. She'd ordered him to come back from the dead, and he'd done so for fear she'd follow him down and spend eternity complaining that he didn't listen.

"I swear," Cunningham mumbled. "I have a hard time believing that woman don't fight for slavery. She's a natural master."

They both laughed. They'd never had slaves or believed in owning slaves. Like most Texans, they'd fought for Texas rights and it had cost both dearly. If either had anyone close to them they wouldn't be doing such a dangerous job. McCord had been alone so long he barely remembered how it felt to have family. The war had left him with nothing but land that had gone wild in the years he'd been gone, and no one who cared.

McCord forced down the pain in his back and his heart. "How long have I been out?"

"Three days, and she's barely left your side."

"I know," he answered. Every time he'd come close to waking, he'd known she was beside him.

Cunningham offered him whiskey, but he declined.

"Water," he said.

The sergeant frowned. "I don't know about that. With all the holes in you, you're liable to spring a leak." He poured a cup of water and held it while McCord drank.

When he finished he asked, "What happened after . . ."

Cunningham knew what he wanted to know. "A dozen of the boys went back for the bodies. Both the men who kidnapped Clark and Anna were dead. The gambler's body and the man on watch, who Clark shot, were easy to recognize, but the man in black is a mystery. We brought the bodies back to the camp, but no one seems to be able to identify him. He could have been Thorn, who headed up the gang. From what I've heard about the man, he might have come alone, thinking he'd have time to torture Anna before the gambler killed her."

Anna entered, ending the conversation. She smiled when she saw McCord propped up.

The sergeant stood away from the table and showed the patient off. "I did what you said. I turned him over. He may look like trampled death, but he's well enough to complain about my nursing skills."

"She can see that," McCord grumbled. "Mind getting me a shirt from my pack in the barracks?"

Cunningham frowned. He didn't seem to like the idea of leaving. "Oh, all right, but she's been looking at that hairy chest of yours for days."

"And take your time," McCord said to Cunningham's back.

The sergeant nodded as he moved to the door. "I should have known you'd wake up meaner than a wet snake. You got no gratitude in your bones, McCord. If it weren't for knowing you'd do the same for me, I'd have left your bloody body out there in the middle of nowhere." He closed the door, still complaining.

Anna's eyebrows pushed together. "Aren't you going to thank him?" She set the soup beside his bed.

"He knows I'm grateful and he's right—I would do the same for him."

"It never hurts to say the words, Wynn." She pulled a chair beside his bed and picked up the spoon as if she thought he'd let her feed him.

McCord watched her, thinking how proper she looked. "Is that why you kept talking to me when I was near death, Anna? You thought there were words that needed saying?"

"I guess." She didn't look up at him.

"I don't know if I heard everything, but I remember you telling me over and over to stay." He took a drink of water and waited for her to say something. When she didn't, he added, "You commanded me to come back, not just from death, but to you."

She set the spoon down and laced her fingers, but still did not look up.

He saw the red burning across her cheeks, but he didn't stop. "You said when I came back to you it would be to stay. You told me I belonged with you." He grinned. "I think I even remember you yelling at me one night about how I was your man and I couldn't die unless you said it was all right." He laughed.

His Anna was a strong woman who'd never hesitated to tell him what she thought, but she remained silent now. Maybe she'd never said those words before. Maybe she had thought he was too far gone to have heard. He didn't care. She'd said them and that was all that mattered to him.

"Give me your hand, Anna."

"Why?" She finally met his gaze.

"I want to touch you." When she laid her hand in his, he tugged her toward him.

"You're still very near death." She tried to pull away.

He grinned. "I'm also very near heaven. If touching you kills me, I can think of no better way to die. Unbutton a few buttons on that very proper dress of yours, darlin'. I've been thinking of how soft you feel and how it might taste to kiss my way down your throat again."

"I will not, Wynn McCord!" She twisted free and opened the pot of broth. "I can't believe you'd even ask such a thing."

"I'm thinking more of doing than of asking," he said, still smiling, "and I'm thinking you'll let me too."

She stared at him and he had his answer in the need shining bright in her eyes. Her fingers trembled as she lifted the bowl of soup. "Now, eat your broth or I'll call the sergeant back and he'll pour it down you."

He didn't push touching her. He knew what lay beneath that plain blue dress and he'd wait. He couldn't stop smiling though. She'd been shy with him when she hadn't known where she stood, but the minute he had pulled her close, she knew how he felt. Nothing had changed between them. They both knew he needed her, but she'd come to him on her own terms, and he'd let her take her time.

He didn't move as she sat on the side of the table and began feeding him. Halfway through the meal he watched as the blush came back to her cheeks. She talked of the broth and how good it would be for him, but they were both very much aware that his hand rested on her dress, just above her knee.

He needed her near and she needed his touch, even if they couldn't seem to find the words.

That night when she checked his bandages and made sure he didn't have a fever, his hand slipped beneath her gown and gripped the warm flesh above her knee.

Her breathing quickened as he tugged her knee so he could brush her skin.

"We going to talk about this, Anna?"

She closed her eyes. "No," she whispered.

His grip tightened. "Am I making you feel uncomfortable, or am I hurting you in any way?" His hand moved a few inches higher.

"No."

"I love the feel of you." His touch turned to a caress. "I might not know how to be gentle, but I'll never hurt you."

She looked at him and smiled. "I know."

Then, without him even asking her to, she leaned forward and kissed him.

Chapter 11

That night set a pattern to their lives. She was all the proper nurse in the morning when breakfast was brought in and several of the men came to visit, but after lunch she'd shoo them all away, saying McCord needed his rest. Then, in the silence of the office, she'd sit on the table that was his bed and face him.

Without a word, he'd unbutton her blouse and brush the tips of his fingers over her warm flesh until she finally sighed, leaned forward, and kissed him fully. Anna had no idea if this was the way couples should act. She was far too old to worry about it. All she knew was that McCord loved touching her and she loved being touched.

His injury prevented them from going further, even though Wynn sometimes told her of what he'd like to do with her while she buttoned up her dress and unlocked the door to the late afternoon sun.

He grew stronger every day, and every night he held her a little longer before she moved away to her tent.

Logic told her he was a man without roots or home. The odds were he'd leave her, no matter what she said or how she cried, but when he did, he'd take her heart. She forced herself not to dwell on the future but only to treasure each hour they had.

On their fifth day together, McCord stood and dressed himself. His back was healing. He'd be whole again soon.

She watched as he reached for his Colts, then thought better of putting them on, but she knew a part of this Ranger would never feel completely dressed without the guns strapped around his waist.

"Anna, there's something I need to tell you," he said the first chance they had alone together. "I'm moving to the enlisted men's quarters tonight. Cunningham said he'd help me with my things."

"No," she said, feeling her back stiffen. Just like that, he was leaving her.

He reached for her, but she stepped away and they both knew he couldn't move fast enough to catch her.

He took two steps to the door and pulled the bolt closed. "This may be the last time we have alone for a few days. I'm not sure I'll have the opportunity or the energy to walk all the way across camp tonight."

She moved in front of him. "You're not well. You need to be here. You still need care."

"No, Anna, all I need now is a little time and you. Cunningham is rounding up an old buggy brought in for a wife who'd already left by the time it arrived. I could tie my horse to it and make it out of here. By the end of the week I'll be able to . . ."

A pounding on the door drowned out his words.

"Annalane! Are you all right?" There was no mistaking her brother's rant. "Why in the hell is this door locked? Annalane?"

McCord backed away to sit on the bed, his strength fading.

Anna opened the door. "Welcome back, Devin. Did you get all your business taken care of?"

"Never mind that—what are you doing here locked in my office with a man?"

Anna couldn't help it—she smiled. "Learning about love and all kinds of forbidden things."

Devin didn't buy the answer for one minute. "Stop being ridiculous. I know you weren't doing anything, but you must think of appearances. You might have just been doctoring a dying man, but someone . . ." Devin paused long enough to stare at McCord. "You don't look that sick."

"I'm not sick. I was shot."

Anna could see the dislike in McCord's eyes. If her brother knew how deadly the Ranger could be, Devin would walk more softly. She half expected even an injured McCord to stomp on her brother like he was a bug.

"He saved my life," she said simply.

Devin threw up his hands as he paced like a windup toy. "So what does that mean? Do you think you belong to him for life now?"

McCord smiled at Anna and she forgot all about her brother.

Wynn held out his hand and she walked into his arms. Without looking at her brother, she whispered to the Ranger, "Something like that."

He kissed her lightly. "You're mine, Anna. You have been since I first saw you, and like it or not, I'm yours."

She laughed. "I like it just fine."

"What's been going on here?" Devin yelled, but no one was listening.

Wynn kissed her, spread his hand over her hip and pulled her against him.

"This is outrageous," Devin shouted, then added, "This is unbelievable."

When McCord let her up for air, he said, "I'll go get the

buggy. There's no use waiting a few days. Can you be ready in half an hour? I want you leaving with me."

"But you're. . ."

"We'll take it slow and the captain will give us an escort to Texas." He collected his hat and Colts, then turned back to her for one more kiss. As his lips moved away, he whispered, "Come with me, Anna."

Devin was five feet away. Her brother seemed to be gagging on the words he'd just heard.

McCord walked out the door without even looking at Devin.

Anna started to pack. She'd need bandages and blankets for Wynn. No matter what he said, the trip would be hard on him, but she didn't argue. She'd had enough of her brother and nothing sounded better than leaving.

Devin was still yelling and complaining about her deserting him when Cunningham helped her into the buggy. Wynn looked as strong as steel, but McCord noticed his side of the buggy had been padded with blankets.

They pulled out of the camp and headed southwest toward Texas. Everything had happened so fast, Anna just sat and tried to think. Change had always struck like lightning, but this time she'd stepped into the bolt.

Wynn didn't say a word until the guard following them waved and turned back. All at once the world seemed wild and empty and they were alone.

She was alone, she corrected, with a man she barely knew. A man who probably hadn't said a hundred words to her since they'd met.

All panic left when his hand closed gently over hers.

They traveled in silence until almost dark, then he stopped and led the horses to a small clearing where they had a stream for water and grass to graze. She insisted he rest while she made camp and offered him bread and dried meat from a basket one of the men said Clark insisted on putting in the back of the buggy.

Wynn looked tired as he lowered himself onto the blankets, and by the time she'd packed the food away he was sound asleep.

Anna curled up beside him and slept. At dawn she awoke to his gentle kiss.

He didn't say a word when she mumbled something about being a mess and crossed to the other side of the buggy to straighten her clothing and wash her face with water from the canteen. After she'd combed her hair without a mirror, she faced him.

Wynn had hitched the horse and was waiting for her. He nodded a greeting as if they were little more than strangers. Neither seemed to know what to say. They climbed in the buggy and began following the ribbon of road made by wagons.

As the cloudy day cooled, he touched her leg. "We're going to hit rain," he said, then patted her skirts as if he thought rain might frighten her. "We'll need to make as many miles as we can before it starts."

They raced the weather, but by midafternoon the rain caught up to them. Wynn pulled the buggy beneath a stand of old cottonwood trees. They climbed out and he watched the clouds as she retrieved apples from their stash of food. When she handed him an apple, Wynn walked away from her and for one panicked moment she thought he might keep walking. He'd asked her to come with him in a hurried moment, with her brother watching. He'd been right about growing stronger, but had he changed his mind about her?

At the edge of the natural shelter, he turned around and walked back, his head down.

He didn't say a word, but took her hand and pulled her toward a cottonwood, where the air hung still and damp and branches almost touched their heads.

Anna waited. If she had any sense, she'd probably tell him to take her back to the camp. But she didn't want to go back. She wanted to stay with him. He was the first man in years who saw her. Not a woman alone, to be pitied. Not a battle-weary nurse. Not a sister to be passed along to someone else just because he "couldn't afford to be picky."

Wynn McCord *saw* her.

She glared at him now, praying he didn't suggest they turn back.

He put his hands on her shoulders and gently pushed her back against the tree. "I need to say the words, Anna. I need to make it plain between us."

She could barely hear him for rain and the wind and her heart pounding.

"I want you in my life." He stopped, but didn't let her move. "Hell!" he added. "That's not right."

She decided he looked like a man fighting the death penalty, but she guessed anything she said right now would not be welcomed, so she waited.

"That's not right," he repeated.

Tears threatened as she whispered more to herself than to him, "You don't want me in your life?"

"No. I mean yes." He swore. "Facing down outlaws is easier than this." He straightened and stared at her. "You might not guess, but I don't usually talk to a woman, any woman. So let me finish and keep your suggestions to yourself."

Anger flared, but she held her tongue. If he told her to drop her accent, she'd clobber him right here, right now, even if he was injured.

"I don't just want you in my life, Anna." He started again with no softness in his tone. "You are my life. I want you with me here in Texas. In my life and in my bed until we both die of old age. I think I was a walking dead man before you came along. The war took all the caring I had in me. I don't even know if I have enough to give you now. But I'd like to give it a try. I want to fight with you all day and make love to you all night. I want to build a house around you and have a dozen kids and stay in one place for the rest of my days. I want to stay beside you."

Anna understood. "What about what I want?"

He raised an eyebrow.

"Let go of me, McCord."

He pushed away, looking very much like he wanted to fight for her, but the only one to fight stood before him. His eyes narrowed, as if he thought she planned to ask for more than he had to give.

"I want you." She poked him in the chest. "Broken down, hurt, hard as nails, you're still the best man I've ever known. I want you."

A slow grin spread across his face.

She held up her hand. "But I have terms. You have to tell me you love me."

"All right, Anna. I love you." He circled her waist and pulled her closer. "I love every inch of you."

"And."

He didn't let go of her. "I had a feeling there'd be an 'and.'"

"You have to tell me you love me every day."

"I'll tell you and show you. How would that be?" He leaned down to brush his lips along her throat. "Marry me, Anna."

She felt his hands moving over her as if there were no clothes between them.

"Marry me, Anna," he whispered again as he cupped her breast. "I'm not alive without you."

She never said yes. She was too lost in the kiss. When they were both out of breath, he walked her back to the buggy and they continued without a word. He'd said the words she'd needed to hear.

Epilogue

Wynn and Anna McCord built one of the finest cattle ranches in Texas. When she died at the age of seventy-four, her husband and four sons placed her in a grave on the ranch. The stone at her head read, *To my angel, Anna McCord. One more time, "I love you."*

Wynn McCord joined his wife less than a year later. Everyone agreed that once she'd gone he was never really alive.

The great-great-grandchildren of Anna and Wynn still work the ranch today. If you ask any of them why they always settle on the McCord land when they marry, they all say the same thing. McCords stay.